Nightchild

Nightchild

CHRONICLES OF THE RAVEN

James Barclay

GOLLANCZ

LONDON

The right of James Barclay to be identified as the
author of this work has been asserted by him in accordance
with the Copyright, Designs and Patents Act 1988.

This edition first published in Great Britain in 2001 by
Gollancz
An imprint of the Orion Publishing Group
Orion House, 5 Upper St Martin's Lane,
London WC2H 9EA

A CIP catalogue record for this book
is available from the British Library

ISBN 0 57507 215 6

Typeset at The Spartan Press Ltd,
Lymington, Hants

Printed in Great Britain by
Clays Ltd, St Ives plc

This book is dedicated to the memory of Stuart Bartlett.
A truly great friend to me, wonderful husband to Viv and
father to Tim, Emma, Claire and Nick.
We all miss you Stuart, so this one's for you.

Once again there are people who have helped smooth the writing process and supplied the right answers when I needed them most. Thank you to Alan Mearns for providing a vital missing link during a walk to the pub in Killarney; to Lisa Edney, Deborah Erasmus and Laura Gulvin for the words they gave me; to Dave, Dick, George and Pete who keep on fighting the good fight on my behalf; and to Simon Spanton, whose support and insight have helped me through what at times was a very difficult year.

Cast List

THE RAVEN

Hirad Coldheart BARBARIAN WARRIOR
The Unknown Warrior WARRIOR
Ilkar JULATSAN MAGE
Denser XETESKIAN MAGE
Erienne DORDOVAN MAGE

THE COLLEGES

Dystran LORD OF THE MOUNT, XETESK
Vuldaroq TOWER LORD, DORDOVER
Heryst LORD ELDER MAGE, LYSTERN
Sytkan LORD MAGE, XETESK
Ry Darrick GENERAL, LYSTERNAN CAVALRY
Aeb A PROTECTOR
Lyanna ERIENNE'S DAUGHTER

THE SOLDIERS, SAILORS AND EARLS

Ren'erei GUILD OF DRECH
Tryuun GUILD OF DRECH
Jasto Arlen EARL OF ARLEN
Selik CAPTAIN OF THE BLACK WINGS
Jevin CAPTAIN OF THE *Calaian Sun*

THE AL-DRECHAR

Ephemere
Cleress
Myriell
Aviana

THE KAAN

Sha-Kaan GREAT KAAN
Hyn-Kaan
Nos-Kaan

When the Innocent rides the elements,
and the land lies flat and riven;
the Sundering shall be undone
and from the chaos shall rise the One,
never again to fall.
Tinjata, High Elder Mage, Dordover

Prologue

Jarrin had fished the waters north of Sunara's Teeth all of his long life. He knew the intricacies of the tides and the petulance of the wind. And he knew the beauty of solitude. His lines and pots were dropped in a sheltered deep-water cove and now was the wonderful wait. It was the time he loved. He lay back along the boards of his eighteen foot coastal skimmer, its single sail furled against the boom, as it rocked gently in the slight swell.

Jarrin uncorked his water and wine, then chose a thick ham sandwich from his daysack, laying it all on the bench by him as he stared at the glorious, cloud-veined blue sky. On a day like today, no life was better.

He must have dozed off for a while because he awoke with a start, felt the boat shifting strangely beneath him and saw the sun had moved a little to his left. Something was upsetting the perfection of the day and a distant roaring noise irritated his ears.

Jarrin pushed himself up onto his elbows, bent his head and dug a finger into his left ear. He couldn't hear a single bird. Over the years he'd become so accustomed to the harsh calls of gulls circling overhead or following his boat after a good day that they'd become part of the background. Now their silence was unnerving. Animals could sense things.

And now he was fully awake, nothing was quite right. The sky above was beautiful but the air felt like rain was coming. The water below the boat dragged him out to sea though the tide was surely coming in. And that roaring sound seemed to echo off the peaks of Sunara's Teeth, filling the air with an unearthly sound that scared him deep in the pit of his stomach.

Frowning, he sat up above the gunwale, his gaze caught by movement out to sea. He froze.

Approaching impossibly fast was a wall of water, behind which a dark cloud mass blew and thickened. It stretched out of his vision to either side of the cove, a towering blue-grey mountain, white-flecked and awesome.

Jarrin just carried on looking. He could have tried to haul up his anchor, raise the sail and run for the shore but it would have been a futile gesture. The wave had to be over one hundred feet high and left no hiding place, just death against the rocky coast.

Jarrin had always sworn he would stare into the face of his killer so he stood up, sang a prayer to the Spirit for his safe passage to the ancestral haven and drank in the magnificent power of nature before it dashed him to oblivion.

Chapter 1

The covered carriage rattled along the western edge of Thornewood, heading in the direction of Varhawk Crags on a rutted and overgrown trail. Wheels bounced off stone, wood protested and metal bolts screeched in their stays. The driver urged his pair of horses on, snapping the reins and shouting his encouragement as they dragged their unstable load at a speed that could only have one outcome.

But not just yet.

With every bump in the trail thudding through his lower back, the driver turned to look over his shoulder. Through the cloud of dust the carriage threw up, he could see them closing. Six figures on horseback, eating up the distance, their pace unimpeded by ground that played havoc with wheels.

He'd seen them closing over half the day, his sharp eyes picking them out almost as soon as they had spotted him and begun the chase. At first, he hadn't had to gallop but, as the afternoon had worn on, it had become clear that his pursuers would ride their horses to death to catch him. He wasn't surprised. What they believed to be inside the carriage was worth the lives of far more than a few mares.

He smiled, turned back to the trail and snapped the reins again. Above him, a fine day was clouding as dusk approached and already the light was beginning to fade. He scratched his chin and stared down at his horses. Sweat poured from their flanks and foamed beneath leather straps. Heads bounced as they drove on, eyes wide and ears flat.

'Well done,' he said. They had given him all the time he needed.

He glanced back again. They were within a hundred yards. A thud signalled the first arrow to strike the carriage. He breathed deep; it had to be now.

Keeping low, he dropped the reins and launched himself on to the back of the right-hand horse, feeling the heat through his hands and legs, hearing their exertion.

'Steady now,' he said. 'Steady now.'

He patted the horse's neck and drew his dagger. Its edge was keen and with one quick slash, he cut the carriage reins. Another and the leather binding the yoke dropped away. He kicked the horse's flanks and it sprang right, away from the carriage which, with the other horse still attached, slowed dramatically and veered left. He prayed it wouldn't overturn.

Unhitching the single reins from where they were tied around the bridle, he fought briefly for control and leaned close to his mount's neck, putting quick distance between himself and the carriage. When he heard the shouts behind him, he reined in and turned.

The enemy were at the carriage. Its doors were opened and riders circled it, their voices angry, filled with recrimination. He knew they could see him but he didn't care. They wouldn't catch him now; but more than that, he had taken them away from their quarry. Half a day's ride following an empty carriage. And now they, at least, would never find what they were looking for.

No time for self-congratulation though. These were just six incompetents he had fooled. There were far cleverer enemies still in the hunt and they would not make their intentions so obvious.

Erienne looked down at her daughter, dozing fitfully in her lap, and wondered for the first time whether she had not undertaken a monumental folly. The first day in Thornewood had been easy enough. Lyanna had been high-spirited and they'd sung walking songs as they'd travelled south, and the sun-dappled forest had smelled clean, fresh and friendly. That first night had been a real adventure for Lyanna, sleeping in the open, covered by her mother's cloak and guarded by her alarm wards. And as Lyanna had slept, Erienne had gone further, tuning to the mana spectrum and tasting its chaos, looking for signs that all was not well.

Not that Erienne had considered them in any danger that night. She trusted that the Guild knew what they were doing and would look after them. And though wolves ran in Thornewood, they were not known to take human flesh. And she, as a mage of Dordover, had more defences than many.

But on this second day, the atmosphere had changed. Deeper into the woods, the canopy thickened and they walked in shadow much of the time, their moods lifting only when the sun broke through to lighten the ground at their feet. Their songs and chatter had become sporadic and then ceased altogether. And though Erienne fought to find things to say or point out to her increasingly anxious daughter, she found her efforts fell on deaf ears or died on her lips as she looked into Lyanna's fearful eyes.

And the truth was, she felt it too. She understood, or thought she understood, why they were having to walk alone. But her faith in the Guild was quickly diminishing. She had expected some contact but had had none; and now every twig that cracked and every creak of a tree in the wind made her jump. She strained for the sounds of the birds and used their song to boost Lyanna's spirits. After all, she had lied, if the birds sing, there can be no danger.

Erienne had kept a smile on her face though she knew Lyanna was only half-convinced to carry on. Even so, the little girl tired quickly and so they had stopped in the late afternoon, Erienne resting her back against a moss-covered tree trunk while Lyanna dozed. Poor child. Only five years old and running for her life, if she but knew it.

Erienne stroked Lyanna's long black hair and edged her doll out from where it was making an uncomfortable dent in her cheek. She looked out into the forest. The sound of the breeze through the trees and the shadowy branches waving above them felt somehow malevolent. She imagined the wolf pack closing in and shook her head to disperse the vision. But they *were* being followed. She could feel it. And she couldn't free herself from the thought that it wasn't the Guild.

Her heart was suddenly pounding in her chest and panic gripped her. Shadows flickered in front of her, taking on human form and flitting around the periphery of her vision, always just out of reach. Her mouth was dry. What in all the God's names were they doing here? One woman and a little girl. Pursued by a power too great for them to combat. And they'd put their lives in the hands of total strangers who had surely abandoned them.

Erienne shivered though the afternoon was warm, the motion disturbing Lyanna who woke and looked up at her, eyes searching for comfort but finding none.

'Mummy, why do they just watch? Why don't they help us?'

Erienne was silent until Lyanna repeated the question, adding, 'Don't they like us?' She chuckled then and ruffled Lyanna's hair.

'How could anyone not like you? Of course, they like us, my sweet. I think maybe they have to be apart from us to make sure no one bad finds us.'

'When will we get there, Mummy?'

'Not long, my darling. Not long. Then you can rest easy. We must be getting closer.' But her words sounded hollow to her and the wind through the trees whispered death.

Lyanna looked sternly at her, her chin carrying a slight wobble.

'I don't like it here, Mummy,' she said.

Erienne shivered again. 'Nether do I, darling. Do you want to find somewhere better?'

Lyanna nodded. 'You won't let the bad people get me, will you?'

'Of course not, my sweet.'

She helped Lyanna to her feet, shouldered her pack and they moved off, direction south as they had been told. And as they walked, their pace hurried by the phantoms that they felt closing in, Erienne tried to remember how The Unknown Warrior or Thraun would have shaken off pursuers. How they would have covered their tracks, moved carefully over the ground and laid false trails. She even wondered whether she could carry Lyanna within a Cloaked Walk, rendering them both invisible. A tiring and draining exercise that would be.

She smiled grimly. It was a new game for Lyanna and it might just keep her happy but it was a game they were playing for the highest of stakes.

They moved through the forest with no little skill but beneath the canopy elves missed nothing. Ren'erei confessed surprise at their ability, the silence with which they moved and their efforts to leave no trace of their passing. She even respected the route they chose, often moving away from the trail they left, to throw off any who might follow.

And for most pursuers it would have worked. But Ren'erei and Tryuun were born to the forest and detected every nuance of change brought upon it by the passage of humans. A splayed leaf crushed into the mulch; loose bark brushed from the bole of a tree at a telltale height; the pattern of twig splinters lying on the ground. And for these particular people, a shadow at odds with the sun through the canopy, eddies in the air and the altered calls of woodland creatures.

Ren'erei went ahead, Tryuun covering his sister from a flank at a distance of twenty yards. The two elves had followed the signs for a full day, closing steadily but never allowing a hint to their quarry that they were being followed.

She moved in a low crouch, eyes scanning her route, every footfall of her light leather boots sure and silent, her mottled brown and green cloak, jerkin and trousers blending with the sun-dappled forest environs. They were close now. The woodchucks nesting in the roots of the tall pines ahead had sounded a warning call, bark dust floated in the still air close to the forest floor, and in the dried mud underfoot, tufts of grass moved gently, individual stalks recovering from the force of a human foot.

Ren'erei stopped beside the wide trunk of a great old oak, placing one hand on it to feel its energy and holding the other out, flat-palmed, to signal to Tryuun. Without looking, she knew her brother was hidden.

Ten yards ahead of her, local turbulence in the air, signified by the eddying of bracken and low leaves, told of a mage under a Cloaked Walk. The mage was moving minutely to avoid becoming visible even momentarily, and again Ren'erei paused to enjoy the skill.

Her fingers all but brushing the ground, Ren'erei crossed the space, identifying the patches of shadow and building a picture of the mage. Tall, slender and athletic but unaware of his or her mortal position. The elf was silent, her movement disturbing nothing, the woodland creatures comfortable with her presence among them.

At the last moment, she slid her knife from its leather sheath, stood tall, grabbed the mage's forehead and bent his skull back, slitting his throat in the same movement. She let the blood spurt over the vegetation and the man shuddered his last, too confused to attempt to cry out in alarm. The Cloak dropped to reveal black, close-fitting clothes and a shaven head. Ren'erei never looked at their faces when she killed this way. The look in their eyes, the surprise and disbelief, made her feel so guilty.

She laid the body down face first, cleaned and resheathed her knife and signalled Tryuun to move.

There was another out there, Erienne and Lyanna were running scared and the day would soon be done.

Denser sat in the fireside chair in the cold study, an autumnal wind rattling the windows. Leaves blew across the dull grey sky but the chill outside was nothing to that inside the Xeteskian mage who sat in Dordover's Tower.

The moment the Dordovan envoy had arrived on horseback to speak with him and ask him to come to the College, he had known circumstances were dire. The dead weight in the pit of his stomach and the dragging at his heart hadn't shifted since but had deepened to a cold anger when he discovered that it had taken them six weeks to agree he should be called.

Initially, he'd been disappointed that Erienne hadn't tried to contact him by Communion but breaks of weeks between touchings weren't uncommon and now, he realised ruefully, sheer distance might be stopping her even making the attempt.

He folded the letter in his hands and pushed it into his lap before looking up at Vuldaroq. The fat Dordovan Tower Lord, dressed in deep blue robes gathered with a white sash, was sweating from the exertion of accompanying Denser to Erienne's rooms. He shifted uncomfortably under the other's stare.

'Six weeks, Vuldaroq. What the hell were you doing all that time?'

Vuldaroq patted a cloth over his forehead and back on to his bald scalp. 'Searching. Trying to find them. As we still do. They are Dordovan.'

'And also my wife and child, despite our current separation. You had no right to keep her disappearance from me for even one day.'

Denser took in the study, its stacks of tied papers, its books and parchments arranged in meticulous fashion on the shelves, its candles and lamp wicks trimmed, a toy rabbit sitting atop a plumped cushion. So completely unlike Erienne, who delighted in untidiness where she worked. She hadn't gone against her will, that was clear. She'd cleaned up and intended to be away for a long time. Maybe for good.

'It is not as simple as that,' said Vuldaroq carefully. 'There are procedures and processes—'

Denser surged from the chair to stand eye to eye with the Tower Lord.

'Don't even think of trying that horseshit with me,' he grated. 'Your Quorum's damned pride and politics has kept me away from the search for my daughter and the woman I love for six bloody wasted weeks. They could be absolutely anywhere by now. What exactly have your searches turned up?'

Denser could see the beads of sweat forming on Vuldaroq's red, bulbous face.

'Vague clues. Rumoured sightings. Nothing certain.'

'It's taken you six weeks to find out "nothing certain"? The entire and considerable might of Dordover?' Denser stopped, seeing Vuldaroq's squinted gaze dart momentarily away. He smiled and stepped away a little, half-turning, his fingers playing idly with a stack of papers. 'She really took you by surprise, didn't she? All of you.' He gave a short laugh. 'You never had any idea that she might leave or where she might go, did you?'

Vuldaroq said nothing. Denser nodded.

'So what did you do? Send mages and soldiers to Lystern? Korina? Blackthorne? Even Xetesk perhaps. Then what. Scoured the local woodland, sent word to Gyernath and Jaden?'

'The search area is large,' said Vuldaroq carefully.

'And with all your great wisdom, none of you had the wit to know her well enough to consider in which direction she might have headed, did you?' Denser tutted, and tapped his head, enjoying, for a moment, Vuldaroq's embarrassment. 'No instinct, was there? And so you sent for me, someone who might know. But you left it so very, very late. Why is that, Vuldaroq?'

The Dordovan Tower Lord wiped the cloth over his face and hands before pocketing it.

'Despite your relationship to both Erienne and Lyanna, they were both under the care of Dordover,' said Vuldaroq. 'We have a certain image to uphold, protocols to observe. We wanted them returned to us with the minimum of apparent . . . fuss.' He spread his hands wide and tried a half-smile.

Denser shook his head and moved forward again. Vuldaroq took a pace back, struck his leg against the seat of a chair and sat heavily, face reddening anew.

'You expect me to believe that? Your secrecy over Lyanna's disappearance has nothing to do with risking public embarrassment. No, there's more. You wanted her back in your College before I even knew she was gone, didn't you?' Denser leaned over the sweating face, feeling the warm, faintly alcohol-tainted breath spatting quickly over his cheeks. 'Why is that? I wonder? Scared she would fetch up at the door of a more capable College?'

Again a slight spreading of the hands from Vuldaroq. 'Lyanna is a child of utterly unique talents. And those talents must be channelled correctly if they are not to provoke unfortunate consequences.'

'Like the awakening of a true all-College ability, you mean? Hardly unfortunate.' Denser smiled. 'If it happens, we should celebrate.'

'Be careful, Denser,' warned Vuldaroq. 'Balaia has no place for another Septern. Not now, not ever. The world has changed.'

'Dordover may speak only for itself, not for Balaia. Lyanna can show us the way forward. All of us.'

Vuldaroq snorted. ' "*Forward*"? A return to the One is a step back, my Xeteskian friend, and one talented child does not herald such a step. One child is powerless.' The old Dordovan bit his lip.

'Only if you stop her realising her potential.' What started as a retort finished as a whisper. Denser paced back, his mouth slack for a moment. 'That's it, isn't it? By all the Gods falling, Vuldaroq, if one hair on her head is harmed—'

Vuldaroq pushed himself out of the chair. 'No one is going to harm her, Denser. Calm yourself. We are Dordovans, not witch-hunters.' He moved towards the door. 'But do find her and bring her back here, Denser. Soon. Believe me, it is important to all of us.'

'Get out,' muttered Denser.

'Might I remind you that this is my Tower,' snapped Vuldaroq.

'Get out!' shouted Denser. 'You have no idea what you are toying with, do you? No idea at all.' Denser sat back down in his chair.

'On the contrary, I think you'll find we have a very good idea indeed.' Vuldaroq stood for a while before shuffling out. Denser listened to his heavy footsteps receding along the wood-panelled corridor. He unfolded the letter they hadn't even found, though it was barely hidden in Erienne's chambers. Denser had known it would be there, addressed to him. And he had known they wouldn't find it, just as she had. No instinct.

He read the letter again and sighed. Four and a half years it had been since they had all stood together on the fields of Septern Manse, and yet The Raven were the only people he could possibly trust to help him, depleted as they were. Erienne was gone and Thraun presumably still ran with the wolf pack in Thornewood. That left Hirad, with whom he had had a bad falling-out a year before and no contact since, Ilkar who was working himself to an early grave in the ruins of Julatsa and, of course, the Big Man.

Denser managed a smile. He was still the lynch pin. And Denser could be in Korina in a little over two days if he flew all the way. A supper at The Rookery and a glass of Blackthorne red with The Unknown Warrior. A pleasant prospect.

He decided he would leave Dordover at first light, and turned to ring for a fire to warm Erienne's chambers. There was a great deal of work still to do. Denser's smile faded. The Dordovans would continue their search and he couldn't risk them finding Lyanna first. Not that that was very likely, given the contents of the letter, but he couldn't be certain. And without certainty, his daughter was at risk from the very people Erienne had turned to for help.

But there was something else too. Something serious nagging at him that he couldn't drag from his subconscious. It was to do with the awakening.

A strong gust of wind rattled the windows, almost over before it had come. Denser shrugged, switched his attention to the desk and began leafing carefully through its papers.

Korina was bustling. Trade had been excellent throughout the summer and the seasonal change had brought little diminishment, other than the falling numbers of itinerant travellers and workers, who had begun to take ship for Balaia's southern continent, following the heat.

After two years of rumours of more battles, increased taxation and Wesman invasion, following the end of the war, confidence was returning to Korina's once deserted docks and markets, with every trader seemingly determined to wring out every last ounce of profit. Market days were longer, more ships sailed in and out on every tide, day and night, and the inns, eateries and hostels hadn't seen such a boom since the halcyon days of the Korina Trade Alliance. And of course, out in the Baronial lands, the bickering had begun in earnest again and the mercenary trade was seeing a return to profitable days. But it was a trade without The Raven.

The Rookery, on the edge of Korina's central market, groaned at the seams from early dawn when the breakfast trade began, to late evening when the nightly hog roasts were reduced to so much bone and gristle on their spits.

The Unknown Warrior closed the door on the last of the night's drunks and turned to survey the bar, catching his reflection in one of the small pillar-mounted mirrors. The close-shaven head couldn't hide the spreading grey that matched his eyes, but the jaw was as strong as ever and the powerful physique under the white shirt and dark tan breeches was kept in peak condition by religious exercise. Thirty-eight. He didn't feel it but then he didn't fight any more. For good reason.

The watch had just called the first hour of the new day but it would be another two before he walked through his own front door. He hoped Diera was having a better night with young Jonas. The boy had a touch of colic and spent a good deal of the time grumbling.

He smiled as he moved back toward the bar on which Tomas had placed two steaming buckets of soapy water, cloths and a mop. His happiest times of the day were standing over his newborn son's crib at night and waking next to Diera with the sun washing through their bedroom window. He righted a stool before slapping his hands on the bar. Tomas appeared from beneath it, a bottle of Southern Isles red grape spirit and two shot glasses in his hands. He poured them each a measure. Completely bald now he had entered his fiftieth year, Tomas' eyes still sparkled beneath his brow and his tall frame was upright and healthy.

'Here's to another good night,' he said, handing The Unknown a glass.

'And to the wisdom of hiring those two extra staff. They've taken a weight off.'

The two men, friends for well over twenty years and co-owners of The Rookery for a good dozen, chinked glasses and drank. Just the one shot every night. It was the way and had become a token these last four or so years. Neither man would miss it after an evening's work together any more than they would give up breathing. It was, after all, to enjoy these moments of magnificently ordinary life that The Unknown had fought with The Raven for more than a decade. Shame then, that with the wisdom of hindsight, he knew they weren't enough.

The Unknown rubbed his chin, feeling the day's stubble rasp beneath his hand. He looked towards the door to the back room, painted with the Raven symbol and scarce used now.

'Got an itch, boy?' asked Tomas.

'Yes,' replied The Unknown. 'But not for what you think.'

'Really?' Tomas raised quizzical eyebrows. 'I never could see it, you know. You settling down and actually running this place with me forever.'

'Never thought I'd live, did you?' The Unknown hefted a bucket and cloth.

'I never doubted it. But you're a traveller, Sol. A warrior. It's in your blood.'

The Unknown allowed only Tomas and Diera to use his true name, his Protector name, and even now when they did, it always gave him pause. It meant they were worried about something. And the truth was that he had never settled completely. There was still work to be done in Xetesk, to press for more research into freeing those Protectors that desired it. And aside from that, he had friends to see. Convenient excuses when he needed them and while his reasons still drove him, he couldn't deny that he sometimes tired of the endless routine and yearned to ride out with his sword strapped to his back. It made him feel alive.

It worried him too. What if he never wanted to settle? Surely his desire would fade to something more sedentary in the not too distant future. At least he didn't feel the urge to fight in a front line anymore and there was some comfort in that. And there had been offers. Lots of them.

He smiled at Tomas. 'Not any more. I'd rather mop than fight. All you risk is your back.'

'So what's the itch?'

'Denser's coming. I can feel it. Same as always.'

'Oh. When?' A frown creased Tomas' brow.

The Unknown shrugged. 'Soon. Very soon.'

Rhob, Tomas' son, appeared through the back door that led to the stables. In the last few years, the excitable youth had grown into a strong, level-headed young man. Glinting green eyes shone from a high-boned face atop which sat short-cropped brown hair. His muscular frame was the product of many years' physical labour around horses, saddles and carts and his good nature was a pure reflection of his father's.

'All in and secure?' asked Tomas.

'Yes indeed,' said Rhob, marching across to the bar to grab the other bucket and the large rag-headed mop. 'Go on, old man, you get off to bed, let the youngsters fix the place up.' His smile was broad, his eyes bright in the lamp light.

The Unknown laughed. 'It's a long time since I've been called a youngster.'

'It was a relative term,' said Rhob.

Tomas wiped the bar top and threw the cloth into the wash bucket. 'Well, the old man's going to take his son's advice. See you two around midday.'

'Good night, Tomas.'

' 'Night, Father.'

'All right,' said The Unknown. 'I'll take the tables, you the floor and fire.'

Just as they were into their stride, they were disturbed by an urgent knocking on the front doors. Rhob glanced up from his swabbing of the hearth. The Unknown blew out his cheeks.

'Reckon I know who this is,' he said. 'See if there's water for coffee will you, Rhob? And raid the cold store for a plate of bread and cheese.'

Rhob propped his mop in the corner and disappeared behind the bar. The Unknown shoved the bolts aside and pulled the door inwards. Denser all but fell into his arms.

'Gods, Denser, what the hell have you been doing?'

'Flying,' he replied, his eyes wild and sunken deep into his skull, his face white and freezing to the touch. 'Can you help me to somewhere warm? I'm a little chilly.'

'Hmm.' The Unknown supported the shivering Denser into the back room, dragged his chair in front of the unlit fire and dumped the mage into the soft upholstery. The room hadn't changed much. Against shuttered windows, the wooden feasting table and chairs lay shrouded beneath a white cloth. That table had seen celebration and tragedy, and it was a source of sadness that his abiding memory was of Sirendor Larn, Hirad's great friend, lying dead upon it, his body hidden by a sheet.

The Raven's chairs were still arrayed in front of the fire but every day The Unknown moved them so he could practise with his trademark double-handed sword in private. If there was one thing The Unknown's experience had taught him, it was that nothing in Balaian life was ever predictable.

Rhob pushed open the door and came in, carrying with one hand a steaming jug, mugs and a plate of food on a tray. In the other was a shovel, full of glowing embers. The Unknown took both from him with a nod of thanks.

'Don't worry, I'll clear up out front,' said Rhob.

'Thank you.'

'Is he all right?'

'Just a little cold,' said The Unknown but he knew there was more. He had seen pain in Denser's eyes and an exhaustion forced upon him by desperation.

He quickly lit the fire, pressed a mug of coffee into the mage's hands and placed the bread and cheese on a table within arm's reach. He sat in his own chair and waited for Denser to speak.

The Xeteskian looked terrible. Beard untrimmed, black hair wild where it protruded from his skull cap, face pale, bloodshot eyes ringed dark and lips tinged blue. His eyes fidgeted over the room, unable to settle, and he constantly fought to frame words but no sound came. He'd pushed himself to the limit and there was no beyond. Mana stamina was finite, even for mages of Denser's extraordinary ability, and a single miscalculation could prove fatal, particularly under ShadowWings.

The Unknown had felt a tie to Denser ever since his time as the mage's Given during his lost days as a Protector. And looking at Denser now, he found he couldn't stay silent.

'I understand something's driven you to get here as fast as you can but killing yourself isn't going to help. Even you can't cast indefinitely.'

Denser nodded and lifted his mug to trembling lips, gasping as the hot liquid fired down his throat.

'I was so close. Didn't want to stop outside the City. We'd have lost another day.' His numbed lips stole the clarity from his words. He made to say more but instead coughed violently. The Unknown leaned in and grabbed the mug before he slopped coffee on his hands.

'Take your time, Denser. You're here now. I'll find you a bed when you need it. Be calm.'

'Can't be calm,' he said. 'They're after my girl. Erienne's taken her away. We've got to find her first or they'll kill her. God's, she's not evil. She's just a little girl. I need The Raven.'

The Unknown started. Denser's tumble of words had shaken him every which way. But it was the solution that troubled him almost as much as the problem. The Raven had disbanded. All their lives had moved on. Reformation was unthinkable.

'Think hard, Denser, and slow down. I need to hear this from the start.'

Night on the southern slopes of the Balan Mountains, half a day's ride from the largely rebuilt town of Blackthorne. The stars patterned the sky, moon casting wan light, keeping back full dark.

Hirad Coldheart tracked down the steep path, his movement all but silent. It was a path he could traverse blindfold if he had to but this time, speed and stealth were of the essence over the treacherous mud and smooth stone. Hunters were coming again and, like those that had come before, had to be stopped. Yet even if these latest fell as had all the others, Hirad knew that wouldn't put a stop to the stupidity.

Not many dared the task but the numbers were increasing, as was the complexity and technicality of their planning, as information on habits and strike points filtered through Balaia, falling on interested ears. It sickened him but he understood what drove these men and women.

Greed. And the respect that would be afforded those first to bring back the ultimate hunter's prize. The head of a dragon. It was why he couldn't leave the Kaan even if he wanted to. Not that they were particularly vulnerable. But there was always the chance. Humans were nothing if not tenacious and ingenious; and this latest group marked another development.

Hirad still found it hard to conceive of minds that so quickly forgot the debt they owed the Kaan dragons; and it had been The Unknown who had put it in context when delivering word that the first attack was being prepared, after overhearing a drunken boast in The Rookery.

'You shouldn't be surprised, Hirad,' he'd said. 'Everything will ultimately have its price and there are those who will choose never to believe what the Kaan did for Balaia. And there are those who don't care. They only know the value of a commodity. Honour and respect reap no benefit in gold.'

The words had ignited Hirad's fury exactly as The Unknown had intended. It was what kept him sharp and one step ahead of the hunters. They had tried magic, poison, fire and frontal assault in their ignorance. Now they used what had been learned by the deaths and by the watchers. And for the first time, Hirad was worried.

A party of six hunters; three warriors, a mage and two engineers, was moving carefully and slowly into the foothills below the Choul, where the dragons lived. Their route had taken them away from any population that might have alerted Hirad sooner and they brought with them a crafted ballista, designed to fire steel-tipped wooden stakes.

Their plan was simple, as were all the best-laid. Unless Hirad was sorely in error, they planned to launch their attack this night, knowing the Kaan flew to hunt and feed under cover of darkness. The ballista would be positioned under a common flight path and it had the power to wound, and perhaps cripple with a lucky shot.

Hirad wasn't prepared to take the risk so descended to meet them before clearing the Kaan to fly. The hunters had made two mistakes in their plan. They hadn't factored Hirad into their thinking and only one of their number was elven. They had placed themselves at the mercy of the night and would soon discover the night had none.

Hirad watched them through a cleft boulder. They were roughly thirty feet below him and a hundred yards distant. The barbarian was able to track their movement against the dull grey of the landscape by the hooded lantern they carried, the creaking of the ballista's wheels and the hoof-falls of the horses that pulled it.

They were nearing a small open space where, Hirad guessed, they planned to set up the ballista. The slope there was slight and a butt of rock provided an ideal anchor point. Hirad knew what had to be done.

Backing up a short distance, he moved right and down into a

shallow ditch that ran parallel to the small plateau. With his eyes at plateau level, he crept along its edge and waited, poised, sword sheathed and both hands free.

The mage led the horses up the incline on the near side, a warrior overseeing their progress on the other. The two engineers walked behind the ballista with the final pair of hunters bringing up the rear.

Hirad could hear the horses breathing hard, their hooves echoing dully through mufflers tied around their feet. The wheels of the ballista creaked and scraped as it approached, despite constant oiling by the engineers, and the odd word of warning and encouragement filtered up the line.

Hirad readied himself. Just before it levelled out, the path became a steep ramp for perhaps twenty yards. It would be slippery after the day's showers. As the hunters approached it, they slowed, the mage out in front, hands on both sets of reins, urging the horses up.

'Keep it moving,' came a hiss from below, loud in the still night air.

'Gently does it,' said another.

The mage appeared over the lip. Hirad surged on to the plateau and dived for his legs, whipping them away. The mage crashed to the ground. Hirad was on him before he could shout and hammered a fist into his temple. The mage's head cracked against stone and he lay still.

Racing low around the front of the suddenly skittish horses, he pulled his sword from his scabbard. The warrior on their other side had only half turned at the commotion and was in no state to defend himself. Hirad whipped his blade into the man's side and as he went down screaming, the barbarian leant in close.

'Believe me, you are the lucky one,' he rasped. Quieting the horses who had started to back up, he ran back to the ballista and slashed one of the harness ropes. The ballista shifted its weight and the horses moved reflexively to balance it, one whinnying nervously. Below him, four faces looked up in mute shock. Blades were drawn.

'I warned the last who came to tell the next that all they would find here is death. You chose not to listen.' He lashed at the other harness rope, splitting it at the second strike. The ballista rolled quickly down the ramp, scattering the hunters and gathering pace as it bounced over rock and tuft. A wheel sprang away and the main body ploughed left to plunge over the edge of the path, tumbling to its noisy destruction in a stand of trees some two hundred feet below.

Below the ramp, the hunters picked themselves to their feet, the engineers looking to the warriors for guidance.

'There's nothing they can do for you now,' said Hirad. *It is safe, Great Kaan.*

A shadow rose from the hills behind Hirad and swept down the path. It was enormous and the great beat of its wings fired the wind and from its mouth came a roar of fury. The hunters turned and ran but another shape took to the air over the path below them and a third joined it, herding them back towards Hirad.

The trio of dragons blotted out the stars, great bodies hanging in the sky, their united roars bouncing from the mountains around them, the echoes drawing cries of terror from the hunters now turned hunted. They huddled together, the dragons circling them, lazy beats of their wings flattening bush and grass and blowing dust into the air. Each one was over a hundred feet long, its size and power making a mockery of the pitiful band who had come to kill one. They were helpless and they knew it, staring into mouths that could swallow them whole, and imagining flame so hot it would reduce them to ashes.

'Please, Hirad,' mumbled one of the engineers, recognising him and fixing him with wide desperate eyes. 'We hear you now.'

'Too late,' said Hirad. 'Too late.'

Sha-Kaan powered in, his wings beating down and blowing the hunters from their feet to sprawl beneath the gale. His long neck twisted and arrowed down, striking with the speed of a snake and snatching up a warrior in his mouth. And then he was gone into the sky, his speed incredible, his agility in the air breathtaking. He was impossibly quick for an animal his size and the hunters left on the ground gaped where they lay, too traumatised now even to think about getting back to their feet.

The man in Sha-Kaan's mouth didn't even cry out before his body was torn in two and spat from the huge maw, scattering blood and flesh. The Great Kaan barked his fury into the night, the sound rumbling away like distant thunder. Nos-Kaan soared high, then dived groundwards, the men below his gaping mouth screaming as he fell towards them. With a single beat of his wings, he stalled his speed, the down draught sending the hunters rolling in the dust, their cries lost in the wind. He looked and struck as Sha had done, his victim crushed in an instant and dropped in front of his comrades.

And finally Hyn-Kaan. The Great Kaan's bark brought him low across the ground, a great dark shape in the starlight, his body scant feet from the rock, his head moving down very slightly to scoop his target into his mouth. He flicked his wings and speared into the heavens, a human wail filtering down, cut off, and followed by the sound of a body hitting rock.

Hirad licked suddenly dry lips. They had said they wanted revenge. And they had said they wanted men to known their power. Yet the elf at his feet was still unconscious and had seen nothing. Lucky for him. Hirad loved the Kaan and theirs was a bond that would not be broken by such violent death. Yet once again, he was reminded of the unbridgeable gulf between man and dragon. They were majesty, men their slaves if they so chose.

Hirad brought his attention back to the lone engineer, alive still and surrounded by the torn carcasses of his friends. He had soiled his breeches, liquid puddling around his boots where he crouched in abject terror of the three dragons circling above him. Sha-Kaan landed and grabbed him in one foreclaw, bringing him close to his jaws. The man wailed and gibbered.

Hirad turned to the mage, uncorked his waterskin and dumped its contents over the elven head. He gasped and choked, groaning his pain. Hirad grabbed his collar and hauled him upright, a dagger at his throat.

'Even think of casting and you'll die. You aren't quick enough to beat me, understand?' The mage nodded. 'Good. Now watch and learn.'

Sha-Kaan drew the hapless engineer even closer. 'Why do you hunt us?' he asked, his breath billowing the man's hair. He tried to reply but no words came, only a choked moan. 'Answer me, human.' The engineer paddled his legs helplessly in the air, his hands pressing reflexively against the claws he could never hope to shift.

'The chance to live comfortably forever,' he managed. 'I didn't realise. I meant you no harm. I thought . . .'

Sha-Kaan snorted. '*No harm*. You thought us mindless reptiles. And to kill me or one of my Brood was, what does Hirad call it? Yes, "sport". Different now, is it? Now you know us able to think?'

The engineer nodded before stammering. 'I'll n-never d-do it again. I swear.'

'No indeed you will not,' said Sha-Kaan. 'And I do hope your fortunate companion pays careful attention.'

'My fortun—?' The engineer never got to finish his question. Sha-Kaan gripped the top of his skull with a broad foreclaw and crushed it like ripe fruit, the wet crack echoing from the rock surrounding them.

Hirad felt the mage judder and heard him gasp. His legs weakened but the barbarian kept him upright. Sha-Kaan dropped the twitching corpse and turned his eyes their way, the piercing blue shining cold in the darkness.

'Hirad Coldheart, I leave you to complete the message.' The Great Kaan took flight and led his Brood out to the hunt.

Hirad stood holding the mage, letting the terrified elf take in the slaughter around him. He could feel the man quivering. The smell of urine entered his nostrils and Hirad pushed him away.

'You're living because I chose you to live,' he said, staring into the elf's sheet-white face. 'And you know the word you are to put around. No one who comes here after the Kaan will succeed in anything but their own quick death. Dragons are not sport and they are more powerful than you can possibly imagine. You understand that, don't you?'

The mage nodded. 'Why me?'

'What's your name?' demanded Hirad.

'Y-Yeren,' he stammered.

'Julatsan aren't you?'

Another nod.

'That's why you. Ilkar is short of mages. You're going to the College and you'll put out the word from there. Then you'll stay there and help him in any way he sees fit. If I hear that you have not, nowhere will be safe for you. Not the pits of hell, not the void. Nowhere. I will find you and I'll be bringing friends.' Hirad jerked a thumb up into the mountains.

'Now get out of my sight. And don't stop running until Ilkar says you can. Got it?'

A third nod. Hirad turned and strode away, the sound of running feet bringing a grim smile to his lips.

Chapter 2

The last few days had been the most tranquil and relaxing period of Erienne's remarkable life. They had been the days aboard ship when she knew that she had escaped the fetters of the Colleges at long last. Not just Dordover, all of them. And in the calm, late summer waters of the Southern Ocean, with the temperature rising to a beautiful dry warmth, she and Lyanna had finally been able to rest and let go the cares of what had gone by and think on what was to come.

Looking back, the voices in her head had become so regular they had seemed a part of her. Urging her to leave and be with them. She recalled the night her decision had been made. Another night in Dordover, another nightmare for Lyanna. One too many as it turned out.

Dordover. Where the Elder Council of the College of Magic had taken her in after she had left Xetesk. Where they had treated her with a mixture of awe and disdain over her chequered recent past. And where her daughter's extraordinary gifts had been nurtured and researched by mages whose nervousness outweighed their excitement.

In the year the Dordovans had tried to help, they had produced nothing Erienne had not already known or that she and Denser hadn't guessed. The fact was that Lyanna was beyond their introverted comprehension. They could no more develop her talents safely than they could teach a rat to fly.

One magic, one mage.

The Dordovan elders hated that mantra and hated the fact that Erienne believed in it so fervently. It went against the core beliefs that drove Dordovan independence. And yet, at first, they had taken on Lyanna's training with great dedication. Maybe now they were aware of the scope of her abilities, it was affecting their desire or, more likely, they felt threatened by it.

But the whole time someone had understood. Someone powerful. And their voices had spoken in her head and, she knew it, in

Lyanna's. Supporting her, feeding her belief, keeping her sane and calming her temper. Urging her to accept what they offered – the knowledge and power to help.

And then had come that particular night. She had realised then that, not only could the Dordovans no longer help Lyanna, their fumbling attempts were putting her at risk. They couldn't free her from the nightmares and she was no longer being allowed the space to develop; her frustration at being kept back would inevitably lead to disaster. She was so young, she wouldn't understand what she was unleashing. Even now her temper wasn't long in the fraying; and in that she was very much her mother's daughter. So far, she hadn't channelled her anger into magic but that time would come unless she learned the boundaries of what she possessed.

The nightmare had set Lyanna screaming, her shrill cries scaring Erienne more than ever before. She had cradled the trembling, sweat-soaked child while she calmed, and knew things had to change. She remembered their conversation as if it had just occurred.

'It's all right. Mummy's here. Nothing can harm you.' Erienne had wiped Lyanna's face with the kerchief from her sleeve, fighting to calm her thrashing heart.

'I know, Mummy.' The little girl had clung to her. 'The darkness monsters came but the old women chased them away.'

Erienne had ceased her rocking.

'The who, Lyanna?'

'The old women. They will always save me.' She had snuggled closer. 'If I'm near them.'

Erienne smiled, her mind made up for her.

'Go back to sleep, sweet,' she had said, resting her back on her pillow and smoothing her hair down. 'Mummy has some things to do in the study. Then perhaps we can go on a little trip away.'

'Night, Mummy.'

'Good night, darling.' Erienne had turned to go and had heard Lyanna whisper something as she reached the door. She'd turned back but Lyanna wasn't speaking to her. Eyes closed, her daughter was drifting back towards what, Gods willing, would be a calmer sleep, free of nightmares. She had whispered again and, that time, Erienne caught the half-sung words and heard the little giggle as if she were being tickled.

'We're co-ming. We're co-ming.'

Their night-time flight from Dordover soon after still made Erienne shudder, and her memories were of anxiety, fear and the perpetual proximity to failure; though it was now clear that they had never really been in great danger of capture. Eight days in a carriage driven by a silent elven driver preceded their uncomfortable three days in Thornewood. At the time she'd thought that ill-conceived but it had become obvious since that the Guild elves had left very little to chance. There followed a final urgent carriage ride south and east towards Arlen before they had taken ship and her cares had eased effortlessly away.

The ship, *Ocean Elm*, was a tri-masted cutter, just short of one hundred feet from bowsprit to rudder. Sleek and narrow, she was built for speed, her cabin space below decks cramped but comfortable enough. Kept spotlessly clean by a crew of thirty elves, *Ocean Elm* was an attractive ship and felt sturdy underfoot, her dark brown, stained timbers preserved against the salt water and her masts strong but supple.

Erienne, whose experience of ocean sailing was very limited, felt immediately comfortable, and their firm but kind treatment by the busy crew helped the air of security. In their off-duty moments, they delighted in Lyanna's company, the little girl wide-eyed in wonder at their antics on deck, juggling oranges, tumbling, singing and dancing. For her part, Erienne was glad for a while to be somewhere other than the centre of attention.

And so they had rested, drinking in the fresh air, the complex smells of ship and sea, and seeing their guides at last smile as Balaia was left behind them. Ren'erei, their erstwhile driver, had found her voice and introduced her brother, Tryuun. Tryuun had done little more than bow his similarly cropped black hair and flash his deep brown eyes, the left of which, Erienne noted, had a fixed pupil and was heavily bloodshot. The socket around it too, was scarred and she was determined to ask Ren'erei about it before they reached their destination.

Her opportunity came late one night, four days into the voyage. Supper was over and the cook pots had been stowed, though the ship's carefully netted fires still glimmered. Above them, the sails were full, the wind chasing up cloud to cover the stars. Lyanna was asleep in her bunk and Erienne was leaning on a railing, watching the water speed by beneath them, imagining what might be swimming just below its surface. She heard someone walk to stand near her and looked along to see Ren'erei mimicking her stance.

'Mesmeric, isn't it?' she said.

'Beautiful,' agreed the young elf. She was tanned deeply from a life around the Southern Continent, Calaius, her jet black hair cropped close to her head and into the nape of her neck. She was young, with angled green eyes, leaf-shaped ears sweeping up the sides of her head, and proud, high-boned cheeks. She was standing a few feet away and in the dark her eyes sparkled as they caught the stars' reflection off the water.

'How long until we get there?' asked Erienne.

She shrugged. 'If the winds stay fair, we should see the Ornouth Archipelago before sundown. Then it's a couple of days to shore, no more.'

'And where is "there"? Assuming you can tell me now, that is.' Erienne had been persistent in her questioning during their carriage ride but had learned nothing of any consequence whatever.

Ren'erei smiled. 'Yes, I can tell you now,' she said. 'It is an island deep inside the archipelago, which we call Herendeneth, which means "endless home" in your language. I don't know if it has a common name. There are over two thousand islands in the Ornouth, many not even on a map. To chart the whole area would be the job of more than one lifetime, which is to our benefit. Herendeneth isn't much to look at from the sea, I'm afraid, all cliff and black rock where so many are all sand, lagoons and trees; but it serves our purpose.'

'Sounds lovely,' said Erienne drily.

'Don't get me wrong, it's beautiful inland. But if you want to get there you have to know the way. The reefs show no mercy.'

'Oh, I see.'

'You don't, but you will.' Ren'erei chuckled. 'None can reach us that don't know the channel.'

'They can fly.'

'It is just barren from the sky, though appearances are deceptive.'

'Got it all sewn up, I see,' said Erienne, her natural scepticism surfacing.

'For three hundred years and more now, yes,' returned Ren'erei. She paused and Erienne could feel the elf studying her face. 'You miss him, don't you?'

Ren'erei's words startled her but there it was. However subconsciously, she'd held out the hope that Denser would be able to follow them eventually but now . . . Gods falling, he wasn't a sailor and with the island's identity apparently disguised from the air as well . . . She supposed she shouldn't be surprised.

But the truth was, she felt isolated, away from everything she knew and she missed him despite the delight that was Lyanna. She missed his touch, the sound of his voice, the feel of his breath on her neck, the strength he brought to everything he did and the support he showed her so unflinchingly, despite their long separations. And though she knew her decision had been right, the unknowables gnawed at her confidence and spoke of unseen dangers for her daughter. Denser would shore her up. They would shore each other up, only he wasn't here and she had to dig deep in her considerable reserves of strength to keep believing.

Ren'erei helped. She was a friendly face. Respectful and understanding. Erienne made a note to keep her as close as she could for as long as she could. The Gods only knew what she would face on Herendeneth.

'You know we would welcome him but there are others who have less sound motives for wanting to find us besides those who have already tried,' she continued, sparing her the need to answer. 'They hunt us day and night and have done so for more than ten years. They and their enemies would all see us fall.'

Erienne frowned. It didn't make sense. Surely the Dordovans were the only ones who pursued them still.

'Who?'

'Witch Hunters,' said Ren'erei. 'Black Wings.'

The strength went from Erienne's legs and she sagged down, clutching at the rail. With astonishing swiftness, Ren'erei moved across the deck and caught her. Erienne couldn't find the words to thank her. Her pulse was pounding in her throat, the blood roaring in her ears, her mind releasing the memories she'd buried so carefully years before.

She saw it all again. Tasted the atmosphere of the Black Wings' castle, the stench of fear in her twin boys' room, the hideous torture of separation from the sons she loved and the sneer of Captain Travers, the leader of the Witch Hunters. Again and again she saw the blood from their slit throats spattered over the bed clothes, their faces and the walls. Her boys. Her beautiful boys. Slaughtered for a risk they didn't pose, by men who were terrified of magic because they could not understand it. Again, she felt their loss, just like it was yesterday, just like everyday.

And the Black Wings hadn't been destroyed despite everything she and The Raven had done. They hadn't been destroyed and now they hunted that which was most pure. Lyanna.

'No, no, no,' she whispered. 'Not again.'

'I am a fool and I'm sorry,' said Ren'erei, wiping a tear from Erienne's face while she clutched the elf's forearm. 'It was wrong to tell you that. We know what you lost to them and we have grieved. But you have to know so that you can understand that you will be safe with us where you weren't before, not even inside the walls of your College. Tryuun has suffered at their hands. You have seen his face. He escaped their torture but not without cost. But one day we will finish the Black Wings. Finish what The Raven began.'

'But they are finished,' mumbled Erienne, searching her eyes for the lie. 'We destroyed their castle.'

Ren'erei shook her head. 'No. One escaped the castle and others have joined him to raise the banner again in the wake of the Wesmen withdrawal. Selik.'

'Selik is dead,' said Erienne. She pushed away from Ren'erei, moving to sit on a crate lashed to the deck, nausea sweeping her stomach. 'I killed him myself.' Ren'erei stood.

'Tell that to Tryuun,' she said solemnly. 'Selik is disfigured, almost unrecognisable to look at, but his manner is all too easy to recall. The left-hand side of his face is cold and dead and his eye droops toward it, blind forever. His hair was scorched in the flame and he bears the scars of many burns, but his strength of arm remains. He is a dangerous adversary and he knows a great deal about us. More than any man living.'

'So kill him.' Erienne's voice reflected the cold dread she felt inside though the night was warm. 'He can't be hard to spot.'

'But we have to find him first. Tryuun escaped him ten weeks ago and we haven't heard of him since. But we will and this time there will be more of us, I promise.' She crouched in front of Erienne who looked into those ocean-deep green eyes. Her smile had returned. 'He can't follow us here. No one can. You are safe, Erienne. You and Lyanna. No one can harm you on Herendeneth.'

She knew Ren'erei was right but the shock of her words kept Erienne from sleep that night. Irrational fears drifted across her tired mind, snapping her to heart-thumping wakefulness whenever she drifted close to its embrace.

Denser was still in Balaia, heedless of the danger that lurked somewhere in its borders. Dear Ilkar too. Both had borne torture at the hands of Black Wings once. That some had survived and would repeat the horror sickened her. Perhaps Selik's disappearance meant they had somehow infiltrated the crew on board. Perhaps when they reached Herendeneth, all that would greet them would be death.

Black Wings were everywhere in her imagination and each one had a dagger with which to slit a helpless child's throat . . .

The Ornouth Archipelago appeared out of the haze of the setting sun the next day, a string of islands that looked almost as one so far as the eye could see in either direction. Through a thin bank of cloud, the sun cast red light across the archipelago, bathing land and sea in a warm radiance.

Erienne and Lyanna stood at the prow of the *Ocean Elm*, drinking in the splendour as the islands became gradually more distinct, with what they thought at first sight to be mountains on one island, resolving themselves as belonging to entirely another.

From tiny rock atolls, jutting from the sea like fists grabbing at the air, to great swathes of white sand, miles long, the Ornouth swept west to east, a tail off the northern coast of Calaius, beautiful but treacherous. Riddled with hidden reefs, beneath even the calmest waters, the power lurked to rip the bottom from any ship and Erienne could feel tension begin to grow among the sailors as they neared the outlying islands.

It was small wonder the archipelago hadn't been mapped. The journey to the island closest to the southern mainland couldn't be risked in anything smaller than an ocean-going vessel, and with shallow-draught boats the only way to be confident of charting the myriad central islands, it would truly be a labour of love. Unsurprisingly, much of what lay deep inside Ornouth was uncharted and, to a large extent, untouched.

The *Ocean Elm* cut confidently across the sea towards the outer islands but as they approached close enough to make out individual trees bordering the beaches, and boulders on the shingle, the tension reached a new level.

From the wheel deck, the first mate rattled out a series of orders that had elves scurrying to the sheets and up into the masts. Much of the sail was furled, leaving only the jib and forward mast topsail to drive the ship. And all those not engaged in rig work leant over the sides or swung plumb lines to measure the fast-varying depth. The skipper steered a course between two islands, keeping very close to the one where a shelf led to deep water just off shore.

With the passengers ignored, the crew waited, tensed, reacting immediately to every quarter turn of the wheel, every order to trim or loose the sails, while a constant stream of calls echoed back from the prow as sailors scoured the water in front of them or measured the depth again and again.

The ship crawled along the channel. Erienne noticed long poles stowed beneath the gunwales and it didn't take much imagination to understand what they were for. She never wanted to see them wielded. Not a word was spoken that wasn't directly relevant to the task at hand and the taut expression on the face of every sailor told its own story about their proximity to disaster, despite their obvious experience.

It was an hour of careful travel before they rounded the port side island and hove-to in a wide channel from where the horizon in every direction was studded with islands. The crew stood down, the light failing quickly, and soon the smells of cooking filled Erienne's nose while somewhere, a flute was playing softly. Hardly daring to move, Erienne and Lyanna shifted where they sat on the netted and tied crates, not part of the relief the crew shared. Ren'erei came over to them, carrying mugs of tea for them both.

'We're stopped for the night. Only a madman would risk the channels to Herendeneth in darkness. We're hidden from the ocean and few could follow us even this far. You have no wish to know how close our hull came to the reef and it will be no better at first light.'

Erienne accepted the tea and watched a while as Lyanna cupped her hands around her mug, breathing in the fresh herb fragrance.

'But surely you've sailed this stretch before?' she asked eventually.

Ren'erei nodded. 'But sand shifts and reefs grow. Eventually the course of channels change. You can't be too careful and there must always be passage. Our charts change almost with every voyage. Never by much, but enough to keep us alert.'

'Will we make land tomorrow?' asked Erienne.

'I want to walk on the sand!' announced Lyanna abruptly, taking a sip of her tea. The young elf smiled and shook her head.

'No sand where we are going, my princess,' she said. 'Not tomorrow. But one day, I'll take you to the sand, I promise.'

Erienne saw the warmth in Ren'erei's eyes.

'Do you have children?' Erienne smoothed Lyanna's hair. The child pulled away slightly, concentrating on her drink. It was easy to forget the depth to which her mind already ran and the power that was harboured there.

'No,' said Ren'erei. 'Though I'd love to. My duties take me away from the attentions of males, but it won't be forever.'

'You'll make a fine parent,' said Erienne.

'For now I can only hope so,' said the elf. 'But thank you.'

The night passed quietly, the crew savouring whatever rest they could get, acutely aware of the rigours dawn would bring. The *Ocean Elm* set sail again in the cool of early sunrise and Erienne had woken to the feel of the ship underway, albeit slowly, and the curious quiet that held sway as they moved through the narrow channel that led inexorably to Herendeneth and the voices that had urged them to their journey.

Washing and dressing quickly in a pair of pale brown breeches, a wool shirt and leather jerkin supplied by Ren'erei, Erienne had taken to the deck, pausing to frown at her daughter's slumbering form. Normally a bundle of energy that rose with the dawn, Lyanna had slept more and more every day of their voyage and Erienne couldn't help but feel that it was sleep not entirely under her control. But on the other hand, she was refreshed and bright when she awoke, and her calm acceptance of the uprooting of everything she had known was pure blessing.

Up on deck, Erienne returned to her position of yesterday, soaking up a watery sun that shone through a thickening cloud bank. The wind was brisk but even and the *Ocean Elm* made slow and steady progress through the archipelago.

Throughout an anxious day, they crawled between islands. An idyllic lagoon setting would give way to a scatter of lifeless rock fists or a sweeping volcanic atoll, its ridges obscured by cloud. Up in the rigging, the crew stood waiting as they had yesterday, ready to reef or unfurl sail on barked command, and the jib was slackened any time the wind picked up pace.

The threat beneath the waves removed the romance of this final leg of the voyage, and though Erienne never ceased to marvel at the sheer scale and beauty of Ornouth, she couldn't help but feel they were somehow unwelcome. A paradise of tranquillity it might be but, lurking close by, a sense of malevolence. The *Ocean Elm* was here under sufferance and failure to show respect would be met with the dread sound of reef ripping through timber.

In the middle of the afternoon, with the cloud blowing away to leave a blanket of blue sky, the temperature rose as the wind dropped. Lyanna, who had joined Erienne late in the morning, scrambled to her feet, using Erienne's back to steady her as she peered forward intently.

'What is it, sweet?' asked Erienne.

'We're here,' said Lyanna, her voice soft and almost inaudible above the creaking of spars and the gentle bow wave that ran past the ship. Erienne looked too. The captain had been holding the *Ocean*

Elm on a starboard tack, taking the ship past a sweeping sandy beach at the back of which cliffs soared hundreds of feet into the air, giving a home to thousands of sea birds whose calls surrounded them.

Skirting the edge of the island, the ship turned slowly to run down a channel barely more than three ship's widths across. Bleaker cliffs towered above them on both sides now, closing in above their heads, the shrill cries of gulls echoing down to them from where they circled high above or sat on precariously sited nests.

But it was at the end of the channel that Lyanna stared, because closing with every passing heartbeat was Herendeneth. Like the cliffs by which they passed, the island was dominated by a sheer rock face that scaled many hundreds of feet into the afternoon sky. And slowly revealed was a shore from which spears of stone protruded and cliffs tumbled down to the sea, the scattering of huge boulders evidence of ancient tumultuous movement.

Moving steadily down the widening channel, the *Ocean Elm* was silent once more. Herendeneth reached out with an aura that demanded reverence and quiet contemplation. Any sailor not tending sails or wheel, dropped briefly to one knee with bowed head, touching the centre of his forehead with his right index finger.

'You are here, Lyanna,' said Ren'erei. Erienne started, she hadn't heard the elf approach. 'Soon you will be standing with the Al-Drechar.'

The name sent shivers down Erienne's spine. Al-Drechar was a name written in legend and ancient texts. They were the holders of the faith, the guardians of true magic. They were the Keepers of the One. There had never been any doubt that a substantial sect had survived the Sundering, the cataclysmic battles that had seen four Colleges emerge from the ruins of the one that had previously dominated Balaian magic. But that had been over two thousand years before and they were assumed to have died out as time passed and peace returned to Balaia. All that was heard were rumours, explained away by the clashing of charged mana or the unpredictability of nature.

Yet the idea that descendants of the One had survived had never been conclusively disproved and through the centuries, enough mages had been strong enough to state their beliefs and perpetuate what had appeared at best a myth.

Now, Erienne knew different. She *knew*. And in a while, she would physically meet with those who many dreamed still lived but more prayed were dead.

'How many are there?' she asked.

'Only four remain,' replied Ren'erei. 'Your daughter truly repre-sents the last hope for furtherance of our cause.' She placed a hand on Lyanna's head who looked up and smiled though a frown chased it quickly away.

'Are they dying then?' Erienne asked.

'They are very old,' replied the elf. 'And they've been waiting for you a long time. They couldn't have waited too much longer.'

Erienne noticed tears standing in Ren'erei's eyes.

'What will we find there?' she mused, not really expecting an answer.

'Peace, goodness, purity. Age.' She looked into Erienne's eyes and the mage saw desperation burning in those of the elf. 'They can't be allowed to fade uselessly. I and the Guild, we've watched them grow steadily weaker over the years. She must be the one.'

'She is,' said Erienne, Ren'erei's fervour unsettling her. Lyanna felt it too and had leant against her mother. She was gazing again at the island that would be her home for the Gods only knew how long.

'Tell me, Ren'erei, how many of you serve them? The Al-Drechar, that is.'

'We are few. Forty-three in all, but our sons and daughters will carry on the work until we are not needed any more, one way or another. We've served them for generations, ever since the Sundering, but the honour is undiminished.' She stood tall, pride on her face. 'We are the Guild of Drech and we will not falter until our service is fulfilled. All else is secondary.' She turned from Erienne and looked towards Herendeneth, touching index finger to forehead as she bowed.

The ship dropped anchor about a quarter of a mile off the bleak northern coast of the island. Only the most tenacious of vegetation clung to the towering rock wall ahead of them and waves raced into crash against hard stone. In the sky, a few birds circled, their calls lost in the breeze.

Immediately they were stationary, the crew began unlashing the three long boats and lowering them into the water. Scrambling-nets and ladders followed, and a brief flurry of activity saw luggage and supplies passed swiftly down to be securely fastened to two of the craft. Each boat took four oarsmen and a skipper. Erienne was invited to climb down a ladder while Lyanna sat on Tryuun's broad shoulders, very quiet and pale, while the elf descended swiftly to the boat that would carry them ashore.

The crews pulled away strongly, heading for a shore apparently barren of landing sites. But rounding a spit hidden from shipboard view, they beached on a narrow stretch of shingle, away from which a path climbed up and disappeared through a cleft in the rocks. Ren'erei helped Erienne and Lyanna out of the boat, smiling as they skipped through the cold shallows to escape the water and joining them as they stared down, wet above their knees.

'Not far now,' she said. 'Just one last climb. The crew will bring up all your things.'

The path was well kept, its steps long, carefully carved and shallow in the rise, and it wound up in a deliberately gentle incline overlooked by birch trees.

Looking back down the stairway, Erienne could see the scope of the illusion. This was no harsh rock island. True, the landing points were difficult and crowded with reefs, but the height of any cliff had been hugely exaggerated. And beyond the shore line, the island rolled gracefully up to a low pinnacle through tumbledown rock and rich green forest under which the heat of the day was captured. Away from the sea breeze, the air was humid and Erienne felt sweat beading and running all over her body.

Beside her, Lyanna trotted along, clutching her doll in one hand, humming to herself, her face intent.

'Are you all right, darling?' Erienne trailed a hand across Lyanna's head.

'Yes,' she affirmed. 'Will you do the walking song again?'

Erienne smiled. 'If you like.' She held out her hand and Lyanna gripped it tightly. 'Here we go,' Erienne said, changing to a shorter stride.

'I step with my right foot,
And the left follows on.
If I do it once again,
Then the journey soon is done.
If I don't move my left foot,
Then the right one gets away.
If I don't move my right foot,
Then just here is where we'll stay.'

Repeating the words over and over while they stepped and double-stepped, Erienne couldn't help but blush as she caught Ren'erei and Tryuun watching her over their shoulders. Both elves were smiling and as they turned back, Ren'erei mimicked the double steps the song demanded.

'One day, it'll be your turn,' said Erienne, joining in their laughter. Lyanna skipped up to the elf and took her hand.

'You're not doing it right. Mummy, sing it again.'

'Just once more, then,' said Erienne. 'Pay attention, Ren'erei.' And while she sang, she watched her daughter, carefree, giggling at Ren'erei's attempts to mimic the steps, and wished fervently that Lyanna had been born without the burden she carried. And with that, came guilt. Because Erienne had planned it to be this way. And though it was a great thing they were trying to do, before they achieved their goal, there was so much hardship to come. And Lyanna, of course, had no choice in the matter. Erienne already grieved for the childhood she was to lose.

Lyanna let go of Ren'erei's hand and trotted on, warbling a vague approximation of Erienne's walking tune. She turned out of sight around a corner of the tree-lined path a few yards ahead. Erienne had upped her pace the moment she heard the song falter. And by the time Lyanna's scream had split the air, she was moving at a run.

Chapter 3

Four years after the last Wesmen had withdrawn, the College city of Julatsa had returned to something like its old self, with one significant difference.

Ilkar stood on one of the few undamaged sections of College wall and turned a full circle, his shoulder-length black hair drifting in the light breeze. On the city's borders, the Wesmen's wooden fortifications had long been stripped away to use in rebuilding homes, businesses, municipal offices and the scores of shops and inns burned and demolished by the invaders during their brief occupation. Original stone was much in evidence, bearing the scarring and scorches of war. The populace, scattered or enslaved, had flooded back once the Wesmen departed and the destroyed city now glowed with energy again, the people bringing with them the pulse of life.

Ilkar shook his head slightly at some of the new architecture. The kindest word to describe much of it was 'enthusiastic'. Yet no one could deny the energy that the rash of twisted spires, white stone domes and flying buttresses exuded. They had been built with tremendous verve but Ilkar couldn't help but wonder what those builders thought now.

Their desire and that, perhaps misplaced, enthusiasm had run out at the gates of the College. It hadn't started that way. In the immediate aftermath of Wesmen withdrawal, the devastated College had been the city's focus as it struggled to come to terms with its trauma. There had been a recognition of the scale of violence visited on the College and in the early months, new building work had forged ahead. Quarters, administration, kitchens and refectory, a long room, the old quadrangle and a library – sadly empty but for a few of Septern's texts, brought there by Ilkar himself following the closing of the Noonshade rip – had appeared from the rubble.

But the job was enormous and, as more Julatsans returned to the city, attention turned quite rightly to its infrastructure. The trouble was that with life able to begin again, it was easy to turn away from the College and forget the work that was still needed there.

Ilkar couldn't. His circle ended with looking down over the new library. He couldn't argue with the quality of what had been done but it left them so far from having a functional college. And vital to it was the building that should occupy the black, scarred, jagged hole, three hundred feet wide, that dominated the centre of the College.

The Tower.

Ilkar knew that what lay below scared the city builders and tradesmen. Gods, it scared him sometimes, but for him it was the enormity the crater represented that was the fear. At its base, covered by an impenetrable black mist, lay the Heart. Buried as Julatsa fell, by Barras, the old elf Negotiator, and a team of senior mages, its raising was critical to the College's return to power.

So much knowledge lay within. Not just key magical texts but, of greater immediate importance, plans and blueprints. Until the Heart was raised, they could not rebuild the Tower, ManaBowl, Cold Room or recovery chambers among others. And until he had enough mages, he couldn't hope to raise the Heart.

Ilkar sat down on the parapet and let his legs swing. There was the nub of the crisis. Hammering echoed up to him. New paint sparkled in the sun under the clear blue sky, its odour fresh in his nostrils. Wood dust covered the stone flags that had been awash with so much blood.

But it would never be finished. There weren't enough Julatsan mages to cast the necessary magic. Gods in the ground, there was barely enough experience to form a council but he'd done it anyway, just to give the place some structure. He didn't particularly want to take on the role of High Mage but there was no other figurehead and at least his reputation with The Raven earned him respect and weight in negotiations.

He'd had to put out wider calls for mages. There had to be Julatsans scattered across the continents, those like himself who rarely visited the College but who owed their lives to it nonetheless. He'd even sent word into the Southern Continent of Calaius, to the eleven homelands where so many Julatsan elves had returned over the years, bleeding Balaia of a crucial resource. The Gods knew what the state of their magic would be. Ilkar only hoped their Julatsan Lore training hadn't lapsed with the passing of time. It was becoming increasingly clear that he needed them badly.

'Ilkar!' called a voice from below. He leaned forward. Pheone, her brown hair tied up in a bun and her long young face smeared with dust and sweat, looked up at the parapet, her green dress flapping gently at her ankles. She was a fine mage but inexperienced, and lucky to be alive after surviving the rout of the Dordovan relief column during the siege of Julatsa at the height of the war.

'How's it going?' he asked.

'The cladding on the long room is complete. A few of us thought we'd run a test. Release a little pent-up emotion, if you know what I mean. Care to join us?'

Ilkar chuckled. He hadn't cast an offensive spell in four years. He flexed his fingers and hauled himself to his feet.

'I don't mind if I do,' he said. He brushed stone chips from his tan breeches and the dark leather jerkin that covered his fawn shirt and headed for the stairway.

A feeling of energy caused him to look up at the sky. A bolt of lightning, pale straw and angry, arced in the unbroken blue heavens, its report echoing dully in his ears. Another flash, and then a third, broke the peace of the day. He frowned at the repetition of the startling and worrying sight.

Ilkar descended the stairs, resolving to mention the subject over supper. Someone, he expected, could provide an explanation.

The Unknown Warrior sat in a chair beside the sleeping form of Jonas. The boy had spent a quieter night than his father, who had come home not long before dawn. And though he had slipped into bed next to Diera to try to grab what little sleep he could, his mind had churned over Denser's words, and kept him from his dreams. Shortly after Diera had risen in response to Jonas' cries, to feed and comfort him until he slept again, The Unknown had ceased his endless turning and come to sit in the calm of Jonas' room to give his wife the chance of uninterrupted rest.

And sat he had, while the sun rose above the horizon to cast cool light over Korina, listening to the gentle breathing of his six-week-old son, still bearing the after-effects of the slight cold that had given way to his touch of colic. He was a strong boy and The Unknown was glad of his brushes with illness; they would benefit him in later years much as they had his father.

Watching Jonas squirming as he fought to change position, his little hands pushing at the soft white blanket that covered him to the top of his chest, he felt both a stab of fear and a kinship with Denser that no man without a child could fully understand. He didn't even have to ask himself how he would feel if it had been his child that had disappeared, with or without its mother. And he didn't have to ask himself what he would expect from his friends should that happen.

But going with the Xeteskian mage, as he had to, carried the risk that he wouldn't see his wife and his own son again. And he would be breaking his promise to Diera – that The Raven would never ride with him at its head.

The Unknown sighed and read again the letter Denser had given him, looking forlornly for clues as to what had him so worried.

My Dear Husband,

I know this letter finds you unopened because the eyes of the Dordovan Council are blind to all that is most apparent. I have been feeling for some time that the masters here are failing Lyanna and her health is at risk from the mana she attracts but cannot properly control.

She misses you terribly at times but seems to understand that you cannot be here, without fully grasping why. One day, I hope we can tell her together but perhaps that is asking too much.

I expect you're wondering by now where we have gone and why I did not contact you by Communion with my increasing worries but it is difficult when you are removed from the day-to-day life of our beautiful child. Besides, this is something that we must do alone, without the council of those who might deflect us from our path. Lyanna knows it. I know it too.

Right now, I can imagine your anger. I knew the Dordovan Council would hide my leaving from you. My only regret is that I am not there to see you humbling Vuldaroq. Please understand that only I can accompany her – to involve you would have exposed us all to danger.

I want you to know that we are safe and going to a place where Lyanna can learn in safety the craft for which she was born, and still enjoy being the delightful little girl she is becoming, more so every day. There are those who understand her talent and wish to nurture it. I have felt them – they are benevolent minds and Lyanna is very happy at the prospect of meeting them. I think that we can help them too; they do sound old and frail despite their power.

I can barely contain my excitement now. I think we have found those we so fervently hoped were still alive. Or rather, they found us. It will be a long journey and not without its risks but please don't worry about us.

*I will send word as soon as I can and when Lyanna is settled,
perhaps we can meet again. For now, I must say good bye. We have
both shed tears at the thought of how long we might be apart from
you but it will be for the best for us all.*

*Lyanna will be the first true mage, I know it now. And that means
we can begin to build a better future for us all.*

Wish me luck and love. One magic, one mage.

Yours forever, Erienne.

Something in that text had bothered Denser more than mere worry
at the journey Erienne had determined to make with their daughter.
And it had to do with the Dordovans' apparently urgent desire to find
them and return them to the College. Denser was anxious to meet up
with Ilkar, with all of The Raven but Ilkar most of all, and The
Unknown had had to order him to rest.

And now the new day was full and Korina swarmed with life.
There was much to be done and while The Unknown couldn't help
the thrill that coursed through him, he hadn't the faintest idea how
they would find one mage and her young child in this huge world. All
they had was a letter, a starting point and a vague hinting of ancient
magic he had neither heard of before nor understood. But if Denser
thought it was important, The Unknown wouldn't question it. Gods,
how they could do with Thraun; but Thraun was lost to them all.

He stood over the crib and smoothed a wisp of blond hair from
Jonas' face before leaning in to kiss his pale forehead.

'I won't be away long, little one. Look after your mother for me.'
He straightened and faced the door. Diera stood there, wearing a
loose-tied bodice and a blue working skirt. Her fair hair tumbled
across her face but it didn't hide her expression. The Unknown
walked to her, making to speak but she raised a finger and placed it
on his lips.

'Not yet, Sol. Tell me later. But if you must go, you can give me
your next hour.' Her mouth turned up and she kissed his lips, her
tongue darting into his mouth to twine with his. After a while he
drew back, his hands on her upper arms.

'Jonas will wake. And besides, I know a more comfortable spot.'
He took her hand and led her to their bedroom.

*The wind savaged the forest, tore roots from the ground and brought
branches crashing to earth with terrible force. The trunks of young
trees blew about the Thornewood like twigs, smashing everything in*

their path until they too shattered, sending lethal splinters to whirl in the maelstrom.

Thraun hunkered close to the ground, in the shelter of the twisted, cracked bole of a sundered oak, his gaze everywhere, thoughts racing. The flying splinters couldn't blind and cut him and the trunks couldn't smash his bone, though they could trap him, but it was not so for the rest of the pack. When the winds had struck without warning on a tranquil day, with the sun beginning to lose its influence, half of the den had been destroyed before the warnings could be barked.

What they had thought of as their strength had turned out to be a deathtrap. The den had been dug deep beneath the root systems of a dense knot of strong pines, but the wind had ripped them down like leaves falling as the weather turned cold, roots had torn free to whiplash into the den, heavy boughs crashed through the weakened roof, crushing so many to death and maiming so many more.

Sleeping away from the carnage, Thraun had woken, howled danger and fought his way back through fleeing wolves to see the damage for himself and help the trapped and wounded. There was little he could do. Blood was seeping into the ground, bone protruded from hide and fur and of the few that moved, none would live, their bodies broken under the weight of earth and branch.

The wind was bringing down more of the den and Thraun had run to the only open way out, escaping as it too had collapsed. Outside it had been little better. A blizzard of splinters had cut and slashed into the survivors, leaving most bleeding, handicapped or blinded. And those who hadn't found immediate shelter from the wind had simply been blown away, one to hang in grotesque fashion from a net of branches higher than any wolf could spring, eyes dulling as its life-blood ebbed from it.

Thraun howled his lament and hunkered down further to think how to save his devastated, panicked pack. He looked around him, at the mothers sheltering the pitifully few cubs that had survived and at the dog wolves, four only, looking to him for help and escape.

Thraun tasted the wind as it surged around them, felt its evil violence and knew they had to move. It came seemingly from everywhere, thrashing in his ears, its blasting force ripping down the forest. He could hear nothing but its fury and knew it hunted them like prey. There was only one place where they could hope to survive until the wind had passed. The crag point where the pack gathered before hunting would provide a barrier the wind couldn't break.

But it was over two hundred paces away. An almost impossibly long distance in the forest with the wind roaring and spitting its ferocity. Lulls were few and relative. Thraun sniffed again. A temporary quiet was coming.

He waited, every fibre tensed, his heart racing. There it was. A lessening of the tumult. Barely noticeable but it could give him the edge. He sprang over to the sheltering mothers, grabbed a cub by the scruff of her neck, growled through clenched teeth for the rest to stay and darted toward the crag.

The way was every bit as difficult as he had envisaged. The trails he knew and the markers he followed were all gone. The whole nature of the forest had changed almost beyond recognition. Everywhere he could see the sky, its heaving dark cloud piling across his vision like a river in flood.

The crown of every tree was shredded, snapped or gone completely. Debris lay thick on the forest floor, waiting to be whipped into lethal frenzy by the next gust. Nothing was as it should be and only Thraun's innate sense of direction, strained by the enforced need to find a new and far longer route, got him there at all.

The relative calm in the lee of the crag was like walking from night into day. The wind whistled around its edges, a mournful dirge that saddened the heart, but in its centre, the crag would protect their lives. He set the cub down, nuzzling the quivering body of the petrified creature and licking its face. His growl was warming and comforting.

Stay. I will return.

And so he did. Five more times. Once with each cub and once with the remnants of the pack.

Finally, he could rest as the wind tore at the ruins of Thornewood. He looked at them, four adult males, two adult females and five cubs all less than two seasons old. Pitiful survivors of a den in excess of forty. But he would save what he had and build again. First, though, it was time to mourn.

He lifted his head and howled to the sky.

Erienne hadn't calmed Lyanna until they were alone in a room in the extraordinary building that was home to the Al-Drechar. It lay between a gurgling stream and a dense palm forest and, from the front, was an astonishing mass of timber and slate. It looked rather disorganised, and perhaps that was how it was supposed to be, but inside the elegance was breathtaking.

Not that Erienne had time to take in much more than a general sense of the place. Detail would have to wait until later. Right now, she cradled her sobbing child in her arms and wondered how she would ever get her from the delightful room which had been decorated just how Lyanna would like it, if she stopped crying enough to look.

And the truth was that they had scared Erienne too, standing there so tall and gaunt, pale robes flowing, every bone in their bodies standing proud. Ren'erei had reacted quickest, snatching up Lyanna from where she stood rooted and running inside with her. Dragging herself after the elf, Erienne had time to pick up the doll and shrug 'sorry' at the crestfallen Al-Drechar before chasing Ren'erei to the room in which she and Lyanna now sat alone.

On the gently toned yellow walls had been drawn waving, smiling bears and groups of rabbits at play. Light came from three shaded lanterns and, in addition to a soft bed and low wooden desk, there was a child-sized armchair and sofa; and all sitting on thick rugs that protected feet from the timber floor. Candles filled the air with a fresh forest scent.

But Lyanna wasn't looking at any of it and her sobs were only just beginning to subside though her body still trembled and shook.

'Shh, darling, Mummy's here. No one will hurt you,' she whispered, putting her lips to the girl's head. 'That's it, calm down, now. Calm down.'

'Are the ghosts gone, Mummy?' she mumbled into Erienne's chest.

'Oh, sweet, they aren't ghosts, they're your friends.'

'No!' wailed Lyanna, her crying starting again. 'They aren't the old women. They're ghosts.'

Erienne could see her point. She knew the fluttering light robes they had worn were for comfort in the humid heat. She was also aware that old elves traditionally kept their white hair long as a demand for respect; and that the muscle and fat faded from their bodies long before they became decrepit, leaving them skeletal in appearance. And these elves were incredibly old. But their appearance was a child's nightmare brought to life and Lyanna had suffered more than her share of those.

'I'll be with you,' said Erienne. 'You'll be all right. Brave girl. My brave girl.' Erienne stroked Lyanna's hair until she pulled away to look up, her face blotched and red where it had been pressed so hard against her mother. Erienne smiled.

'Look at you!' she admonished gently. She wiped away the damp on Lyanna's face with the cloth she had held ready for some time. 'Don't be scared. Are you still scared?'

Lyanna shook her head but said, 'Just a little. Don't leave me, Mummy.'

'I'll never leave you, darling. Do you want to sleep with me tonight or in here?'

Lyanna examined her new surroundings for the first time, the flicker of a smile on her anxious face.

'This is a nice room,' she said.

'It's yours if you want it.'

'Where's your room?'

'I'll make sure it's next door, so I can hear you. Is that all right?'

Lyanna nodded. There was a knock on the door and Ren'erei poked her head round.

'How are we doing?' she asked.

'Come in,' said Erienne. 'Much better, thanks.'

Ren'erei had changed into loose cloth trousers and a woollen shirt, reminding Erienne that she still carried around the dirt and sweat of the day, as did Lyanna.

'Good,' she said, not approaching too close. 'They are anxious to meet you. They didn't understand your reaction.'

Erienne stared at Ren'erei, a frown on her face. 'Then I take it they haven't spent much time around children recently. You have explained, I presume.'

'As far as I could,' affirmed Ren'erei. She smiled. 'They have changed into more formal clothing.' She turned to go. 'When you're ready, just come out. I'll be waiting.'

'Thank them for not intruding into our minds. That was thoughtful,' said Erienne.

'They may not understand children but they aren't without conscience. Don't let the way they look affect your ideas of who they are.' She closed the door quietly behind her.

'If there had been any other way, I would have taken it,' said The Unknown. He was at the doorway to his house. It was mid-afternoon. Out in the street, Denser was astride his horse, agitated, his mood communicating to the light brown mare who shifted her hooves, unable to remain still.

'You've made your position quite clear,' said Diera, her face red from tears, her hair rough tied in a tail that trailed over one shoulder. Jonas was inside. She hadn't wanted him to see the parting.

'Diera, it's not like that. Think how I'd feel if it were you and Jonas. I'd expect the same of them.'

'Oh, I understand your damned honour and your damned code. What about the promises you made to me?' She hissed her words, not wanting Denser to hear.

There was no answer to that. He was breaking his word and the knowledge of it tormented him. Yet it had seemed at first that she understood and their love-making had been tender and passionate. He had lost himself within her, never wanting the feeling to end and yet, lying next to her, basking in the afterglow, his head above her, his hand caressing her breast, her tears had warned him it would be no gentle goodbye. Their shouts had wakened Jonas and it was only his cries that broke the argument and brought them ultimately to this cold exchange.

'I cannot excuse what I do but I cannot apologise for it either,' said The Unknown, reaching out a hand. Diera pulled away. 'I couldn't refuse him just as he couldn't refuse me if you had disappeared.'

'But you never really considered saying no, did you?' The Unknown shook his head. 'You haven't stopped to think about what you leave behind and you ride off to reform The Raven.' She spat the word out as if it left a bad taste in her mouth.

'Because they . . . we are the best. Together, we have the best chance of finding Erienne and Lyanna and all coming back unharmed. This isn't for money, Diera. I owe Denser my life, you know that.'

'And what do you think you owe me and Jonas? Nothing?' Her expression softened a little. 'Look, I know *why* you're leaving. It's why I love you.

'But you didn't ask me, Sol. It feels like my opinion isn't important. You made promises to me and Jonas, and though you don't want to walk away from them, you are. And the thought that you might not come back at all is breaking my heart.' She gazed deep into his eyes. 'We are your life now.'

'What would you have me do?' he asked.

'Whatever I may feel, I do understand you. I would have you go and I will take comfort that should I ever encounter trouble, The Raven will help me. But I would also have you think about me and Jonas before everything you do. We love you, Sol. We just want you back.'

She moved forward and held him tightly and he was surprised to find tears on his cheeks. He clutched at her back, his hands rubbing up and down it.

'I will come back,' he said. 'And believe me, I never do anything without thinking of you. And your opinion is important. It's just that I never had any choice that you could influence.'

Diera put a finger to his lips, then kissed him. 'Don't spoil it now. Just go.'

He broke away and mounted his horse, turning it towards the north and Julatsa. And as he spurred the animal on, Denser following close behind, he prayed to the Gods that he would see her again.

Vuldaroq sat at the centre of a long table. Flanking him, four to either side, were the humans and elves who made up the Dordovan Quorum.

In front of them stood one man, tall and proud, a semi-circle of fifteen College guards behind him. The small auditorium was chill, but not because of the icy wind that howled outside. It was the aura that bled from the man and the repugnance in which he was held that cooled the room. He was the most hated of men among mages and he was standing on the hallowed ground of Dordover, his wrecked face displayed now his hood was thrown back, the black tattoo on his neck a symbol of his reviled beliefs.

His arrival at the College gates had triggered a flurry of activity, culminating in the hastily arranged meeting; abhorrence of the individual was outweighed, at least temporarily, by incredulity and a desire to learn what had brought the man to a place from which he could never hope to leave.

'The risk you take is unbelievable, Selik,' said Vuldaroq. 'Indeed, I'm amazed you aren't dead already.'

'Lucky for you that I'm not,' said Selik to snorts of derision from the Quorum, his speech slow, thick and incomplete, the result of his horrific facial injuries.

Vuldaroq studied Selik's features and could barely suppress a smile of satisfaction. The left-hand side of his face appeared as if it had been smeared by the careless swipe of brush on wet paint. The bald eyebrow angled sharply down, the sightless eye beneath it milky white and unmoving. The cheek was scored as if by the drag of heavy claws and it pulled the mouth with it, forcing Selik to speak through a perpetual sneer. It was a fitting expression, completed by left side upper and lower jaws slack and devoid of teeth.

And all caused by the spell of a Dordovan mage. It had been believed that Erienne's IceWind had killed the Black Wing and number two to Captain Travers but somehow he survived it and the fire that The Raven had laid in Black Wings' castle. And with him the Witch Hunter order. Less numerous now but no less zealous.

'I can never envisage a time when your not being dead would be lucky for any Dordovan mage,' said High Secretary Berian, his face curling into an unpleasant smile.

'Then envisage it now,' said Selik. 'Because, like it or not, we are after the same thing.'

'Really?' Vuldaroq raised his eyebrows. 'I would be fascinated to know how you reached that conclusion.' A smattering of laughter ran along the table. Selik shook his head.

'Look at you, sitting there so smug it nauseates me. You think no one is aware of what you do yet I know you have lost a great prize and you want it, her, back. And I am the only one who can really help you. And help you I will, because in this quest we are in accord. This magic cannot be allowed to prosper or it will destroy us all. I know the direction of their travel and I know at least one of those who helped them.' He stopped, studying their faces. Vuldaroq could taste the silence his words engendered.

'Got your attention now, haven't I? The Black Wings see all and always will. Remember that, O mighty Quorum of Dordover. As you are well aware by now, the Al-Drechar are no myth; we just don't know where to find them. But if we work together, we will, believe me.'

'Your front is extraordinary as is your blindness, If you think for one moment that we would suffer to join forces with *Black Wings!*' Berian's face was contorted and red with rage. 'Have you taken leave of what remains of your senses?'

Selik shrugged and smiled, a grotesque leer on his ruined face. 'Then kill me and never learn what we know. The trouble is, you haven't the time to risk me being right after killing me, have you? Late at night in Dordovan taverns, your mages are not always as discreet as you might wish. Much has reached our ears and it is very interesting. Very interesting indeed.'

'But you haven't come here to exercise your altruistic streak, have you Selik?' asked Vuldaroq. 'You want something. What is it?'

'Ah, Vuldaroq. Not always as fat in the head as you might look. It's quite simple. You want the girl back, to educate, control or dispose of as you see fit. You can have her and I will help you get her. But in return, I want the witch that did this to my face.' He poked a finger at his hideous scarring. 'Give me Erienne Malanvai.'

And in the storm of protest that followed, Vuldaroq allowed himself a small chuckle.

Chapter 4

Ren'erei took Erienne and Lyanna along a wide, picture-hung, timbered and panelled corridor. It stretched fully seventy yards to a pair of plain double doors flanked by Guild guards. Other doors ran down its left-hand side and windows to the right overlooked a lantern-lit orchard.

On seeing the outside, Lyanna had forgotten her fear temporarily and run over to the window, mesmerised by the lanterns which swayed in the breeze, sending light flashing under the branches and broad leaves of the trees in the early evening gloom.

It was still very warm and Erienne had chosen a light, ankle-length green dress and had tied her hair up in a loose bun to let the air get to her neck. Lyanna wore a bright red dress with white cuffs, her hair in her favoured ponytail, the doll clutched, as ever, in her right hand.

'Just how big is this place?' asked Erienne, standing behind Lyanna and looking at another wing of the house over a hundred yards away, across the orchard.

'That's not an easy question to answer,' said Ren'erei. 'It has been standing since the Sundering and building has hardly stopped, even now when there are so few living here. It must cover much of the hillside. You should take a flight; you can see it all if you stay beneath the illusion. Suffice to say that though it is now only home to four, it was home to over eighty.'

'So what happened?' Erienne turned Lyanna away from the window and they walked on, passing ancient, faded pictures depicting burning cities, great feasts and running deer. It was an odd collection.

'I think they were complacent about ensuring the line continued, until it was almost too late. As you're aware yourself, producing a true adept is very difficult. Numbers soon dwindled and it was made worse by those that just didn't want to stay their whole lives here. Despite the importance of the order, the will ebbed away. Who can explain that?'

They reached the doors, which were opened for them. Inside, a huge ballroom, decorated in red and white, decked with chandeliers and mirrors, took the breath away, though the covering dust told of its redundancy.

'I'll let them tell you the rest,' said Ren'erei, taking them right across the ballroom to an innocuous-looking door. She knocked and opened it, ushering them into a small dining room. Oak-panelled and hung with elven portraits, it contained a long table around the far half of which sat four elderly women. They were talking amongst themselves until Lyanna and Erienne entered, the little girl clutching her mother's leg.

'It's all right, Lyanna, I'm here and they're friends,' whispered Erienne, taking in for the first time, the majesty of the Al-Drechar.

Erienne had no doubt that she was in the presence of Balaia's most powerful mages. Their faces told of people tired of life yet determined to survive, yearning for fulfilment to their long lives. It was the way she would always remember them.

Superficially, they were ancient elves, friendly enough but with the fierce expressions taut flesh dictated. Erienne saw shocks of white hair, bony fingers, long necks and piercing eyes. And then one spoke, her voice like balm on an open wound, quelling anxiety.

'Sit, sit. We must all eat. You, my child, must be tired and scared after your long journey. We won't detain you long. Your mother we might keep a little longer, if it's all right with you.'

Lyanna managed a little smile as Erienne pulled out a chair at the opposite end of the table and ushered her to sit before taking the place next to her. Ren'erei took up a neutral position between the two groups.

'You won't hurt my mummy,' said Lyanna, her eyes fixed on the blue cloth that covered the table.

'Oh, my child, quite the reverse,' said another. 'We have been waiting too long to do anyone harm.' She clapped her hands. 'Introductions in a moment. First some food.'

Through a door to the left, a slim middle-aged woman came, carrying a large steaming tureen by ornate wooden handles. Behind her, a boy of no more than twelve carried a tray with a stack of bowls and plates piled with cut bread. Swiftly, beginning with Lyanna, they served a thick soup that smelled rich and wholesome and set Erienne's stomach growling. She could see lumps of vegetable floating under the surface and the fresh aroma filled her nostrils.

'Eat, dear child,' said one of the Al-Drechar. Lyanna dipped a corner of her bread into the soup, blew on it and put it gingerly into her mouth. Her eyebrows raised.

'It's nice,' she said.

'Don't sound so surprised, Lyanna,' laughed Erienne. 'I'm sure they have good cooks here too.'

'I hope so.' Slightly clumsily, she scooped liquid on to her spoon. For a time, they were quiet, all eating the soup, which tasted as delicious as it looked and smelled, before Ren'erei cleared her throat.

'I think we've gone long enough without those introductions,' she said. 'Erienne, Lyanna, it is my great honour and pleasure to name for you the Al-Drechar.' Erienne smiled at the light of reverence in her eyes.

'To my right and moving around the table, Ephemere-Al-Ereama, Aviana-Al-Ysandi, Cleress-Al-Heth and Myriell-Al-Anathack.' She bowed her head to each in turn.

'Oh Ren'erei, you're so formal!' Cleress-Al-Heth laughed. 'You make us sound completely unapproachable.' The other Al-Drechar joined the mirth and Ren'erei blushed, the corners of her mouth twitching slightly. 'Please, Erienne, Lyanna,' she continued. 'We are Ephemere, Aviana, Cleress and Myriell, though you may hear us address ourselves with various other names which you are of course welcome to use.'

Erienne felt more at ease than she had done for days. The aura of the Al-Drechar dissipated a little though she remained mindful of their power and the clear magical vitality that they possessed. They were, on one level at least, just old elves and that was a comforting thought.

She studied them as the soup was drained, and her immediate impression was that they looked very much alike. It was inevitable, she supposed, after so many years living so close to one another, that they would share mannerisms, dress and even broad physical attributes. And though they were different enough through shape of nose and mouth, and through eye colour, she expected Lyanna to have trouble telling them apart for a few days.

'You've lived together a long time, haven't you?' she asked.

Cleress smiled. 'A very long time,' she agreed. 'Three hundred years and more.'

'What?' Erienne was taken aback. She knew elves had a potentially very long life span but three hundred years was extraordinary. Impossible.

'We have waited here, scanning the mana spectra, conserving

ourselves and planning for the next coming of someone who can take
on the Way,' said Aviana. She smiled ruefully. 'We were getting a
little desperate.'

'How long have you been waiting?'

'Three hundred and eleven years. Ever since the births of the
babies: Myriell and Septern,' replied Aviana.

Erienne gaped. Septern having been an Al-Drechar wasn't really a
surprise but the scarcity of the adepts certainly was. 'And there have
been none since then?'

'Oh, there have been whisperings and our hopes have been raised
and dashed more times than you have years in your body,' said
Cleress. 'But let's leave that for later. I see your beautiful daughter is
wilting and we do need to talk to her before she sleeps. It's been a
long day.'

Erienne looked down. Lyanna was playing with the remains of her
soup, trailing a piece of bread across its surface.

'Lyanna, the ladies want to talk to you. All right?'

Lyanna nodded.

'Are you still feeling shy, darling?' asked Erienne.

'A little,' admitted Lyanna. 'I'm tired.'

'I know, darling. We'll have you in bed soon.' Erienne nodded for
the Al-Drechar to speak.

'Lyanna?' Ephemere's soft voice reached across the table and
Lyanna raised her head to look at the friendly face of the Al-Drechar.
'Lyanna, welcome to our home. We hope you want to make it your
home too, for a little while. Do you want that?'

Lyanna nodded. 'If Mummy stays here, I do.'

'Of course she will, my dear child, won't you, Erienne?'

'Of course I'll stay,' said Erienne.

'Now Lyanna.' Ephemere's voice took on a slightly harder edge.
'You know there is magic inside you, don't you?' Lyanna nodded.
'And you know that in your old home, it was starting to hurt you and
your teachers couldn't help you any more, and that's why we came
into your head and your dreams. To help you. Do you understand
that?' Another nod. Lyanna glanced up at Erienne who smiled down
and stroked her hair.

'Good,' said Ephemere. 'That's very good. And how do you think
we will help you?'

Lyanna thought for a moment. 'You'll make the bad dreams go
away.'

'That's right!' said Myriell, clapping her hands. 'And we'll do more. I know that the hurt inside you makes you angry sometimes. We'll teach you how to stop the hurt and make the magic do the things you want it to do.'

'You have a great gift, Lyanna,' said Cleress. 'Will you let us help you make it safe for you?'

Erienne wasn't sure that Lyanna had understood the last question but she nodded anyway.

'Good. Good girl,' said Ephemere. 'Is there anything you want to ask us?'

'No.' Lyanna shook her head and yawned. 'Mummy?'

'Yes, my sweet. Time for bed, I think,' said Erienne. The cook and serving boy came back and started clearing away the soup plates as Erienne picked up Lyanna. 'I'll get her settled and be back. It could be a while.'

Cleress shrugged. 'Take your time. We'll still be here. After this long, I think we can bear to wait a little longer to speak with you.'

Lyanna was asleep in Erienne's arms before they had reached her room and barely stirred as she was put into her nightgown.

'All too much for you, my sweet,' whispered Erienne, tucking the doll under the sheets beside her and experiencing another wash of guilt. 'Sleep well.' She kissed Lyanna's forehead and left the room, closing the door gently behind her. Ren'erei was waiting.

'I'll stand here and listen,' she said. 'If she stirs and calls for you, I'll come for you.'

Erienne kissed her on the cheek, a sudden relief running through her.

'Thank you, Ren'erei,' she said. 'You're a friend, aren't you?'

'I hope so,' she replied.

Erienne hurried back to the dining room to find the table laid with meat and vegetables in serving dishes sitting over candles. A flagon of wine stood on a tray with crystal glasses, and smoke from a long pipe in Ephemere's hand curled towards the plain ceiling. A clear memory of Denser flashed through her mind; of him sitting against the bole of a tree, calmly smoking his foul-smelling tobacco while The Raven debated the end of everything. She smiled to herself and wished again he was with her.

'She went straight to sleep then?' asked Aviana. Erienne nodded. 'Good. Good. Help yourself to food and wine and sit closer, then we shan't have to raise our voices.'

Erienne took a little food and poured half a glass of wine before sitting next to Ephemere, who wafted smoke away from her.

'I do apologise for this appalling habit,' she said, sounding hoarse. 'But we find the inhalation eases our lungs and aching limbs. Unfortunately, as you can hear, it rather affects our voices.' She passed the pipe on to Aviana who sucked deeply, coughing as she swallowed the smoke that smelled of oak, roses and a sweet herb she couldn't quite place.

As if seeing them for the first time, Erienne took in their age and frailty. In the candle- and lantern light, Ephemere's skin looked so stretched across her face it might tear at any moment. It was very pale under her thick white hair, giving a stark backdrop to her sparkling deep emerald eyes, that displayed her magical vitality so effectively.

Her robes hung on a fleshless body from which her long, narrow neck, tendons and veins standing proud, jutted like a rock from a dark sea. Her hands were long, almost spidery, unadorned by jewellery and shaking slightly, her fingers ending in carefully tended short nails.

Erienne returned to those eyes and saw the light and warmth burning within them. Ephemere smiled.

'I expect you're thinking you didn't get here a moment too soon,' she said. 'And you aren't far from the truth.'

'Oh Ephy, don't be so dramatic,' scalded Myriell, her voice ragged from the pipe.

'Is it so?' hissed Ephemere, tone hardening. 'I, for one, will not hide from the risk we all take and the likely outcome for us all.'

'The girl must know the truth. All of it,' added Cleress.

'Know what, exactly?' asked Erienne, feeling a shiver in her mind. All the warmth had gone from Ephemere's eyes though the power still burned there, as it did from all their eyes.

'Off you go, Ephy,' said Cleress.

'Erienne, as you can see, we are old, even for elves and there is a limit to how long even magic can delay the inevitable,' said Ephemere.

'And it would be fair to say we none of us would still choose to be alive were it not for our enforced wait,' said Cleress.

Ephemere nodded. 'You're going to see things here that you won't like. You're going to want to stop us doing what we do with Lyanna. You will fear for her safety and you have every right to, because she will be in danger every day of her training. I'm afraid this is an unfortunate consequence of the damage done by her Dordovan teachers.'

'Damage?' Erienne stopped chewing, heart thumping in her chest, her head thick with a growing fear.

'Calm yourself, Erienne, there is no lasting damage, either physical or mental. We have calmed the nightmares that threatened her in your College. The problem lies in that she is so very young to be accepting an Awakening. And if she fails to understand our teaching, the harm to her could be severe,' said Aviana.

'Death?' Erienne hardly dared mouth the word.

'That is the ultimate price any mage may pay for attempting to realise the gift of magic,' said Cleress. 'But for Lyanna, the consequences before death would be most distressing.' She held up a hand to stop Erienne's next question. 'We know that Lyanna had already accepted Dordovan mana as if it were the most natural thing in the world, and it was this that first alerted us through the mana trails we have studied for so long.

'But in her mind there is a conflict caused by her Dordovan training. Only part of her ability has been stirred and now we must awaken the rest, but we fear that the Dordovan-trained part of her mind will resist unless we can retrain it not to. It's a difficult enough concept to grasp for anyone but for a child so young . . .' Cleress shrugged.

Erienne put down her fork and held her hands to her mouth, searching for a way out. 'Can you not just wait until she is older. Protect her from harm until she's ready somehow?'

'If we could, we would. But the process of her Awakening has been started. Unnecessarily.' Myriell's eyes bored into Erienne's.

'I beg your pardon?'

'Whatever they may have told you, the Dordovan masters hoped their magic would stifle the rest within her, so like fools they went ahead to bring it out. No doubt they told you it was the only way to save her,' said Myriell.

'Well yes, but . . .' There was a clamouring in Erienne's mind, like an alarm bell ringing but far too late. She felt on the edge of panic.

'What they wanted was to save themselves from her. But they had no real conception of what they were dealing with, Erienne, and your trust in them has put Lyanna in great danger from her own mind. And us with it.'

'No, no, no.' Erienne shook her head but couldn't make sense of the tumble of thoughts. 'You're supposed to be able to help. Make her like you. How can she be in danger now? We've come here to be safe.'

Ephemere put a cold hand on Erienne's arm.

'Child, relax,' she said, her tone soothing despite its roughness. 'Here is what you must know, but first keep in mind that you are not to blame for anything that has happened and that your bringing Lyanna here was her only hope. And ours too. Had she stayed in Dordover, she would surely have perished.'

Erienne breathed deep and felt her heart slow a little. She nodded and looked up into Ephemere's deep green eyes and waited for the Al-Drechar to continue.

'Within Lyanna is an ability none but one of her own can understand and nurture. She doesn't merely have the capacity to understand all College lores but has the innate knowledge of the base single force of magic that all mages once had. But to release it, she must first learn how to harness the individual strands. For her it will be like visiting the ManaBowl in each College to accept the mana and lore. This should be learned as one but Dordover has upset the balance.

'I cannot begin to explain to you the sheer power she holds inside her but her ability to shape mana can already be felt over hundreds of miles. If we don't teach her how to control her power, she could do immense damage before she inevitably kills herself. I'm afraid that in teaching her there will be problems. And while she learns, her mistakes will be a beacon for those who would do her harm. You will be the steadying influence on her life while she is at her most vulnerable. You must protect her.

'She is so young and physically frail. The poor girl should not have had to face this until she was your age.'

'But you can make it happen?' Erienne searched those eyes.

'We have to.' It was Aviana who spoke. 'Because if we fail, there will be no Al-Drechar.'

'Why, what will happen to you?' Erienne thought she knew the answer and so did Ephemere, who laughed.

'Why Erienne, it takes all our energies to maintain ourselves and the illusions that protect us. I'm very much afraid that training your lovely daughter will be the death of us all.' She smiled and squeezed Erienne's arm. 'But that is the way of things and death never comes quickly to an Al-Drechar.'

'When will you begin?' asked Erienne, not sure whether she should let them. Not just for Lyanna's sake but for theirs too.

'Tomorrow morning. Time is pressing. Ren'erei feels that our enemies are closer to us than they have ever been, as poor Tryuun's wound demonstrates. We must be vigilant. Nothing must deflect us from our task,' said Aviana.

Erienne had lost her appetite. In her dreams, she had seen the Al-Drechar as simply lifting the veil that fell between Lyanna and her understanding of the One. But now, with this talk of enemies, she was scared of what Denser would find in his way as he searched for her. And she found herself hoping he wouldn't find her.

'And now we should all take to our beds. The time for hard work and great strength is here. Sleep is the healer of the mind,' said Cleress.

'I'll finish my wine,' said Erienne, not able to even contemplate sleep. She took a sip and watched as the Al-Drechar helped each other from their chairs and made painfully slow progress to the ballroom door, each supporting another; Ephemere bowed under a curved back, Myriell ramrod straight but limping, Cleress tottering as if true balance eluded her and Aviana clearly plagued by arthritis in her knees.

They were just four terribly old women muttering to each other as they made their way to their chambers somewhere in the huge house. Erienne almost laughed at the thought that it would be almost dawn by the time they reached their destinations but managed to stifle it.

She poured another glass of wine and held it under her nose, letting its deep fruity aroma enclose her. What in all the hells had she done? She was entrusting the life of her daughter to a quartet of witches who all looked as if their final breaths were imminent. It should have appeared utter madness but somehow it made perfect sense and, through her fading anxiety Erienne saw what she had been searching for but that had eluded her until now.

A purpose for her and a chance for Lyanna.

Perhaps she would sleep well, after all.

Chapter 5

Ilkar awoke to the familiar sounds of hammering from outside on the College grounds. By the smell of it, the day was another dry one and a steady light shone around the gently billowing drapes covering the open window. Beside him in the bed, Pheone shifted and turned over to face the wall. Ilkar smiled, as he had been doing every morning since the night of the long-room testing five days before.

That had been a wild night. They'd set up rough carved and painted wooden blocks depicting Wesmen Lords and members, past and present, of the Xeteskian Circle Seven and the Dordovan Quorum. Taking turns, they had destroyed them using an imaginative range of offensive fire and ice spells, some better prepared than others.

Twenty mages had joined in the barrage, easing a frustration that had been building up for weeks. It had been a spectacular sight, with mage fire thrashing off the walls, ice shattering wood and forming deep icicles in the corners of the long room, that were subsequently burned away with tight-beamed flame, filling the place with steam. And every time he wasn't casting, Ilkar had stood ready to deploy shields for those who didn't have the targeting skills of their companions.

Ilkar had felt Pheone's closeness the whole evening and in the drunken feast that followed, he'd found his arms around her and her head on his shoulder more times than he could count. His memories, though indistinct, were full of her flashing smile, her laughter and the revealing shirt she had worn.

The alcohol-fuelled sex had been abandoned and fantastic, though he had to confess to himself that time had blurred. He wasn't sure it had been a lengthy experience but the feeling of a female body against his, even that of a non-elf, had been wonderful.

Pheone had quelled his concerns once their hangovers had cleared enough for their brains to function. Elves shouldn't become involved with humans, the lifespan differences leading to inevitable heartbreak and, too often, the suicide of the almost-always elven survivor.

'I don't think either of us believe this will last,' she had said. 'But we need each other now. Try and enjoy it and don't think too much about tomorrow.'

Ilkar wasn't sure Pheone really believed her own words and their passion on subsequent nights had been physically if perhaps not emotionally profound. She had been right. Their sexual union had given him a new outlook on everything. He had allowed himself to become so wrapped up in the rebuilding of Julatsa, all else had paled. He had even found himself beginning to resent The Unknown's infrequent visits, which was unforgivable. Pheone had reminded him how to relax and he found himself beginning to love her for that at least, if love was the right word.

More than that, though, he had started to look beyond the physical rebirth of the College to the longer term. The rebuilding of its psyche. There was so much to be done to attract mages back to Julatsa, to help it begin again, and he knew that, ultimately, he would need to leave to spread the word that his College of magic lived and breathed again.

But right now it was dormant and the place he had to be was here. He leaned over and kissed Pheone's sleeping face before jumping out of bed on to the cold stone floor, grabbing green breeches and rough woollen work shirt. He pulled on a pair of sturdy calf-length boots, pushed his hands through his ruffled hair and, hunger building, walked out into the passage, heading for the refectory which lay across the courtyard.

Outside, the day was fresh and warming. Dawn was an hour gone and he glanced at the work being done on the library roof and to a new structure whose foundations had been laid over the last seven days. As he always did, Ilkar paused for a while at the hole in which the Heart lay, contemplating their greatest remaining task.

One day, it would see light again and the bodies of those entombed within, including Barras, the last elven negotiator, could be paid proper respect. He mouthed a short prayer that the Gods would deliver him the tools to do the job.

'Ilkar!' He spun at the sound of his name, recognising the voice instantly. There he came through the gap that had been the north gate, leading his horse, and behind him, a second sight that gladdened his heart still more.

'Denser!' He strode towards the gate. 'Gods, they'll let anyone in here these days.'

'Sorry. I thought I had the freedom of the place after last time I was here.'

'That you do.' The two old friends embraced. 'Let's look at you.' Ilkar stepped back and took in Denser's face. 'A bit dusty, perhaps. And certainly a touch of grey here and there. Oh, and you need a haircut. But still recognisable.' He shook his head. 'It's great to see you. You've brought your hammer and chisel, I hope.'

Denser smiled. 'Sorry, never did go in for it much. I brought my pipe, though.'

'And I've missed its rank stench.' Ilkar patted him on the upper arm and looked past him. 'Hey, Unknown, it's been a while.' Ilkar tried to keep a smile on his face but seeing these two men riding through his College gates together could only mean one thing. Something bad, probably very bad, had happened.

The Unknown walked over and shook his hand warmly, his grip, as ever, crushing.

'Too long,' he said.

'So.' Ilkar returned his attention to Denser. The Xeteskian was tired despite the hour of the morning and seemed solemn. 'How's Erienne and Lyanna?'

Pain flashed in Denser's eyes and his brows pinched slightly. Instead of answering, he looked to The Unknown for help.

'That's what brings us here,' said the Big Man.

Ilkar nodded, his suspicion confirmed. 'Oh I see. Are you hungry? We could talk over breakfast.'

The refectory was a long, low building set with a series of bench tables. It was quietening with most of the mages and paid workers already on site. Ilkar indicated a corner table and while the travellers made themselves comfortable, he went to the servery and packed a long wooden tray with bacon, bread and a large jug of coffee.

'Here,' he said as he sat. 'Help yourselves. There's more if you need it.'

While they ate, Denser talked of Lyanna's progress and her nightmares, of Dordover's obstructive Quorum, and of the disappearance of both Erienne and their daughter. Finally, he passed Ilkar the letter, which the elf read in silence, frown deepening with almost every line. He passed it back after he'd read it twice and refilled all their mugs.

'If they find them first, they'll kill them,' said Denser.

'Who will?' asked Ilkar.

'The Dordovans. Don't you see?'

'That's a little extreme, don't you think? There's more to it than simple conspiracy. There's potential risk to all Balaian magic systems.'

'Don't you start,' said Denser. 'Lyanna is the future for all of us, not our death and destruction. The Dordovans are just scared. All they need is education. No one is talking about an enforced return to the One Way, for God's sake. No one alive is capable of practising it.'

'Except Lyanna.'

Denser shrugged. 'Yeah, except Lyanna. Possibly. Look, Ilkar, Vuldaroq is not interested in any multidisciplined mage being nurtured by anyone. He told me Balaia didn't want another Septern. That's why, if he can't control her, he'll kill her.'

'So you want to find them?' said Ilkar.

'No, I want to offer them up to Dordover, chained to sacrificial altars,' replied Denser.

'Just checking you hadn't completely lost your sense of humour.'

'Of course I want to find them.'

'And do what, exactly?' asked Ilkar. 'And that's a serious question.'

Denser regarded him as if he were an imbecile.

'Ilkar, they are my family. I have to protect them.'

'I think we both understand that,' said The Unknown. He put down the sandwich he had made but not eaten while he'd listened, and leant forward. Ilkar had to smile; he'd lost none of his instant authority. 'But you have been depicting the might of Dordovan magic lined up against us. What do you hope to achieve?'

'A warning, if it's needed. Organisation too. Erienne and Lyanna are already well protected, I know it. But we can help. We even the odds.'

'Who?' asked Ilkar.

'The Raven.'

Ilkar took a long draw on his coffee, feeling the strong bitter taste flood down his throat. He'd known his fate the moment he'd seen The Unknown and Denser come through his gate together. Whatever The Raven could do, he had to help. Futile, possibly. Deadly, probably, if Lyanna and Erienne were in the hands of the power Denser thought they were. But whatever, he had to make sure they understood what they were up against.

'Denser, there's something you need to know.'

'Go on. I feel sure it won't be to my advantage.'

'We've been seeing random mana activity in the sky. Lightning, flaring, showers, that sort of thing. Not a lot but definitely odd. We got talking about it a few days ago. Have you heard of the Tinjata Prophecy?'

Denser shook his head.

'Didn't think so. Neither had I, though perhaps you should have done. Haven't you researched the Sundering at all?'

'Not really,' said Denser. 'Beyond conditions for producing a child with the correct potential and those are well enough documented in Xetesk, I don't think Erienne even disturbed the dust in the open vaults. Who was this Tinjata, then?'

'Well Erienne should certainly have heard of him. He was first High Elder mage of Dordover.'

'She probably has,' said Denser. 'But she hasn't told me about him.'

'Never mind. We'll ask her when we find her. The point is that Tinjata was instrumental in the Sundering and culpable in a number of horrific actions against mages of the One, the Al-Drechar. He formulated a prophecy based on some kind of extrapolation of mana theory and dimensional connectivity – the roots are long gone – and he posted it as a warning to all who believed in the continuation of the four-College structure.'

'How do you know all this?' Denser was frowning.

'I asked around. Do you remember Therus? He helped you in the library during the siege? Well, he survived. He's an ancient writings archivist and the time around the Sundering is an area of particular specialisation for him. And that includes the Tinjata Prophecy.'

'And?' Denser beckoned Ilkar to speak it.

'Right. Well, Therus' knowledge is incomplete because the Dordovans would never let him into their library but the summary is enough. "When the Innocent rides the elements, and the land lies flat and riven; the Sundering shall be undone and from the chaos shall rise the One, never again to fall." Pretty clear, don't you think?' Ilkar felt his heart beating as he spoke the words, finding it impossible to imagine Lyanna, a child he had never seen, presiding over the destruction of Balaia. The idea was frankly ludicrous.

Denser and The Unknown were quiet. The big man finished his sandwich while he thought, the Xeteskian's brows arrowed in as he digested Ilkar's words.

'And that's what Therus thinks your lightning flashes are all about, does he?' asked Denser. 'My child being this "Innocent"? One flash of lightning and the end of the world is coming?'

'Denser, you know what you hoped Lyanna would be. And perhaps she will be the first of a new race of mages, but there are wider implications,' said Ilkar.

'Well, what's certainly clear is that if the Dordovan Quorum believe the prophecy, they'll be desperate to recapture Lyanna,' said The Unknown. 'Or do something to stop her.'

'So what you're saying is that Lyanna is some form of destructive power, according to Tinjata,' said Denser.

'Or maybe the catalyst for something. We've seen lightning in a cloudless sky already and that is a clear elemental anomaly. And you know as well as I do the stories that have been going round. Tidal waves, hurricanes, thunderstorms lasting for days . . . hardly one bolt of lightning, Denser. Therus says they're all mentioned in the prophecy.

'And who are these people you think Erienne has gone to? What if they don't want to train Lyanna but to use her as a focus? We have to consider the possibility.'

'But don't forget on the other hand that, whatever the evidence, Tinjata would have had a vested interest in painting his findings as black as he could,' said Denser.

Ilkar nodded. 'Also true. Look, I'm not for one moment saying that we should leave Lyanna to the Dordovans, or anyone for that matter, besides you and Erienne.'

'What are you saying then?' asked Denser.

'That we should be aware of the wider picture while we search. Putting aside whether the prophecy is true or not, or even relevant to this debate or not, Dordover will act on the premise that it might be; and their actions, if not stemmed, will divide the Colleges, and none of us want that. It doesn't take a genius to see Dordover and Lystern seeing a threat to their independence and identity, and Xetesk looking to broker power and ultimately force a reunion as the dominant party. It all hinges on who controls Lyanna. As for Julatsa, well—' he gave Denser a rueful smile '—we're nowhere, but no less determined to see our magic and beliefs survive.'

Denser rested his head in his hands, pulling them down his face and talking through his fingers. 'Ilkar, you're taking this too far,' he said. 'She's one child. She can't do anything alone.'

'From what you've told me yourself, the Dordovans clearly don't share that view,' returned Ilkar.

'And we are fairly sure she isn't alone,' added The Unknown.

Ilkar sighed and drained his coffee. 'Look, Denser, you have to make a full report to Xetesk on this. You know you do. Gods, I don't suppose they even know Erienne is gone yet. The point is that they can apply significant pressure on the Dordovans to curb any designs they may have on Lyanna's life. That leaves us to search for your family unmolested, so to speak.'

'Officially, anyway,' said The Unknown. He stretched his arms above his head, his shoulder muscles bunching, shirt stitching pulling.

'One more thing,' said Ilkar. 'This is going to spread. The rumours about Lyanna have been around even here, though as no more than a point of interest. But soon there'll be a lot of questions, particularly if Colleges start throwing their weight around. Tinjata's prophecy intimates a return to the One Way and that bothers most mages, me included.

'We can't afford a conflict so let's tread a little carefully, eh?'

Denser shrugged and his mouth twitched up at the corners. 'You're right. I know you're right. That's probably why I came here first. I needed a level-headed view. Thanks, Ilkar.'

'A pleasure. Right, I suggest a day's rest for you while I sort out my affairs here and make my excuses, then a ride to Dordover and then to Xetesk.'

'Why Dordover?' asked Denser.

'Because Therus is away from Julatsa and you really need to read the prophecy, and that's where the original lore script and translation are held. Assuming they'll let you in.'

'And someone must have seen something of Erienne at the time she was escaping,' said The Unknown. 'You just have to ask the right questions. Hmm. We could do with Will or Thraun. They knew Dordover's underbelly well. Still, perhaps their names will open a few doors.'

'There's something missing here,' said Ilkar.

'Hirad,' said The Unknown, nodding.

'We'll collect him after we've been to Xetesk,' said Denser.

'It won't be that simple,' warned The Unknown. 'After all, his dragons are still here.'

Hirad kicked sand over the fire outside his single-roomed stone-and-thatch hut and walked into the Choul. It was not ideal, not for a Kaan dragon. The wind echoed down the gaping maw of a cave forty feet wide, spreading a chill in the winter months for which even three dragons nested together could not fully compensate.

What they really needed was the heat and mud of a Kaan dwelling, but for that Hirad had to have builders, ironsmiths and labourers. And as with so much that concerned the saviours of Balaia, people simply turned their backs and chose to forget.

To a point, Hirad understood. Half a day's ride away in Blackthorne, the Baron still struggled to rebuild his dismembered town. And he alone had sent people to help make the mountain as comfortable as it could be. At least Hirad had a roof separate to that of the Kaan, and a lean-to stable for his nervous horse.

Lighting a lantern, Hirad turned the wick low, aware that his dwindling oil supply would force a trip to Blackthorne before long. Increasingly, he was anxious at leaving the dragons, even for a day and a night. One day, hunters would attack while he was gone.

Walking into the Choul, Hirad pulled his furs tight about him. It was a cold night, unseasonably so, and rain had fallen for much of the day. He yearned for a warm inn with roaring fire, ale in one hand, woman in the other. But he couldn't forget what he owed Sha-Kaan. It seemed, though, that he was the only one.

The stench of dragon filled his nostrils. Undeniably reptilian, it was layered with wood and oil and a sour taint that he knew was exhaled from huge lungs. It wasn't a smell you could ignore but it could be endured. Around a sweeping shallow bend, widened by Blackthorne's men, was a low, domed cavern, big enough for ten dragons. In its centre lay three, and their enormity staggered Hirad no less than it had the first time.

An initial glance revealed a mass of golden scales, moving with indrawn breaths and glittering faintly in the lantern light. A second glance, along with a boosting of the lantern wick, revealed three Kaan dragons. Nos- and Hyn-Kaan lay to either flank, tails coiled, necks laid inwards, bodies dwarfing Hirad as he watched, wings furled tight, claws skittering against the rough floor, tiny movements giving great comfort.

And in their midst, fully a quarter and more their size again, lay Sha-Kaan, Great Kaan of his Brood, exiled by choice to save two dimensions. His head lifted as Hirad entered the Choul and his one-hundred-and-twenty-foot body rippled along its ageing, dulling golden length. Hirad walked to the Great Kaan, standing before the mouth that could swallow him whole.

'I trust you enjoyed your meal, Hirad Coldheart,' rumbled Sha-Kaan, voice sounding only in Hirad's head.

'Yes, thank you, it was an unexpected feast,' replied the barbarian, recalling the sheep Sha-Kaan had deposited outside his hut, undamaged but for a neatly broken neck.

'When we can, we provide,' said Sha-Kaan.

'Though the farmer might right rue the fact you chose his flock.' Hirad smiled.

'Surely a small price for our continuing sacrifice.' Sha-Kaan did not share Hirad's humour.

The barbarian's smile faded and his heart beat a flurry as unsettling thoughts crowded his head for an instant. He stared deep into Sha-Kaan's eyes and saw in them an intense sadness, like grief at a loss; the kind of enduring emptiness The Unknown spoke of when his link with the Protectors was severed.

'What's wrong, Great Kaan?'

Sha-Kaan blinked slowly and breathed in, Hirad feeling the air flow past him.

'This place ages us,' he said. 'It dampens our fire, dries our wings and starves our minds. The Brood psyche cannot sustain what it cannot touch. You have done everything you can, Hirad, and our gratitude will not fade. But our eyes dim, our scales dull and our muscles protest our every movement. Your dimension drains us.'

A chill stole down Hirad's neck and spread through his body.

'You're dying?' he ventured.

Sha-Kaan's startling blue eyes reflected the lantern light as he stared.

'We need to go home, Hirad Coldheart. Soon.'

Hirad bit his lip and strode from the Choul, his anger brimming, his frustration complete. There would have to be action.

In the warming early morning, following a breakfast of fruits, milk and rye bread, Lyanna played in the orchard, skipping around trees and singing to herself, engrossed in a game the rules of which Erienne couldn't fathom as she watched from a bench.

The night had been quiet and peaceful. Lyanna hadn't woken and as a result, had risen refreshed and full of energy. Erienne was glad, knowing she'd need it all and more. This was the calm soon to be shattered and Erienne felt a dreadful anxiety grip her as she watched her little girl play. Her innocence, her essential childishness, her carefree spirit, all were about to be deluged by an overwhelming need to unlock and then control the power within her.

And last night, as she had sat alone in the dining room, sipping at her wine and thinking, she had reached an inescapable truth. Lyanna was to be changed forever and it didn't take a great leap of understanding to realise that the risk of this change was mortal. If for any reason her teaching went astray, Lyanna would die.

'Come here, my sweet.' Erienne held out her arms, the desire to hug her child so strong it hurt. Lyanna trotted over and Erienne crushed her in an embrace she never wanted to release. But all too soon, Lyanna struggled and Erienne allowed her to pull away.

'You promise me you'll be good and listen to your teachers?' she asked, stroking Lyanna's hair.

Lyanna nodded. 'Yes, Mummy.'

'And you'll try to do everything they ask?'

Another nod.

'It's important, you know. And I'll be here if you need me.' She looked into Lyanna's eyes. All the Dordovan training had been taken in her stride, accepted like learning to use knife, fork and spoon. This could be the same but somehow Erienne didn't think so. 'Gods, I wonder if you have any real idea what's happening?' she breathed.

'Of course I do, Mummy,' said Lyanna. Erienne laughed.

'Oh, darling, I'm sorry. Of course you do. Tell me, then.'

'The teachers will help me chase away the bad things. And then they will open the other magic doors and then show me how to hold the wind in my head.'

Erienne gasped. Her heart lurched. She was too young, surely, to have any concept. Erienne had anticipated rote learning. It seemed she was wrong.

'How do you know all that?'

'They told me,' said Lyanna. 'They told me last night.'

'When?'

'While I was sleeping.'

'Oh, did they?' Erienne felt a sour taste in her mouth and a quickening of her pulse.

The door to the orchard opened and Cleress stepped outside, a broad smile on her face. Gone was the tottering of the night before, replaced by an almost youthful stride.

'Is she ready?' she asked brightly.

'Well, apparently you know more about that than I do,' said Erienne sharply.

'What's wrong?'

'Next time you wish to invade my child's mind while she sleeps, you will have the decency to ask me first, is that clear?'

Cleress' smile was brittle. 'We must prepare her, and there are many things she will not accept awake that her subconscious mind will.'

'Cleress, you aren't listening.' Erienne stood up, putting Lyanna down and holding her close. 'I didn't say, don't do it. Gods, I brought her here because I believe you know exactly what you are doing. I merely want you to check with me first. No one understands Lyanna like I do. Sometimes she needs her solitude.'

'Very well.' Cleress scowled.

'She's my daughter, Cleress. Don't any of you forget that.'

'I understand.' She nodded at last. 'We've been alone a long time.'

'Let's just get started, shall we?'

Chapter 6

Denser had no trouble gaining access to the Dordovan College library despite it being after dark, when the grounds were closed to all but College mages and staff. Indeed, on The Raven's arrival in the city the previous day, Vuldaroq had been anxious to help them in their investigations and offer any information available. He had even welcomed Denser and Ilkar's suggestion that they read the Tinjata Prophecy but had extended his official invitation to Denser alone.

Denser was, of course, extremely suspicious. But, with The Unknown and Ilkar out combing the streets for contacts and anything the Dordovans had missed, there was nothing for him to do but read and hope it became apparent why Vuldaroq had been so accommodating.

The original Tinjata Prophecy was kept under airtight glass in another part of the College. What Denser's assigned archivist produced for him was a large leather-bound volume, light brown and titled in embossed gold leaf. It contained upwards of sixty thick parchment pages, the left-hand pages being a transcript of the original lore, the right, a translation, which was incomplete.

Denser had asked why there were blanks in apparently random places, to be told that those parts of the lore were for the eyes of lore scribes only. He had frowned, curiosity aroused, and read what he could.

The early pages turned out to be a rambling account of the dangers of inter-College sexual union, the threat to Balaia of a return of the One Way of magic, and the importance of identifying and retarding the development of any such mage identified.

Denser raised his eyebrows. It seemed that Dordovan thinking hadn't advanced too far on this subject in the intervening millennia.

He read on, past some blank and fractured passages of translation, the prophecy moving to encompass the likely results of ignoring the threat or of failing to control the developing mage. Denser's heart began to beat faster, his mouth drying. Balaia had already been struck by tidal wave, hurricane and days of unbroken thunderclouds and here they were, all laid out. It was hard to believe it was a prophecy, not a diary because, not only did Tinjata foresee the weather systems, he also knew where they would strike.

' "The sea will rise and smite the mouth of the land." ' It didn't take a genius to deduce that Tinjata had meant Sunara's Teeth. ' "The sun shall hide its face and the sky's smears will grow thick and deliver floods upon the earth. And when the gods sigh, the tall will be stunted where they felt most secure and the proud will be laid low, their stone temples the graves of their families." '

And further on, Denser shivered at what might be to come. ' "The beasts from below shall rise to gorge themselves and the mountains will crumble, their dust seen by none, for the eyes of the world will be blinded, awaiting the new light of the One. It shall be the light of hell on the face of the land." '

'Dear Gods.' He looked up and found the archivist looking at him. 'It really is happening, isn't it?' The mage nodded. 'Is there more?'

'It's worth you reading,' said the archivist. 'It might help you understand our fears more fully.'

Denser blew out his cheeks. 'I already understand. I just don't agree with your methods. This is my daughter we're talking about.'

'What can I say?' The archivist shrugged.

'You could say, "can I get you some coffee and a sandwich".'

'I'll be back in a moment but don't leave the library. There are still those who are very bitter about what happened the last time you were in our Tower.'

The archivist bowed slightly and walked away, Denser hearing the door shut gently. It wasn't so much Denser they were bitter about, he assumed, more his Familiar who had, at his bidding, killed a Dordovan mage in a room high up in the Tower. He had never felt any sympathy for the man – his had been a stupid action in capturing the mind-melded demon in the first place – but he had regretted the necessity of his death nonetheless. Dawnthief and the salvation of Balaia had been at stake and there was nothing that couldn't be sacrificed.

Denser turned his attention back to the prophecy, flicking on, the pages creaking against their bindings. He frowned, looking again at one of the partially blank pages. There was something not right about the parchment. He brought the lantern closer and looked, smoothing down the opposite pages. They were different colours, the translated paler than the transcript. And the clinching evidence was there in the spine and the bindings. He quickly checked all the blank and part blank pages, six of them. There could be no doubt. They were newer.

He really had no choice. With his heart thumping in his chest, and his ears straining for any sound of the returning archivist, Denser drew a dagger and slit the untranslated pages from the volume, folding them hurriedly and stuffing them inside his shirt. He resheathed his dagger and turned to an undamaged spread as the door opened.

'Thank you,' he said as a tray containing coffee and bread were placed on the table. He poured a mug with a slightly quivering hand. That had been a little close.

'Anything you need help with?' asked the archivist.

'No,' said Denser, smiling. 'I'm all but done. Just a few more passages.'

The Dordovan moved away. Denser leaned back and watched him, blowing on his coffee and taking a sip. It wasn't too hot and he gulped down half the mug. He took a bite out of the cold meat sandwich. The archivist disappeared behind a shelf and Denser took his chance, closing the volume and snapping the clasps into place. To him, it looked so obvious that pages were missing; to one who wasn't looking, there probably wasn't anything to arouse suspicion. Probably.

Deciding not to take the risk, Denser drained his coffee, grabbed another mouthful of sandwich and stood up, chair scraping slightly on the smooth wood floor and picked up the book. Heading back to the shelf where he thought the prophecy sat, he was intercepted by the archivist.

'Don't trouble yourself,' he said. 'I'll take it.' He held out his hands.

'It's no trouble.'

'I insist.'

Denser smiled as generously as he could muster. 'Thank you.' He followed the Dordovan to the gap in the eight-row-high shelves. The man raised the book to slide it home and paused, a slight frown on his face. He hefted it, feeling its weight. Denser held his breath. It could only have been a heartbeat but it felt a lifetime before the archivist shrugged and replaced it, turning to see Denser's renewed smile.

'Thanks for your help,' he said.

'My pleasure.' The frown hadn't quite disappeared from his face. 'Take the food on your way out. The guard will see you to the gate.'

Denser proffered a hand, which the Dordovan shook.

'Goodbye,' said Denser. 'Let's hope this ends well for all of us.'

'I can second that.' At last a smile.

Denser walked as calmly as he could to the door of the library and summoned the guard to see him out of the Tower, across the grounds and into the streets of Dordover. Only there did he start to relax, a broad grin spreading across his face. He had to find the others and quickly. Vuldaroq might not welcome them for much longer.

It wasn't until early the next morning that the archivist's nagging itch led him back to the Tinjata Prophecy for another look. His swearing shattered the calm of the library.

The Raven, if you could call them that, had come and gone in two days. So far as Vuldaroq and his network could gather, they had found out nothing new, which was something of a shame but hardly a surprise. The Dordovan College guard and mage spies had interrogated every possible contact and lowlife in the City. Spies and assassins were tracking every lead but so far, though some clues to her direction were known, there was nothing as to her final destination.

Yet still he felt satisfied that his plans were forming well. The bait had been taken and Vuldaroq felt he could relax in the knowledge that Balaia's finest were immersed in the search. All that irked him was that, though Denser had taken in the information Vuldaroq had wanted him to from the prophecy, he had stolen that which was not on offer. And the Tower Lord did not want to risk him finding someone to translate the lore for him. Someone, for instance, like his lore scribe wife, Erienne.

He had come to a bar well away from the College and just east of the central cloth market, a well-to-do area where a senior mage could relax without interruption and meet discreetly with whom he pleased. This time, his companion was less brash and arrogant than at their first, rather difficult meeting, but was no less driven.

'You have to understand that the nature of mages has changed since the Wesmen invasion. We cannot afford to wantonly sacrifice each other to satisfy the cravings of a maimed Black Wing. We are trying to regain our strength, not pare it still further.' Vuldaroq took a long drink from his goblet and refilled it from the carafe of very expensive Blackthorne red. A serving woman brought another bowl of Korina Estuary mussels and oysters. 'Excellent.'

'But you understand my price cannot be reduced,' said Selik, his face hooded. 'I will have the bitch, with or without your blessing, but together it will be easier for us all to achieve our ultimate goals.'

Vuldaroq chuckled. Selik had been lucky to escape with his life from the College and had done so only with Vuldaroq's personal intervention. Even so, the Black Wing had left pale and shaken, freed from the entrapping spells in which he had been so quickly entwined. There had been shouting, pushing and recrimination but most of all there had been a shocked disbelief, and it had been this that had allowed Vuldaroq to get Selik away.

'Erienne is still one of our most talented and fertile mages. Her death would be a blow the College would feel keenly. I do not necessarily share the College's view.'

'So?'

'So I will meet your price but you must operate only through me. And now I have organised for you a little assistance.'

'Who?' Selik's single eye stared bleakly from his cowl.

'The Raven.'

Selik laughed, a pained, rasping noise that shuddered his ruined lung. 'And what help can they give me? I am already closer to your precious prize than they will ever be.'

'I would advise you never to underestimate The Raven or their resourcefulness. And for all your torture of the elf you suspect of belonging to this Guild of Drech, he revealed nothing. The Raven are a useful extra force. Monitor them as I will and use what you find as you see fit. As I will.'

Selik rose. 'Then I am already late. The Raven left some hours ago.'

'And headed south,' said Vuldaroq. 'One more thing, Black Wing. Remember with whom you are dealing. Erienne left in response to a signal that pierced our mana shield as easily as a knife through water. They retain great magical power and I need to know where they are. See that Erienne does not die before she tells you their location. But see that she does die.'

Selik bowed very slightly. 'My Lord Vuldaroq, strange though this union of ours is, we both understand that magic is a necessary force. The Black Wings only seek to cut the mould from the otherwise healthy fruit. We are both fighting for the same cause.' He left the Inn, Vuldaroq's eyes on him all the way.

'I don't think so, Selik,' muttered the mage to himself as he prised open another oyster. Unexpected pieces were being added to what could turn out to be a very satisfying conclusion. Perhaps more than one enemy would be laid to rest forever. In a while he would have to organise the interception of The Raven and the taking of the stolen parchment, but for now he had more oysters to enjoy and Vuldaroq was not a man to let excellence go to waste.

Outside, the wind was getting up, rattling the windows of the inn. Dordover could be in for a stormy night.

The day dawned bright, light streaming through cracks in the barn walls. Ilkar, The Unknown and Denser had begged the shelter from a farmer, happening upon his land late at night with the wind battering at their bodies. But it had blown over quickly and now was just an unpleasant memory.

Ilkar rolled over and sat up in his makeshift bed of hay, in the loft above the animals, and came face to face with Denser.

'Gods, but I shouldn't have left Julatsa,' he said. 'Every morning for days, I've been waking next to a beautiful face and figure and for some twisted reason, I've exchanged that for your bloody beard and stinking armpit odour.'

'You know you've missed them,' said Denser, scratching at his short-trimmed beard.

'No,' said Ilkar, heading for the ladder. 'I have not.'

'Hey!' The Unknown's voice came from below. 'Stop chattering and get moving.'

'You heard the man,' said Ilkar, smiling.

'Just like old times,' muttered Denser.

'Absolutely nothing like old times whatsoever,' returned Ilkar.

Outside the barn, they followed The Unknown who was striding up towards the farmhouse across an empty paddock. All the horses were still in the barn and stables. Inside the two-storey house's kitchen, a plate of ham steamed on a long table and the aroma of a sweet leaf tea filled the air. Ilkar raised his eyebrows.

'Very decent of him,' he said, sitting next to The Unknown and forking some meat on to a thick slice of bread.

'Not really,' said The Unknown. 'I've paid him.'

The farm was fifteen miles south of Dordover and one of a cluster lying in a shallow valley near the main trail to Lystern. Occupied during the Wesmen invasion, they had been rebuilt, their fields replanted and animal stocks replenished, restoring them to their key position, supplying both Colleges. Mage-friendly, Ilkar had been confident they'd get a good reception from any of the farms and, since neither he nor Denser had been keen to remain in Dordover, the settlement had been the obvious choice.

'Now listen,' said The Unknown. 'It's apparent that the Dordovans are very serious in their attempts to find Erienne and Lyanna and that means we have to be efficient. So far they've squandered their fifty-day advantage but it can't go on forever and their mage spies will be everywhere, just listening. We should also consider the possibility that we'll be followed.

'Now, that curious friend of Will's told us about activity to the south of the City on the night Erienne left, if you can believe what he said, and even more unreliably, that drunk you found, Denser, reckoned he'd seen a woman and a girl getting into a carriage in about the same place.'

'So what?' asked Denser. 'We already knew they left Dordover. It tells us nothing.'

The Unknown shook his head and sipped the tea. 'Think, Denser. You've spent too much time dabbling in Xetesk's politics. It tells us two things and we can infer a third. First, that they had help, wherever they were going. Second, a carriage suggests a longish trip. Third, they headed south.' He held up a hand to stop Denser speaking. 'Now I'm sure the Dordovans have guessed as much and no doubt they have representatives in every town and city south of here. What they don't have is the information I found out yesterday afternoon.'

'What information?' Ilkar frowned.

'Sorry not to share this until now but too many people knew why we were in Dordover. I bumped into an old merchant friend of mine who travels a good deal between Greythorne and Dordover. He saw a carriage driven by an elf leaving Greythorne three weeks back and heading for Arlen. I know it's not much but it's more than Vuldaroq knows. I think that's where we should be headed.'

'Will this friend talk to anyone else?' asked Denser.

The Unknown cocked his head. 'Hey,' he said. 'It's me you're talking to.'

'Arlen's a long way round from Xetesk and the Balans,' said Ilkar.

'Just what I was worrying about,' said The Unknown. 'Here's what I propose. Denser, you get to Xetesk as fast as you can. ShadowWings would be best and we'll bring your horse. Ilkar and I will head for the Balan Mountains and talk to Hirad. This could get nasty and we need his blade and his strength. Then we meet up as soon as we can in Greythorne.'

'You reckon you can persuade him?' asked Denser.

'Well we've got more chance if you're not there, put it that way,' replied The Unknown. 'He had some particularly legitimate grievances.'

'I know, I know,' said Denser sharply. 'But you know Mount politics, Unknown. Gods' sakes, how far have you got in pressuring the completion of research into safe release of the Protector army?'

'The group I am funding is considerably more advanced than yours which seeks understanding of the realignment of the dimensions. Besides which, I cannot be in Xetesk for long periods. I don't live there, unlike you. And however much Diera understands my desire to see the Protectors have some sort of choice, I am supposed to be retired. Anyway, I don't think this is the time to debate the rights and wrongs of the Mount's organisation,' said The Unknown. 'But you haven't helped yourself, Denser. You haven't kept him informed so he's gone and sought his own information. All he's heard is about your ascension to the fringes of the Circle Seven, and nothing about serious dimensional research.'

'He has to be patient,' protested Denser. 'It's a delicate—'

'Denser, don't try it with me!' snapped The Unknown. 'For one, Hirad has never had any patience and you should always have borne that in mind. For another, it's been more than five years and nothing has happened. Those dragons saved Balaia and so far as he's concerned, Balaia, and more particularly Xetesk, has turned its back on them. And I have to say I have a good deal of sympathy for him.'

'We need him, Unknown. Dordover are a real threat to my family, I can feel it.'

'I am aware of that. All I can say is, we'll do what we can and we'll see you in Greythorne in fourteen days or so.'

'That's a long time,' said Ilkar.

'Then we'd best not hang around,' said The Unknown. 'Come on, eat up. It's time we were on our separate ways.'

Erienne sprinted through the orchard and flung the door aside, her daughter's screams resounding in her ears. She turned right and ran down the corridor towards the Al-Drechar teaching chambers buried in the hillside.

Lyanna was sobbing now, the sounds a torture in Erienne's mind. Her anger flared. Through a set of double doors she all but flattened Ren'erei, who caught her by the arm, arresting her progress.

'Let me go, Ren'erei,' she hissed.

'Calm down, Erienne. What's wrong with you?'

Erienne struggled against her grip, unable to break it.

'Those bloody witches are hurting my daughter.'

'Erienne, I can assure you that is the very last thing they intend.'

But her dismissal and the laughter in her voice merely sent Erienne's blood racing yet higher.

'Let me go. Right now.'

'Not until you calm down.'

Now she looked at Ren, seeing her eyes flinch involuntarily. 'Let me go or I'll drop you where you stand,' she whispered. 'I will see my daughter now.'

Ren'erei stepped away and Erienne ran on without a second glance, following the sounds in her mind, reaching the door to the Whole Room and throwing it open.

'What the hell is going on?' she demanded, but the last words almost died in her throat. Lyanna, apparently happy, was drawing on a chalk board with bright coloured chalks, the Al-Drechar clustered around her desk, staring intently at her work.

Ephemere glanced up. 'Erienne, you look flustered. Has something happened?'

Erienne frowned. The wailing sobs in her head were gone, the screams a distant echo.

'I heard—' she began and took a pace forward. 'Lyanna, are you all right?'

Not even looking up, Lyanna nodded. 'Yes, Mummy.'

Erienne turned back to Ephemere who, with Aviana, was walking towards her across the bare but warm, firelit chamber, the flames dancing across the polished stone walls and ceiling.

'Do you feel all right?' she asked.

'No, I—' Erienne's frown deepened. 'I heard . . . in my head. Lyanna was crying and screaming. It was horrible.'

'I can well imagine,' said Aviana. 'It's probably memories she's exorcising subconsciously. I'm sorry that they are affecting you. This isn't a side effect we'd anticipated. But, as you can see, Lyanna is quite contented.'

The two Al-Drechar continued to move toward her and Erienne felt herded back to the door.

'It wasn't a dream,' she said. 'I wasn't imagining it.'

'No one's suggesting you were,' said Ephemere, her arm out, shepherding Erienne away. 'Perhaps you need some air.'

'Yes,' said Erienne. 'Lyanna, do you need Mummy?'

'No,' came the bright reply.

'Fine.' She couldn't fathom it. The cries had been of pain and fear. She had felt them and come running as she had done a hundred times before in Dordover. Yet Lyanna was completely untroubled, on the outside at least. It didn't make sense. Exorcising memories. Perhaps. She had to think. 'I'll take that flight above the house, if you don't mind,' she said.

Ephemere smiled. 'Of course. An excellent idea. Clear your head. Come back when you're done. Lyanna will be finished by then, I'm sure.'

'See you later then, darling.'

'Uh-huh.' Lyanna continued her drawing.

A loud, flat crack, echoing in the distance brought Lord Denebre to a slightly confused wakefulness in his chair by the roaring fire. Taking a nap in his warmly decorated tower chamber as he always did after lunch, with the sun streaming in through the widened castle window, the old Lord shook his head, wondering whether the sound hadn't been part of a dream. His health had never fully recovered since his town's occupation by the Wesmen and the pain that periodically gripped his stomach was getting worse and more prolonged as the seasons went by. It was an occupation that had claimed the life of Genere, his wife of forty-five years, and the pain in his stomach was eclipsed by that still in his heart.

Lord Denebre levered himself from his chair and walked slowly over to the tower window which overlooked the castle courtyard and across into his beloved town, from which every scar of Wesmen invasion had been scrubbed. It was a warm late afternoon, though there were clouds sweeping up from the south that promised rain.

Looking down over the beautiful lakeside town, Denebre saw that the noise hadn't been a dream. Everywhere, people had stopped to look. Though he was old, Denebre's eyes retained all their sharpness. He could see his townsfolk point or shrug, shake their heads and continue on their way. The market was picking up again after the midday meal, the hawkers' cries floated above the hubbub, men and women had turned out of the handful of inns and traffic moved sedately down the cobbled, impeccably clean streets.

Lord Denebre didn't have a vast fortune but what he could spare, he set to keeping the place of his birth as he remembered it as a child. His people respected and protected the town and those who travelled in and sought to take advantage of what they saw as a soft underbelly soon discovered a hard edge to the Lord's governance. He wouldn't have gibbets on display in the town, but on the approaches they occasionally swung with the corpse of robber or thief. In his naïveté, he had thought a couple of examples were all that it would take but over the years he had never ceased to be amazed at the arrogance and stupidity of criminals.

Mainly, though, his life had been a joy and his sons and daughters had pledged to keep the idyll when he was gone. That had made it all the harder when the Wesmen had come, threatening the destruction and death of all he held dear.

Gone now, of course. Back across the Blackthornes. He doubted they would ever incur again. And certainly not before he was long entombed. Denebre smiled to himself and took a deep breath at the window. A second crack shattered the calm of the day, bringing silence to the market. It was an unearthly sound, reverberating through the ground and sending a tiny shudder through the castle walls.

Denebre's face creased into a frown and he squinted out, shading his eyes with a shaking, mottled hand and peering away towards the low hills that bordered the small lake's southern shores where he had fished as a boy.

A black scar ran down the face of the grass- and bracken-covered slope. Denebre had not recalled it being there before . . . perhaps a fire during the hot, dry summer. He dismissed the notion; it was not something he would have missed.

His heart skipped a beat and raced. The scar was moving. Outwards and down, swallowing more of the lush green and belching a cloud of dust into the sky.

'No, no,' he whispered, breath suddenly ragged. Two more cracks assaulted the ears, two more fractures appeared, land falling into the instant chasms, the hideous brown-black lines rushing down the hillside accompanied by a low, dread rumbling.

The vibration through the castle increased. In the market place, voices were raised in anxiety and incomprehension. Stalls were rattling, a stack of oranges spilled and bounced onto the street as stallholders rushed to make their goods secure, first instincts for preservation of business, not self.

Moving impossibly fast, the ruptures, which the town's people couldn't see, tore through the south shore and disappeared beneath the lake. For one blissful moment, Denebre thought the water had halted the charge but the rumbling never died and the tremors increased their intensity. A picture fell from the wall behind him. The logs shifted on the fire.

Turmoil churned the placid surface of the lake. Waves fled out from its centre in every direction, great bubbles boiled to the surface and finally, with a huge, sucking thud, a wall of water erupted, sending a mist into the air, falling back like a deluge of rain.

Denebre gripped the window sill, the vibrations through his feet leaving him uncertain of his balance. Dust shivered from every crevice and his chair rattled against the stone flags.

Devastation was coming. The farmland north of the lake fell into the void as if hell were pulling it down. Tears were streaming down the old Lord's face. What the Wesmen couldn't achieve, nature would wreak in the blink of an eye.

He leaned out of the window. Down in the town, milling confusion reined. People were screaming or barking warnings. Feet slithered on heaving streets, doors were closed, windows fell from frames and the roar of approaching doom still had no face.

'Run, run.' Denebre cursed his voice. Weak with age, it couldn't hope to carry and though he waved an arm frantically, even if anyone was looking, they couldn't hope to understand what he was doing. He was helpless, and the earth was swallowing his town.

Land folded inwards at its borders, the fractures tore into the first building and moved on, faster than a horse could gallop and straight as an arrow, heading for the castle. The world was shaking. Sudden subsidence robbed Denebre of his purchase and he fell heavily, feeling a bone in his hand snap as he tried to absorb the fall.

He cried out, his breath coming in short gasps, but no one would be hearing him. Outside, the rumble had become a deafening roar, as of some earthbound leviathan finding its voice at the surface.

Denebre clawed his way back to his feet, the floor around him shaking, the window frame creaking, glass long since gone. A timber crashed down behind him, thumping into the fire, scattering burning logs across the floor, embers filling the small room. The old Lord ignored it all.

Panic had engulfed the streets and market place. Men, women and children ran blindly away from a threat that showed no mercy. Timbers split, stone cracked, and whole buildings heaved, struck by giant ripples of land before collapsing into the maw of the beast, crushing anyone in their path.

A choking dust mixed with smoke thickened over Denebre. People scrabbled desperately against the tilting land only to lose grip and slip shrieking into the depth of the earth. The castle gatehouse rocked violently and crumbled, huge gashes fled along the courtyard walls and orders from guardsmen were lost in the awful wailing of horses and the chaos of a hundred poor souls trying to save themselves from a fate from which there was no escape.

Lord Denebre's tower shifted ominously. Behind him, another timber hit the floor. Slates from the roof fell past the window to land in the crevice opening up before the front doors of his own house and not pausing before sweeping under the keep.

'May the Gods have mercy upon us,' he whispered.

The tower shuddered again, the window frame loosened and fell. The air was filled with dust and the creaking of protesting stone and wood. Denebre stood firm, leaning against the shifting wall but the keep groaned, a mortal wound struck in its foundations.

Beyond the walls, the market place was gone, replaced by piles of rubble, mounds of earth thrown up by the leviathan and scattered with bodies, precious few of whom were moving.

Lord Denebre took one last look at the sky, blue and peaceful, the sun shining down. Beneath his feet, the tower moved sickeningly sideways, the violence of the movement all but breaking his grip on the loose window sill. His knees gave way and he sagged forwards, determined not to lose sight of his beloved town. A thudding far below him, reverberating through his feet, told him of central supports breaking.

The tower teetered, the roar of hell pounding at his ears, the sounds of collapsing stone only just audible. His chamber shifted and sagged. Slabs of rock fell through the ceiling to smash into and through the floor and the fall of slate outside became a torrent.

A third massive shudder and the tower leaned outwards at an impossible angle, slipping, sliding on inexorably. Denebre wiped his face clear of dust and tears.

'Not long now, Genere, my love. Not long now.'

The air was clear, warm and pure in her lungs, as Erienne's ShadowWings took her slowly higher, revealing more and more of the quite extraordinary structure that dominated Herendeneth's single shallow peak.

She'd meant to let the air blow through her, dismissing confusion to allow her to think about all that was going awry. But the scene below her changed all that and for an age it seemed, it filled her eyes and her mind.

The house of the Al-Drechar was sprawling, disorganised and magnificent. She hovered, identifying the orchard where Lyanna loved to play, and worked outwards

Immediately below and towards the path to the landing, she could see what would have been the original grand entrance to the house when it had first been built. Half-towers and gallery-sized rooms were covered with a slate roof which itself was bestrewn with vibrant green creeper. More recently built and making the new frontage, was a lower structure of wood and glass, a long slender entrance corridor that Erienne remembered running along after Ren'erei, on their arrival that now seemed a long time ago.

To the left of the orchard, three slate-roofed wings jutted like the legs of a monstrous insect, not quite straight as if built around immovable natural features. Swooping a little closer, she could see these features were gently steaming rock pools and delicate waterfalls none but a fool would destroy.

To the right, one massive structure dominated. She moved slowly over it, seeing courtyards and follies built into the intricate multilevel building of white stone, grey slate, dark wood and an extraordinary abundance of flowers as if the Gods had sprinkled them from the heavens. A gorgeous confusion of reds, yellows, blues and purples, strung with emerald green, every pigment strong and pure.

But the real majesty was to the rear of the orchard and it dwarfed the rest of the house. Cut into steps up the shallow incline to the peak of the hill were terrace after terrace of arches, statues, pillars, domed roofs as of small temples, grottos, pools, intricate rock gardens and perfectly formed trees. And on the peak itself, a stone needle, thirty feet high and six across its base, pointing to the sky, swarming with ivy, covered with weathered carvings and exuding a deep and ancient aura of mage power.

Erienne flew lower, extending her wings for a long slow glide across the extraordinary architectural and cultural diversity of what she saw. Approaching, she looked for a likely landing place, already imagining herself walking in the tranquillity, lost from herself and everyone for a few precious moments. But as she neared, the air chilled and she retreated upwards, feeling all at once like a trespasser in the past.

She wasn't flying over the fanciful notions of artists brought to fruition, she was flying over graves. One, surely, for every Al-Drechar that had lived to dream of the reunification of the colleges and died, unfulfilled and fearful of the end of all in which they believed.

To land now would be to desecrate the memories. First, she had to carry through her mission, despite her burgeoning misgivings. She flew a little higher and tried to make sense of it all.

Lyanna's training had performed an almost instant change on her, exactly as Erienne had feared. Gone was the carefree spirit that sang nonsense songs to her doll, to be replaced by a considered, almost introverted, quiet. And though she would still talk, Erienne could see there was more than just the thoughts of a child behind her eyes. It was as if she were assimilating everything she saw, felt and heard; and presumably it was the same on the mana spectra.

Erienne was at once scared of what her daughter would become, proud that she was the future of the One Way and jealous of the wonders she might see.

It was all so different from her time in Dordover, where Lyanna's training, based on generations of developing the minds of infants, left her with all her innocence and gave her the gift of mana acceptance. Erienne felt yet another sweep of guilt as she rode the warm thermals above Herendeneth. She knew Lyanna's mind was suffering in Dordover and they had had to leave, but was this really any better? She still shouted out in the night, she still awoke crying from the pain in her head. There was comfort, though. Here, at least, Lyanna stood a chance of living and giving Balaia back the gift that stood on the precipice of extinction.

But she couldn't banish the worries. She'd seen the Al-Drechar leave the Whole Room and fail to disguise the anxiety in their faces. She had seen them become visibly more frail at the end of each day though the training was barely seven days old. And she had interrupted whispered conversations that stopped too abruptly when she was noticed.

Determining to speak to Ephemere later, she rose higher, interested to see where the illusion began. She was perhaps only fifty feet from the ground when the house started to become indistinct. Like grey cloud washing across the sky, blotting out detail, the house disappeared under the enormously complex spell with every beat of the ShadowWings. At a little over sixty feet, all she could see was the top of a mist-obscured long-extinct volcano.

As she watched, the illusion flickered and steadied. She thought it a trick of her eyes until the shimmer was repeated. To her left, a roiling in the spell left a wing of the house plainly visible for several beats and closer inspection revealed light shining through illusory rock.

Erienne's heart raced and she dived for the orchard. She'd seen enough poorly maintained static spells to know the illusion was decaying towards the point of collapse.

Something was badly wrong. Surely the Al-Drechar's strength

could not be so seriously impaired this soon. A failing illusion was worse than none at all, sending flares of mana whipping through the spectra. To the trained eye, they'd be like a beacon fire in the dead of night. No clearer signal would be needed. All it would take was a master mage searching the southern coasts of Balaia and out to sea.

And then Dordover would come in force. It would be no contest.

Chapter 7

Two days after leaving Ilkar and The Unknown Warrior, Denser sat in his chambers, a warm fire heating the small study, its crackling frequently drowned out by the storm assailing Xetesk. Lightning flared and spat across the darkened heavens, thunder rolled and crashed, reverberating through the stone of the College, while rain drove against the shutters like the furious knocking of a thousand angry demons.

But no sound came from the pair in the study; Denser at his desk and the promising young lore diviner, Ciryn, in a chair by the fire. She was one of a relatively new breed trained to develop an empathy with certain aspects of another lore, in this case Dordover's. And scattered around the room was every text and scrap of information Xetesk had on Dordovan lore and its meaning. It amounted to precious little but they had shed fragmented light, held together by educated guesswork, on one of the Tinjata passages Denser had stolen. It had been easy to see why Vuldaroq had ordered the translation removed.

Denser seethed at the danger Lyanna had unknowingly been in every day of her stay in Dordover, a death threat hanging over her. And Erienne could not have known of it, though she would surely have researched Tinjata during her years in Dordover. But, he reasoned, Vuldaroq would have seen this abhorrent passage withheld from her just as he had from Denser.

He reread the words they had pieced together, his anger and relief clashing uncomfortably. '. . . silenced forever . . . ritual . . . order of casting . . . and only then can the breath be stopped and the celebration begin . . . scattering of ashes accordingly . . . lore demands.'

'There's no mistake in this?' he asked.

Ciryn shrugged, her lank brown hair lifting on her shoulders as she did so, and looked at him though dark eyes set in a face too long to be anything but plain.

'Almost certainly in the words, Master Denser, but not in the meaning.'

He shouldn't have been surprised, he supposed. But the ritual magical killing the words implied made the Dordovans no better than the Black Wings. Just a little more precise.

Denser returned to a passage towards the end of the prophecy. So far, Ciryn had determined that it dealt with another danger to the Dordovan order. There were words describing some odd type of shielding but no apparent reference to a casting. It also suggested, Ciryn thought, that the shielder would die as a result of the process, or at least become what she called, 'irrevocably altered', but that the One Mage would grow in some undefined manner.

Much as Ciryn did, but less logically, Denser scoured the texts at his left hand, looking for anything that might unlock just one of the words of Dordovan lore for which they had, as yet, no clue. Their knowledge was so frustratingly slight. And the Prophecy was written in a lower lore. Had it concerned spell construction or generation, they would have read nothing whatever: the higher Dordovan languages remained completely closed to Xetesk.

Denser sighed and Ciryn looked up, frowning, her finger propping open a scroll, her teeth irritating at her bottom lip.

'Master Denser?'

'Sorry, but I can't make any sense of this.'

'But I'm afraid I think I can,' said the diviner.

'Why afraid?'

'Because you are the child's father. I'll write down the piece I have translated,' said Ciryn.

'No, just tell me,' said Denser.

'Oh. All right.' She took in a deep breath. 'I don't think it's a shielding, I think that was the wrong interpretation. But it's a way of bringing a One Mage from Night undamaged.'

'How?' A chance to really help his daughter was there for him to grasp.

'By the father opening his mind to the storm and surrounding his child with the power of his mind, so showing the light the mage needs to complete Awakening.'

Denser felt suddenly cold. 'But that would mean I would d—'

'Be irrevocably changed, yes.'

The Circle Seven had taken Denser's words in complete silence the following mid-morning. Deep under the Tower of the Lord of the Mount in the Laryon Chamber, they had granted him unwilling

audience then sat transfixed as he recounted recent events in Dordover, spoken of Erienne's letter and the work he and Ciryn had
completed the night before.

The Circle Seven, Xetesk's Tower Masters, chaired by Dystran, the
fortunate incumbent of the Mount, had been expecting more pressure
for research. What they heard was a cry for help and the raising of the
spectre of a threat from another College.

'How long since her disappearance?' asked Ranyl, an ageing
master, hairless and hunched but still vital in his magic.

'More than sixty days.' There was a hiss of indrawn breath.

'And you still hope to find her,' said Dystran. His tenure had aged
his young face, his eyes looked heavy and his black hair was shot
through with grey.

'Yes,' said Denser firmly. 'There seems little doubt who she has
gone to.'

Dystran chuckled. 'Indeed, but we are now entering the realm of
myth and blind belief. And we have no idea where these one-magic
mages of yours live, should they turn out to be real.'

'You should read more,' responded Denser. 'Ilkar says there's
significant evidence that they're on or near Calaius and that's backed
up, albeit tenuously, by the leads we found in Dordover.'

'So what do you want of us?' Dystran regarded Denser over
steepled fingers, affecting a pose of studied contemplation. Denser
almost laughed. This Lord of the Mount was a ridiculous figure who
had done nothing but engender political instability since his surprise
tenure had begun more than five years before. A bigger surprise was
that he remained alive. Ranyl was doubtless the architect of his
continued survival. Denser wandered how long it would be before the
old man made his move.

'I need Xetesk to keep Dordover away. Their intentions are clear
enough and we can't let them take Lyanna back, or worse.'

Dystran's eyes flashed fanatically cold. 'Oh we'll keep Dordover
away, all right. We can't have them meddle any further with the
natural order. And you clearly understand your role. It's certainly
fortunate we've delayed implementation of the volunteer release plan
your Unknown Warrior so desires, isn't it?'

Denser shuddered. The Protectors would be marching again. The
Unknown wasn't going to like it.

Selik rode with a guard of eight Black Wings, his journey from
Dordover to Arlen pausing in the ruins of Denebre. He wanted to

show his men what it was they were fighting for. Not that they were wavering. It just never hurt to reinforce beliefs.

But what he saw didn't merely do that, it added a whole new dimension. And for Selik personally, it set his anger raging afresh and brought an ache to his dead eye. The nine men rode slowly around the edges of the once beautiful lakeside town. They couldn't even get to what had been the centre; chasms in the earth blocked their way.

And perhaps that was fortunate. The stench of death was everywhere. Above the wind, the buzzing of myriad flies was a warning to keep away and everywhere they looked, rats scurried. Disease would be running into the rivers and soaking into the ground. Selik hated to think about the state of the poor innocents lying dead and unburied.

He could imagine all too easily the panic that had engulfed the town. As the earth heaved and buildings plunged, people would have abandoned everything that was dear to them. Their homes, their possessions. Their families. The air would have been filled with the screams of the terrified and the wounded and dying. Dust would have clogged lungs, chips of stone and glass would have slashed faces and hands; and everywhere they ran, the people of Denebre would have encountered the ground at their feet tearing itself apart, swallowing them whole or ripping their bodies to shreds.

Looking across the ruins it was hard to imagine the life that had been there so recently. Not one building was left standing. On the opposite side of the town, the castle was rubble. Selik could make out parts of the keep, piles of tottering stone and snapped timbers suggested where the walls might have been. But the outer structures were gone. A gash seventy yards wide had driven through the centre of the courtyard in front of the keep and taken it all down.

Nearer to where they sat, mute, the Black Wings couldn't make out a single road or where the market place had stood. Debris littered the ground, great boulders and shelves of earth had thrust from below and, here and there, a ragged piece of cloth or the smashed remnants of furniture were all that signified the life that had been so brutally snuffed out.

Selik was amazed that anyone had survived and indeed only a handful had, taking their story to Pontois or Lystern, some south to Erskan. But who was to say it wouldn't happen again in any of those places?

Selik turned to his men and took in their disbelieving expressions and the hands over their mouths to keep out the worst of the smell that drifted by on the breeze.

'This is why we fight magic,' he said. 'This is why we are right. Magic caused all of this, never forget that. It is a force of evil and we are the only ones who can see it. The rest of the world is blind.'

But not for long, he thought. The destruction across Balaia had to change the perceptions of its people. They would demand more control. The mages couldn't be trusted to keep their power benign and innocents were dying in their hundreds and thousands, taken by forces they couldn't understand.

The worst of it was that *she* was behind it all. The bitch had given birth to the abomination whose mind was destroying the land. All in the cause of greater power, of domination. Selik seethed and as he put his heels to his mount and spurred it on southwards, leaving Denebre to rot, he began to imagine the pain he would cause her before he allowed her to die. Justice for the righteous. Agonising death for the mage.

The rain was falling hard on the Balan Mountains when Ilkar and The Unknown Warrior arrived, tired and hungry, late one evening, eleven days after parting company with Denser. It was a bleak and cold night following a chill and sunless day. The rain had fallen incessantly and the pair had ridden into the teeth of a biting wind, every part of their bodies soaked despite cloaks and leather. Bemoaning the sharp change in the weather from the sun and warmth of Julatsa, Ilkar was walking his horse and wishing fervently he was caressing Pheone's body when a movement in the rocks above caught his eye.

'Unknown—' he began, but with a shriek, a huge shadow tore through the clouds, sweeping low over them. Ilkar's horse reared and bolted, the elf making no attempt to hold on to the reins. The Unknown was pitched from his, landing in a heap on the ground, a flurry of hooves narrowly missing his head as his mount followed Ilkar's in a desperate attempt to escape.

The dragon banked and turned, its black outline only just visible against the heavy cloud in the darkness. Ilkar, shield spell on lips and heart hammering, moved towards The Unknown as the big man surged to his feet. He was swordless but no less imposing and his face was creased in irritation.

'Hirad!' he barked over the noise of wind, rain and wing. 'That is not funny.'

Nos-Kaan flew overhead, heading back to the Choul.

'Can't be too careful,' came the shouted reply. A figure moved down from the rocks above them. He had a few days' growth of stubble on his chin, long unkempt hair blowing about his head and heavy furs covering his trademark leather armour. He moved quickly and surely over treacherous wet rock, displaying no fear of the steep falls any slip would bring. Ilkar expected nothing less from Hirad Coldheart.

He leapt the last few feet, his tough leather boots smacking in a small puddle, and pulled Ilkar into a rough embrace.

'Gods, it's good to see you, Ilks,' he said. Ilkar pulled away, his nose wrinkling.

'You haven't built the bathhouse yet, then?' he said. Hirad grinned, his teeth white against his dark stubble.

'Sorry, it's these furs. I haven't got much in the way of curing tools up there. I'm taking them to Blackthorne in a couple of days, get them seen to.'

'I don't think so, Hirad,' said Ilkar. The barbarian's smile disappeared and he looked from one old friend to the other.

'This isn't a social call, then?' he asked.

'In this weather?' said Ilkar, wiping a sheen of water from his face.

'We'll tell you all about it once you've found our horses and kit,' grumbled The Unknown. 'Was that little display really necessary?'

Hirad's face was sombre. 'I can't take chances, Unknown. I couldn't see who it was and neither could Nos until he was closer. The hunters are getting too clever.'

The Unknown nodded. 'Later,' he said. 'Let's get ourselves out of this rain first, eh?'

It was a beautifully warm sunny day in Dordover, quite at odds with the chill that had swept over the city the day before. The scent of late-flowering blooms hung in the air of the College grounds and the chittering of birds gave an almost spring-like atmosphere. But it was moving towards late autumn and Vuldaroq did not enjoy sweating in the heat in this season. He bustled along the cloister corridor to the Chamber of Reflection where visiting College dignitaries were met, sighing in satisfaction at its cool ambience as he swept in, dark voluminous robes flapping behind him.

The Chamber of Reflection was a room built entirely of polished granite slabs, in each corner of which a fountain or waterfall had been built to engender peace and calm. Woven reed chairs sat about a low marble table and beyond the doors opposite the cloister corridor was the rock garden. It was a place much loved by mages for its intricate arrangements of pools and plants but hated by Vuldaroq for its ability to trap the sun's heat. He would not be entering it today.

Waiting in the Chamber were two men recently arrived from Lystern, Balaia's fourth and smallest College. Heryst, Lord Elder Mage, and General Ry Darrick, Balaia's brilliant young soldier. He was scowling beneath his mass of light brown curly hair and plainly uncomfortable, shifting his tall frame as if in a hurry to leave as he stood behind the seated Heryst. Three goblets and a jug sat on the low table next to a large wicker bowl of fruits.

'You took your time,' said Vuldaroq, bridling at Heryst's refusal to rise as he entered.

Heryst merely smiled. 'There are many issues demanding my attention in Lystern. We travelled as soon as was practicable.'

'Pour yourself some juice, Vuldaroq,' said Darrick. 'Sit down. You're looking a little flushed.'

Vuldaroq met Darrick's eyes. The General didn't flinch, staring back placidly until the Dordovan reached for the jug.

'Your Communion was not detailed,' said Heryst. 'I take it you have a problem too severe for Dordover to handle alone.'

Vuldaroq eased himself into a chair, his bulk causing the weave to creak and protest. He took a long draw on the cooling mixed apple and orange juice, determining to retain a modicum of control.

'As you may be aware, the child has left Dordover. This would not be a problem in itself but she and her mother have disappeared, to all intents and purposes, and we believe them to have been contacted by servants of the One Way.'

Heryst laughed. 'Vuldaroq, you always did have a penchant for the dramatic. For you, the most outrageous of conclusions for any series of events has always been the most likely. No doubt Erienne is relaxing with her husband. Or perhaps she and Lyanna have merely taken a break from the rigours of training. They are not your prisoners, remember; they can go and do whatever they like without your permission.'

Vuldaroq mopped his sweating brow and allowed himself a patronising smile.

'Busy your College may be but it faces inwards from dawn 'til dusk. Lyanna is a child of the One, that much is now achingly obvious, and her effect is already being felt across Balaia. Presumably you are aware that Greythorne Town and Thornewood have been struck by winds the like of which none have ever experienced, and that Denebre has been all but swallowed by the earth.' He leaned back, waiting for reaction. Darrick's shrug disappointed but did not surprise him.

'Portents of some greater doom, are they?' The soldier couldn't keep the cynicism from his voice.

'Absolutely,' said Vuldaroq, hoping his sombre response would disconcert the cocky General. 'You are clearly not conversant with the Tinjata Prophecy. Your High Elder Mage, of course, is.'

Heryst was suddenly a shade paler, his swagger gone. Vuldaroq watched him replay the words of the prophecy in his head before he spoke, his voice quiet.

'Are you sure?' he asked.

'About what?'

Heryst shrugged. 'All of it.'

'How much more evidence do you need? Surely the word is spreading around Lystern as it is here. Denebre has gone, swallowed by the earth. Thornewood has been flattened by a hurricane, we've had reports of flooding from a dozen and more towns, and Blood Lake now covers over twice its original area. Even Korina hasn't escaped. And that's not to mention all the stories of lightning storms, hail lasting days and cloud so dense the sun never penetrates.

'Look, Denser was here a few days ago with Ilkar and The Unknown Warrior. The Raven is reforming to search for her. They share our concerns. This child must be found and returned to the College before more harm is done.'

'And Xetesk?' ventured Heryst.

Vuldaroq blew out his cheeks. 'We can expect them to be troublesome. Though they too are at risk from the elemental forces battering Balaia.'

'But surely they believe the outcome will be better for them if the girl is not found and returned,' said Heryst.

'Indeed, so long as the storms cease,' agreed Vuldaroq. 'We must be very wary of them.'

'So what do you require of us?' asked Darrick, mindful of Heryst's reaction.

'Both The Raven and the child will need protection. I have people shadowing The Raven. When the time is right, I want you, General, to be in the right place to help them. That could be before or after they find the girl. If Heryst agrees, I want you to lead a force of Dordovan and Lysternan cavalry to achieve that aim.'

'Naturally,' said Heryst. 'Anything.'

Vuldaroq smiled. 'Thank you, Heryst. Your cooperation will see both of our Colleges remain independent.' Darrick was frowning, looking down at his feet. 'General, is anything bothering you?'

'There's something not right about this,' said Darrick. 'I don't see why The Raven were called upon so late and I don't see why Xetesk would cause any trouble. Surely they share your – our – interest in the child?'

Vuldaroq's lips thinned. 'My dear General, The Raven had retired. And while Denser was fully in support of our early efforts to find Lyanna alone, it subsequently became clear we needed more help, hence The Raven and your good selves.

'And you are right, Xetesk does share our interest, but they have an agenda other than our own. They want to see a return to the One Way of magic and that would spell, if you'll pardon the pun, the end of Dordover, Lystern and, for that matter, Julatsa.'

'I can't see why Xetesk would desire that. Not now – surely they are as anxious as any of us to maintain equality among the Colleges?'

'Well, that rather depends on whether they feel they can survive and become the dominant force without the need for battle. And I believe that's exactly what they think.'

Darrick nodded, though Vuldaroq could see he remained unconvinced. 'And what of Erienne and Lyanna's feelings and desires?'

'They are Dordovans,' said Vuldaroq sharply. 'And it is our right as well as our duty to train them in the Dordovan ethic. Lyanna will, of course, be allowed to expand her compass to other disciplines but she should remain, at root, one of ours.'

Darrick raised his eyebrows. 'Surely Lyanna is a child of Dordover and Xetesk, at the very least, and perhaps of all Colleges.'

'Ry, please? I'll explain later.' Heryst looked over his shoulder.

Darrick shrugged. 'They are my friends, my Lord Mage. I am merely anxious to see right done by them.'

'And it will be,' assured Heryst.

'There is far more at stake here than friendship,' said Vuldaroq.

Darrick regarded him coolly. 'No, there isn't,' he said. 'Not for me.' He bowed to both mages and left the Chamber of Reflection.

Vuldaroq scowled. 'You keep your General in line,' he said. 'We've already got The Raven out there and I can't have any more mavericks. This is too big.'

'Don't worry, Vuldaroq. Darrick may be possessed of a big heart but he is also possessed of an unflinching loyalty to Lystern. He'll do as I ask.'

'See that he does.'

*

Lyanna was walking alone down the corridor to her room as Erienne hurried into the house, a confrontation with the Al-Drechar on her mind.

'Lyanna?' she called, a little more sharply than she'd intended, taken aback that Ren'erei wasn't shadowing her.

The little girl stopped and Erienne felt the air move about her. She turned a scowling face to her mother and walked towards her. Erienne had seen that scowl a hundred times before but this time she felt threatened, though the notion was absurd.

'Oh Lyanna, what's happened? Don't look like that,' she said gently, crouching down. 'Come and give me a hug.'

'I don't feel well,' said Lyanna. 'Ephy's very tired and Myra was sick. I hurt them, Mummy, and I hurt you.' She was close to tears.

Erienne frowned. 'You didn't hurt me, darling. I was just worried about you, that's all.'

But Lyanna shook her head. 'No, Mummy, I know what I did.' A tear rolled down her cheek. Erienne wiped it away then pulled Lyanna close.

'You could never hurt me, Lyanna. I love you.' She stood, picking her daughter up and taking her to her room, setting her on the bed. 'Tell you what, why don't you tell me what you did today? What made Ephy so tired?'

'I draw pictures,' said Lyanna, her tone a little brighter. 'Of what the magic inside me shows me. Then they tell me how to hold the wind it makes in my head.' Lyanna looked up and more tears were in her eyes. 'But I can't make it work and they have to help me and it makes them ill and things happen. I know they do because they all look so frowny and then they have to stop and make my mind quiet again.'

She started to grizzle and Erienne held her tightly, her heart lurching. She couldn't grasp exactly what Lyanna was trying to explain but one conclusion was clear enough. The Al-Drechar weren't coping.

'Will you be all right here on your own for a little while?' she asked.

'Yes. For a little. Maybe Ren will come.'

'If I see her, I'll ask her to visit you.' Erienne smiled and leant to kiss Lyanna's cheek. It was wet with tears. 'Don't worry, my sweet. Everything will be fine.'

But as she hurried along to the dining room where she hoped to find the Al-Drechar, her words echoed in her mind like betrayal.

They were there, as she had hoped, sitting around one end of the table as always. Myriell had the pipe in her hands though it was only late afternoon.

'Sit, Erienne. Sit.' Cleress waved a hand wearily at the empty chairs. Erienne chose one where she could face them all.

'I think it's time you told me what is really going on,' she said.

'You sound as if you think something's wrong,' said Aviana.

'And it's time you dropped that illusion too. It's as full of holes as the one I flew over just now.' There was no reaction. Erienne pointed at her eyes. 'These work, you know.' Then her ears. 'And so do these. So why don't you drop the high and mighty all-conquering Al-Drechar bit and tell me what's happening.' Erienne felt her anger stir. She saw a frown flash across Ephemere's face but it was Cleress who spoke.

'Your daughter is an exceptionally talented individual but her abilities are unfocused. It is taking longer than we anticipated to calm her mind. Then we can begin to train her to use the Way.'

'Gods, I get straighter answers from Lyanna,' Erienne said. 'Look, I don't know whose benefit all your bluff is for but I'm not buying it. I may not be Al-Drechar but I know when I see a major illusion disintegrating and I know what that causes in the mana spectra. I also know when I see four exhausted old elves and I'm looking at them right now. I'm asking you, please, don't fail because you're too proud to call on me to help.'

The Al-Drechar were silent, expressions neutral while they conversed with each other. Erienne waited and presently Ephemere focused on her.

'Erienne, the depth of your daughter's potential power exceeds our hopes but brings such problems. Her youth makes her mind so vulnerable to surges and uncontrolled expression of mana and we have had to absorb and refocus so much as she learns to accept the feelings within her.

'She is not currently at risk because we are able to accommodate her energies but, as you have made clear, it has depleted our own and leaves us somewhat exposed.'

'Somewhat? Look at you Ephy, Myra – all of you – taking the pipe in the afternoon, sitting like it takes all of your remaining energy to stay upright. And that illusion above our heads is a liability. Why do you even sustain it?' Erienne felt a crawling in her chest. The

Al-Drechar looked so frail. Such power and venerability reduced to sunken-eyed exhaustion.

'It is our only defence,' said Aviana. 'We are so few and our enemies are so near.' She sounded close to panic.

'But how long can you go on, Ana? Gods, you're killing yourselves. Let me help, I implore you. Tell me what I can do.' She searched their faces through the wisps of smoke. 'Clerry? Ephy?'

'We have already taken steps,' said Cleress.

'Ren'erei is leaving on the pre-dawn tide,' said Ephemere.

'To do what?'

'To seek mages who can sustain the illusion and allow us to focus all our energies on Lyanna,' replied Cleress.

'Where's she going? I mean, do you have mages you can trust?'

Cleress shook her head. 'I'm afraid it's a little more urgent than that. We have no mages in the Guild and Ren'erei goes to Calaius to recruit those who believe in our myth.' She tried to smile. Erienne was horrified.

'You're going to invite total strangers here? Think of the consequences.'

'And think of them if we don't,' said Myriell harshly, her voice thick with pipe smoke.

'No, no. Sorry, Myra but you misunderstand,' said Erienne. 'I'm talking about trust and betrayal. You've spent so long keeping your location secret, you can't afford even the slightest risk that Ren'erei finds the wrong people.' She paused, her heart swelling in her chest, ashamed at the rush she was feeling. 'I'm going with Ren'erei but not to Calaius because you need people, and not just mages, that you can trust utterly. We're going back to Balaia. You need The Raven.'

The vanguard of the Protector army scouted half a day ahead of the rest, at the limits of contact with their brothers. Twenty men, masked and silent, accompanied by four mages directing their movement but no longer with the ultimate punishment for disobedience available to them.

The Protectors represented a declining but still awesome Xeteskian calling. The last man had been taken more than six years before and subsequently freed in a ceremony that could not be repeated until it was further researched. He was The Unknown Warrior and they would never forget him.

A frighteningly short time ago, a Protector transgressing the harsh rules of the calling would have suffered soul torment by demons for as long as his Given mage wanted. That was no longer sanctioned although the demons hadn't been told that. Souls to torment was their part of the bargain for maintaining the DemonChains that linked each Protector to his soul held outside his body in the Soul Tank, deep in the catacombs of Xetesk.

In truth, the punishment wasn't needed now anyway. Aeb, at the head of the vanguard, could barely remember the years before he was taken. He would have been in his late teens, he thought. What he knew now was that the Soul Tank, where his soul linked with those of his hundreds of companions, meant brotherhood beyond all human meaning. It meant strength, comfort and understanding on the most basic level. It was what made them the power they were.

He understood that one day, he might be asked to choose freedom. He wasn't sure what he would say.

But some rules remained. A Protector could make no decisions except in a battle situation unless his Given was lost. And Protectors were never told to where they marched. They followed and fought or threatened as directed. Aeb accepted it had to be this way. And though the souls often swam in unhappiness in their Xeteskian containment, their abiding joy was their closeness and the power it gave them. There were no dissenters. It had ever been so and the concept was alien. It would undermine the whole and that was unacceptable. Abhorrent.

Aeb was aware that research would break the brotherhood and it saddened him. But for now, people feared the Protectors and that was right. People like the Dordovan cavalry they had encountered.

They had been travelling south and east from Xetesk for four days, stopping late in the night and setting off at dawn each day, their pace fast, their rests dictated by the tiredness of mages and horses. An hour from the borders of the mage lands, in an area once rich for farming but now battered by incessant rain, they had paused for refreshment.

All day, low cloud had released a shifting rain mist that eddied in the wind and made visibility poor. The damp penetrated armour and mask, the land was quiet as if every other living thing had sought shelter, and the mist played with the eyes, making shapes where there were none. For some time before the Dordovans had ridden up, they had heard hoof falls echoing dully, the rain and wind making their direction of approach difficult to determine. Eventually, the Dordovans had appeared, their lead warriors pulling up sharply as the Xeteskians loomed at them out of the mist.

Aeb permitted himself the tiniest satisfaction at their manner. He could see the mask of Elx, dark and shining, and knew that they must have startled the horsemen. Aeb signalled the body of the army, using his nineteen brothers to augment him over the range. The mages stepped into the centre of the trail as a rider trotted up from the middle of the Dordovan column. He was another mage, but fat, the skin of his face unhealthy under the hood of his cloak. His horse had the girth to match.

Their lead mage, Sytkan, spoke.

'Vuldaroq. What an unpleasant, if predictable sight.'

The fat mage smiled. 'Likewise, Sytkan. We've heard reports of you and your abominations on the move for days. I suppose it's pointless to enquire after your destination.'

'A waste of your breath, but more a waste of mine.' Sytkan looked about him. He was a young mage, a junior master but being schooled for greatness. He was tall, quick and heavy-boned, his grey eyes glaring out from under his tight-fitting skull cap. 'You know something, I do believe these lands to be under the care of Xetesk.'

'Care? An interesting term. And I believe we have full rights of passage as laid down in the Triverne Agreement on Mage Land Propriety.'

'An old and dusty legislature,' said Sytkan. 'And rendered void in times of open conflict between Colleges, as I recall.'

'Is that what you call this?' Asked Vuldaroq.

'Since your insults directed at the Lord of the Mount, yes.'

Tension flared. Aeb watched the ripple through the Dordovan cavalry. He could count more than a hundred but guessed that twice that many stood hidden by the chill swirling mist.

Stand down ready. No weapons. Check left, aggressive intent, centre is fear, right neutral, Aeb pulsed to his brothers. None of them so much as moved a muscle.

In the centre of the trail, the four Xeteskian mages stood calm but Aeb could feel one preparing a HardShield to defend against projectile attack. Beside her, another prepared spell defence. He assumed the Dordovans were doing the same.

'It would be unwise to threaten us, Sytkan,' said Vuldaroq. 'I have three hundred cavalry here. I'd hate to see them run you down.'

'And you will not,' replied Sytkan, voice firm but cool. 'A clear act of aggression in Xeteskian lands would be a great mistake with the bulk of the Protector army not far behind you.'

Vuldaroq chuckled and dismounted, his horse twitching its gut and back as the considerable weight was removed. The mage walked forward.

'There. Far more civilised. Now, I think this little spat should end here. Let's agree to differ on our agendas and move on.' He was a few paces from Sytkan and Aeb could see the fear in his eyes though he covered it with overconfident bluster.

'Absolutely,' agreed Sytkan. 'But for you that means journeying by the quickest route from Xeteskian lands. You understand you cannot be allowed to ride ahead of us. So, north, I think that means. Aeb, do you concur?'

'The lands north are easier for horses, Master. It is a quicker route than south.'

'Exactly. I am sorry, Vuldaroq, but I have instructions from Dystran himself. Due to the unfortunate reaction of Dordover and Lystern, our lands are temporarily closed to your traffic. I require you to respect that.'

'You expect me to accede to the word of a Lord of the Mount who is nothing more than a puppet to his Circle Seven and the advice of a masked thug?' Vuldaroq spun on his heel and stalked back to his horse.

'Retract your remarks concerning my Lord of the Mount,' demanded Sytkan.

'I never retract the truth.'

'Aeb, deploy,' muttered Sytkan, signalling his mages to cast their shields.

Space across the path. Move to ready.

Like ghosts in the mist, the Protectors reacted, their movements precise and efficient. In moments they had blocked the path in a slightly concave line. As they came to ready, axes and swords snapped from back mounts in a clatter of steel which echoed across the windswept space, its chill sound accentuated by the silence that followed. Aeb looked and saw fear. It was expected.

Sytkan spoke into the void. 'This is not a bluff. Your insults are crude, Vuldaroq, but our threat is not. Ride north. Leave our lands and take some advice. Go back to Dordover. You'll find nothing but death in Arlen.'

Vuldaroq sniffed. 'I will ride where I please.'

'North.'

'And if I refuse?'

'Then we will attack you. Aeb has freedom to act. He needs no further command.'

Vuldaroq considered and smiled. He shrugged.

'Horses are quick. Your creatures are on foot. I can order the cavalry to ride north a mile if it will assuage your conscience. We will return to the path at a time that suits us and well ahead of you.'

'How little you understand about the mind of a Protector. He is bred to snuff out threat and aggression against Xetesk. You can only ride so fast and we will track you down. Don't challenge us.'

'I am getting very tired of this. We are three hundred horse and one hundred and fifty mages. You are twenty and four. Stand aside.'

'You are a split force,' said Sytkan. 'And no, we will not yield. All Xeteskians are pledged to defend their land, as you are yours. If you can't show civility, at least show respect.' He tempered his tone and added. 'Come on, Vuldaroq, neither of us needs to fight here. You know I can't move. You aren't losing face. You're just doing the right thing.'

'So be it.' Vuldaroq wheeled his horse and began to trot back down the centre of the four-abreast cavalry column. At once, FlameOrbs soared up from its middle, arcing across the space to splash against the shield covering the Xeteskians. It held, the fire lashing over its transparent surface, searing and cracking as it dissipated into the ground, sending steam clouding up.

'Damn you, Vuldaroq,' muttered Sytkan.

Aeb needed no invitation.

Front rank, horses, second rank, flank support. Force width, pincer in.

Standing at the centre point of their formation, Aeb, with Elx and Ryu at his sides, stepped up just as the Dordovan cavalry started moving. Dropping to his haunches, Aeb swung his axe right-handed into the lead horse's front legs, catching the left just above the knee and slicing clear. The animal screamed and reared, Aeb already moving forward and away from the flailing limbs. Its rider crashed off, seeing nothing but the Protector's sword thrash through his undefended neck.

Left and right, Aeb's brothers struck low with axe, high with sword, horses and riders collapsing as the frightening onslaught gathered momentum. Blood fizzed into the air, painting the mist a hideous shade of pink and, all around, the terrified cries of horses mingled with the urgent shouts of riders attempting to force their mounts to forward action.

Aeb was pressed on all sides. He lashed out with his axe, feeling it bite deep into an unguarded flank. The horse leapt sideways, rider hanging on, sweeping his sword down where it connected with Aeb's protective block. But the man was unbalanced and the next axe strike knocked him from his saddle, to die under the hooves of his stricken mount which, eyes rolling, searched for a way out of the death, the scent high in its flaring nostrils.

Aeb let it go, to add to the confusion, and turned for his next target. Ahead of him, the cavalry had stopped and left Elx decapitated a rider who had made the mistake of leaning down to strike at what he had been sure was an unguarded back.

Regroup. Withdraw centre. Outer flanks hold. They are massing. Charge imminent.

Aeb looked along the line. No Protectors were lost and a dozen cavalry lay slain. He backed off, each footstep sure, guided by a brother. Overhead, more FlameOrbs covered the sky, boiling the spray of rain as they travelled, detonating harmlessly on the Xeteskian shields. There was no return.

The Dordovan cavalry had disappeared back into the mist but in the eerie half-silence, shouted orders filtered out. Visibility was perhaps sixty yards. The Protectors stood in two ranks of ten, ten paces from the carnage they had created. Their weight was towards the flanks, eighteen each side, with only Aeb and three others holding dead centre. Long before they could see anything, the ground vibrated as the cavalry advanced at a trot. Clashing metal sounded from the mist, and the snorts of horses impatient for the charge.

Aeb waited, his Protectors solid and unmoving. Shadows moved in the mist ahead, ghosts in the rain. Slowly, they resolved and Aeb could see the outline of their formation. He felt his pulse quicken and his brothers joined him in the surge that came before battle. Behind him, the mages were mounted, spell shields doubled, HardShield dropped, ready to run but confident in their Protectors.

Perhaps fifty yards away, at a barked order, the cavalry charged, the riders roaring as they came, weapons glistening in the rain, their horses sleek and powerful, bred for the run.

Aeb had assessed the charge before it came. 'Front ranks, Master Sytkan. Break the flanks.'

They will attempt to flank, be ready. Low stance, quick strikes. Axes front. We are one.

We are one, came the response.

Xetesk had a weapon and Sytkan, having already suffered spell attack, was not shy of retaliating with it. He had been preparing since the skirmish began. As the first horses in the eight-wide column broke into the gallop towards the bodies of their fallen comrades, he and his spare mage crossed arms over their chests before pushing their hands out to cover the cavalry's flanks.

'HellFire.'

Blasting away the mist, steam trailing and gushing, a dozen columns of fire hammered down from the sky, each seeking a living soul. To the left, the Dordovan shield held, sending the flame lashing and spinning into the ground where it scorched the wet earth to ignition, panicking horses and riders alike. But to the right it cracked, and beneath it, the cavalry never stood a chance.

Men blew apart under the sudden tumult, with no time to scream before their bodies were splashed to the winds, the fire driving on, breaking horses in two, finally spending itself against the ground.

The right flank disintegrated in terror, surviving horses bucking and twisting, taking their hapless riders back into the teeth of the charge that smashed into them, unable to pull up in time. Horses tried desperately to jump others in their path, catapulting riders out of saddles and the slap of horse on horse and the agonised cries of riders with legs crushed between two beasts filled the air.

To the left, the splashing fire caused similar chaos, though less pain and only in the centre did the charge come on. Skittish but well-trained, the wild-eyed mounts drove steadily on, slower now, picking their way over the bodies of the fallen.

In front of them squatted Aeb, axe cocked and ready in both hands, his sword discarded, lying in the mud at his feet. He fixed his eyes on their strides, establishing the pattern and calculating the fast diminishing distance. At the last, he rolled left and forward, returning to the crouch and swinging up and out with his axe. He felt it slice flesh and he hardened his grip, letting the blade bite deep and his body be dragged forward by the momentum of the horse, keeping his body tucked.

The animal shuddered. Aeb looked up and saw the axe deep in its thigh. He clung on, dragging it down, its rider unable to strike out effectively as he fought his wounded mount. The horse stuttered and pitched on to its nose, other cavalry milling behind it, disconcerted by the belligerence of the Protectors. But two broke through, bowling over the men in their path, horse clattering over bodies, riders exhorting them on.

Taken by surprise for an instant, one of the second rank was taken by a wheeling sword that whistled through his chest, lifting him from his feet. But the rest were so fast. Forming up seamlessly, Protectors crouched and swung to slow the horses while more brothers dived at the riders, bearing them from their saddles to the ground and with sharp twists, ending their lives in a snapping of necks.

Aeb wrenched his axe clear of the fallen but struggling horse.

Aeb, three brothers down. Sword underfoot. Right lower rear quarter strike.

He struck without looking. A cavalryman died.

Stooping, he swept up his sword, straightened and saw the end game. Protectors forged in on both sides of the crumbling charge. Wide spaced and with weapons free, they struck without error, bringing down horse before taking rider, a relentless advance. Aeb moved up. In front of him, a cavalryman wrestled his blade from a tangle of reins and forced his horse around. He blanched as he saw the Protector advance but was already too late. Ignoring the animal, Aeb lashed round-armed with his axe, lifting the rider clean out of his saddle, the blow catching him high in the chest, his last breath exhaled as a fountain of blood.

They are broken. We are victorious. We are one.

We are one.

Aeb surveyed the enemy. They were wheeling and galloping away down the trail, shouts of recrimination echoing through the swirling mist that smelled so much of death. Satisfied, he turned, counted all the mages safe and knelt to take the mask from Elx.

The brother had taken a hoof clear in the face, splitting the mask and snapping his neck. His face, bloodied and bruising, stared sightless to the sky. He was released. In the Soul Tank, they would grieve. His body, they would burn. His weapons, they would take.

Aeb walked back down the path to where Sytkan sat on his horse, his young face angry, his body tired from the HellFire casting.

'Will they attack again?' he asked.

'No, but we will track them, master. Now they are running south.'

'Good. Then tend to your wounded and dead. We need to be away from here. It's still ten days to Arlen.'

Chapter 9

'Has the water clogged your ears, Ilkar? I said no.' Hirad slammed his tin cup down on the stone table and stalked to the door of his hut, leaning against its frame and looking out at the dreary night.

The rain hadn't stopped and by the time they'd found the horses, all three men were drenched and miserable. Hirad had banked a good fire in his hut and now their clothes were steaming on a rail hanging in front of it while they each wore a blanket. But despite the ridiculous picture they made and the meal they shared, Hirad's mood had not lightened enough to hear what Ilkar and The Unknown wanted of him with any real reason.

'You shouted it, actually,' said Ilkar evenly, picking at some lamb stuck in his teeth. 'And I heard you the first time. I just hoped I'd heard wrong.'

'Well you didn't,' growled Hirad, turning half face. 'Why the hell should I help that prat? Everything he promised, he failed to deliver. The Kaan are still here.'

'It was never something that was going to be solved quickly,' reasoned The Unknown.

'I know. I didn't expect quickly. But it's been almost five years. And nothing has happened. Nothing.' Hirad's voice was cool and angry. 'They're dying, you know.'

'I understand your feelings,' said The Unknown. 'But Denser's not been idle, he's—'

'Oh yeah, I gathered that. Close to the Circle Seven, has the ear of the Lord of the Mount, good chambers. Not idle at all.' Hirad cleared his throat and spat out of the door. 'Tell you what, when he comes here with clear evidence Xetesk is working on getting my dragons home, I'll help him find his family.'

'He doesn't have that sort of time,' said The Unknown.

'He's had five years!' Hirad stormed back across the room. 'Five bastard years! My dragons are dying and the only people capable of helping them are sitting on their fat arses congratulating each other about how they beat the Wesmen. The real heroes are being left to rot.' Hirad stared at The Unknown and Ilkar in turn, taking in their faces in the firelight.

'I'm not getting through, am I?' he said quietly. 'Get your boots on and come with me. The Choul's right next door. Saying hello is the least you can do.'

The three men scurried across the short space to the cave, blankets held tightly around them. Hirad's lantern lit the way in the chill, damp gloom.

'Gods, Hirad, it's cold,' said Ilkar.

'Yes, isn't it,' said Hirad. They rounded the corner into the Choul proper, the stench of dragon nauseatingly strong. Hirad grinned fiercely at his friends' gasps.

'Great Kaan, visitors for you.'

Sha-Kaan raised his head and opened a shining blue eye.

'Well met, Ilkar. Well met, Unknown Warrior.' His voice was low and tired, that of a dragon close to sleep.

'And you, Sha-Kaan,' said Ilkar. 'I won't ask about your health. Hirad has already been forthright. I am sorry.'

'Sorry will not take us home.' The lack of lustre was plain. The immensity of the Kaan's size and presence was undiminished but the verve was gone from his voice and his languid movement was a sign of his growing inertia.

'Hirad mentioned your desire,' said The Unknown.

'It has always been a desire. Now it is a necessity.' Sha-Kaan gazed at the pair unblinking. 'You have picked a curious time for your visit. Rain and dark, I understand, are not to human liking.'

The Unknown shrugged. 'We need Hirad. The weather is inconsequential.'

'And I told them I wouldn't be helping,' interrupted Hirad.

'With what?' asked Sha-Kaan.

'Finding Denser's daughter.'

'Ah.' Sha-Kaan opened his mouth wide, his jaws stretching impossibly wide, fangs glinting in the lantern light. 'I might have guessed the thief was at the heart of your anger, Hirad Coldheart. Presumably he isn't yet offering a way back to Beshara.'

'No,' said Hirad curtly. 'He hasn't quite finished worming his way to the top of the Xeteskian mage society.'

Ilkar sighed.

'You have something to add?' asked Sha-Kaan.

'Hirad knows I believe he's being harsh on Denser, though I

understand his and your frustration at the length of your wait. But we're talking about the safety of Erienne and her child, Lyanna. They are in considerable danger though they probably don't know it. Right now, Dordover is searching for them both and Denser thinks they don't necessarily want to catch Lyanna alive.'

'And I said he's creating shit,' said Hirad. 'Dordover has been *training* her. Why would they want to kill her?'

'I tried to explain but you weren't listening. It's because of what she represents and where they think she's gone,' Ilkar said.

Sha-Kaan breathed out, a low rumbling sound that sent echoes through the air.

'This child is a mage?' he asked.

' "Mage" hardly covers it,' said Ilkar. 'She is almost certainly a four-College adept and probably capable of encompassing the One Way.'

Nos- and Hyn-Kaan's heads snapped up and all three dragons stared at Ilkar, who took an involuntary pace backwards. The Kaans' necks moved, giving the impression of a three-headed beast with a single monstrous body.

'Where has she gone?' demanded Sha-Kaan.

'Denser suspects she's with practitioners of the One Way but we don't know if they even still exist, let alone where they might be.'

'Al-Drechar,' breathed Sha-Kaan. 'If they live, they must be found. Hirad, you must help.'

'Who are these Al whatever?'

'Keepers of the One,' said Sha-Kaan. 'Septern will surely have shared his knowledge with them. He was one of them. They can send us home.'

Dordover had ignored Xetesk's call for a Triverne Lake meeting. That in itself would have been an act of aggression had they not invoked a dusty but very useful clause in the four-College treaty which in this case, covered Julatsa. The College was inquorate, temporarily at least, and unable to fulfil its duties. More, its acting High Mage, Ilkar of The Raven, was absent.

Vuldaroq fully expected the deputation he received a few days later, particularly as it came in the aftermath of his mobilisation of a one-hundred-and-fifty-strong Dordovan mage force, enhanced by three hundred mounted swordsmen. That, added to Darrick's Lysternan and Dordovan cavalry, however reluctant their commander, amounted to a significant troop movement. Xetesk were bound to be unhappy but, as in all things, it was the way in which they were told that was important.

This was not a stroke Vuldaroq would have pulled with Styliann still incumbent on The Mount. Whatever his personal feelings, Vuldaroq had respected Styliann's intelligence and political acumen. But the pup, Dystran, had no respected network, no quality advisers and no sure thoughts of his own. Even Denser wasn't on hand to help. Everything seemed to be working rather well and Dystran's entirely predictable responses merely added to Vuldaroq's feeling of control.

He chose to meet Dystran and his unimpressive entourage in the austere surroundings of a student's study chambers, the small living area of which contained a round table and four straight wooden chairs, a basic iron-grated fireplace and plain brown drapes which hid ill-fitting shuttered windows. Candles cast a wan illumination amid gaunt shadows, and the air was heavy with old damp.

The only concession to the seniority of his guests was the ubiquitous bowl of fruits and an insulated jug of Dordover's much vaunted herbal tea. It was cold, wet and very windy outside and the enlivening infusion would banish thoughts of that particular un-pleasantness and stop tired minds from wandering.

Vuldaroq and High Secretary Berian were ensconced early in the chambers, situated in an outbuilding off the central courtyard behind the Tower. As the door opened to admit a scowling Dystran, Vuldaroq had positioned himself to greet him with a perfectly modelled expression of apology on his face. Behind Dystran, came Ranyl, an average mage in Vuldaroq's opinion, and a pair of Protectors.

'Gentlemen, I must apologise for the sparseness of our surroundings but your arrival finds us at rather a loss for quality accommodation.' He held out his hands in a gesture of supplication. Dystran regarded him coldly before moving to sit opposite Berian.

'We have come here to talk, not debate the fine points of your College's architecture and wallhangings,' he said.

'Indeed not,' said Vuldaroq, smiling thinly. 'Berian, tea for our guests. My Lord Dystran, your Protectors?' Vuldaroq found it difficult to contain his distaste at the abominations that insulted his College by their presence. They should all have been put to the sword years ago.

'They need nothing. If they make you feel uncomfortable, they can remain outside.'

'Most kind.' Vuldaroq took his seat and waited while the tea was poured. Ranyl selected an apple but he was the only one who ate. The Dordovan Tower Lord watched while the Xeteskians drank, noting with satisfaction their obvious pleasure.

'Very good,' admitted Dystran.

'Perhaps our best kept secret,' said Berian, inclining his head.

'Hmm, and you keep very few of those these days, it seems,' said Dystran, turning to face Vuldaroq.

'You have issues you wish to discuss,' said Vuldaroq smoothly.

'I have not ridden here to idly pass the days,' said Dystran shortly. 'And I will not keep you from my point. Your mobilisation of forces is a clear act of aggression and an insult to the peace not only between the Colleges but that presiding across Balaia. And, I will add that your Arch Mage's decision to send, with all due respect to yourself, a lesser lord, to attend me is a personal slur that I find both mystifying and unnecessary.'

Vuldaroq lifted his hands in a placatory gesture while he seethed behind his carefully neutral expression.

'As I'm sure you are aware, my Lord Dystran, Arch Mage Herolus is in very poor health and his death is close. I and Berian act as his voice and his ears in his stead, as it has always been during times of Arch Mage sickness. There is no slur.' He sipped his tea before continuing. 'Furthermore, I find your use of the term aggression a little surprising. I fail to see who it is that we threaten. My meagre forces are acting on reputable intelligence suggesting a threat to our child, Lyanna, and her mother. We are naturally concerned and have dispatched a protective force to travel south, where we believe we have most chance of finding our people before our enemies do.

'I fear the same cannot be said for your considerable number of, and I use the term advisedly, "Protectors" now marauding along the borders of the mage lands blatantly intimidating any Dordovans they and their masters encounter.'

Dystran frowned. 'Against what are you protecting the child? You haven't even found her yet and indeed probably never will. The Raven may bring her back but I fear even they will be left searching for spirits in the wind.

'As for my Protectors, they are there as a reminder to Dordover that shows of strength and force will not go unchallenged or unmatched. They also provide a security net for those within and without the mage community who do not share Dordover's parochial views.'

Vuldaroq chuckled and leant back in his chair, taking a mouthful of tea that he sloshed over his tongue, letting the flavours enrich his mouth. At least the pup had spirit.

'My dear Dystran, Dordover's views can hardly be considered parochial, shared as they are by Lystern and Julatsa. It is Xetesk that is out of step with College thinking and College desire.'

'But surely your desire to control Lyanna will lead to her losing her life,' said Dystran.

'I have mentioned no one losing their life,' replied Vuldaroq. 'Our intention is to return the girl here to continue her training.'

'Which, as I think we are both aware, will result in her quick and painful demise.'

'I beg your pardon?'

'Don't play me for a fool, Vuldaroq. We both understand what is happening here and we both know that Erienne left Dordover because she believed your training was harming her daughter. We both think we know to whom she has gone and we have both read the Tinjata Prophecy. But instead of being excited about the possibility that the Al-Drechar still live, your sole concern is grasping at something that is not even yours to take back.'

Dystran's eyes burned while beside him, Ranyl drank tea as if he hadn't a care. In contrast, Vuldaroq could sense Berian's discomfort without the need to look. He let the tension settle, choosing to refill their mugs, the new burst of revitalising herbal scent a perfect tonic.

'I have never thought you a fool,' he said at length, the lie slipping easily from his tongue. 'But the chaos and destruction visited on Balaia is the principal reason Lyanna must be returned to us quickly. It's clear to the Masters here that whoever holds her, and I'm not at all convinced it is these Keepers of the One you seem to think it is, haven't the skill to prevent her from unleashing these mana storms. There was no such problem while she was here, was there?'

Dystran gave a slight nod. 'Stories of freak weather were around well before Lyanna left Dordover. Still, a predictable response. However, Xetesk considers Lyanna a Dordovan by fluke of birth-place only. We believe her to be a child of the One and that while Tinjata was mainly accurate, his conclusion was flawed and based in fear of a return to the One Way, not in real belief of ultimate disaster.'

'And you don't consider earthquakes, hurricanes and tidal waves the prelude to ultimate disaster?' Vuldaroq was surprised by the basic flaws in the Xeteskian take on events. 'If we're right, and by we, I mean you and us, then just one small child is causing all this. She must be properly controlled until she is able to harness her undoubted powers effectively.'

Dystran shook his head. 'Let's not pretend, Vuldaroq. Lyanna represents a threat to the magical order that Dordover wishes to maintain. But she is the future for us all. The way forward, not back as you seem to believe. And we will not stand by and watch her destroyed by you while you hide behind your pretty words.' Dystran set his body and pushed his mug away from him. 'We will stop you taking her. Recall your forces. Let The Raven see her safe.'

'The Raven?' Vuldaroq couldn't help but scoff. 'Pawns in a greater game and in too deep. They are a help to us all but no solution. Surely you can see that.'

'Yet you let them run because part of you believes them to have the best chance of finding the child.'

Vuldaroq inclined his head. 'Their skill is unquestioned. Their strength as the years pass is more open to debate.'

'And assuming you should recover the child by whatever means, when will you be handing her to Xetesk for further training?'

The Dordovan Tower Lord was taken by surprise by the question and blew out his cheeks while giving an involuntary half shrug. 'Dystran, that is a decision for our lore masters and not one that can be given now.'

Dystran leaned forwards, clasping his hands in front of him on the table. 'On the contrary, Dordovan, it can. The girl is to be left with the Al-Drechar, if it is they who hold her. And that is because we believe they have the best chance of halting the mana storms in a timely fashion. Or she is to travel to Xetesk before enjoying training in both Lystern and ultimately Julatsa. She will not be returning to Dordover.'

Vuldaroq felt his jaw drop a mote before he caught it. 'You dare to threaten this in the halls of my College?' he managed.

'Oh, please, Vuldaroq, this is no threat and my Protectors are not marching for pure effect. I tried to ask you politely but now I demand that you withdraw your forces and those of Lystern and allow this matter to be settled in the natural way.'

'Meaning?' snarled Vuldaroq.

'Meaning Lyanna be allowed to develop unhindered in the place that her mother and father deem the most appropriate. That place clearly not being here.'

Vuldaroq turned to Berian and raised his eyebrows. Berian responded with a slight shake of the head.

'I'm afraid that we cannot agree to such conditions. We have a vested interest and will see it through.'

Dystran stood abruptly, followed a heartbeat later by Ranyl. The door to the chambers opened and a Protector stood in the frame, his sheer presence imposing and frightening even to the mages.

'Then I am afraid that relations between our two Colleges, and presumably Lystern, are not, for the time being, on a cordial footing. You are so notified and warned. Good day.'

The Xeteskians swept from the room. Vuldaroq leaned back in his chair and poked his tongue into his cheek.

'Stupid young pup,' he said and turned to Berian. 'Oh dear, old friend. It does look rather as if we have a little trouble on our hands. Heryst and Darrick must be informed immediately. See to it, would you? I have others to contact and we both have journeys to make.'

Erienne found herself more than a little hurt that Lyanna hadn't cried when told her mother was leaving. In fact, she displayed precious little emotion bar a smile when Erienne explained the reason for her abrupt departure.

'They are tired,' Lyanna had said. 'And I think they look older. Daddy can help.'

And much as she had tried to dismiss her feelings as a purely selfish reaction, Erienne couldn't help but think that Lyanna's response was simply too calculated. Not right for a five-year-old girl.

Erienne waved again and Lyanna waved back as the long boat pulled out of the tiny bay to dock with the *Ocean Elm*. Ephemere stood to one side and, as the long boat reached the less sheltered water, ushered Lyanna away back up the path to the house.

Inside the failing illusion, the trees flanking the path waved in a light breeze and the rock that flanked the small beach and the path closed in quickly as they moved further from the shore, taking from Erienne her last view of Lyanna's hair and back.

Erienne let her head drop, her heart already heavy. This was going to be her first break of more than a couple of days from Lyanna and she wasn't at all sure how well she'd cope with the separation. She felt a lump in her throat, tears behind her eyes. It would have been easier if she thought Lyanna felt the same.

Ren'erei didn't approach her until the ship was underway, joining her leaning on the port rails, watching the deep blue waves passing by.

'She'll be fine. The Al-Drechar will care for her,' she said.

Erienne smiled to herself. She couldn't help but like the young elf despite her deeply ingrained serious nature but sometimes she missed the real issue completely.

'Oh I have no doubt she'll be fine. It's me I'm worrying about.' She didn't lift her head, letting the white-flecked water fill her eyes.

'You'll miss her terribly.'

'Yes, I will. Let's just find Denser fast.' She looked across. Ren'erei wasn't looking at her but she was nodding as she gazed down at the sea.

'It will be a pleasure to meet him,' said Ren'erei. 'The father of Lyanna and the keeper of your heart.'

Erienne blushed and was glad for the elf's studying of the *Ocean Elm*'s load line.

'Don't get too excited. He's Xeteskian first and my husband second, I think.'

'Then his priorities are askew.'

'Not really. I am a mother first and a wife second. We both have tasks to fulfil before our lives together can really start. I think it's best we're honest in the interim.'

Ren'erei contemplated Erienne's words. She could see the elf raise her eyebrows as she thought, and suck in her lips. Erienne felt very safe in her company. She was solid and dependable and her thoughts ran deep. And her naïveté was endearing. Ren wasn't streetwise like anyone with a normal education in the ways of Balaia but she harboured great strength of feeling and inside the elf there was the confidence to kill. The Raven could have done with her a few years ago.

'How will you find him?'

'Communion. When we arrive in Arlen, I think I have the range to reach Xetesk. I'm sure he'll still be there. Or possibly Dordover. Either way I can contact him. Then we wait.'

'And The Raven?'

'He'll bring them. If I know Denser, he's already contacted them.'

'You sound very sure.'

Erienne shrugged. 'They're all such different people but when one is troubled, they all do the same thing.' She smiled, a little surprised by another surge of longing. Not for Lyanna but for them. The Raven. To stand among them once again. Should that happen, she knew they'd be all right. After all, The Raven never lost. Erienne suppressed a laugh at her own ludicrous arrogance and looked back to the beautiful blue sea.

Chapter 10

Hirad's meeting with Denser was never going to be warm but the devastation he saw at Thornewood and then Greythorne took much of the venom from the barbarian's mood. Ilkar had watched him brood ever since they'd left the Balan Mountains, unwilling even to entertain the thought of cordial relations with the Xeteskian. He had grumbled about leaving the Kaan who were all but shovelling him from the Choul and his temper had remained frail for the entirety of the three-day ride.

But Thornewood had changed him. The three original members of The Raven's first ride, almost fifteen years before, had seen signs of wind damage while they were over a day from the forest. Flattened grassland, bushes uprooted and drifts of broken twigs, leaves and dirt, all told of a powerful gale.

But nothing could prepare them for Thornewood itself. It was gone. Just a tangled mass of twisted and shattered trunks, scattered debris and piles of foliage covered in dirt. It was as if some giant claw had gouged across the forest, scooped it up, crushed it and then let it fall once again. Where once a stunning landscape had been, there was now just a smear on the face of Balaia.

'I can't even see where the farms might have stood,' whispered Ilkar. 'There are no borders to the wood. Nothing at all.'

The Unknown pointed north and east. 'There's the trail though it's mostly hidden now. We should see if there's anything we can do.'

But close to, it was clear that what little could be done, had been done. A few foundation poles from one of the farmsteads that had lived off the forest could be seen snapped off low to the ground and, here and there, a piece of treated hide was wedged in a shallow crack in the earth. All other signs of life had been swept away.

Hirad stared into the havoc that had been visited on Thornewood and voiced the fear they all felt.

'Thraun?'

'We just have to pray he escaped,' said The Unknown quietly. 'But even he would have been hard pressed to survive a falling tree.'

'And as for the pack . . .' Ilkar left his words hanging. Though he was a wolf, Thraun would always retain vestiges of humanity in his mind. It was the way of all shapechangers, even those lost to their human form, and Thraun had already experienced more sadness than most of his fragile kind could bear. The Gods only knew what he would do if he lost the pack.

'What caused this?' The Unknown shook his head.

'I'm scared to even think about it,' said Ilkar.

'What do you mean?' asked Hirad.

'Let's get to Greythorne,' said Ilkar by way of reply. 'Find Denser.'

They rode on, expectations of finding the town undamaged dismissed. But as they travelled the decimated lowlands surrounding the wrecked forest, it became clear that their worst fears were liable to be realised.

It was like a journey through a foreign landscape though they all knew the land well. So many landmarks and waypoints had gone. Trail posts, cairns, copses and spinneys, all had been scratched from the face of Balaia. Any remote homestead had been destroyed, timbers scattered wide and even the topsoil had been ripped away on the exposed slopes, bringing rock to the surface for the first time in centuries.

The wind, if such it was, had been utterly indiscriminate and totally ruinous.

They were under a day's ride from Greythorne with the morning all but over when The Unknown turned in his saddle for the third time in as many miles. He dropped back slowly before shifting in his saddle and pulling up.

'Hey!' he called, dismounting and scrutinising the girth buckle and strap. 'Wait up.'

Hirad and Ilkar wheeled their horses and trotted towards him, slipping off as they approached.

'Girth slipping?' asked Hirad.

The Unknown nodded. 'No,' he said. 'Don't look up. We're being followed. Tell you what, get out your waterskin and let's have a break, all right?'

Hirad shrugged. 'Sure.'

The Unknown unbuckled the strap and tugged it back to the same position before joining his friends sitting at the side of the trail. The horses grazed a few feet away.

'How many?' asked Hirad, handing him the waterskin.

'Impossible to say.' He took a swig and rinsed his dry mouth, handing the skin back. 'I've seen metal glint and shapes moving against the background.'

'Distance?' Ilkar pushed a hand through his hair and lay out on his back.

'Three miles, maybe a little more. Certainly horse-borne. I think they've been trailing us since the Balan Mountains.'

'But you didn't want to worry us, eh?' Hirad's tone was only half joking. The Unknown's lips thinned.

'No, Hirad, I just wasn't sure. You know how it is,' he said. 'It's of no importance anyway. They haven't attacked us so we have to assume they're just trailing us for information. That also means they'll probably have a mage to communicate with whoever.'

'Dordover,' said Ilkar.

'Most likely,' agreed The Unknown. 'And suffice to say, we can't let them find out any more than they can already guess.'

'So where do we take them? The forest?' Hirad nodded at the wrecked woodland. They had been skirting it to the south having ignored the north-east trail through the farmsteads as they headed for Greythorne.

'Yes. At the rock.'

Whatever the state of the forest, the crag at its centre would still be intact until the earth opened up to swallow it.

'Assuming we can persuade them to follow us in there.'

Thornewood was a mess, just a shamble of dying vegetation and twisted wood. The birds had returned and their song could be heard above the wind that was gusting stronger again, clouds bubbling across the fast greying sky.

'I don't think they have any choice,' said The Unknown. 'They can't simply watch the hunter trails because there are none, not any more. We can pick our way in and out anywhere. And they can't go on to Greythorne and risk us not stopping there.'

'But they'll assume our decision to go in means we've seen them, won't they?' queried Ilkar.

The Unknown shrugged. 'Possibly. But it hardly matters. It'll make them wary perhaps but it doesn't change what they're doing. And if we lose them, then so much the better.'

'So, Unknown, any ideas about how to get in?' Hirad smiled. The Unknown blew out his cheeks. The force of the hurricane had snapped off almost every tree at a height varying between eight and a dozen or so feet. Tangled foliage was knotted across the forest floor and banked up in huge drifts against close-packed stands of trunks and, further in, no doubt against the rock itself. It had left no obvious entry point and the Raven trio would have to pick or hack their way through the least dense obstructions.

'We'll find a way. C'mon, break over, no time like now.'

They mounted up and trotted gently to the borders of the forest, indistinct now with debris scattered so widely. Making their way inside, the destruction was brought into stark focus. In places, the forest floor had been swept clean, the mulch and dust of years, the loose topsoil and every plant, flower and shrub scoured away. No tree was undamaged and everywhere arches of fallen boughs crisscrossed just above their heads or impenetrable, forced a change of direction, as if they wished no living thing to see the death of Thornewood.

For three hours, The Unknown ensured they left a traceable trail as he bullied his horse through the debris. Where it thickened too much to be trampled, he dismounted and used his sword one-handed, sweeping through leaf and branch alike. Behind him, Ilkar and Hirad followed, saying nothing until they reached the crag.

'Make sure you clean your sword. Sap's a real killer for rust,' said Hirad, sliding from his horse. The Unknown looked at him, his expression carefully blank.

'Really? Thanks, Hirad. I'd have hated to have lost my sword through ignorance of sap's rust-inducing qualities.'

Ilkar chuckled.

'Just saying,' muttered Hirad.

'I have been at this a couple of years myself,' said The Unknown. 'And don't get comfortable. You've twenty yards of path to make thataway—' he waved his sword across the clearing around the crag '—while Ilkar goes and listens for them and I work out our best point of contact. All right?'

Hirad nodded. 'What about the horses?'

'Take them down the path to tether when you're done. I'd help you but I can see little brown spots on my blade. What do you think they mean?'

Hirad pulled his sword from its scabbard. 'Funny, Unknown, but leave the jokes to me next time, eh?'

'To prove you're even less amusing, presumably,' said Ilkar.

'All right, come on,' said The Unknown. 'They won't be far behind.'

*

Hirad was convinced it wouldn't work. Dordovan spies or assassins weren't the type to blunder into a hastily laid ambush. But he had to concede they couldn't lead anyone straight to Denser or Erienne at this stage; and if all it served was to throw them off the scent, then he'd take that as a positive result. And there was no desire to kill those that followed them, after all, they might have some very useful information. They were merely under orders. What they needed was some clear guidance on why following The Raven was an occupation with no future.

It was with some surprise then, that he heard Ilkar whisper that they were coming, just as the wind picked up suddenly, gusting through the remains of the forest and sifting at what it had so brutally created.

The Raven had taken up position a few yards from the crag itself, hidden from the path they'd made by a tangle of pine branches and thick, sharp gorse.

There were four of them, leading their horses, treading carefully and not uttering a sound, as if aware that all was not right in Thornewood. All were men, clad in varying shades of dark leather armour, long swords in free hands, helms framing faces older than those watching them. Hirad raised an eyebrow at the oddity. They were clearly an experienced team but the carelessness with which they'd revealed themselves to The Unknown made him wonder why Dordover had chosen them to follow The Raven. At least with no elves or willowy athletes in the party he could be fairly sure they weren't mage-assassins. Just trackers.

They entered the crag clearing and were edging around it cautiously, two by two, when The Unknown stepped out directly in front of them, the point of his sword down, tapping on the earth before him, its sound dull but music to Hirad's ears as he moved next to his old friend.

'Lost or looking?' asked The Unknown, not unpleasantly. The quartet had stopped abruptly and Hirad saw the front pair share a glance, sudden fear in one's eyes, confusion and surprise in the other.

'I don't like being followed,' said The Unknown.

'We're not—' began the left of the pair, a heavyset man with greying temples and long brown hair beneath his helm. He had a few days' growth of stubble, thick eyebrows and a stooped forehead.

'I don't like being lied to either,' said The Unknown, interrupting smoothly. Hirad felt Ilkar step up behind them, a spell shape no doubt already formed.

'Now,' continued The Unknown. 'We aren't looking for any trouble. We're just helping a friend. I understand this is all of great interest to your masters but they'll find nothing by sending people to follow us. Just bodies. Do I make myself clear?'

The men shifted a little, one dropped his gaze from The Unknown but the other held firm, brow creasing.

'You'll kill us if we continue to follow you?'

'Quick, isn't he?' said Hirad.

The Unknown ceased tapping his sword point.

'We don't want to but we can't risk you jeopardising what we have to do either. So turn around now and go back the way you came.'

More hesitation. Behind the front pair, the second whispered urgent words.

'Is there something you're confused about?' asked Hirad, his voice loud and harsh in the silence of the forest. The wind stilled momentarily before a fresh gust plucked at cloak, hair and mane, whistling through the jumbled branches.

'I'm not used to being threatened,' said the heavyset man.

'It's not a threat,' said The Unknown. 'Call it heartfelt advice.'

Hirad couldn't stop the smile touching his face. The Unknown had used the same words to face down Styliann, a former Lord of the Mount of Xetesk and a rather more powerful adversary.

'I don't see this as a laughing matter,' said one of the second pair, stepping forward between the horses. He was mid-height, younger than his companions, with a long nose and small mouth below hooded eyes.

Hirad felt the tension rise. The four men hadn't been ready for a fight before. Perhaps they were now. He and The Unknown gazed on unmoving. From behind them, Ilkar spoke.

'Please don't make this difficult because it's really very simple,' he said. 'You were following us, we don't want you to, and we've asked you very politely to stop doing so. I suggest we all calm down and go our separate ways. What do you say?'

Hirad and The Unknown both nodded and Hirad saw three of the men relax but the heavyset one pursed his lips.

'We have direct orders,' he said, more in explanation than anything else.

'Well now you have new ones,' said Hirad.

'Hirad, shut up,' hissed The Unknown. 'Look, no one's watching you. Just report back you saw us headed in the direction of Greythorne but lost us in Thornewood.' He shrugged. 'But before you go, tell me who sent you to follow us. Dordover?'

The man nodded. 'And losing you was not an option we were given,' he said, and as if he'd reminded his colleagues of a forgotten fact, the tension returned.

Ilkar chuckled gently. 'Oh, come on. I know Vuldaroq and the Dordovan Quorum are keen to get their prodigy back but they'll hardly have your heads for losing us, will they?'

The answering silence hinted that they believed otherwise.

'Either way, fighting us will not help you,' said The Unknown. 'Because whoever wins, you will have "lost" us, won't you?'

For a moment, they stood on the verge of fatal indecision. Then, the heavyset man's face twisted in what passed for a lopsided grin. He inclined his head and put up his sword.

'Let's not spill blood here,' he said. Hushing his companions, he turned them round and they mounted and left the crag clearing.

The Unknown put a finger to his lips and the three of them stood silent until the hoofbeats died away.

'You know what they'll do, don't you?' he said.

'Of course,' said Ilkar.

'Then if you'd be so kind, Ilkar,' he invited.

The elf smiled, formed the shape for a CloakedWalk, stepped forward and disappeared, his footfall utterly silent in this mockery of his ancestral home.

'C'mon Hirad,' said The Unknown. 'Let's go. They won't be tracking us back through here.'

'Ahead, you think?'

'No doubt about it.'

Hirad smiled and they led all three horses on an angled path to exit the wood about half a mile from where they'd entered it, a slow enough passage to give Ilkar time to find their followers and let them believe The Raven had swallowed the lie.

Ilkar was disappointed. They really weren't very good at all. Having exited Thornewood the way they'd entered it, the quartet had turned east and trotted along not far from its edge, leaving a trail only the senseless could fail to follow. He broke into a jog and skirted the boundaries of the wood, the wind steadily picking up in strength at his back, clouds now thick and threatening overhead in the grey, dank afternoon sky.

He found them a couple of miles down, slowed to a walk and deep in discussion, one of them making angles with his hands and pointing first into the woodland and then away over the open ground towards Greythorne. Apparently arriving at a decision, they ducked back under cover, having to force their way into the tangled foliage. Ilkar noted their position before walking back to where he estimated Hirad and The Unknown would be waiting. Knowing the way through the forest would be difficult, particularly while leading horses, he took his time.

'Well?' came The Unknown's voice from a deep patch of shadow.

Ilkar grinned and pushed into the foliage, its shelter cutting the strength of the wind that was gusting up to gale force. It was gone mid-afternoon and the light was beginning to fade.

'A mile and a half ahead, just under the eaves, probably split to cover a wider angle. How do you want to play it?'

The Unknown thought for a moment. 'Hirad, fancy a little forest stroll?'

Hirad knew they'd be there. He hadn't fought with either of them for four years and more but his confidence in them was undimmed. He'd been able to move quickly through Thornewood now he wasn't encumbered by his horse, the increasing wind creaking through shattered trunks and twisted limbs of trees, rustling dead leaves to a parody of life, dancing in the air and along the dusty floor.

Hirad was a quiet mover but not like Ilkar. The elves had something with the forests that he had never been able to fathom, let alone replicate. Only Thraun, of any human he had known, had come close and there was tragic reason enough for that.

The Dordovan trackers were well-spaced and well-hidden along the perimeter where they expected The Raven to either exit or pass by before turning to Greythorne. But Hirad had done enough hunting to understand shadow and silence and he was only scant yards from the right-handmost man before he drew his sword and spoke.

'Was there something we said you didn't quite grasp?' he growled.

The man started violently and spun round as he stood, twigs snapping underfoot.

'Trouble!' he called.

'I never strike at unarmed men,' said Hirad. 'So I suggest you arm yourself.' He came to ready in the tight space of tangled branch, leaf and bramble.

The man pulled out his long sword. 'I need help over here!' There was an answering call but it was troubled, not supportive. He was scared. Hirad could see it in his eyes and in the set of his body, and chose to be wary. Scared men were unpredictable and there was no room for manoeuvre.

'No help is coming,' said Hirad, and stepped back a pace, beckoning his opponent on with one hand. He heard other urgent shouts echoing on the wind and knew he was right.

The man sprang forward, unleashing a swift attack, his tall frame and long arms giving him good reach. Hirad stood his ground, blocking high, then to his midriff, eventually pushing away with his free hand as he deflected a second strike to his neck. The man stumbled back off-balance, one arm flailing out at an outstretched branch as he sought to steady himself, feet slipping on a dusting of leaves.

Hirad moved in, thrusting straight at the stomach, expecting and getting a half-block. He used the pace and change of direction to wheel his sword in a tight circle around his head, left to right. Almost too late, the tracker saw the blow coming and ducked, the blade skipping hard off his helmet.

Hirad swore, his assailant gasped and swayed but didn't go down, shaking his head, clearly groggy. He formed an uninspiring defence, wobbling slightly and backing away. Behind him, he could see two more shapes, one advancing on and hulking over the other, his sword low, no doubt tapping at the earth.

Hirad grinned harshly, batted aside the attempted jab and buried his blade in his opponent's neck, stepping smartly aside as blood spat from the severed artery. Gurgling, the victim fell, his life blood draining away into the forest floor.

Looking up, Hirad saw The Unknown straight-arm his enemy in the face before smashing his sword through his legs. The man dropped, screaming his last. Two down. Hirad moved. Ilkar had the other two. The ghost of concern flickered across his mind but an icy blast roared across him some twenty yards away and he knew he shouldn't have even begun to worry.

The Unknown appeared at his shoulder, sheathing his cleaned sword.

'Good work. Ilkar wanted the other two. They were a mage pair.'

'Oh, I see.' Hirad scrambled towards the source of the IceWind he'd felt surging into the dead woodland. 'Ilkar?' There was no answer for a while.

'Over here.' Hirad changed direction and came upon the elf kneeling by the twisted corpses of the tracker mages. He'd always found the sight of IceWind victims unnerving. Frozen in the attitude of life but with the pain etched in their faces of the instant of death, like paintings depicting the onset of terror.

'Didn't think you were keen on that spell,' he said.

'I'm not,' said Ilkar vaguely. 'It's somewhat indiscriminate. Still, nothing much else in the firing line on this occasion.' He hadn't looked round.

'What's up?' asked Hirad.

'See for yourself.' He moved away and indicated the exposed neck of one whose helmet lay nearby. 'This isn't right at all.'

Hirad frowned and bent to look. The light wasn't good but it was enough to show him the telltale tattoo below the ear.

'What the—?' He looked up and round. 'Unknown, what the hell is going on?'

The men hadn't been sent by Dordover. They were Black Wings.

Chapter 11

Selik finally found an outlet for his anger and frustration a day north of Arlen. The ride towards the town, where all of his reports indicated he should station himself and the bulk of the Black Wings, had been brooding and unpleasant. The changeable weather had alternately frozen and soaked him, practically blown him from his horse on more occasions than he cared to count and finally, a hailstorm had bitten lumps from his face.

Yet still most of Balaia just thought it was freak weather. They hadn't grasped what was behind it. Why would they? After all, the mages held such sway over their minds most of the time that the truth would be denounced as something akin to heresy. But he couldn't keep silent and still sleep at night. Magic was causing chaos all across his country and it was a cancer that had to be excised.

Vuldaroq had been fulsome in his explanations of the Tinjata Prophecy and how the bitch and her child were the only ones to blame but Selik knew it ran deeper than that. When magic was the problem, all mages closed ranks, making them all as guilty as each other. The time for tolerance of any College was past and what he couldn't use from them, he would discard.

He finally lost his tenuous hold on his temper on the borders of Easthome. A small farming community numbering perhaps one hundred and fifty families, Easthome lay close enough to Arlen to enjoy healthy trade from the prosperous port. Its hardworking people had farmed the land for generations, their crops feeding themselves and selling into Arlen's busy markets, their grain reaching as far as Calaius. But not this year.

With late afternoon waning towards evening, Selik and his eight cohorts rode up to the village, looking for lodging before joining the rest of the Black Wings in Arlen the following day. The calamity that had befallen Easthome unfolded before them as they neared. Crops lay flattened, fences and hedges had been uprooted, barns and farms had lost roofs. Stables had collapsed.

Outside one farm house, Selik reined in by a man who stood staring out across his ruined fields, barely acknowledging the men who stopped beside him. Selik dismounted and the farmer turned to him, the expression on his face one of disbelief and defeat. He was a young man, not yet thirty, with a broad muscular frame, fair hair and a heavy brow.

'What happened?' asked Selik.

The farmer looked at him closely and then past him to his men who remained mounted.

'Black Wings?' he said. Selik nodded. 'Come to try and stop the wind from blowing, have you? Best you leave us to sort ourselves out. We don't want trouble.'

'And I will bring you none,' slurred Selik, attempting a smile. 'Wind did all this?'

The farmer nodded. 'Blew out of nowhere just a night ago. From a clear sky. Every one of us has lost his crop. Some have lost their animals and houses too. I've been luckier if you can call it that.' He turned back to his fields. 'I mean, we'd be all right but . . . We've grain in the store to see us through but no one else, and four days ago a hundred and more from Orytte came here. They've lost everything.'

'I didn't know,' said Selik, though he could guess exactly what had happened. The farmer confirmed it.

'The sea came and took the town,' he said. 'Most of them are dead, so the survivors say. We'd have sent them on to Arlen but none of them want to see water again. I guess you can understand that. So we took them in and now we can't feed them. Not for long.'

Selik glanced back at his men who were listening to the exchange, some shaking their heads. Selik breathed out, his chest suddenly painful where the cold had touched him so deeply. It merely served to stoke his determination.

'So what are you doing about it?' he asked not unkindly.

The farmer jerked a thumb towards the village centre. 'There's some meeting about it now down at the inn. There's a lot of anger down there. People want answers before they starve this winter. Apparently Evansor's going to appeal to the Colleges for help. They've got the wealth, haven't they.'

'And Evansor is . . . ?' Again, Selik knew the answer.

'Our mage,' confirmed the farmer.

Selik spat. 'Mages. You'll get nothing from them.' The vehemence of his words made the farmer start. 'Gods, man, they are the cause of all this. Do you really think it's natural? A hurricane from a clear sky, the sea taking Orytte? And there's so much more it would break your heart. Magic is to blame.'

The farmer frowned. 'Well we've heard stories but Evansor . . .'

'Evansor, yes,' said Selik, his voice chill. He ached to confront him, to declaim him for the fraud he undoubtedly was 'Very persuasive. Very understanding, no doubt.' He leant in. 'But believing a mage is offering your life to a murderer.' He swung away and hauled himself back into his saddle. 'And why aren't you there, at the meeting?'

'Because I have to look out for my own. And because there'll be trouble there before the night's out.'

'Yes, there will,' said Selik. 'But it's the start of something righteous.'

'So what do we do when we find her?' asked Hirad.

The Raven had stopped not long after leaving Thornewood, dismounting to sit on the top of a slope up which the wind roared, blowing away the scent of blood and death. They were sitting in a line, the harsh cold wind in their faces, sharing a waterskin before riding the last leg to Greythorne. They planned to arrive a couple of hours after nightfall.

The Unknown put down the skin, ramming home the stopper with the heel of his palm.

'Good question? But don't you mean "if"?'

'No, I mean "when",' said Hirad, looking across at his friend, his close-cropped scalp dull under the heavy cloud, his eyes suggesting his mind was elsewhere. 'Like always.'

Ilkar chuckled. 'Glad to see you haven't lost any confidence in your ability, Hirad.'

'It's just a job, when all's said and done.' He shrugged. 'Pay's not up to much but still, once taken, always completed. The question still stands, though. The way I see it, we've got Witch Hunters and Dordovans, Xeteskians and the Gods know who else after this girl. Where will she be safe?'

'Where she is, I expect,' said Ilkar a little gruffly.

'And you think that's a bad thing?' asked The Unknown. 'Surely, we're not necessarily doing anything with her. Perhaps we are just making sure she's safe. Lyanna's Denser and Erienne's daughter, let's not ever lose sight of that.'

Ilkar made a growling noise in his throat. 'It's not that simple, Unknown, and you know it. You can't dress it up as a search for a little girl. Who she is and what she represents are driving this whole mess. Look around you. Gods, look above you now. See what she is unwittingly creating.'

They all looked. The heavens were filled with a dense dark cloud, driven hard across the sky, unbroken and malevolent. When the rain inevitably came, it would be torrential.

'You're blaming Lyanna for it being cloudy?' asked Hirad. 'I've got to tell you, I'm finding this all rather far-fetched.'

'Hirad, the evidence is overwhelming,' said Ilkar.

'Is it? An ancient mage writes a prophecy two thousand years ago and all of a sudden he's talking about Lyanna?' Hirad shook his head. 'Look I know we've had some unseasonal weather lately but—'

'*Unseasonal?*' Ilkar gasped. 'We're supposed to be bringing in our crops in the next few weeks under the warming autumn sun. Instead we're having earthquakes and hurricanes and I've forgotten what the sun looks like. Gods, Hirad, in the Balan Mountains, it rained so hard I thought my head would shatter. You can't possibly think this is normal.'

Hirad shrugged. 'Fair enough, it's not normal but nothing you've said points the finger at Lyanna. I mean, it could be anyone.'

'Like who?' snapped Ilkar.

'He's right, though, Ilkar,' said The Unknown. 'This is all so much theory.'

'But back in Julatsa you said—' began Ilkar.

'I said that Dordover believe the Tinjata Prophecy. And now it seems that the Black Wings have jumped on the wagon, which is hardly a surprise. And that's why I'm chasing Erienne and Lyanna. To stop them. That doesn't mean I believe it myself.'

Ilkar paused to think. He pushed a hand through his hair. 'I can see I won't persuade you both now but you'll see. I just need you to trust me on this. Lyanna is an innocent child but this elemental mess is caused by magical forces and I believe she is the focus, just like Dordover does. I can all but smell the mana playing around us now and it's not the natural way of mana. If we're proved right then there are ramifications for the whole Collegiate system. This has to be handled right.'

'Meaning what, exactly?' The Unknown wore a deep frown.

'I don't know yet. That's one of the reasons I'm here. As a Julatsan, scared of what she may symbolise. I know it's probably of no concern to either of you right now but Lyanna and the Al-Drechar could so easily herald a return to dominance of Xetesk under the guise of the One Way. That would be bad for all of us.'

'But particularly Julatsa, eh Ilkar?' The Unknown said. 'Doesn't matter now, though, you're right. So securing Lyanna and Erienne is paramount, don't you agree?'

Ilkar hesitated before replying. 'Like I said, it's not that simple.'

'So tell me what's so damn complicated,' demanded The Unknown. Hirad started at the anger edging his voice.

'I just have,' snapped Ilkar. 'No one wants to see her harmed but I'm not sure what we're securing her for or from, all right? And I don't know how we stop her causing this mayhem. Denser thinks the Dordovans want her dead and I can believe that very easily. I think we can dismiss the Witch Hunters. They surely aren't numerous or powerful enough to really threaten. But I also think Xetesk will have an entirely selfish agenda and that does threaten my College – particularly with us being so weakened. The Al-Drechar want to perpetuate themselves and I'm not so sure that's something we should support.'

'So where does that leave Lyanna?' asked Hirad. 'Strikes me your little outline has her surplus to Balaia's requirements.'

'Yes, Ilkar, perhaps you'd like to put your foot down in one camp or another,' invited The Unknown, his eyes cold and body tensed.

Ilkar's ears pricked and he sucked his top lip while he thought. 'I want the magical balance of Balaia maintained. I think that's best for everyone, not just Julatsa. I think Lyanna should not be allowed to return to Dordover, Xetesk or any college. She should be taught by the Al-Drechar to contain the outbursts that are causing all the trouble but that's as far as it should go. There shouldn't be a return to the One. Not ever.'

'And if Denser or Xetesk or whoever doesn't agree with you?' asked The Unknown. 'If they determine her training should continue to its natural conclusion?'

Ilkar shrugged and looked away over the wilds in the direction of Greythorne, still obscured by rolling heather-covered moors ahead.

'You would, wouldn't you? I bloody knew it!' The Unknown stormed to his feet and took a pace towards Ilkar. Hirad scrambled up and stood between them.

'Take it easy,' he urged, putting up a hand in front of The Unknown. 'What would he do?'

The Unknown stared past him at the elf. 'He'd see her die.'

'*Kill* her?'

'No, I don't suppose so. But I don't suppose he'd stand in anyone's way, either. Would you Ilkar, eh?'

Ilkar didn't turn his head.

'See?' The Unknown's face burned and Hirad realised he couldn't move aside. 'She's just a little girl, you bastard. And she's Denser's daughter. How could you even contemplate it? Gods, I thought better of you, Ilkar.'

Hirad was desperate to turn but was fearful of The Unknown's next move. It dawned on him sickeningly that this powerful man was a genuine threat to Ilkar for the first ever time. From behind him, Ilkar spoke.

'You know me well enough, Unknown. Perhaps it's me that's misinterpreted you.'

'I'm a father, Ilkar. And I understand what Denser must be experiencing.'

'And he's an old and trusted friend of mine and I would see no harm come to him, Erienne or Lyanna. But she's a child of the One, that's becoming clearer to me at least, by the day. And Tinjata's Prophecy is so far proving depressingly accurate. Or so I believe. Lyanna's Night has only just begun, Unknown, and it promises devastation for us all if she isn't controlled. Or stopped. And I don't see anyone coming forward with ways to control her. Clearly the Al-Drechar haven't yet, have they?'

Hirad felt The Unknown's body relax. It was enough for him to turn and look at Ilkar, who was still seated. The expression on the elf's face, and the desperation in his eyes, told of the depth of his belief in what he had said.

'But aren't you being overdramatic?' he asked. 'What do you mean, "night"?'

'No, Hirad, I'm not. Unless you count Thornewood as over-dramatic. And that, as we know, is far from being a one-off storm. Look, when a mage tries to learn to accept the flow of mana, there is a period, usually short, of darkness for the mage. Where the senses are uncontrolled, and the mind turns inwards while the mana batters inside the head. It's like being in a gale in the pitch black and that's why it's come to be called "Night". Mages training in the Colleges have the ManaBowl around them to direct and control the otherwise overpowering flow of mana. Lyanna only has the Al-Drechar and they clearly aren't up to shielding her from her Awakening or her from us. Her Night could last a long time. And again, that's just what I believe but I'm better placed than you to make a judgement.'

'And you think it would be better if she died?'

'Dammit, Unknown, no!' Ilkar pushed himself to a standing position. 'It may come to that but I certainly will have no hand in it.'

'Denser hears nothing of this,' warned The Unknown.

Ilkar shook his head. 'If he doesn't already know it inside, I'd be very surprised. He is a mage and no fool. He knows what he and Erienne wanted to create and so far as I'm concerned, he has rather unfortunately succeeded.'

'Then we'd best get to him, hadn't we? Sounds like he might be needing our help.'

The three old friends mounted up and rode for Greythorne, their silence as angry and dark as the sky above them.

Selik listened to the angry voices inside the inn for a few moments before slapping open the doors and striding inside, his men crowding behind him but for one who stayed by the horses. Three men stood against the bar opposite, looking out over a crowd of approaching fifty men and women who sat on chair or table, or leant against walls and beams. The inn was lantern-lit and low-ceilinged. Pipe smoke lay thick across their heads in the poor ventilation, its sweet odour obscuring that of ale and wine.

His loud entrance having had the desired effect of silencing the crowd and having every head turn in his direction, Selik walked calmly to the bar, coming to stand between the three men. He kept the man he knew had to be Evansor on his right and the two older farmers on his left. The mage was young and slender, his body not used to hard physical work, and his clothing was of a cloth too fine-woven to be of any use in the fields.

Selik took in the gathering with a lazy sweep of his head. Some were fearful, others burned too deeply with anger to worry about what he represented, while most just looked on, waiting for him to announce himself. Perfect. He hushed the objection of one of the older farmers with a raising of his left forefinger and spoke.

'I am Selik and some of you may have heard of me and the work I and my associates undertake on your behalf.' He indicated his men who had spread themselves around the inn. 'I have seen the wreckage in your fields. And I have heard of the extra mouths you have to feed. I feel for you all.'

Beside him, the mage scoffed quietly. Selik ignored him for the moment. He threw back his hood and waited for the sounds of revulsion and sympathy.

'You can see what magic has done to me, and now you experience its malignancy for yourselves.' He held up a hand as voices became audible. 'I know you don't understand but your mage does, don't you Evansor?' He sensed the mage flinch as his name was mentioned. 'Because this was no natural wind, was it? Magic did this to your village.' Selik affected a look of surprise. 'Oh, did he neglect to tell you? Well, perhaps he might choose to do so now?'

Selik turned to face Evansor and felt the gathering do the same. This was easier than he expected. Evansor's pale face pinched into a half-smile and he spread his hands.

'My friends, the Black Wings have always hated magic. Don't let him sway you. We have more important matters to discuss. Like how we are to survive the winter if the weather does not improve.'

He'd mollified a few but Selik wasn't even nearly done. 'You have dodged answering the question. A simple yes or no will do. Was the wind that destroyed the livelihood of this village natural or not?' Selik let his voice soften. 'Come, Evansor, you're among friends. You said so yourself. Answer the question.'

Evansor looked around at the gathering, Selik watching him squirm. The net was tightening beautifully. The silence grew and with every heartbeat, suspicion grew with it.

'I-I tasted magic on the wind,' he said. 'But, but . . .'

'But you didn't think these people worthy of knowing? That the filth your kind creates has visited ruin on them all?' He swung round to face the crowd whose expressions ranged from the confused to the red-faced furious. He could see his men whispering in certain ears, guiding thoughts, suggesting actions. 'And how do you feel about that, eh?'

'I don't understand,' said one voice. The query was taken up by others.

'What's there not to understand?' said Selik. 'The wind that wrecked your crops was fuelled by magic, not by an act of the Gods. And this "friend" of yours didn't want you to know that. Do you think Orytte's flood was a natural disaster? Or Denebre? Or any of a dozen others I could mention. Magic is tearing our country apart and yet you sit and ask him what to do. You've going to starve and he and his kind are the cause of it all.' He heard the crowd stirring and muttering. Close, so very close. 'Would you ask the devil the way out of hell?'

Selik heard a voice say 'no' and there was a sudden rise in the volume of noise, angry voices shouting out for answers and only quietened by one of the older farmers to his left.

'He's taking this too far,' the man said, half-pleading. 'Marching in here, spreading his poison. Evansor is our friend.'

' "Friend"?' Selik spread his hands theatrically. 'And who needs the sort of friend that won't tell you the truth when it suits him? Who's happy to take your money to keep the rats from your barns and the sores from your hands but who is only loyal to his cursed College? Because believe me, he isn't loyal to you. Any of you. Don't be fooled like I was. Don't let my face be your face.' Selik let his voice rise in strength. He had them, he was sure of it. 'This travesty of a man is the problem, not the answer. And problems have to be stamped out!'

He smacked a fist into his palm and glared at Evansor, hearing the clamour of the crowd grow. The mage was badly frightened but Selik knew he would speak and condemn himself.

'Please, my friends,' he said, shouting to make himself heard. 'I'm not your enemy, I can help you.'

'Yes, by getting out!' came a voice. It was a Black Wing voice but nobody cared. The crowd was shouting.

'Out! Out! Out!'

'Please!' Evansor's eyes were desperate, flitting around the room. Selik grabbed the collar of his shirt.

'Don't touch me, Black Wing, or I'll—'

'What?' And Selik's voice stilled them. 'Cut me down like your kind have the crops of these good people? Which spell will it be? Fire or ice?'

Selik dragged him closer, then shoved him into the crowd. The fist of a Black Wing came out of nowhere and slammed into his cheek, snapping his head back and sending him stumbling. The crowd was roaring now, but none would move forward. Evansor, though, was losing control. Selik smiled as he saw the mage's eyes narrow in anger then unfocus as he prepared.

'He's going to cast!' shouted a voice. A Black Wing voice.

Selik gestured at two of his men. They rushed in. Evansor let the spell go. It was a ForceCone, hard enough to fling the men back, where they clattered into those behind them.

'Get back. I mean you no harm!' shouted Evansor. 'Please.'

A bottle came flying across the bar, missing the mage by a fraction.

'He's broken my arm!' moaned a man. And the surge was triggered.

Selik stepped smartly aside as they came, leaving his foot out to trip one man who fell into those in front, pushing them on. They'd surely only meant to grab him, take him to the village borders and sling him out but Selik's men were in the rush and after the first punch was thrown, Evansor didn't stand a chance.

With the old farmers desperately trying to pull their people away, blow after blow rained down on the helpless mage, whose shouts and begging cries were swallowed up in the pack howl and the desire to mete out punishment on the blameless.

Selik saw a chair leg flash across Evansor's face, splitting his nose; he saw boots stamping and kicking his body and he saw a knife flash in the lantern light and plunge into his heart. They were still punching him long after he had died.

The Black Wing commander gathered his men to him as the hatred dissipated as quickly as it had grown. Village men started to back off, stunned at what they had done. Voices began to rise, expressing shock, and in the background a woman was crying.

Selik smiled and walked to the door of the inn and turned.

'The path of the righteous is ever drenched in the blood of the evil,' he announced into a gathering that was only too willing to hear justification for the murder it had collectively committed. 'This is a great day for Balaia. Magic has wreaked its havoc on our country for too long. It's time we sought recompense. Tell everyone you meet. We shall be second to mages no more.'

He swept from the inn, a swell in his heart and his anger assuaged. Next, the bitch.

Lyanna didn't understand it, only that it hurt and she wanted the hurt to stop. They had promised her peace from the nightmares that made her wake so frightened. And they had promised that they could calm the wind that blew inside her head.

But they couldn't.

Well, they did at first, but now Mummy was away looking for Daddy and they seemed to grow older. They walked slower and their eyes were all dark, inside and out. And that made them cross so much.

So the nightmares had come back. And the wind roared in her head and made it hurt and sometimes she felt like it was dark although it was day. They always helped her when that started to happen. She wished Mummy was here to cuddle her and lie with her when she cried.

Lyanna looked up into the blue sky through the trees in the courtyard orchard. The leaves on the branches blew patterns across her eyes, like little sprites waving hello. She smiled. Perhaps the sprites would talk to her. Ephy and the others never seemed to find the time. Too busy with that smelly pipe.

For a moment, the wind stopped inside her. It was a relief. She thought hard and the branches of the nearest trees moved towards her, bringing the sprites to where she could talk to them.

This would be a fun game.

Cleress dragged deeply on the pipe, feeling the inhalation throughout her wracked and tired body. The mixed weeds calmed her muscles and anaesthetised the arthritis twisting her left knee into a gnarled, swollen parody of a joint.

Beside her at the table, Myriell slumped in her chair, the exhaustion plain on her face. She could sleep soon, much as Aviana did now. Only Ephemere watched over the child who was destroying them all so fast.

They had disastrously miscalculated her power, or rather, the power they would have to expend in shielding such an unbalanced Awakening. And the girl had such energy outside of magic too. She was a lovely child but was becoming more demanding every day. Her moods swung wildly between joy and wonder; and fear and darkness.

Cleress had been at pains to remind them all that, despite the ravaging mana surging barely checked through Lyanna's head, due to the Dordovans' clumsy Awakening, she was still just a small child. And that brought its own rash of idiosyncrasies, demands and responsibilities. With Erienne gone, however temporarily, all four of them had to assume the role of understanding grandmother. And though Lyanna undoubtedly trusted them, while she didn't trust any Guild elves now Ren'erei had gone, they had not practised that particular quality of care for decades.

So there were mistakes, the worst of which was to assume Lyanna could always amuse herself when at play. They kept a watching brief on her mind and the flow of the mana around her, yet that wasn't really the point, and Cleress knew it. But they had to rest and the temptation to do so at any time they weren't actively teaching or shielding was overwhelming.

Cleress took another long draw on the pipe, ensured it stayed lit and passed it to Myriell, having to place the stem between her sister's lips before she acknowledged it was there.

'What time is it?' she mumbled before inhaling.

'Too early to be relying on the Lemiir in that pipe, Myra. The sun is riding down but night-time is way away.'

'Or maybe not so for the child.'

'No,' agreed Cleress.

Myriell's brief assessment nagged at all their shattered minds. They supported each other, gave each other their strength and tended their bodies and minds as carefully as they could. But the question remained. Would Lyanna learn even a modicum of self-control before their capacity to teach, control and protect her was finally gone?

Cleress feared the worst.

Cleress, orchard, now. Ephy's voice rang through her head, an alarm that sent her heart racing.

'Trouble, Myra. Stay here. I'll call you if we need you.'

'Try not to,' muttered Myriell.

Cleress dragged herself to her feet and hobbled towards the orchard, the effects of the Lemiir not strong enough to fully dampen the pain that shot up her leg and through her back every time she put pressure on the arthritic knee.

Out of the dining room and through the ballroom she moved, worry hurrying her step, Ephemere's anxiety dusting across her mind.

Ephy was standing at the doors to the orchard, staring out, one hand on the frame to brace herself. When Cleress joined her, she didn't know whether to laugh or cry.

In the centre of the orchard sat Lyanna in her favourite blue dress, cross-legged. Her arms were outstretched before her and her face turned up, a beatific smile across her features. And all around her, the trees moved at her bidding. Whole branches turned down towards her, their leaves rippling, flowers opening, embryonic fruits shifting in colour.

Like a dance, choreographed by Lyanna, eight or nine trees moved to her order, their boughs swaying, crowns dipping and twisting. But it was the leaves that held Cleress rapt. Their movement, like a pulsing wind over the top of a corn field, sent them shimmering in surely impossible directions. Their synchronicity was beguiling, their dark green top surfaces and silver undersides blinking like ten thousand eyes as they twisted gracefully on their slender stalks. And the noise they made was like voices, whispering and laughing, joyful and so real.

Beneath them all sat Lyanna, still but for her lips, which moved soundlessly as if . . .

'She's talking to them,' breathed Cleress.

'Yes,' agreed Ephemere. 'Or trying to. A child's imagination has no boundaries and Lyanna's has the power to animate what she dreams. The trouble is, she's flaring. She'll have a headache when she's done.'

'And Balaia will have another gale,' said Cleress. She attuned her eyes to the mana spectrum and saw what Ephemere meant. Though the mana shape Lyanna used unconsciously to manipulate the trees was a stunning spiders' web formation, all around it dark brown spears of mana tore away, creating eddies and vortices which gathered in size and strength as they whipped away beyond vision – beacons for those who searched for her and would do her harm.

She had no idea what she created but the after-effects were felt all over Balaia, where her birthplace was and where the core of her mana strength would always reside. Cleress could only imagine the problems her flares were causing but knew the dissipation of focused but unfettered mana energy of this magnitude typically manifested itself as terrifying elemental forces.

Tinjata, for all his senile meanderings those thousands of years ago, had been right about one thing. An awakened Child of the One could lay waste to Balaia in less than half a year. It was up to the surviving Al-Drechar to stop that by keeping her from the worst excesses of herself until she was old enough to understand the control she had to master. If she couldn't, the Al-Drechar would be left with one alternative and its mere contemplation was hideous.

Not for the first time, Cleress cursed the Dordovans for disturbing something in which they should never have meddled.

'What do you want me to do, Ephy?'

'Go in and speak to her. Hear how she describes it. I'll cap the flaring and monitor the mana shape.'

Cleress nodded and entered the orchard. It had an eerie quality to it, though the late afternoon sun cast a warm yellow light. The birds weren't singing and the creak of boughs and branches under Lyanna's control was alien in the windless air.

Close to, Cleress could see Lyanna's eyes darting from leaf to leaf, her mouth moving, her smile alternately thinning and broadening as if the answers she thought she received to her questions pleased her. Her outstretched arms trembled with the effort of maintaining the mana shape and a frown creased her brow. She was tiring.

Cleress knelt by her and smoothed a loose hair from her forehead.

'Lyanna, can you hear me?' she asked, her voice soft despite the effects of the Lemiir.

'I've got my friends here, look, Clerry,' replied Lyanna, not turning from her work, her voice distant with effort.

Cleress looked and had to smile at what kept Lyanna spellbound. From an arc in front of her, branches flowed in, almost touching her face, caressing the arm in front of her and moving over and floating across each other, like the tentacles of a benign sea creature, the stiffness of the bark and grain gone, replaced by a flesh-like suppleness.

And in the branches, the leaves danced and rustled, twisting and bending along their lengths, their gentle susurrations almost musical. It was a beautiful sight and Cleress gazed back at Lyanna, wondering what it was the little girl imagined she saw and heard.

'Are they good friends?' asked Cleress. 'They look pretty.'

'Yes they are, but they can't talk to you because you wouldn't understand.'

'Oh, I see. And what are they saying to you?'

'There are bad people coming here but good people too, to help us. And you're very tired and it's because of me but it's all right really.'

Cleress was speechless. She glanced over to Ephemere but her sister was deep in concentration, eyes closed, hands held at her midriff.

'How do they know that? They must be very clever.'

Lyanna nodded, the leaves rustled as if in applause.

'They know because that's how it feels, silly.'

The elderly Al-Drechar stifled a gasp. Lyanna was feeling communication through the nuances of the mana flow. Some of it she probably picked up from conversations with Erienne but the rest was somehow being filtered from the random force roaring through her head. Had to be. But it also had to be terribly draining and dangerous. She only hoped Ephemere was in control of the flaring.

'And have your friends told you anything else?' Cleress almost feared the answer.

Another nod from Lyanna but this time her smile was gone and her eyes moistened.

'It's going to get dark soon and I won't be able to see them for ages. And I might get lost but you will help me.'

'Oh, Lyanna, dear,' said Cleress, her heart brimming with sorrow. 'Say goodbye to your friends. I'm afraid Night is coming.'

Chapter 12

There it was. Quite unmistakable. Like the first breath of wind on a becalmed sea. And again.

Far to the south, north of Calaius, the mana spectrum was in flux. This far away, the movement was slight but its very abnormality was its fascination and its betrayer.

The experienced mage could sense the casting of spells throughout Balaia with the mind tuned to the base spectrum, brief oases of order rising from total chaos. But these eddies were altogether different, almost alien and undoubtedly emanating from a collapsing static spell. Interpretation was still difficult, though. They were slight, mere nudges at the random whole.

The Dordovan master, Gorstan, stood and sensed until he was completely sure. This was not Balaian magic. It had a quality of completeness even in its distress, that he could not have achieved. This was magic from another power, a greater power, and through his distaste, he felt awe.

Gorstan turned, reattuning his eyes to the dull grey light from the heavy Balaian sky.

'I have them,' he said.

Selik smiled, a twisted sneer affecting only half his disfigured face. 'How far?'

Gorstan shrugged. 'Days. It's impossible to be more accurate from here but I suspect its base to be in the Ornouth Archipelago.'

'If you'll excuse me, Gorstan.'

'With great pleasure,' replied the Dordovan. Selik nodded curtly and swept away, the hood of his cloak back over his face, two aides by his sides.

Gorstan watched him go then turned back towards the south, head down, eyes fixed on the ripples on the largely still waters of the River Arl as it fed into the Southern Ocean.

He supposed Vuldaroq was right and that Selik was a useful ally for now. But he couldn't help thinking that Dordover would be forever mired by their now open contact with the Witch Hunters. Gorstan was nominally in charge of the one hundred mages and two hundred foot now billeted all around Arlen and it wasn't hard to sense the nervousness among the sleepy port's populace. And, with rumours of Xetesk on the way, backed by Protectors, he wondered whether it wasn't really Selik who was driving it all.

Vuldaroq was due in Arlen shortly and the sooner he arrived, the better.

Hirad, The Unknown and Ilkar led their four horses into Greythorne late in the evening. Cloud still hung heavy in the sky, the wind whipping across open land. Everywhere, the ravages of the wind had been evident as they had ridden in: flattened plains grass, interspersed with sections of dirt where stalks had been torn out at the roots and, here and there, the corpses of animals and even two people that none of the survivors had yet found.

They had been a middle-aged couple, huddled together inside a barn that had collapsed on top of them, crushing their bodies beneath thatch and beam. Ilkar had spotted them as The Raven had ridden past to see if they could help. All that was left for them was a burial.

Not long after leaving Thornewood, they'd come across a ragtag column of refugees heading south to Gyernath from Rache in the north. Rache had been struck by gales off the Northern Ocean and a massive mudslide from surrounding hills. It had engulfed most of the town, burying many alive. Those that had survived had fled, believing it would be safer in Gyernath, a warm, tranquil southern port. The Raven hadn't the heart to tell them that nowhere was safe.

The last leg of the journey had been slow and largely silent, each of them brooding on what they had seen and heard on the road. Greythorne was the worst of it.

As The Raven approached, the multiple lights had given them hope that the quiet market town had escaped the hurricane. But closer to, the gathering gloom could not obscure the reality.

What Hirad thought were sloping roofs revealed themselves as part-collapsed walls, leaving angles of broken stone spearing into the sky. The lattice of swept cobbled streets that ran to the market place was filled with rubble and debris. Dust blew through the town and the only roofs standing were tented ones, raised as emergency shelter.

The Raven had seen this sort of destruction before, albeit not on such a scale, but it was the people that brought home the horror of what had befallen Greythorne.

Although the hurricane must have struck two or three days before, the shock was only now setting in. Hirad could well imagine what had happened in its immediate aftermath. Adrenalin and panic would have banished fatigue as teams of survivors battled to find loved ones, free the trapped and salvage anything useful. Indeed, stacks of crates under skins and canvas spoke of the scale of the effort.

But the first night without proper shelter, sleeping in the ruins of once proud houses and, following that, the first dawn, would have sapped wills and leached morale away. Those awash with energy the previous night would have woken dark-eyed and exhausted as they looked on their town, and realised that all they were going to uncover now were bodies.

And this is how they were. Faces streaked with dirt, men and women worked as hard as they could but the spirit was gone. Eyes were wide and uncomprehending, still disbelieving.

They walked past a child wrapped in a blanket and sitting under a small, staked-out leather bivouac. No more than five, he was too traumatised even to cry. He just sat, stared and shivered. The Gods only knew what he had seen and the fate of his parents.

Walking into the main square, The Raven, who had been largely ignored, saw signs of the organisation behind the desperately slow but determined activity. The town hall and grain store were gone but for a corner which still supported windows, their glass reflecting lantern light like malevolent multifaceted eyes. An open-fronted marquee was pitched below it, lit up like daylight, and within, men and women swarmed around tables marking maps and parchments or prepared hot and cold food and drink.

In the centre of it all, sat a man bandaged around the right eye and right leg. Even from twenty yards, he was pale and haggard, a deep-etched face, grey hair and a drained body fighting hard against exhaustion.

'We need to speak to him,' said The Unknown.

'You two go on. I'll find somewhere for the horses,' said Ilkar.

The Unknown nodded and he and Hirad walked into the warm tented space to be stopped by a young man, scared and tired.

'Out-of-towners? Come to help?' he asked, long blond hair hanging all over his pale, thin features.

'We are The Raven,' said The Unknown by way of reply. 'We're looking for Denser.'

The young man drew in sharp breath.

'He said you'd be coming.' He nodded them on towards the bandaged seated man. Hirad put a hand on his shoulder.

'And yes, if we can do anything to help, we will.'

A smile brought a spark of life to his bloodshot eyes.

'Thank you,' he said. 'Thank you.'

The Unknown walked up to the man who still wore his mayoral chains and dark green cloak of office around his shoulders. He put out a shaky hand which The Unknown took and shook warmly.

'Gannan. At least you're alive.'

'Barely, Unknown, barely. I'd say it was good to see you but I fear your appearance here has little to do with salvage and much to do with the causes of all this mess.'

Ilkar had walked up to Hirad's shoulder.

'Is there anyone he doesn't know?' whispered Hirad.

'Apparently not,' replied the elf. 'I've left the horses with a local. There's a makeshift picket and stable in the west of the town.'

The Unknown ignored them.

'You've spoken to Denser?' he asked.

'Not at great length, but yes.' Gannan shifted on his chair, using both hands to adjust the position of his injured leg. 'He's very agitated, Unknown. Not making too much sense.'

'Where is he? We need to speak to him.'

Gannan gestured towards a table nearby. 'Some refreshment first, surely?'

'No,' said The Unknown. 'Save it for your people. We'll find our own.'

'He was behind the grain store a while back, wanting some peace and quiet. You could try there.'

'Thanks Gannan, we'll talk later.' He turned away. 'Hirad, you staying or coming?'

Hirad shrugged. 'I've got to talk to him sometime. It may as well be now.'

The Unknown nodded. 'Good.' He led the way outside.

The grain store had butted on to the town hall but was little more than a pile of rubble. Beyond it, to the north end of Greythorne, the activity and light were lessened, though the devastation was equally as severe. Clearly, there were simply not enough survivors to work everywhere.

But someone was moving through the debris, punctuating the windblown quiet with the shifting of slate and the grating of stone on stone.

'Denser,' said Ilkar, pointing away into the gloom.

For a time, Hirad couldn't make him out against the drab, dark background, then he saw his head move.

Denser was crouched in the rubble of what had probably been a house. Timbers were scattered around and slate, thatch and stone was piled where the corners of the walls still stood, defiant. He was holding something and, as they moved closer, they could see it was a tiny human hand.

He appeared not to notice them as they approached, just held the hand in one of his and stroked it gently with the other. Close too, over the noise of the wind, Hirad could hear he was murmuring but couldn't make out the words.

'Denser?' The Unknown's tone was soft. The Dark Mage started and turned to them, his face streaked with tears, his eyes black holes in the shadow of the night.

'Look what she's done,' he whispered, his voice choked and thick. He swallowed. 'This has gone too far.'

Ilkar crouched by him. 'What are you talking about?'

Denser indicated the hand in his. Ilkar followed it. It belonged to a young boy, no more than five, though in truth it was hard to tell. His head had been crushed by falling stone.

'You can't blame Lyanna for his,' he said.

'Blame Lyanna?' Denser shook his head. 'No, but she's the cause of it all. You can feel what drives the wind even now. Imagine it fifty times as strong and tearing down your walls. It's a miracle any of them lived. If anyone's to blame, it's me and Erienne.'

'I don't think it's that simple,' said Ilkar. He shifted his position and took the child's hand from Denser's unresisting fingers and placed it back in the rubble.

'Only I can stop this thing. Only me,' said Denser, his eyes wild, his voice wavering. 'You have to get me to her. You have to.'

'I think it's time you stopped torturing yourself and came away from here.' Ilkar looked up. 'Reckon we can find anywhere private?'

Hirad shrugged. 'If we build it ourselves.' Ilkar's eyes flashed anger. 'We'll sort something out. C'mon, Denser. Time you had a hot drink.'

Every covered and sheltered space was crammed with people, the very young, the injured and the precious few carers. The Raven walked out of the centre of the town and laid a fire in a scrabbled together circle of stone from a building that had been cleared of any victims. With borrowed water heating in The Unknown's old iron jug, Denser calmed a little but his hands were jittery and his attention wandered fitfully.

'Surprised you're even here, Hirad,' he said, attempting a smile. Hirad didn't return it.

'I wouldn't be but Sha-Kaan needs the Al-Drechar. Apparently ancient mages are the last chance now everyone else has let him down.'

'Can we leave that for another time?' Ilkar's voice was pained. 'How long have you been here, Denser?'

The Xeteskian shrugged. 'A day. I was delayed. There's so much mess. I had to try and help, didn't I?'

'You can't hold yourself responsible,' said Ilkar.

'Can't I? Isn't this what Erienne and I wanted? The Child of the One. Balaia's most powerful mage.' He spat out the words. 'But she's out of control and we must stop her. I must stop her.'

Ilkar looked at The Unknown and Hirad. 'What did I tell you?'

The Unknown nodded. 'If he believes it too, then I guess I'm prepared to. But that doesn't change why I'm here, and don't you forget it. Denser, we'll find her and help her control this. Or rather, you will, if you say so. Ilkar's explained it may be her Night.'

'And what will be left when dawn breaks for the Night Child, eh?' Denser swept an arm around him. 'Just look at this place. All the death. And I've heard the other stories. They're all over the town. Not just what we've heard. This is happening *everywhere*.' He put his head in his hands. 'Magic has done this. That's what the survivors are saying here. But it's not just that, is it? It's my daughter. Mine. You've got to get me to her.'

'Come on, Denser, calm it down now. You need some rest. Hirad, we need a hot drink for him,' said Ilkar.

Ilkar sat back and let the silence roll over them all. Denser was biting back more tears. The Unknown and Hirad presumably were digesting Denser's words. There seemed little more to say and Ilkar found he'd lost the energy. He hoped that daylight would bring some level-headed talk.

But it was a long time until daylight.

All was not right. Thraun had left the remnants of the pack in safety, hidden deep within Thornewood, in a shallow den dug under a stand of trees the wind hadn't managed to destroy. He had chosen to scout Greythorne where the humans lived. To forage for food and look for any sign of the ones with the mist he recognised from a dim and confused past.

But when he'd arrived, with night full and blustery under a sky hidden by cloud, all he'd found was more sorrow and more destruction. He'd sat on a rise above the town, gazing down, his lupine heart beating strangely as if sympathetic to a race he considered a threat. There would be no food. No fowl to take, no dog or cat to chase down, no scraps from the tables of the humans discarded in alleyways.

Because though it was night, the town still moved as if it was day. Men carried stone from fallen buildings. Lifeless bodies, once exposed, were moved to an open space in the centre of the town and everywhere, lanterns and torches dazzled his eyes. He could not risk venturing in – he didn't want to bring the hunters back to Thornewood.

And so he had returned to the pack but decided on a different route to the new den, hoping for a kill. It was there that he had found them. Four humans, two killed by metal and two by something else, their faces telling of sudden terror and brief agony.

But there was something more. A scent in the air and on the leaves that he recognised, a cleanliness in the kills and a residual knowledge within him that sparked into life. He knew who had done this. He could taste them in the air. It had to be linked with the two he had seen in Thornewood before the wind had come. They and their tree-shadowpeople.

Thraun stopped, his mind clearing slowly. Thornewood felt bad. Not because of the breaking of so much, but because of how it had happened. The suddenness, the wind out of all keeping with all that was natural and its links to the mist he could sense but never touch or feel around him.

And that sense of wrong was still everywhere. With every gust his heart lurched, and with each drop of rain he feared flood from a clear sky. It had to be stopped. The threat to the pack had to be removed. And somehow, those humans he recognised so faintly were involved. Perhaps they sought what he now sought. Perhaps they didn't. But one thing was clear, he couldn't stay in Thornewood and live on hope alone.

Thraun had always known he was different from the rest of the pack. He understood things. He didn't get damaged. He felt a curious kinship with humans that led him to forbid the pack to hunt them. Now, though, he needed the wolves.

*His mind set, he trotted back to the pack, left the cubs with the
female least able to fight and took the rest back towards Greythorne.*

Somewhere out there were the answers.

Hirad was poking at the fire, sending new flame spiralling into the air
and embers scattering. Beyond the fire, the night was anything but
quiet. Although it wasn't raining, the wind was blowing more cloud
across the sky and, closer to the ground, savage gusts were whipping
up dust, mourning around the broken ruins of Greythorne's once
proud homes.

Down in the centre and south of the town, the lanterns still burned
as the work to uncover the dead continued. Hirad had enormous
admiration and pity for the townspeople who clung to each other for
what support they could get, while their inner strength drove them to
sift the ruins for their dead so that those who survived could begin to
live again.

Hirad added another dried-out branch to the fire and looked away
from the town centre to those he guarded. The Raven. It felt
undeniably good. He hadn't imagined ever watching over Denser,
Ilkar and The Unknown again, yet here he was, and their sleeping
postures said everything about their confidence in him.

There were so many memories to recall, he didn't know where to
begin. He hooked the hot pot off the fire and refilled his mug, the
soaking herbs Ilkar had gathered good enough for one last infusion.

A gust of wind played across the campsite, sifting through the
cloaks and furs of his friends as they slept, the whispering pickpocket
that stole nothing. He smiled, recalling the countless times he'd seen it
before.

But the smile died as his eyes rested on Denser's form. Because the
gust had gone, yet the riffling went on, his cloak moving under the
order of some unseen hand. Unseen.

He'd witnessed more magic than most non-mages would see in a
lifetime and he knew a CloakedWalk attack when he saw it. Mindful
that the mage, who would be moving very slowly around Denser to
avoid becoming visible, would not be alone, Hirad stood leisurely, his
gaze never slipping entirely from Denser, his mind framing the likely
position of the mage-thief.

Denser was the other side of the fire from him, with The Unknown
to his left and Ilkar his right. Hirad stretched, his heart rate increasing. Another gust blew across the ruins. Hirad half-turned as

if to look down in to Greythorne, swung back, took a single pace and launched himself across the fire.

Fists clenched and arms outstretched, he dived to land beyond Denser's body but connected with the Cloaked mage's shoulder and upper back as he bent to steal. Hirad heard the mage grunt in surprise and suddenly he was there; a long figure, dressed in close-fitting black clothes, his arms flailing as the barbarian slammed him to the ground.

'Raven! Mage attack!' called Hirad as he landed, hands grappling for a hold. The mage was fast, sinewy and supple, scrabbling furiously and jamming an arm between himself and Hirad, pushing the barbarian away.

Hirad rolled again, letting go his grip and coming to a half crouch, seeing the mage still disorientated and, behind him, The Raven surging to wakefulness. The mage made to run but Hirad was quicker, lashing out a leg to trip him, the mage tumbling head over heels, sprawling in the dust.

The Raven man jumped after him, the mage quickly on to his feet and facing the barbarian. He swung a fist which Hirad ducked, stepping inside the man's long reach to slam a punch into his midriff and follow up with a left hand which caught him square on the nose. Hirad felt it crack under his fist and felt the blood wet and warm on his hand.

The mage staggered back, gasping in pain. Hirad went after him, double jabbing to the mouth with his left and swinging with his right in a hook that the mage swayed away to avoid. Hirad squared up but never landed his next punch, taken off his feet by a body slamming into his side.

He tumbled to the ground, aware of shouting and seeing another figure all over his vision as he rolled. He heard The Raven shouting.

'Three! There are three!' Denser shouted.

A sword was drawn. Hirad saw the glint of metal and blocked instinctively left to right, connecting with a forearm. He scrambled back, trying to gauge his surroundings, seeing people everywhere.

Denser shouted something unintelligible and rage filled the space. In front of Hirad, his attacker jumped to his feet but doubled over as soon as he straightened. Hirad felt the spray of blood over his face and the man collapsed.

'Gods!' he shouted, getting to his feet and looking for the mage with the broken nose but Denser had seen him first.

'Bastards!' shouted Denser. The Xeteskian swept by Hirad, blood-ied sword raised to bring it down, again and again.

'Stop! Stop!' The Unknown was shouting.

By Hirad, the other mage lay writhing, clutching his side, screaming his agony. Hirad lashed a foot into his face to quiet him while behind, the dull thud of metal on dead meat sounded in his ears.

'It's over. Denser, it's over!' The Unknown again.

'No!' shouted Denser.

'It is over!' The Unknown's voice had finality about it and quiet reigned.

Hirad dusted himself down. He flexed his fists, feeling the knuckles and rubbing at the soreness he found.

On the ground near him, the body of one mage lay twisted in the rubble. His kick to the face had snapped the man's neck but given the gaping wound in his back, it was probably a blessing. A few paces away, a second body. There was blood everywhere. In the garish light of the fire, it glistened on seemingly every stone, trailed over the churned mud and slicked in pools by the bodies. The third was nowhere to be seen and Hirad drew his sword, staring around into the night.

'The third one's still out there somewhere,' he warned.

'He won't be back,' whispered Denser. 'He knows we'll be waiting.'

Denser still stood over his second victim, blood dripping from the blade he clutched, dragging in huge breaths, his head down, face blank. The Unknown and Ilkar stood near each other and to Denser's left. Neither had drawn a weapon and both looked on in almost comical shock at the carnage Denser had so quickly wrought.

'Denser, it's time to clean and sheath,' said The Unknown quietly.

The Xeteskian nodded and knelt to wipe his sword on the dead mage. They watched him make his very deliberate movements and walk back to the fire to retrieve his scabbard, refusing to catch their eyes. He sat on his bedroll and stared into the fire.

'Who were they?' asked Hirad.

'Dordovans,' said Ilkar.

'Assassins,' grated Denser.

'I don't think so,' said Hirad. 'Or it'd be your blood on the ground, not theirs. What the hell *happened* to you?' He gestured at the bodies and walked back into the warmth of the fire, Ilkar and The Unknown joining him. 'I can't believe you did this.'

Denser shrugged. 'They attacked, we defended.'

'Interesting angle,' said Ilkar. 'Someone else might say you ran after an unarmed man and hacked him half to pieces.'

'They didn't attack,' said Hirad. 'They wanted something from you.'

Denser looked at Hirad, his fury still burning. 'And they didn't get it.'

'Didn't get what?' asked The Unknown.

'It doesn't matter,' said Denser, hand reflexively touching his stomach.

'No?' Hirad saw the wildness in Denser's eyes and chose to keep himself calm. 'It mattered to the Dordovans. And it mattered enough for you to kill them.'

'That's not why I killed them.'

'Then tell us,' said The Unknown. 'You're keeping secrets from us again and, again, we couldn't be prepared. You're putting us at risk and that's not The Raven's way.'

'Gods, you sound like Hirad,' said Denser.

'That's because, on this, he's dead right,' said Ilkar, adding his weight. 'We need to know, Denser. And we'll sleep easier if we know now.'

The Xeteskian raised his eyebrows and nodded, somehow making it a grudging gesture.

'The Prophecy wasn't all translated. And I was curious. So I took the pages that weren't translated to Xetesk and found out Dordover's intentions, all right?'

Hirad breathed out sharply and looked down into the town. Lights were weaving through the streets, heading their way. Not surprising. The screams of the dying mage were bound to have been heard despite the wind. At least it would keep the third mage away. He sheathed his sword and sat down.

'And you thought this little snippet not important enough to mention?' said Ilkar, voice quiet but angry. 'You've put us at risk ever since we left Dordover and didn't bother to mention it. Thanks very much.'

'I didn't think they'd find out,' said Denser.

'That isn't the point,' said Hirad. 'I hope it was worth it.' He looked over at Denser and could see that, to him, it was.

'If they get hold of my daughter now, they'll conduct a ritual spell sacrifice. They'll murder her but they won't do it quickly. She'll die in agony. And I won't let that happen. Enough for you?' Denser stared back into the fire.

'For now,' said The Unknown.

Hirad looked at the big man. He suspected there was more. Time would tell but he was seldom wrong. Right now, though, with the lanterns bobbing nearer, there was some explaining to do.

Erienne knew they had made good speed but to her their passage still felt so slow. She knew it was her anxiety but the nagging feeling wouldn't go away. She'd have blown into the sails herself but the stiff wind whipping white horses across the surface of the water, and without doubt a product of Lyanna's mind, was obviously power enough. Indeed at times, the captain of the *Ocean Elm* could be seen frowning out from the wheel deck, confused as to the direction of the wind which didn't necessarily accompany cloud or follow its direction.

But he was a skilful sailor, used to the vagaries of the Southern Ocean and the tides around Calaius; and though clearly irritated by the conflicting information he could see and feel, had enough faith in his judgement and kept the sails full.

Erienne had risen with the first signs of dawn, as she had each morning, marvelling at the sight of light breaking across the eastern horizon as she stood at the bow, dressed in thick woollen breeches, shirt and cloak. This morning, she could see Balaia on the horizon. It was a clear, bright day without a hint of haze and the sight boosted her spirits, quelling the impatience that Ren'erei had found both funny and frustrating.

'Be calm,' she had said. 'There's nothing you can do. The wind and the ship are beyond your control. If you relax your mind, the days will pass more quickly.'

Erienne smiled and half-turned to see the pretty young elf standing on the wheel deck next to the captain. She had tried to teach Erienne mind-calming exercises which were surprisingly similar to those taught at the Colleges to mages suffering severe mana drain. Ren'erei asked her to think of her tensed mind as a muscle, cramped by fatigue, before imagining it slowly unwinding and stretching, then feeling the cool wash of blood begin to flow again.

She knew she could do it, she just didn't want to, and her smiling admission had caused Ren to throw up her arms and stalk away.

Now, of course, Erienne wished she'd tried harder. She was tired, having not had a solid night's sleep since leaving Herendeneth. Lyanna's cries of pain and fear still echoed around her skull in the dead of night and her own anxiety surfaced to wake her a dozen times from her rest.

She'd survive. The coastline was looming large and the trip up the river to Arlen quick, if the captain timed the tide well. Erienne had no doubt that he would.

Her emotions were so mixed. She was desperate to see Denser but feared his reaction after so long out of contact. She needed his strength and thought but disliked the admission of failure it had come to represent within her. And she still thrilled at the prospect of standing with The Raven once again despite knowing the confidence it would give her was entirely unfounded. After all, how could they possibly help? She had to smile at that. They had achieved enough against the odds to make the question ridiculous. The fact was, they'd find a way.

There would be problems, though. She knew Ilkar would be ethically opposed to a return to the One and she could well understand the conflicting thoughts that would be running through his mind. Perhaps he wouldn't even be with them. But somehow, she thought he wouldn't miss it – if only to ensure right was done by his College. As for Denser, well, Denser's College had a vested interest and they'd no doubt be irritated he wasn't working directly with them. But he was a father before he was a Xeteskian and he'd fight his own College if he thought they threatened Lyanna. And in that, as in so much, Erienne and he were one.

But through all her feelings at what she would find back in Balaia, her strongest tie was to the child she had been forced to leave behind. Poor Lyanna. The innocent in a game with no rules, no defined sides and no obvious way to win. Erienne yearned to see her little face, her delightful smile and her beautiful eyes. And she feared that if this mission went astray, and the Dordovans found Herendeneth, she would not.

The strengthening wind drove the bow of the *Ocean Elm* into the next wave, sending spray flying into the air and across the foredeck. Erienne wiped a film of water from her face, turned and walked to the wheel deck, her balance true and confident after six days at sea.

Trotting up the eight-runged ladder she came to stand by Ren'erei, the elf smiling at her, green eyes sparkling.

'Getting a little rough down there, was it?' she asked.

'No. It's just that I've already washed this morning, that's all,' she returned. 'How close are we?'

The Captain turned to her, reddened face pinched, his strong hands rocks on the wheel. 'A day and a half, no more. Less if we go upriver through the night and I have a mind to.' His voice was melodic and gentle, so different from when he bellowed orders to his crew.

Erienne nodded. 'Then it's time I tried to contact Denser. I'll be in my cabin and I need to not be disturbed.'

'Then I'll be standing outside the door.' Ren'erei's face was solemn.

'You don't have to.' Erienne smiled.

'Nevertheless.'

Erienne led the way below decks, turning to Ren'erei as she reached the door to her cabin.

'You should hear nothing,' she said. 'But even if you do, don't worry. Occasionally, dispersal of Communion is a little painful.'

'Good luck,' said Ren'erei.

'Thank you.' She closed the door, lay down on her bed and closed her eyes. As she settled into the mana spectrum, searching for the spike that she would recognise as Denser, she prayed he was within her compass and, more importantly, that he would answer her at all.

She was not to be disappointed.

Chapter 13

Darrick faced down the angry Dordovan mage master in front of him. The young General hadn't slept, though his cavalry and mage charges had grabbed a few hours after arriving in the ruins of Greythorne in the middle of the night. Having overseen the picketing and feeding of the horses, he'd toured the ruins, resolving immediately to leave half of his four hundred cavalry to help the salvage effort, taking the balance on after a day's rest and assessment.

What he didn't need, with the stubble itching his chin, his eyes red and smarting and still wearing his riding garb, was the mage, Tendjorn, to disagree.

'These people need our help,' said Darrick. 'While you were resting, I was walking these streets. My decision stands.'

Tendjorn, not yet forty and with a flat, supercilious face, looked along his wide, veined nose from where he stood in the centre of Greythorne, clearly able to see the situation for himself.

'Your orders, if I'm not mistaken, General, are to support the forces now in and around Arlen and rendezvous with Vuldaroq on his arrival with your entire force. Our latest intelligence from Gorstan indicates we are close to finding the girl but will need to move fast. Ornouth is a long way and Xetesk and the Protectors are not far behind.'

'Open your tiny eyes, and see what I see, Tendjorn. I see a small town destroyed by a hurricane. And it was a hurricane that, by your own admission, was probably a result of Lyanna's awakening power.

'Now I understand your need to recapture her to stop all this but we have a duty as responsible ambassadors of magic to help those who have become innocent victims of whatever this actually is.'

Tendjorn smiled, a patronising gesture that sparked Darrick's anger, though he kept himself in check.

'General, I think you fail to fully understand the situation. This is not the end, though if we don't find the girl soon, it will be the beginning of the end. Every hour spent here is an hour wasted.'

'My decision stands and I would advise you to lower your voice next time you choose to utter such an insensitive remark. We do have the time.'

Tendjorn shook his head, his untidy dark hair flapping around his small round ears. 'I don't think so, General. Might I remind you—'

Darrick grabbed Tendjorn's shirt at the neck with both hands and dragged the mage close.

'Listen to me, Dordovan, and listen very well,' he grated, his eyes cold. He could see the sudden fear in the mage's eyes. 'These people need our help now. Not in a day, not in seven, but now. Do you really believe that I, as an emissary of Lystern, can ride out of here without lifting a finger? Never mind the unconscionable moral wrong, what the hell sort of a message do you think it would send them about us?

'This operation is under my control. It is two and a half days' ride to Arlen from here. It will take twice that time to secure and provision enough ships to sail as far as Ornouth. My cavalry are tired, my horses exhausted. We will stay to oversee the cleaning up here. Only then will half of us move to Arlen. There, I will decide if Izack and his men stay here or join us. Do you understand me?'

Darrick let the mage go and stepped back. 'Attempt to remove me from command if you dare.'

'Don't challenge me, Darrick,' spat Tendjorn, straightening his clothing and failing not to appear ruffled.

'It's not a challenge. I'm in charge here, remember that.'

'And remember who wields the real power,' returned the mage.

Darrick laughed. 'Yes I do. But we're not in Dordover now, are we? And you are among Lysternans.'

The young General stalked out of the square towards the camp to rouse his tired men to uncover more of the dead.

There had been no trouble with the townspeople who'd come to check on The Raven after the attack by the Dordovan mages. They had no energy to question their story and anyway, The Raven could always be trusted. A further blessing was the dry weather overnight and The Raven woke shortly before dawn, at the insistence of The Unknown. The Communion to Denser had come with a pale light filtering beneath fast-moving, thin, high cloud across the wrecked town, the renewed noise of activity drifting up to them. Another weary day.

'Who is it?' asked Hirad.

Ilkar regarded him blankly. 'Well, it's a little difficult to tell, strangely enough.'

Hirad made a long face. 'Thought you mages knew this sort of stuff.'

'Tell me, Hirad, if someone gives a friend of yours a letter while you're standing there, do you immediately know who it's from?' Ilkar's ears pricked in irritation.

'Well, letters aren't magical, are they? Isn't there an aura or something?'

'Gods, Hirad, how many Communions have you seen? Isn't it obvious that it's a personal and private conversation?'

'But that doesn't mean you don't know who's talking,' said Hirad evenly but a smile was edging the corners of his mouth.

Ilkar pointed at his face. 'See these? They're eyes. See that? That's Denser, lying on the ground, receiving Communion from the Gods know where or who. I am a mage, not a seer, all right?'

'You know, I've really missed our intellectual debates,' said The Unknown dryly. He knelt by Denser and moved the mage's head further on to his rolled-up cloak. 'So well constructed and delivered.'

'Glad you think so,' muttered Ilkar, throwing a sideways glance at Hirad.

'What I think,' said The Unknown. 'And you think too, Ilkar, is that Denser is most likely in contact with Erienne. After all, few enough know his signature, let alone can guess or have worked out his likely whereabouts.'

'That presupposes Erienne to be not too far distant,' said Ilkar, nodding nonetheless.

'A meeting was always inevitable,' reasoned The Unknown.

'A bit convenient though, isn't it? I mean, we show up here in the middle of basically nowhere and Erienne drops a message in after weeks of nothing?'

The Unknown shrugged. 'I think we've been together long enough not to believe in coincidence or convenience. Erienne left Denser a letter knowing he would try to find her and that we would help him, should he ask. If her need for him has grown, she'll try to find him now too. It just makes sense for them to meet where she believes he will come to.'

'Clever lady,' said Ilkar.

'I never doubted it,' said The Unknown. He straightened and looked back down the small rise into the centre of Greythorne.

'Some horsemen arrived last night. Cavalry by the order of the hoofbeats. We should find out who it is.'

'Dordovan, no doubt,' said Ilkar, scowling.

The Unknown nodded. 'In all probability. We can show them the bodies of their colleagues, can't we? When Denser comes round, we'll go and look. Just keep your ears open and your eyes sharp. It's looking like we aren't on the same side. All right?'

'Mummy! Mummy!' Lyanna's repeated screams woke Cleress before Aviana's urgent message reached her tired mind. The Al-Drechar's house was dark as she came to but even as she fought for focus in mind and eye, she heard the urgent speech of Guild elves and the snap of Ephemere's voice ordering calm.

But as Cleress emerged into the corridor from her room, a shawl about her shoulders, feet rammed into sandals, night dress floating about her skeletal frame, it was clear Herendeneth was anything but calm.

Outside, a wind howled down the wood-panelled passageway, rattling the pictures hanging on the walls and ruffling the rugs underfoot. Behind Cleress as she limped towards the guest wing where Lyanna slept, a vase crashed to the floor and the breaking of glass echoed from a distant part of the house.

Ahead of her, Ephy had stopped at a set of doors and was speaking to a Guild elf, Cleress couldn't make out who. She saw him nod, bow slightly and hurry back up the passage towards her.

'Ephy!' called Cleress. Ephemere turned, her face grey and anxious.

'Let Aronaar help you,' she replied. She opened a door but the wind snapped it shut, the dull bang reverberating along the corridor. Ephemere frowned.

Aronaar trotted up to her, deep green eyes tight with recent sleep, shirt and trousers hurriedly put on. He was barefoot.

'Thank you,' said Cleress, leaning gratefully into him, taking the weight from her stiff and painful right knee.

'You set the pace, my Lady,' said Aronaar, inclining his head slightly.

'Then we'd better make it quick.' They started towards Ephemere. 'We're following you, Ephy. Is she in bed still?'

Ephemere had dragged the door back open and braced it with a foot. She nodded.

'Sitting up but still asleep, Ana says. This could be trouble. She's in danger of becoming uncontained.'

Cleress felt fear shift through her, tensing tired muscles and catching her breath.

'Faster, Aronaar. Much faster.'

It was the flow of the mana they had to assess. The depth of any flaring and the vortices it produced. Without that knowledge, they could do Lyanna incalculable harm, shutting off streams that, with no escape, would disperse themselves inside her mind. Hurrying down the corridor, towards her room, Cleress wondered if that wasn't already happening.

Outside, the orchard was largely still, but every window overlooking it had smashed outwards, leaving jagged spears of glass and warped frames swinging on the wind that gusted strong into their faces.

Above it, Lyanna's wails ran like acid through Cleress' veins and she could but imagine the torment of the young child as she fought a desperate battle to bring her burgeoning power under control.

For days now, the four elderly Al-Drechar had kept unflinching vigil over Lyanna as she descended into her Night. At no time was she left alone in her mind; it was the only way to monitor her acceptance of the mana as part of her being and discern any hint that she was understanding control.

Only now would the Al-Drechar find out whether their terribly short time of teaching had given Lyanna the knowledge that would save her life. But what nagged at them all was that, though Lyanna was obviously bright and a talent with no bounds or equal to her potential, she shouldn't have had to deal with her full Awakening until her teens. Not just her mental wellbeing but her physical state too had to be monitored.

The Al-Drechar did everything they could, though in truth it wasn't much. They kept her exercised and fed during the moments she was awake and shielded her from the excesses of mana strength while she lay semi-conscious. But so much of the battle was within her undeveloped psyche and they were helpless to aid her there.

The lucid periods were shortening dramatically and, more and more, Lyanna either lay on her bed or walked the corridors of the house, oblivious to all around her, Al-Drechar shadowing her every step of the way.

A keening cry split the whistling of the wind and with it, a jolt in Cleress' mind as Aviana's tenuous grip on Lyanna's mind slipped again.

'Hurry, please,' came the exhausted thought. 'She's breaking me.'

'Almost with you,' pulsed Ephemere. 'Be calm, Ana.'

Aronaar reached out with his free hand and pushed open Lyanna's door. Ephemere strode in first, with Cleress unwrapping her arm from the elf's shoulder before following her in while he stayed outside.

Lyanna was sitting on the bed, legs not touching the ground. Sweat matted her hair and ran down her face and across her tightly closed eyes, dripping from her cheeks and chin. Her mouth hung open and she dragged in great breaths, moaning for her mother or whimpering, her brow creased by some savage inner pain.

In a chair near the bed slumped Aviana, her face white in the gloom and drooping to her chest. Her arms were gripping the sides of the chair and her legs were tucked hard under it. She was shivering, her eyes restless as they searched the mana spectrum.

Immediately, Cleress and Ephemere attuned their eyes to the spectrum, revealing the full enormity of what they had sensed on walking in.

Rippling and shimmering, unstable but holding, Aviana's mind-mana shield played like a hood around Lyanna's consciousness, its deep brown cut through with a brilliant emerald green that was Aviana's alone. Beneath it thrummed the chaos of Lyanna's desperate fight to accept and control the mana flow coursing through her head, drawn there by what she represented as if it was alive.

And what the Dordovans had done was there for them all to see. Dominating the gentle brown that gave them cause for hope, indicating as it did her Drechar capabilities, was the poisonous orange of the Dordovan College. Here was where the fight would take place.

Looking deeper, Cleress could see striations of deep green, pale yellow and dark, dark blue assimilated in the streams. Much of it appeared calm but at the centre of the helical structure was the pulsing orange that signified Dordovan Awakening.

Like a lunging animal, no, a snake preparing to strike, the rogue Dordovan mana bunched and coiled before expanding explosively, ripping the gently modulating brown as it did so; and punching outwards as flares or, intriguingly and worryingly, part constructs.

Aviana, with minute adjustments to her shield, accommodated her instant decisions, letting the flares and stronger constructs escape or, if she could, containing them, allowing them to disperse harmlessly away from Lyanna and almost certainly taking damage in her own mind in the process. It was impossible to see how she could do otherwise.

Cleress' pulse quickened. It was an onslaught, unintentional and quite without malice, but one under which Aviana, even Aviana, was beginning to wilt. The power it represented was quite without precedent. Should Lyanna complete the miracle and survive, she'd be a mage with no peer. It was something for the Al-Drechar to cling onto. At least they wouldn't be surrendering themselves pointlessly.

'Cleress, apply yourself to the shield,' said Ephemere. 'I need to calm the inner structure.'

'Be careful,' urged Cleress, already plucking at Aviana's mana strands to knit together the shield and provide a fresh and safer outlet for the flare. 'She's attempting to cast.'

'She's trying to contact Erienne,' said Aviana, relief in her voice as Cleress accepted some of the brunt of Lyanna's outpourings.

Through the jolt she felt and the concentration she partitioned to help Ana, Cleress had enough about her to be irritated she hadn't spotted it straight away.

'Of course,' she muttered. Though Lyanna hadn't been taught even the rudiments of Communion, her innate knowledge led her subconscious mind to attempt it. Her constructs were ill-formed and impossibly unstable, lasting a few heartbeats at most, but they were there nonetheless as she attempted the flow across the spectrum that would lead her to her mother's mind.

It was lucky she had no hope of success. The base power of her casting occasionally reached dangerous peaks which would have slammed into Erienne with the force of a MindMelt. It was these Aviana had been filtering through the shield to dissipate away from that young, helpless mind. Even so, the pain must have been at times intense. Small wonder Lyanna cried out for Erienne so often.

'Aviana, let go if you need to,' said Cleress. Despite her tiredness, she felt able to sustain the shield while Ephemere cut off the source of the flares.

'I'm all right. I'll just pull back a little,' she said. 'Ephy, you'll have to talk her down quickly. The Gods only know what this is doing outside.'

'No, I'm not going to talk. I've got a better idea. I'm going to mana meld with her.'

'Risky,' said Cleress. The mass of trapped mana in Lyanna's mind coiled and sprang, spitting out another embryonic Communion. It was weak as Lyanna began to tire and Cleress was able to disperse it within the shield; a containment that represented a small victory for the seas around Herendeneth.

'She needs to understand how to bind the Dordovan magic into the One at source. She may be able to stand the reaction in her mind of not doing so but I don't think we or Balaia can.'

'Then do it, Ephy, if you believe you can,' said Aviana. 'Just hurry.'

Cleress watched closely as the smooth brown sphere that represented the calm of Ephemere's mind began to reach out, all the while never letting her concentration slip on the shield.

Strands of mana waved out from the sphere. Tiny filaments like hairs on an otherwise bald skull, probing so gently into the multi-coloured confusion that was Lyanna. At first, the little girl seemed unaware her mana coil was being touched and Ephemere was able to spread the gossamer tendrils wider, linking and diffusing areas of deep Dordovan orange, melding their flow with hers, removing its aggression.

But though Lyanna herself had no formal training in defence against such magical intrusion, her innate abilities, unschooled and uncontrolled, fired within her mind.

'Now it starts,' whispered Ephemere. 'Be ready. Accept the pain.'

Cleress frowned but in the next heartbeat understood only too well. The coiling core of Lyanna's mana focus dragged inwards at extraordinary speed, moving from the size of a skull to that of a fist quicker than the mind's eye could follow.

Ephemere gasped, her probing tendrils whipping away from their tenuous hold. Immediately, she constructed a convex surface and suspended it, base down, above the fist which punched outwards with blurring energy.

'Dear Gods,' whispered Cleress as the mana energy deluged Ephemere's deflector, disintegrating against the unyielding surface held by a mind of huge experience. Mana strands flashed away, tearing into the shield held by Aviana and Cleress, the two Al-Drechar modulating desperately to absorb the impact or let it pass through on its way to play havoc with Balaia.

Absorption was a hammer, pounding on her exposed brain. Lyanna's flares coursed the shield, seeking a path, their outlet Aviana and Cleress. Naturally, the Al-Drechar could have completed a circuit, building a contained sphere, but Lyanna would have been irrevocably damaged at the very least as her mana energy gorged itself in the active mind that had so recently given it its freedom.

And that could not be allowed to happen. So the Al-Drechar's old but strong minds had to take the force of it, letting go only that which would have compromised their concentration and hence the shield, so risking catastrophic flaring into the mana trails that covered Balaia. It was an acceptable state, but only for now.

Lyanna's resistance was violent but brief and Cleress realised that Ephemere had fully expected it to be so. Quickly, the mana flow subsided, the coil relaxed and the girl's breathing returned to a regular pace from its fevered speed.

'Join me,' said Ephy. 'She is spent.'

'We should keep the shield,' said Aviana immediately.

'It's done its work,' replied Ephy. 'Trust me.'

Together, the three Al-Drechar forged a lattice of tendrils that stroked the angry, tired coil of Lyanna's failing defences, teasing out the Dordovan strands and calming them to brown. Doing so, Cleress felt Lyanna's energy seep away, as did her own, and she reacted just quickly enough in the physical world to hold the child as she slumped, peaceful for now, to a deep and dreamless slumber.

'We should wake Myra,' said Ephemere. 'She can take the rest of the night.'

'No,' said Aviana firmly. 'I can do it. Just pray she keeps quiet through the day too.'

Cleress knew what she meant. They couldn't cope with another outburst like this without rest. Ideally, Myriell shouldn't be woken until noon and Aviana would have to sleep the whole of the next day and night. She and Ephy were in little better shape but had the rest of this night before having to once again take their stints guarding Lyanna from her own mind. Her Night was far from over.

Cleress and Ephemere made their way slowly and painfully back to their own rooms, spurning the Lemiir for the totality of rest. In truth, neither had the energy to sit and smoke.

Closing her door, Cleress mouthed a silent prayer that Erienne would return soon.

Chapter 14

The Raven walked purposefully back towards the centre of Grey-thorne, their direction clear at last. All their clues, thoughts and suspicions had been proved right. Erienne had travelled south, she had received help and she had met with the Al-Drechar. But not on Balaia.

Denser had woken thoughtful, quiet but determined from his Communion, his fury of the night gone and giving them only a brief summary of his conversation. He was very anxious to be on his way but The Unknown was determined to make proper assessment of Greythorne, both in terms of support for its beleaguered survivors and the potential threat of the cavalry force.

They would leave town after midday all being well which, with Erienne probably arriving in Arlen the following morning, depending on wind and tide at the river's mouth, was all Denser would stand. It would still leave Erienne alone for two days but Denser had advised her to stay aboard the *Ocean Elm*, advice she had been given by the Guild elves already.

'Like I said earlier, keep your eyes open. We've heard all sorts of rumours about College mobilisation and we don't know where allegiances have finally fallen, if anywhere. Don't necessarily trust anyone. And remember, even within a College, not everyone thinks the same way.'

'Meaning what?' asked Hirad.

'Meaning Dordover don't want us to find Lyanna first,' said The Unknown. 'They want us to lead them to her and then they want her back inside the College and probably dead. All right?'

Hirad nodded. 'I'll be careful.'

'Good.'

It was a short walk through the ruins to the centre of the shattered town, coming again to full, painful life, such as it was. The smell of porridge and the steam from water vats drifted across the main square. Squads of men and women moved with dread purpose to their next tasks and inside the marquee a babble of voices signified the day's activities being organised.

The Unknown Warrior stopped one of a group of men heading past them with shovels. 'I heard some cavalry come in last night. Do you know where from?'

The man shrugged. 'West. One of the Colleges.'

'Which one? Dordover?'

A shake of the head. 'I'm not sure. Lystern, I think.'

The Unknown nodded and walked on, heading for the marquee.

'Good news,' said Ilkar.

'If it's true,' said The Unknown.

'Will you ever stop being sceptical?'

'Will you ever stop being an elf?' The Unknown smiled.

'I think you've said that before, sometime.'

'I know I have.'

'But he was right about Lystern, that man. Look,' said Hirad, pointing towards the marquee. Standing just under its awning and talking to Gannan was a tall young man in plated cavalry leather. A cloak was about his shoulders, deep green with gold braiding at the neck, and his curly brown hair waved in the breeze that blew without pause through Greythorne's streets. He was obviously tired, his shoulders having the minutest droop, but he was still unmistakable.

'Darrick,' said The Unknown.

The Raven walked faster across the square to their old friend who didn't look up as they approached, his face half-turned from them.

'Well, well, well,' said Hirad. 'There's a face it's good to see in bad times.'

Darrick's head snapped round and he took in the four of them, a rare smile crossing his face.

'But why is it always the bad times, Hirad, eh?' The smile faded as he gripped hands with them all in turn, his habitual serious expression replacing it. 'I didn't expect to see The Raven together again. The situation must be worse than I thought.'

'We're just helping a friend,' said Ilkar. 'Old habits die hard, you know.'

'I do know.'

'So what brings Lysternan cavalry to Greythorne?' asked The Unknown.

'Orders,' said Darrick. 'Some of my, um, superiors deemed it necessary to increase the weight of our already significant forces in Arlen.'

'Already significant?' Denser's face displayed his agitation.

'Look,' said Darrick, 'I know I'm not speaking to fools. There's been plenty of College mobilisation and the potential for trouble in Arlen is high.'

'Someone else knows Erienne's landing there tomorrow, do they?'

'Hirad!' snapped The Unknown, his voice an angry hiss.

'No, they do not,' said Darrick, but he couldn't help a glance over his left shoulder where a cloaked man was standing hunched over some papers.

'But they do now,' said Denser. 'Nice work, Hirad.'

'What's wrong with you? This is Darrick we're talking to,' said Hirad, though his tone betrayed knowledge that he'd made a bad mistake.

'And you think Lystern alone sent him and his cavalry, do you?' The Unknown scowled. 'Gods, Hirad, sometimes I wonder whether you understand anything at all.'

'Can we conduct this somewhere else?' suggested Ilkar.

Denser nodded curtly and strode back into the square, heading for the makeshift stabling.

'Sorry,' said Hirad, shrugging. 'I didn't think—'

'No, you didn't,' said The Unknown. 'C'mon. Time for a slight change of plan.' He looked deep into Darrick's eyes, the General nodding almost imperceptibly. 'Thanks.'

He turned and followed Denser out into the wan sunlight, Ilkar and Hirad behind him.

Tendjorn straightened and turned, watching The Raven hurry away. To his right, Darrick stood impassive, his eyes glinting, his body still. The Dordovan mage could feel his anger though and found it a comfort. He opened his mouth to speak.

'Don't say it,' warned Darrick. 'You will leave them to do what they have to do.'

Tendjorn snorted. 'Sentimentality is something you can ill afford,' he said. 'They have done what we expected and located Erienne. We can handle it from here.'

'Meaning what exactly? If you've used The Raven, you'll pay. Not by my hand, by theirs. You'll do well to remember that.'

'Five years ago, when they rode the dragons to save us from the Wesmen, I would have believed them capable of anything. But now?

Look at them, General. They're looking exactly what they are. Past it. You're supposed to be a friend of theirs; perhaps you should start acting like one.'

'I beg your pardon?'

'I will be contacting Gorstan at Arlen presently,' said Tendjorn, ignoring Darrick's anger. 'We'll have Erienne as soon as she docks. I expect you to be ready to ride with however many you consider necessary as soon as you have completed your assessment of Greythorne.'

'And The Raven?'

'Will be kept away from causing trouble. Now that can be by you, or by Dordovan forces already in Arlen. Either way, they are not to be allowed contact with Erienne.'

Darrick looked at him, his jaw clenched, eyes betraying his feelings, but said nothing, choosing to walk away. Tendjorn enjoyed his discomfort.

'Oh, General?' Darrick stopped, his back to the mage. 'We don't want bloodshed in Arlen, do we? Like I said, The Raven are your friends. I do hope you decide to, how shall I put it, look after their wellbeing. Stop them doing anything foolhardy.'

The General walked on.

Thraun had tracked the scent of the ones for which he had dim but certain memory. Trotting with the pack towards Greythorne, other disturbing recollections fought to resurface, distracting him and worrying the pack, who kept a wary distance behind.

Like dreams while he was awake, the flashes rocked him. Of standing on two legs; of a friend he knew as man-packbrother; of great winged beasts and of primal fear reaching down from the sky. At least they confirmed that those humans he followed were known to him sometime.

And that they were strong and, he thought, good.

The pack kept above the trail the humans and their animals used as it wound past the remains of Thornewood and arced across open ground, latterly turning full south to enter the town itself.

It was a habit born of caution but he shouldn't have bothered. Nothing travelled the trail and, with the moon shining dully through a cloud-covered sky, there would be no one. Just the spirits of the wind to keep the fear alive within them.

The pack had stopped to rest and watch on a shadowed rise above Greythorne. The scene was much as the previous night, with lights

burning, voices calling and stone and wood rumbling, cracking or
falling.

Well before dawn, horses and riders had thundered into the
western end of the town and Thraun had taken advantage of the
disruption to scout the empty streets. He had picked up the scent of
his humans very quickly and, satisfied he knew where they were, by
smell and the embers of a fire he could see like a puddle in the dark, he
had returned to the pack.

But they hadn't stayed in Greythorne. With light across the sky
once more, the humans had taken to their horses and ridden south
and east. Thraun hadn't known what he expected but it wasn't this.
Perhaps the wrong in the air covered more than he dared imagine.
Perhaps the two female humans he had seen in Thornewood were not
returning to Greythorne. Or perhaps those he knew were doing
nothing to change the wrong to right.

Whichever way it was, the pack had to follow him. He ignored
their desire for food. That could come later. Choosing to track by
scent rather than shadow by eye, Thraun took the pack on to a
destiny none of them could guess at or hope to understand.

The Unknown hadn't even paused to say goodbye to Gannan, such
was the haste with which they left Greythorne. With their horses'
hooves kicking up mud and the surprised and disappointed faces of
the town's survivors following them, they galloped through the
wreckage and out in to the countryside, heading east and south to
Arlen. It was just under a three-day ride and though they were bound
to have a good start on any pursuit, that wasn't Denser's principal
concern.

They rode hard for two hours before the horses needed a break.
Ilkar took the horses to a stream while Hirad built a fire to make
coffee.

The barbarian didn't look up when Denser stalked up and ignited
the damp timber with a brief but intense FlamePalm. The Unknown
dumped a few more short branches by the growing flames.

'Hirad, you are a bloody idiot,' he said, squatting down by his
friend. 'What did I say about being careful?'

'It should be all right. We can trust Darrick,' said Hirad, though
the pit in his stomach told him it wouldn't be.

'Darrick isn't the problem,' said Denser. 'The Dordovan behind
him was.'

'But even so—' began Hirad.

'There isn't an "even so",' snapped Denser. 'Unless they've made a major tactical error, that mage will be able to commune as far as Arlen easily and will have already done so.'

'Always assuming there's anyone there.'

'Oh, assuming that, of course.' Denser cast his eyes skywards. Above him, the cloud was moving and rolling, pushed by a quickly strengthening wind. Already, Hirad had changed his position to shield the fire over which The Unknown hung his pot.

'Hirad, it's become obvious to everyone that Erienne took Lyanna off Balaia. It was a just a question of where. Dordover will have been covering every port for weeks. After all, they've had a fifty-day advantage over the rest of us,' said The Unknown.

'So what do we do?' Hirad at last picked his head up and looked at The Unknown. There was no anger in his expression, just frustration.

'Well we have to assume any Dordovans in Arlen are already aware of Erienne's imminent arrival. And so we have to stop her walking into trouble for a start.'

'Which means Denser communes, right?'

'Yes, Hirad,' said Denser curtly. 'Not exactly how I'd planned to deplete my stamina but still.'

'I'm sorry, all right?' Hirad couldn't keep the irritation out of his voice. 'We'll sort it out.'

'Will we?' Denser's eyes flashed angrily. 'There's four of us. What exactly do you suppose we'll do if the Dordovans get to her before we do?'

'They're not going to hurt her, Denser.'

'But they'll take her from me and time is so short,' he said, fidgeting again. 'And capturing her is all they need to get to Lyanna. Only I can save her.'

'So you keep saying. So get them to avoid Arlen and we'll meet them further down the coast. Don't panic.' Hirad stabbed another branch into the fire, sending a few sparks past the gently steaming pot. Ilkar scrambled over and sat the opposite side of the fire to the barbarian.

'I'm not panicking, Hirad. I'm worried for my wife and daughter. I hope that's all right.'

'And I'm worried for my dragons but I'm still here helping you.'

'Oh, Gods,' muttered Ilkar under his breath. 'Must you?'

'Yes, *such* helpless creatures,' said Denser. 'So vulnerable. I can't imagine how they'll survive without you.'

'They're already dying, Denser,' snarled Hirad. 'Not that you'd know, eating delicacies in your comfortable tower.'

'That's not how it is,' said Denser, leaning back deliberately, attempting to calm the situation a little.

'No, sure, I mean the fruits of your hard work are everywhere, aren't they?' Hirad waved his arms expansively. 'Do you see Protectors freed? Are the Kaan dragons any closer to going home?'

'Those are just two issues in—'

'"Just?" In case it's escaped your attention, Denser, those two issues saved Balaia. One knowingly exiling themselves in the process, the other at great cost outside the Septern Manse. Unfortunately, it was some time ago, and perhaps your memory has dimmed over the years.' Hirad's caustic tone echoed around the fireplace. There was a contemplative silence.

'Hirad, I know this is critical to you,' said Ilkar. 'But temporarily, we have more pressing matters. And getting to Erienne and then the Al-Drechar could solve your problem anyway.'

Hirad nodded. 'I know I made a mistake and I'm sorry. I just want him to know what he's done. Or rather not done.' He jabbed a finger at Denser.

'At the risk of seeming stupid, what does finding the Al-Drechar have to do with Hirad's dragons?' asked Denser.

'The Kaan think they can solve the dimensional riddle,' said The Unknown. 'They have Septern's knowledge after all. And one other thing. Hirad's right, the Kaan *are* dying and the Protectors aren't free—'

'Hold on, I—'

'Don't interrupt me, Denser,' warned The Unknown. 'I know Mount politics are complex but you're a senior master now. We've seen no results. No progress. And we want answers. Just as soon as Lyanna is secure.'

Denser regarded The Unknown with a slight frown on his face. A corner of his mouth turned up as he spoke, a little nervous reaction.

'Let's face it, unless we can secure Lyanna, and the Al-Drechar for that matter, dragons and Protectors will be the least of our worries.'

'All the worse that you've let it go this long, then,' said Hirad. He lined up a row of mugs and tipped the coffee into them.

Denser shook his head. 'You see, the trouble is, you haven't grasped the seriousness of all this yet, have you?'

'Credit me with some notion,' said Hirad, thrusting a mug at Denser roughly enough for coffee to spill over. 'If we don't get to

Lyanna first and keep her from Dordover, we'll have this bad weather
for longer.'

Denser gaped. 'Haven't you told him anything?' he demanded of
Ilkar.

The elf shrugged. 'We tried . . .'

'I understand,' said Denser, nodding in resignation. 'Let me try and
put this in words you'll understand.'

'Don't patronise me, Xetesk man.'

'Sorry. I didn't mean that the way it came out.' He took a sip of his
drink. 'This isn't like a passing storm front. "Bad weather" does not
cover what might happen – this is only the start. We've already seen a
raising of the earth, a hurricane, floods and tidal waves. Imagine that
happening a hundred times worse and all across Balaia. Because if
Lyanna is taken from the Al-Drechar and slips into unfathomable
Night, as would be inevitable, that's what'll happen until she dies.
And that's why the Dordovans will kill her.'

'And can we, or rather you, control her?' asked Hirad, his voice
quieter as the weight of Denser's words sank in.

'Yes, I keep telling you,' Denser replied, anxiety back in his voice.
'But we have to get to her quickly. The Al-Drechar can't contain her
for long, even at this level of mess. At least the fact that Erienne has
left her means she believes the Al-Drechar are capable for the time
being.'

'But then she won't know the extent of what's already happened,'
reasoned Ilkar.

'I think the Al-Drechar will have guessed,' replied Denser. 'But the
point is that letting Erienne fall into Dordovan hands would be a
disaster. They'll either try and fail to control her because they don't
understand or they'll kill her because they're scared of her. I need my
wife. We haven't got long.'

Hirad opened his mouth to speak, saw the depths of worry in
Denser's eyes and chose to drink some coffee instead. What he had
been about to say was inflammatory anyway. Perhaps another time.

'We have to deal with the here and now,' said The Unknown.
'Denser, Communion. If you can get Erienne to persuade them to
anchor in the bay we can ride down the estuary to find them. Hirad,
go and check the horses. Ilkar, a word if I may.'

'Are you all right, Unknown?' asked the Julatsan.

'Yeah, fine,' said The Unknown but they could all see a distant look
in his eye.

Hirad shrugged and walked over to the stream, a smile breaking over his face as his irritation faded. The horses looked relaxed and ready and were grazing contentedly. He patted one on the neck and ran a hand down its foreleg, feeling the fit muscle and bone beneath his fingers.

His smile broadened. They may have been apart for five years but still, when The Unknown spoke, they listened. That fact alone would, he considered, give them the ghost of a chance in the days to come. And it sounded like they might need every ghost they could grasp.

Chapter 15

Selik leaned back in his richly upholstered red and gold chair in a private room of the Lakehome Inn and allowed himself a smile. It still felt like a smile to him though the humour was gone. Another would have seen little more than a grotesque distortion of his face.

He wouldn't have described the feeling as 'happiness' either. A bitter satisfaction, maybe, an easing of the burning hate in the knowledge of its ultimate extinguishing through sweet revenge. But happiness, no. That was an emotion he hadn't experienced since the bitch had frozen him. Lesser men would have died. His strength and breastplate had saved his life when the IceWind had struck him. Nothing so resistant had been protecting his hands and face, though, and he'd borne the stigma for six long years, just waiting his chance.

And now, he was to be presented with it.

It had been good news Gorstan had given him as they'd stood at the mouth of Arlen Bay and he'd ridden hard for the town to set about hiring ships and crews and buying provisions. But there'd been a nagging anxiety. It was one thing knowing where the bitch and her abomination of a daughter hid. It would have been quite another getting there through the famously treacherous rock and coral straits. Many men would have been lost and he didn't know how many, if any, he could afford to lose.

He'd dismissed the mage who'd bought him the latest, far finer news and now sat alone in front of an open fire, a rug beneath his bare feet, mulled wine steaming on a table in front of him and the other three chairs in the tapestry-hung room empty. He enjoyed the peace, broken only by the crackle of flame.

He relaxed, feeling the anxiety slip away. He was not a keen sea traveller and the thought of danger he couldn't see lurking beneath the water at Ornouth made him nervous.

Now, though, the answer to his prayers was sailing up the Arlen River. And he would be waiting at the dock to welcome her.

He sipped his mulled wine, then took a long swallow, draining the glass. Gods, but it tasted good.

Denser ceased his probing, released the Communion shape and opened his eyes. The Raven were around him and the concern on their faces told him he'd shown facial expression during his search for Erienne. He felt tired and lost, somehow, and his heart beat hollow in his chest. He moved gingerly to a sitting position and felt for his pipe and weed pouch.

Ilkar laid a hand on his shoulder.

'That didn't look comfortable, Denser. What happened?'

Denser filled his pipe and lit it, suppressing an unwanted smile at Ilkar's choice of words. The Communion hadn't merely been uncomfortable. It had been like searching in a hailstorm. He felt battered and a little confused by what he had encountered in the mana spectrum.

He knew he'd searched the right area and he knew Erienne's signature intimately. She wouldn't attempt to hide from him. But he'd found a sudden impenetrability, like coming across a bank of fog in a sheltered valley. And it had been a painful experience.

He looked up into Ilkar's face and past him at Hirad, who was examining the blade of a dagger, apparently uninterested.

'I couldn't reach her,' he said quietly. 'Couldn't even feel her. There was something in the way.'

Ilkar frowned. 'How do you mean?'

'Well . . .' Denser fought for the right words. He scratched his head and took a draw on his pipe, the smoke funnelling pleasantly into his mouth. 'Like there was another power there, occupying the space. I couldn't feel her because there was focused mana in the way, I suppose.'

'What shape was it?'

'That's why it's so confusing, there was no shape. It was a coalescing of mana, like a wall.'

'Produced by another mage, though?' Ilkar frowned.

'Presumably.' Denser shrugged. He sighed. 'I guess it doesn't really matter. The fact is that I can't contact her.'

'Not now, anyway,' said The Unknown. 'Come on, we'd better get away. Try again when we stop this evening.'

Denser nodded. 'Yes. It's unlikely to be a long-lived effect. Or I hope it won't.'

'Unless it's a deliberate obscurement,' said Ilkar.

'Hmm. How, though? It's not a structure I recognised. It wasn't right, though.' He bit his lip, frustrated.

Hirad sheathed his dagger and got to his feet. 'It'll be all right, Denser.'

Denser blew out his cheeks. 'Nothing like a non-mage to give you confidence, is there?'

Erienne leaned over the post and retched again, her muscles convulsing, the taste of bile strong in her throat. Her stomach was long empty but the nausea sweeping through her didn't subside and hadn't for most of the morning.

Ren'erei had stood just far enough away to give her comfort but not too near to crowd her and add to her acute embarrassment. As Erienne straightened and turned to let the wind blow into her face, cooling the sweat on her brow, she walked forwards.

'It isn't seasickness,' she said. 'How can it be after this many days?'

'I know,' managed Erienne, her head thumping, her belly aching and protesting every time she took a breath.

'It must be something you ate,' she said, helping Erienne to sit on one of the net-covered crates on deck.

Erienne shook her head; she didn't have the energy to speak. She knew where the nausea originated but didn't want to have to explain it to Ren'erei. It wasn't food, it wasn't the gentle motion of the *Ocean Elm*, which was speeding towards Arlen Bay on a stiff and consistent wind. It was nothing that Ren'erei could comprehend even though she was an elf and so inherently magical. She didn't understand what it was that touched and aided her in everything she did. After all, she wasn't a mage.

Erienne was under attack. She didn't know from where or by whom and that scared her almost as much as what she was feeling. On the mainland, only The Raven knew she was coming, so how she could have been targeted, she didn't know.

It had crossed her mind that she had fallen victim to a mana sickness. There were always claims bouncing around the Colleges that mana within a mage could become somehow infected. Erienne had always dismissed them but in the first flush of her nausea, she had been prepared to believe anything that would provide an explanation.

But as the hours passed and she regained some rationality, she'd ignored the notion in favour of hard fact. Her nausea had come on her like a blow from a hammer, and stirring her head like thick soup so she couldn't focus on her hand in front of her face. It had provoked a reaction in her body that was nothing to do with any physical sickness. And it had gone on long after she'd established in her own mind that there was nothing wrong with her mana capabilities.

So there was no infection, there was no food poisoning and there was no focused drain on her mana stamina.

This was something no textbook had ever covered. It was what happened when someone who knew your signature launched spells at you without knowing exactly where you were. Enemy or friend, Erienne couldn't tell but she could guess. Lyanna. Seeking her mind. But in her innocence she was damaging her mother and until it stopped, the world of magic was closed to Erienne.

The realisation rocked her. It was a powerful weapon. It made her defenceless. Fortunately, she'd be meeting Denser in a couple of days.

He would know what to do.

It was the same that night. While the fire burned and The Raven waited, Denser tried and failed to make contact with Erienne. If anything, the fog obscuring her was thicker than either of the times he'd tried before.

He dispersed the Communion and lay still, desperation beginning to steal over him, a feeling of tears behind his closed eyelids. He was tired. He had never found Communion an easy spell and his three attempts so far had left him depleted of stamina. He needed to rest and pray, to rebuild his strength for another casting, but his mind raced with possible solutions and he could see sleep would be a long time coming. He didn't have time for this. None of them did.

'Denser?' It was Ilkar. He didn't open his eyes. He could feel the fire warm the left side of his body as he lay, its flickering glow orange on his eyelids.

'C'mon Denser. I know you've released the spell. There's tea here for you. Herbal. It should help you sleep later.'

Denser opened one eye. Above him, through the trees that part sheltered them from the strengthening wind, he could see cloud tumbling across the sky. It was darker than the night it covered. There was going to be heavy rain. Very heavy.

'I hate herbal tea,' he said. He tried to smile but nothing happened. He dragged himself to a sitting position and accepted the mug Ilkar offered, wrinkling his nose at the heady, sweet smell. Across the fire,

The Unknown was building a makeshift spit and he could see Hirad laying snares through the gloom about fifty yards away.

'Food could be a while,' said The Unknown, following his gaze.

They lapsed into silence. Denser forced his tea down, wincing at its syrupy texture. He could see Ilkar smile but it was an effort. Denser looked back at the sky. There were no stars at all now, just thick darkest grey cloud. The wind blew chill through the evening air and despite the shelter of the trees, it would get cold. The Unknown clearly intended to keep the fire stacked, not considering the blaze as a risk.

'Anyone in Greythorne who wants us that badly will find us anyway,' he'd said. 'And anyone coming from Arlen is too far away to get to us tonight.'

Too far away. The words haunted Denser.

They were two days' ride from Erienne and that was a day and a half too many. He felt angry that he couldn't reach her, frustrated she wouldn't hear his warning and scared of what they might find in Arlen if he failed in his contact at dawn.

Bloody Hirad. This could prove one indiscretion too many. And despite the barbarian's confidence, Denser still boiled inside. His wife and daughter were at stake here. Hirad seemed to forget that and he clearly had not grasped how desperate Dordover was to get hold of them both.

The wind rattled the branches and blew dying leaves over the ground. The rain was in the sky now and the odd spot hit his face. Dust kicked into the air and the flames of the fire blew hard, tinged with a telltale blue-brown corona.

It was so wrong. Denser wasn't a man of the woods but he was a sensitive mage. And this was deeply disturbing. It even tainted the air they breathed, or so it seemed to him. Perhaps it would be better if the Dordovans found Lyanna first. At least then . . .

He quashed the thought, ashamed it had even arisen. But the rational part of him acknowledged it as a solution to the ravages Balaia was increasingly suffering. Hideous, but a solution.

Hirad walked back into the firelight and sat down. He dumped an armful of leaves and roots on the ground by him.

'There's not exactly a mass of wildlife around here. I've set for rabbits but it might not be rich pickings tonight.'

Ilkar chuckled. 'Get your excuses in early, Hirad.'

'You're funnier than usual tonight, Ilks,' returned Hirad. 'Which isn't hard.'

'Right,' said The Unknown and the moment's levity was banished. 'We have to face the possibility that Erienne will sail straight into Dordovan hands.'

'I take it the Communion was no better?' Hirad looked up at Denser who shook his head, his eyes not quite holding contact. 'Maybe in the morning.'

'Maybe,' said Denser.

'But the worst case is that Erienne is captured,' said The Unknown. 'What then?'

'Well presumably the Dordovans will demand Lyanna and that means all of them going back to Ornouth with her,' said Ilkar. 'It's pretty simple.'

'Agreed,' said The Unknown. 'But there are variables.'

'Aren't there always?' grumbled Hirad.

Ilkar patted his knee. 'Wouldn't be the same otherwise, would it?'

'No indeed.' The Unknown drew a mark in the soil. 'One. We don't know whether the Dordovans are there in sufficient numbers to take the ship. Even if they are, it will take two days to resupply, maybe more, depending on exactly how unhelpful Erienne and the Guild are able to be.

'Two. The Dordovans may only be able to stop the ship putting back to sea themselves. Given Darrick's arrival at Greythorne it's clear they aren't there in the numbers they'd ideally like in order to go back to sea. We also have to assume that Dordover are working with Lystern on this. But that leaves us still not knowing the numbers in Arlen now.

'Three. The Guild could manage to put back to sea having rumbled the Dordovan presence. We need to think how to get out to sea and meet them – assuming Denser still can't get in touch with Erienne.

'Four. Earl Arlen. He isn't going to sit around and watch people fighting on his docks. He may be a good starting point for us because he may well not be aware what is happening in his town. On the other hand, of course, he may be entirely complicit in the whole thing.

'Five. Because of that latter point, we can't be sure that anyone we meet or talk to is with us or even neutral. One thing that we can be sure of is that the Dordovans in Arlen will be looking for us. And it all means that getting to and helping Erienne is going to be extremely difficult. There are other possible factors but I think you get the picture.'

'And what help can we be if the odds are overwhelming?' asked

Denser. He shook his head. The rain began to fall steadily. Not hard but that was just a matter of time.

'We can always help,' said Hirad. 'We're The Raven.'

'Well you'd better start thinking how. This mess is all down to you in the first place.'

Hirad nodded, brushed his hands together and stood up. He walked past Ilkar and The Unknown, heading for the horses.

'Where are you going?' asked the elf.

'Away.'

'What do you mean?'

'I mean I don't need to hear his smart-arsed superior remarks any longer. I made a mistake and it was a bad one and I'm sorry. But I can't undo it, only try and make it right. But every opportunity, he's going to remind me and I don't need it. So you people who never ever make mistakes can rescue Lyanna on your own.'

'So you'll find your own way to the Al-Drechar, will you?' asked Ilkar, ears pricking. A gust sent rain thrashing around the clearing, stinging the face and sending spats of dirt from the ground as it struck. The fire hissed and crackled in protest, shadows speared across the ground, flickering and jumping.

'I expect we could work it out, me and the Kaan,' said Hirad. 'All I'm asking is a little respect for the fact that I'm helping a man who hasn't lifted a finger to help me in the last five years.'

'A little respect, I can grant you,' said Denser.

'Drop it, Denser,' said The Unknown, his voice a growl.

'One more word, Denser,' Hirad raised a finger. 'And you'll be riding to Arlen alone.'

'Run off to your precious dragons, Hirad. And you can all die together in your chilly cave while I try and save Lyanna, and Balaia along with her.'

Hirad spun round and ran at the Xeteskian, hurdling the fire and kicking over the pot, scattering water to steam and hiss in the hot ashes. Putting a hand up he pushed Denser in the chest, knocking him back a couple of paces. He might have been a few years older than when The Raven last rode together but he'd lost none of his speed; there had been no time for Denser to react.

'You'd like that, wouldn't you, Denser, eh?' His voice grated low, his eyes, hooded, his face muscles bunched and taut. 'You and your powerful friends up in your towers.'

He pushed Denser with both hands this time, forcing him to fight to retain his balance.

'Let them waste away, you thought. People will forget, you thought. We'll play a little at research but we know we aren't going anywhere with it. No one will really care. Bet that's how it was in nice warm fire-bright Xetesk, wasn't it?'

Denser met his gaze but said nothing. Hirad grabbed his cloak at the neck and marched him backwards, spitting out his words, his whole body shuddering with his anger.

'But I haven't forgotten, Xetesk man. And neither have the Kaan. You've made them suffer, you bastard, and you never gave it a thought. They are no closer to going home now than they were five years ago are they? But you're too wrapped up in your petty politics and power climbing to give a shit.

'But I've been there. Every day and every night. Seeing their eyes dim and their scales go dull and dry. Seeing their confusion grow and their minds seethe. Because every day they die some more while every day the ungrateful scum they saved forget a little more.'

Denser was backed against a tree with nowhere to go. Rain was running down its trunk and thunder barked overhead. The torrent increased its ferocity, its hammering in the leaf cover a cacophony into which Hirad shouted.

'Get where I'm coming from, Denser? Understand even a little bit?' Hirad made a tiny space between thumb and forefinger. 'Because right now there's a death sentence over the Kaan. It's long and slow but it's certain because no one's going to help them, are they?'

'Hirad, enough.' It was The Unknown's voice but Hirad ignored it, pushing his face very close to Denser's.

'But now, it's your wife and child. Now, it's different. And we're all expected to drop everything and help you, aren't we? No, more than that. We *have* to.' He leaned in until their noses all but touched.

'Well I've got an answer for you, Xetesk man, and it'll stop bloody magic tearing up my country. Let the Dordovans kill the child. Problem solved. Death sentence carried out. What do you think. Eh? Eh?' He shook Denser, banging the back of his head against the tree and seeing the mage's eyes burning hatred into him.

'Hirad, that's enough.' The Unknown's arm came between them, levering the barbarian away. He fought it.

'Lost your tongue, Denser, have you? Have you?'

'I think you spend too much time with reptiles.'

'Fuck you, Denser!' He drew back a fist but The Unknown caught his arm and thrust his body in the way, forcing Hirad back.

'Don't do it,' he said, holding his hands out, his massive frame hiding Denser completely. But Hirad was too far gone.

'Get out of my way, Unknown.'

He came forward again. This time, The Unknown shoved him hard. He stumbled back on to his haunches, feet slipping on the slick ground as the rain beat down with ever increasing force, a net of water obscuring his vision. His hand reached reflexively for his sword but The Unknown stooped to the fire and shook the scabbard from his huge blade in one fluid movement.

'You aren't going to hurt him, Hirad. Back off.' The menace in The Unknown's voice shocked Hirad who could only stand and stare at what he saw.

'Unknown, stop this!' shouted Ilkar. 'Hirad, you too. We're The Raven, for Gods' sake!' He marched in between them, trying to take them both in, unable to keep the disbelief from his voice or his expression as the rain washed down his face.

Hirad had taken his hand from his sword hilt and was gazing slack-jawed at the blade in The Unknown's hands.

'He'd see Lyanna die,' said The Unknown. 'And I can't have that. He'd see her die.' He didn't switch his eyes to Ilkar as he addressed him. 'A feeling you're familiar with, I believe.'

Ilkar ignored the comment. 'Put your sword up, Unknown, and do it right now. There will not be any fighting here, understand?'

The Unknown Warrior looked down at Ilkar, rain splattering across his shaven head, his eyes glinting orange in the wind-whipped firelight.

'I won't let him harm Denser,' he said. 'You know why.' He threw his sword to the ground.

'It's not about that,' said Ilkar.

'Isn't it?' said Hirad. He wiped a sheen of rain from his face and flicked his hand to disperse it. 'Trouble is, Unknown, you're still a Protector in here.' He tapped his chest above his heart. 'And you can't shake it off. And the ridiculous thing is, he's done the same to your brothers as he's done to the Kaan. Let you fester and hope you'll go away.' Hirad made no attempt to move closer.

'How little you know, Hirad. I'm a father, that's what I am. And I won't see someone else's child tossed aside.' The Unknown turned away but swung back. 'You're my friend, Hirad. Probably the best I've ever had. You brought about my release from Protector thrall. But I won't see you threaten a man through his child. That's a bond you won't understand until you experience it.'

'Yet you pulled a sword on me,' said Hirad, his anger gone now, replaced by a feeling of loss. 'We're The Raven and what you did doesn't belong. It was wrong.'

'Listen to yourself,' said the big man. 'It was your actions too, Hirad. Yours too.'

'Think I'll make a camp somewhere else,' said Hirad, and he walked from The Raven's fire.

Chapter 16

Jasto, twelfth Earl of Arlen, was a proud man who had paid the price of overstretching his resources and who, as a result, was now under the firm, fair but unshakeable grip of Baron Blackthorne.

Even in Blackthorne's weakened days following the destruction of his town towards the end of the Wesmen wars, Arlen had perceived himself too weak to challenge the younger man with any certainty of success. But that had not made him a weak man, as some of his resident merchant lords had intimated. It had made him wise and, latterly, very wealthy once again.

He recalled his hard-pressed merchant and shipping families coming to him those six years ago and urging him to break free of the bonds Blackthorne had imposed. They were weary of being beneath the Baron's fist and he, they had said, would never get a better opportunity to demand and achieve his autonomy.

And he had seen their point. There had not been a mercenary to be hired anywhere in Balaia, and Blackthorne's own men were either dead or tired of fighting. However, to Arlen, an attack would have been like betrayal of a man who had sacrificed so much to keep Balaia free of Wesmen domination. So instead of sending men armed with sword and spear, he had equipped them with pick, shovel, saw and hammer. Instead of riding to demand freedom of movement and impose conditions of their own, they had offered help and comfort.

Arlen had recruited quarrymen and stone masons to replace or reshape what the Wesmen had destroyed, carpenters and joiners to work the wood; and he'd encouraged as many of his people as could be spared to be willing pairs of hands.

The Earl smiled as he thought it all through again, his greying, bushy moustache accentuating the movement of his top lip, his leathery, ocean-toughened skin wrinkling on cheek and forehead. It had been help where help had been needed but Arlen had never been a purely altruistic man. Blackthorne had seen that. It was business.

Craftsmen do not come cheap. Wood, stone, iron and steel all have their prices and in such a sellers' market, those prices had been high. Food too, can always be managed to be expensive. And every one of Arlen's merchants, shippers and fisher fleet owners had seen the profits. Blackthorne had not raised an eyebrow. Indeed he had laughed, shaken the Earl's hand and fetched a bottle of superb wine from the cellars the Wesmen had found but left intact. Even savages enjoyed fine wine.

Arlen remembered sitting in a marquee, supplied by his town, and clinking glasses with the wily Baron. His words at the time would forever remain simple vindication of Arlen's decision.

Blackthorne had taken a long swallow, leaned back in his chair, shrugged and had said, 'It's what I would have done.'

And he'd still reduced the travel levies across his lands that had squeezed Arlen's merchants so hard. As a mark of gratitude, he'd said.

Riding away from Blackthorne that day, Arlen had wondered how long the gratitude would last. Almost six years later, he was still expecting the letter of withdrawal. He supposed he shouldn't have been surprised. Blackthorne's honour was unquestionable.

It had left Arlen in peaceful charge of a burgeoning town, attracting trade from Calaius and Korina to his docks. More and more farmers were attracted to his fertile lands on the town's northern borders, knowing the price for their produce would not be driven down by traders passing on the burden of Blackthorne's safe passage levy.

But now something smelled bad in his town. It had blown in on the foul breeze of magic and had taken root to the south along the River Arl. First it had been Dordovans. A few mages and their escorts. Nothing out of the ordinary. But ten days ago, they'd been joined – *joined* – by forty of the Black Wing filth and since then, the Dordovan military and mage numbers had swelled until over three hundred and fifty camped downstream.

His innkeepers and whores hadn't complained. Neither had his fresh food market stalls. There's even been some profit for his fine cloth and silk men but the pilfering had been rather more unwelcome, however well it had been contained.

But there was only so much you could forgive in the name of trade and that line had been breached this morning.

Word had reached him of aggressive buying of supplies and attempted secondment of ocean-going vessels. It had been the Black

Wings putting on the pressure and they weren't prepared to take no for an answer.

He didn't mind the movement of supplies. That was easily balanced. But ships? There was a carefully maintained balance between supply and demand for vessels capable of travelling the tricky distance to Calaius. It was a balance his shipping owners were anxious to keep to maintain their lavish lifestyles.

But at this juncture it wasn't the owners he was concerned about. The trade in salted meats, wine, armour and weapons was lucrative but reliant on regular transport, and the return of coffee, cloth and jewellery among others was equally critical. Arlen could ill afford to lose transport space for these valuable commodities for an unspecified length of time.

He had already sent guardsmen to break up a dispute over a ship already chartered by a consortium of traders. Apparently, Black Wings had offered double the rates for troop passage to Ornouth of all places. When the shipping agent had refused, choosing to remain loyal to his regular paying customers, he had been threatened and one of his clerks beaten for attempting to intervene.

That had been yesterday.

This dawn had seen Arlen forced to drag his very tall frame from his bed at an unseemly hour, with the sun barely cresting the horizon. A deputation waited in the drawing room of the castle. They were a merchant, a farmer and a shipper. He pulled on a white silk shirt, plain deep blue wool-weave trousers and a black three-quarter-length coat. His silver rings decorated three long bony fingers on each hand and the heavy gold chain, passed on to each successive Earl, was placed reverently around his neck.

He drained his tea, dragged on white stockings and simple black, double-buckled ankle boots and loped from his bedroom, his long, easy strides eating up corridor and stair as he marched to what could prove to be a difficult meeting. At the door, a servant brushed the back of his coat to remove dust and the odd stray hair fallen from his fast balding head before opening the door.

'Gentlemen, good morning,' he said as he strode in. A murmured greeting met him from the three men, two seated and one standing near the fireplace. All were dressed well, though the farmer, a sour middle-aged man named Alpar, was garbed in working clothes having already no doubt been at work for two or three hours. Those seated began to rise until Arlen held up a hand.

'Please, let's not stand on ceremony here, I doubt we have the time.' He sat in his gold upholstered armchair across from the deputation and waited for a servant to pour him a cup of tea and withdraw before gesturing for his old silks merchant friend, Hancross, to speak.

'The situation on the docks is getting worse, Jasto. These Black Wings are nothing more than thugs intent on getting their way and wrecking our businesses into the bargain. Stealing from the outlying farms is getting worse by the day and now they have stooped even lower. Erik?' Hancross gestured at the son of Arlen's most successful shipping agent, a man being groomed to take over the family business.

Erik Paulson nodded, fighting to keep his emotions in check. His eyes shone with tears. 'I think this is really why we felt we had to appeal to you directly, my Lord. While it was intimidation aimed at us, it was different. Now it's our families, it's unacceptable and we need action.' He paused, breathing deeply. For a moment, his chin wobbled. He gathered himself and spoke. 'Yesterday evening, my wife and daughter were returning from the market to our house. Three of those bastards knocked my wife to the floor. One held a dagger to my daughter's throat while the other two pawed at my wife's body, threatened her with rape and my daughter with murder.

'I can't believe I can hear myself saying these words,' he swallowed hard. 'Not here. Not about my family.' He shook his head and a tear escaped to roll down his cheek. 'You should see them. They are both in shock in my house, too terrified to venture outside the front door. And this is *Arlen*. What the hell is going on?' He looked at Arlen then, his expression pleading. 'This is a peaceful town, my Lord, but unless you act, we fear people taking the law into their own hands.'

'In fact we promise it,' said Alpar, his throaty voice grating on Arlen's ears. 'Paulson has suffered the worst but we are all losing here. Each morning, my flock is short by a little more, despite the guards I post. Hancross won't tell you but there's been a fire at one of his shops and we all know who started it.'

Arlen nodded and raised both his hands to ask for quiet. He felt a growing anger in his gut. He had worked so hard to rebuild after the austerity of the Wesmen wars. He had brought peace and prosperity to Arlen, not just the town but across the Earldom. And he deserved respect. The Black Wings would have to be taught how to show that respect.

'Gentlemen, this is my town and I abhor violence of any kind being committed within its borders or in the lands I also control. I therefore implore you not to raise arms as I will come down equally hard on either side in this dispute should violence ensue.

'However, your coming here together tells me all I need to know about your sincerity and your trust in my stewardship, and for that I thank you. Now, I will, as soon as I am able this morning, visit the Lakehome Inn, where I understand their leader to be in residence. He will be ordered out, never to return. Any monies that he has paid for goods he has not received will be returned minus costs for damages, stolen goods and sundry expenses.'

'Jasto—'

'No, Hancross, don't say it,' said Arlen. For the third time, he raised a hand. 'The reputation of this town is built on honesty, particularly in dealings for trade. Money exchanged in good faith will be returned. And petty thieves clutter jails to no purpose. However, Erik, if your wife wishes to identity her assailants, they will not leave Arlen before paying for their crimes.'

Arlen looked hard at Paulson and could see the man's fury burning in his hooded eyes. He wrung his hands and his tanned skin had an unhealthy grey tone. He didn't sit on the chair, more perched like some predatory beast. It was clear his chosen justice would be vengeful and violent.

'Erik?'

'They touched her. They *touched* her,' he said, another tear easing from the corner of his eye, his control so admirable, cracking a little more. 'This is a violation. They should pay.'

'Then pay they will,' said Arlen. 'Trust me.'

Erik locked eyes with him then and it was clear that he did not. 'Yes,' he said. 'I just want them to be able to walk in the streets of their own town without fear.'

Arlen rose from his chair and walked over to Paulson, placing a hand on his shoulder and squeezing gently. 'I know, Erik. Leave it to me. They won't escape my justice.' He looked up at Hancross. 'Take him home and keep an eye on them all. I want the word passed around the dock that it will be cleared and I want no one getting in my way. I want word sent to Lakehome to delay Selik however is necessary. I will be there within the hour. Anything else I should know?'

The Unknown Warrior stared at his sword as if it were a snake waiting to strike at him. There it lay where he had thrown it during the downpour and where it shimmered in the dying glow of the fire, ignored now that dawn was close. It was a symbol. Of the death of The Raven, finally. Of the ending of the trust they had in each other, he and Hirad. It had been everything to him. Even through the years they hardly saw each other, let alone spoke or fought together. Something he always had was Hirad's unconditional belief. And last night, he had betrayed it.

And worse, Hirad had been right. When it had come to it, he had been driven to protect Denser. *Protect.* How hollow that word sounded now. All he had done was drive away the man that could keep them together long enough to save not just Denser but his whole family, and Balaia too.

The Unknown's reaction had been much more than just desire to see a family saved, though, and that fact worried him deep in his soul. He should have been thankful he had a soul to feel worried but he wasn't. Too much within him was still wedded to the Protectors and despite the relatively short time he had spent as one of them, he lamented the loss of the brotherhood. Even after six years and more, he had to accept it was a loss he would always feel and that was something he had not yet been able to fully come to terms with.

And they were coming again. They were close. He could feel them and had told Ilkar so the day before. He couldn't describe to Ilkar the clash of emotion it sparked within him. The joy of being near them and the tragedy of their existence linked with the exclusion he felt now his soul was again his own. That was the most acute pain for him. He would always be able to feel them but he would never again feel the oneness that, despite its dreadful reality, the Soul Tank bestowed. He wondered if they could feel him too.

He looked over at Ilkar and Denser, sleeping under the hasty and inadequate shelter of leaf, branch and leather they'd created. He'd been glad for Ilkar last night. His sense had stopped a catastrophe. The Unknown had wanted to go after Hirad but Ilkar had stopped him doing that too. The elf thought Hirad would turn up in the camp come dawn. The Unknown wasn't so sure.

The rain had stopped at last but the wind was cold and whipped through the trees, chilling him as he sat by the fire. How they needed Hirad, now more than ever. After he'd calmed down, Denser had agreed to Commune with a contact in Korina to pass a message to Diera. All that he'd heard was yet more bad news.

The contact was preparing to leave the city as, apparently, were tens of thousands of people, fleeing inland. Two days before, after an unceasing torrent of rain, the tide had risen along the estuary and, fed by run-off from the hills and mountains and whipped up by gale force winds, had kept on rising.

The docks were under water, as were all of the low-lying areas in the estuary basin. Further up into the centre of Korina, conditions were better but the waters were still rising. The Unknown's house had been in the estuary basin. The contact had no idea of the level of casualties in the city but knew The Rookery still stood and still served its patrons. He had promised to deliver The Unknown's message there.

All The Unknown could do now was pray his wife and son were still alive and under Tomas' welcoming roof.

He wanted to saddle his horse and ride to Korina now but knew he couldn't. If he wanted to save his family and friends, he had to get Denser to Lyanna. Hirad was central to that. The big warrior rubbed his hands over his face and shook his head, cursing himself for his actions.

It wasn't until the man walked into the camp that he realised the watch he had been taking had been nothing more than an excuse to sit in the cold and damp, and disappear inside his own mind.

'Nursing a problem, Unknown?'

'You could say,' replied The Unknown after looking up to see Darrick walk in, leather cape around his shoulders, sword scabbarded at his waist, dark rings about his eyes. He must have ridden most of the night. 'Sit down. I'll put some water on for coffee.' But that wasn't why Darrick was there.

'I don't think we've got time for that,' he said.

'No,' said The Unknown. He looked hard into the woods but could see nothing but the shadows of trees moving in the wind as the sun gradually pierced the clouds that threatened more rain. 'Bring many with you?'

'A couple of hundred.'

'You were quiet,' The Unknown smiled.

Darrick nodded and almost chuckled. 'Well, we didn't ride right in, if that's what you mean.'

'Two hundred, eh?' The Unknown glanced again at his sword lying in the mud of the wood. 'That's probably enough.'

'I thought so.' Darrick walked around in front of The Unknown and stood across the fire from him. 'I thought you deserved overwhelming odds to help you make up your mind.'

The Unknown looked up into the General's eyes and saw the guilt painted there like the mark of plague on the front door of a stricken house.

'So what do you want?'

'To stop The Raven getting killed needlessly.'

'Really?' The Unknown raised his eyebrows.

'Yes, really.' Darrick scratched at his forehead with a leather-gloved hand. 'Look, you're in the middle of something bad and I don't think you fully understand how Dordover sees the stakes.'

The Unknown felt a flash of anger. 'Let me assure you, we know exactly how Dordover sees everything. That's why we're with him, trying to get to his daughter before anyone else.' He jerked a thumb at Denser.

'It's not that simple.'

'So Ilkar keeps saying. Only, it is that simple. Denser asked for our help. We're The Raven, so we helped him. He's one of us and he says he can save her and Balaia with her and that's enough for us.' There was silence. The Unknown could see Darrick understood but couldn't do anything about it. His loyalty was to Lystern and, through them, Dordover. 'So where are you planning to take us?'

'Arlen.'

'Well that's fortunate. We were headed that way ourselves.'

'I know. But you aren't doing anything when we get there.'

'Prisoners?'

'Something like that.' Darrick looked away.

'Funny how things change, isn't it?' said The Unknown.

'Not really,' said Darrick. 'Now, are you going to wake them or must I?'

The Unknown smiled again. 'I'll do it. You know how fractious mages are if woken suddenly. Have you already got Hirad?' He saw no reason to hide the barbarian's absence. Darrick wasn't a fool.

But Darrick just bit his lip and gazed down at the ground. 'No,' he said. 'I'm afraid we were too late.'

'Good old Hirad,' said The Unknown. Hope flickered again but Darrick extinguished it.

'Unknown, you don't understand. We tracked him all right but we were there second.' He wiped his gloved hand through his matted curls. 'Gods, how do I say this? The wolves were already closing in when the scouts arrived. I'm sorry.'

Arlen eschewed his horse in favour of marching through his town accompanied by twenty of his guard in a very obvious show of strength. There were faster routes to the Lakehome Inn but Arlen wanted as many people as possible, friends and enemies, to see his intent.

So, with the sun trying to warm a cloudy day and dry the streets that had been swept once again by unseasonably heavy rain, Jasto Arlen strode from the gates of Arlen Castle. Walking quickly up the wide, stone-chipped avenue between his private gardens and the barracks, he turned right on to Market Approach, a meandering street that linked the town to the north trails. Market Approach was peppered by cross-streets the whole of its length, while to the east, increasingly sumptuous merchant and shippers' houses culminated in the magnificent Park of the Martyrs' Souls. To the west, south of the barracks, the silk and fine goods market and the playhouse fronted a less affluent quarter including Arlen's castle workers' cottages and tenements, the stables and the plain but most important Temple of the Sea.

Arlen headed straight down Market Approach, a slightly sloped, cobbled street that opened out into Centenary Square, which housed the main market, selling everything from food to weapons to fine carved furnishings, and ringed all round with eating houses, inns and even the odd gallery. This early, the square was only just beginning to fill but word would spread quickly and Arlen felt his anger rising further. His was a well-formed, prosperous town built on hard work and a tight business ethic. No one would be allowed to change that.

Waving at his townspeople and trading greetings with anyone he knew, Arlen turned right out of the square to walk through poorer tenement streets into the long-nicknamed Ice Quarter where the trawler men had traditionally lived and cold-stored late-landed fish before selling catches in the dockfront fish market each mid-morning. Arlen walked past the iron foundry and fish market on his way to the dockside, taking in the empty harbour that housed the fishing fleet and the first of the deepwater berths, before turning left and walking past an attractive, sleek elven vessel, obviously just tied up, and stopping finally at the doors to the Lakehome Inn.

Looking along the dock past the timber yard and on to the Salt Quarter, Arlen could see a few people about, including some of the Black Wings lounging around jetty-posts. They, like his townspeople and visitors, straightened quickly, and before his sergeant-at-arms had finished hammering on the inn's door to demand attention, a crowd was beginning to gather, a hubbub of noise filling the air and taking men and women from their work as curiosity got the better of them.

Locks were slid back and the left-hand of a pair of painted black wooden doors squeaked open. One of the innkeeper's sons, a scrawny lad in his early teens, peered out, his freckled face blanching under his shock of tangled orange hair.

'Don't worry, Petren,' said Arlen. 'Just wake your father. I need to talk to one of your guests. Now.'

The frightened boy said nothing in reply, just bobbed his head and turned back into the gloom. Presently, they could hear his voice echoing through the inn, reedy and high, unbroken.

'Father. Pa! The Earl's at the door, the Earl's at the door.'

Arlen allowed himself a brief smile, catching the eye of his sergeant-at-arms.

'At least he knew who I was,' said Arlen.

'Yes sir.'

During the short wait, the crowd swelled and amongst them, Arlen counted over a dozen of the Black Wings. Right now, the atmosphere was calm and curious but it wouldn't take much to turn it ugly. He leaned towards the sergeant-at-arms and ordered him to place men near the Black Wings.

'My Lord?' It was the innkeeper, Denat.

'Sorry to wake you,' said Arlen.

'Not at all, my Lord. I've been up cooking breakfasts a while now.'

'Busy time for you?'

'I'm full,' confirmed Denat.

'Hmm.' Arlen nodded. 'Unfortunately, I fear you are about to lose much of your current custom.'

'Pardon, my Lord?' Denat frowned and fidgeted at the door. He was a heavier set but balding version of his son.

'I want Selik, is it? Yes, Selik, at this door immediately.'

'Oh.' Denat hesitated. 'Of course. I'll fetch him for you.'

'Thank you.' Arlen's smile was thin. He regretted the necessity for men like Denat but had to concede his type was useful to the town's economy.

'I am quite capable of fetching myself,' drawled a voice Arlen hadn't heard before. Disabled. Not true. And when the misshapen figure appeared around the door and forced himself past the retreating Denat, the Earl could see why.

'Earl Arlen, I take it?' The figure proffered a hand which Arlen ignored.

'Correct. And you are unwanted in this town.'

Selik raised an eyebrow. 'Really? By whom?'

Arlen regarded him blankly. 'Me. And that is enough. However, I'm not an unfair man and I've watched your activities for longer than I should.'

'I—'

'Be silent.' Arlen raised a finger but not his voice, unused to being interrupted. 'And listen to me. Trade in this town is run by word, bond and delivery of goods and payment, not by threat, fist and intimidation. Goods stolen are accepted losses only if the perpetrator cannot be apprehended. And violations of the person, particularly the female person, are not tolerated under any circumstances.

'These key laws and numerous others have been transgressed by you or your men. So here's what happens now. With two exceptions, I want every one of your men accounted for and out of my town by midday. Any found still here after that time will be deemed in breach of the fair trading laws and suffer the appropriate penalties.

'Any goods you have bought legitimately but not received will be delivered to you beyond Arlen's borders. Any shipping deals you have struck, whether fairly or under duress, will be deemed void and any monies due will be returned to you.

'You, Selik, will remain here not only until your men have gone but more importantly, until you identify and hand over the two scum who molested a woman and threatened her young child in my peaceful streets.

'Do I make myself clear?'

Arlen's speech had brought a hush to the crowd that now numbered in excess of one hundred, every one craning to catch every word. Even this close, the blustery wind off the lake snatched away the odd phrase yet enough was clear to send a ripple of applause around the gathering. Arlen did not acknowledge it.

Throughout, Selik had met Arlen's gaze, a sneer evident on his smeared face. He had not attempted to interrupt. The applause died down quickly, the crowd anticipating Selik's response.

'I understood this to be a free town. It appears I was mistaken.'

'No, not mistaken,' said Arlen. 'But freedom has to be bounded by rules to avoid it becoming anarchy. This is what you have attempted to bring here and I will not tolerate it.'

Selik nodded, his sneer broadening into what might pass as a smile.

'We asked for co-operation and received none,' he said quietly. 'Yet we had to have what we tried to buy and I am afraid some of your traders did not seem to understand that. You see, Earl Arlen, there is a war coming, though you might not see it as such. And I am on the side of the just, fighting against the rising threat of dominion over Balaia of a single magical power.'

Arlen scoffed. 'War. Selik, we are all aware of problems with the mana spectrum, I do talk to my mages, you know. But these problems will pass, and with them this irritating wind and chilling rain. Don't attempt to hang your perverse actions on a magical uprising.' Arlen took half a pace forwards, feeling revulsion grow for the man he confronted.

'I know your beliefs and you are free to hold them. But you are not free to impose them on my people or to use them to justify your simpleminded thuggery. Now do you understand what you are to do, or do I take you to the jail to think on it at greater length?'

Selik straightened and raised his voice.

'I will grant you this futile and very short-lived victory, merely because it would be a waste of my time to stand against you at this moment. But mark my words, Arlen. There is war coming. We will have what we need to conduct it and the innocent will die and their blood will be on your streets and your hands unless you turn to me for help. Mark what I say. And let your people hear it too.' And he tapped Arlen's chest with his forefinger.

The Earl grabbed Selik's hand and turned it away.

'There will never be war in Arlen,' he snarled. 'Unless you make the grave mistake of returning, that is, and, believe me, you will meet my steel if you try. Now get your men, give me the guilty and get out of my town.'

Selik laughed. 'Believe what you will, Arlen. But right will triumph over innocence and ignorance.'

The look in Selik's eye left Arlen cold.

Chapter 17

Hirad made a hasty camp between the trunks of a trio of young oaks, lashing his treated leather sheet to them at an angle to give him some protection from the weather. On leaving the Raven camp, he'd gathered his saddle and unhitched his horse, unsure of how far he'd travel. In the end, he'd walked for a mile, maybe a little more, while the rain pounded down, soaking him through his furs and completing his miserable but unforgettable evening.

With the wind at his back, beating the rain on to the leather, which thrummed and pulled, he set a fire with the dry sticks and kindling he habitually carried inside the leather, before collecting a few more to dry by the small blaze on the sodden ground.

He let his horse wander, knowing it wouldn't stray unless endangered and, with his saddle as a pillow of sorts, lay back to contemplate the mess in which he found himself. There was a pit in his stomach that stole any appetite and a burning in his throat that had nothing to do with his earlier shouting. But above it all in his mind rode a deep sense of unease and wrong, coupled with loss. He'd walked out on The Raven, the only family he'd ever really known. This was nothing like the sad, if inevitable and certainly amicable parting of the ways they'd shared a few years before. This had been an act of finality.

Hirad sought fruitlessly for a comfortable position on the soaking leaf mould, his mind distracted by the howling wind that tore at his sheet, threatening to rip it loose; the incessant heavy rain that poured from the leather, pooling on the ground before running downhill and away.

He wasn't a deep and clever thinker like the others, never had been. He just reacted to what he saw, heard and felt. It was his strength and his curse. He had no idea what had snapped in him earlier. It would have been easy to blame Denser completely but he had to shoulder much of the blame himself.

It was a culmination of things. The way he was always expected to jump to and help other people though, when matters were reversed, those others always found reasons not to bother. And Denser was the worst of them. He'd been acting very strangely since they'd met him in Greythorne.

But still, Hirad knew he shouldn't have done what he did. Clearly, the man was scared for his family's lives and it unbalanced him. Made him say stupid things; and bringing the Kaan into it had been a mistake that had triggered so much.

Once more, Hirad brought the image of The Unknown's blade to his mind, saw its unwavering point and the intent in the grip. It had been no warning and although Hirad knew The Unknown's reaction had been purebred instinct, he also knew that the Big Man would have killed him had he threatened the Xeteskian further. It was, after all, what he had been born to do; and even though he had been released from Protector thrall and had his soul returned, the legacy remained.

And now Hirad didn't know how to feel. Angry at Denser, yes. Sad for what he had pushed The Unknown into, certainly. Disappointed he had walked out without solving the problem as well. That had always been The Raven's way until now. Not to run. But he had.

There was nothing more to be done that night. Ilkar would know he wouldn't come back immediately and there was no way The Unknown would sanction a search for him until dawn. But there was one question he wanted to answer before he slept. Did he want to be found? Actually, as the hours slipped by and he drifted in and out of sleep, disturbed by wind, rain and the odd rumble of thunder, the answer had become rather obvious.

Hirad awoke in a tight position that was scant protection from the chill. The dawn brought with it a strengthening of the wind but a welcome cessation of the rain. Hirad opened his eyes and stared at the taut leather bivouac vibrating against its ropes. He frowned as he blinked back the brightness of the morning, surprised he hadn't woken sooner. But that wasn't all that was amiss. Despite the wind, he should have been able to hear the sounds of forest birds, only it was very quiet and the wind rushed through what to the ear was a dead wood. Like Thornewood.

He stretched where he lay before rolling over and sitting upright, rubbing his face and scratching at an itchy scalp. It was time, he thought ruefully, for Ilkar to clear his head of mites.

Pushing himself up, he ducked out from under the edge of his shelter, he stretched again, his eyes coming to rest on his horse.

'Hello, boy, I—' he began but faltered. The stallion was standing stock still, eyes wide, legs quivering, too terrified to move. Hirad looked left, following its stare to where five wolves stood, partly hidden by shadows.

'Oh dear Gods,' he said. His sword lay by the ashes of the fire. He could grab for it but if he triggered a charge, he'd be killed in moments. So he stood, hoping against the odds that they would move on.

'Easy boy,' he said to his horse but the words were as much to himself.

The wolves stood in a close pack, the leader in front of two pairs. They didn't growl, didn't threaten and didn't give any indication of intent. Like Hirad, they stood and waited. It wasn't normal behaviour and Hirad, not blessed with patience, was anxious for any outcome. Any outcome.

He took a pace forwards, ignoring his blade, knowing that open aggression could be fatal.

'So what is it?' he demanded of them. 'Do something. We're not going anywhere.' His gesture included his horse, who suddenly pissed on the forest floor.

The lead wolf sniffed the air and then, with a low growl to its fellows, padded out into the dappled sunlight. It was a huge beast, four feet at the shoulder, its eyes yellow-tinged and its coat pale brown but for a sprinkling of grey flecks and an absolutely un-mistakable white stripe down the front of its neck.

Hirad felt momentarily weak at the knees.

It was Thraun.

The Unknown, Ilkar and Denser rode in resentful silence but it could have been worse. The Dordovan mage guard had wanted the Raven mages bound but Darrick had instructed them otherwise. The Unknown had smiled at that, a fleeting amusement. The instruction had been little more than thinly veiled threat.

And so the trio rode weaponless but not helpless in the midst of a Lysternan cavalry force heading at good speed towards Arlen. It had become clear to The Unknown that none in the column had any idea what they might find at the busy but sleepy fishing town whose docks had latterly attracted profitable attention. All they knew was that Erienne was due in on an elven ship and that The Raven weren't to be allowed access.

The big warrior could see confusion in many eyes, including

Darrick's but he could also see loyalty and the drive to follow orders. As every soldier knew, not every action had an immediately obvious motivation. So long as the war was won, battles were immaterial. Achieve the desired objective, that was what was expected and required.

The Unknown Warrior recognised and deferred to it, as did Ilkar, who'd seen enough battles to understand every nuance of conscript obedience and the unquestioning respect a fine general commanded. Denser was another issue and his hostility wasn't merely directed at his captors.

'I understood you to be pledged to protect me,' he said, riding a little closer.

'Pledged, no,' said the Unknown. 'Not any more. Protect, yes. You're Raven.'

'I saw how you reacted last night. Don't make me remind you.'

The Unknown regarded him evenly. 'You don't have to, I remember it perfectly well. I experienced an unfortunate throwback. It's a reaction that will pass eventually. However, I will always be your friend. And Hirad's.'

'Unknown, he's dead,' said Denser, a heaviness in his tone.

'Believing it on seeing it.'

'Come on, Unknown, you heard Darrick—'

'Who saw nothing,' said Ilkar. 'Until we have confirmed sighting of a body, he's still alive. And there's something else. He's Dragonene and I don't see any Kaan.'

'Whatever you say.' Denser shrugged.

Ilkar shook his head.

'What have I done now?' demanded Denser.

'All these years and you still miss the point sometimes, don't you?' said Ilkar.

'Get what? Hirad lost it and now he's gone, dead, missing or whatever. I get that. What else is there?'

'He's angry, Denser. He feels betrayed by you and he's going to be confused and distressed by what happened between him and The Unknown last night. But he's Raven. We've been his whole life's focus despite his work with the Kaan and he won't walk out on us. He agreed to help you, under duress I know, but he agreed and he'll never fail a contract until it kills him. That's what being one of us means.' Another shake of the head. 'You should know that by now.'

'But we haven't been The Raven for almost six years.'

'It doesn't make any difference. Not to Hirad,' said Ilkar.

The Unknown listened to the exchange and wondered if Ilkar was right. He wanted to believe it but he had seen the look in Hirad's eyes before he left and it hadn't been distress, it had been shock. And if the barbarian couldn't rationalise what had happened, he wouldn't come back because The Raven as he understood it would have ceased to exist.

'That doesn't change the fact that we're caught, I haven't been able to attempt another Communion and he,' – he stabbed a finger at The Unknown – 'was supposed to be on guard. Some Protector you turned out to be.'

'Is alienating the only people you can trust just a recent hobby of yours?' Ilkar's ears pricked and reddened. 'Because you seem pretty well practised.'

'True, though, isn't it?' said Denser, glaring back at Ilkar.

'I am no longer your given Protector, Denser,' said The Unknown, his voice low and menacing as he attempted to disguise the hurt inside. Perhaps he had failed them all. It was a thought not simply quashed though he had ample justification. 'None of us could have suspected this lot would have ridden all night to get to us – why would they?'

'But you didn't hear them,' insisted Denser. 'How could you not? There are two bloody *hundred* of them.'

'But only Darrick entered the camp.'

'So why didn't you kill him?' asked Denser.

'Because I was protecting you,' replied The Unknown calmly. 'And because I didn't fancy becoming target practice for the elven archers Darrick would have had positioned out of my sight. You may consider yourself able to outwit archers, two hundred cavalry and two dozen mages with range spells prepared but I'm not. You are alive because I chose not to fight.'

'But to what purpose? It's pretty clear your good friend Darrick is fighting on a different side to ours. He's hardly likely to let us go once we reach Arlen. What good can this do? Haven't you been listening to a word I've said? Only I can stop this.'

'Patience,' said The Unknown. It was easy to see how Hirad had lost his cool. But The Unknown could see further than that. He could see the desperation in Denser's eyes and had watched him fidget and heard him sigh, frustrated though they were still going in the right direction.

And what Denser hadn't seen was Darrick's unhappiness. The

General was plainly not in favour of holding The Raven. But the ability to follow orders was just one reason he was such a fine soldier.

When they reached Arlen, the situation might well be very different and The Unknown planned to talk with his captor, fairly sure that he could turn the unhappiness to doubt and the doubt to insubordination.

The Unknown always liked to think there were options. If nothing else, he was riding with two of Balaia's more powerful mages. That couldn't hurt their chances. Deciding to say no more, The Unknown smiled instead and turned his eyes, as ever, it seemed, to the sky.

Thraun stared long at the human he recognised as a man-packbrother and bade the pack spare him. They would also spare the prey though the scent of the meat had them all drooling. The night before, he had howled into a tempest, his voice lost, drowned by the rain and tattered by the wind. It was a bad wind. It had scared him.

Others had been stalking those he needed. Whether to kill them he couldn't be sure so he had watched the forest until man-packbrother had left the fire, taking his horse with him. And when the stalkers found the others, and he knew the pack couldn't help them, he had left them and watched the one.

Man-packbrother had been scared but now he was not. He would help them. And they would help him. Alone, he was surely vulnerable. He was alone no longer. Thraun licked the man's hand, then sniffed the sky again, hoping for comprehension.

Hirad knelt in front of Thraun, feeling the roughness of the wolf's tongue on his hand and watching as he pushed his snout into the air. The barbarian ran a hand across Thraun's head and looked briefly to the other wolves. All four sat alert, staring at him, animal confusion written across comically expressive faces.

'You can feel it, can't you?' he said and pointed skywards.

It was fascinating and it was an immense relief that the shapechanger was still alive, though the term didn't necessarily apply to Thraun any more. But, Hirad reasoned, if he were truly a pure wolf, his behaviour would have been very different.

Hirad supposed The Raven had been followed all the way from Thornewood. And the only possible reason Thraun would have done that was because he remembered them somehow. After almost six years, he should have been wild, with almost no vestiges of his human life to trouble him but that was plainly not the case.

'There's something still going on in there, isn't there, Thraun?'

Thraun growled gently in his throat and locked eyes with Hirad at the sound of his name. The barbarian saw recognition there, and something he was sure wasn't lupine. It was a calmness, an assurance of purpose. And knowledge. Hirad understood wolves to be animals of instinct but Thraun *knew* things. That meant he had to retain memory.

Hirad leant towards him. Thraun didn't flinch.

'Remember.'

The wolf pawed at the ground and shook his head, actually backing up a pace.

'You can understand me, can't you?' said Hirad. 'But can I reach you to bring you back? And do you want to come back?' He remembered the spark in Thraun's eyes the times before when he'd assumed his wolven form. That wasn't in evidence now, so many years later, but he still had intelligence, there was no doubt about that.

Hirad pushed himself to his feet and looked around at his horse. The animal was still badly scared but would have some sense by now that its life wasn't immediately threatened. Walking back to his camp, Hirad untied and rolled the leather, strapped on his sword and scooped up his saddle. Placing it on his horse's back, he felt the animal calm further and the stallion even managed to nuzzle his back as he bent to tie the girth strap. Attaching bit and bridle, Hirad planted a kiss on the top of its nose.

'Good boy. Now then.' He put his head close to its left ear and stroked its cheek gently, his voice carefully soothing, in the tone he knew would work. 'Remember you're the one that shares a home with dragons. These are just a few wolves. You aren't going to let me down, are you?'

The horse snorted softly and nickered, trying to turn its head to him, to look at him through a big dark eye.

'I knew you wouldn't. Come on then,' he said.

Never leaving his position close to its cheek, his free hand now caressing the front of its face, he led the still reluctant horse gently towards the wolves, speaking to Thraun as he came. 'We need to get to the others. To The Raven.' He pointed the way he wanted to go but Thraun growled and immediately the pack stood in his way. He stopped, grip tightening on the bridle, his horse digging in its back hooves.

He frowned and shook his head. All five wolves were looking at him, almost pleading. It wasn't a threat, it was a warning.

'What is it?' he spread his arms wide, bridle hand slipping down the reins. As if in answer, Thraun trotted past him towards the risen sun and in the direction of Arlen. He paused and looked back at Hirad, the growl in his throat sounding like an order.

'Come on, Thraun, the camp's that way.' Hirad pointed away into the forest. Thraun barked once and changed direction, the rest of the pack hesitating momentarily before following.

Hirad hauled himself into the saddle and goaded his unwilling horse after the wolves. He leaned forward and stroked the stallion's face, whispering words of encouragement into his ears.

He had only half expected The Raven to be at their campsite but was still disappointed to find it empty. But as he rode in, it was clear something was badly wrong. The fire hadn't been doused and cleared. A small pile of dry branches still sat near it. Surely they should have been taken for the next blaze. He dismounted and looked around.

There were no signs of any struggle but The Raven had left in a big hurry, the mud churned by hoofprints as if horses had been galloped out. Hirad squatted down, his frown deepening. He dragged gloved fingers through the mud and looked over at Thraun. The wolf was standing with the pack, watching him.

'What happened here, Thraun?' he asked.

He walked along the route the horses had taken out of the small clearing. Then he saw it. The churning wasn't down to galloping. It was because more than three horses had been in the camp when The Raven had left. Many more. Hirad could see the widening column of prints as it drove away, back to the edge of the woodland.

They had been taken, surely. Ignoring the growls of Thraun, he remounted and rode along the trail carved into the sodden ground. Wherever they had gone, he would follow them and free them. He couldn't leave them as prisoners. They were Raven.

And so was he.

Chapter 18

After the heavy seas of the past seven days, the River Arl was placid by comparison. Coming across the estuary on the rising tide, the *Ocean Elm* sliced calmly through the water, all sails full on a run with the wind blowing dead north, funnelling along the tree-lined shores. Further north, the trees would give way to rolling hills westwards, and spectacular escarpments eastwards, before open lowlands came to dominate the miles until the Arl opened into the beauty of Lake Arlen.

Ringed from its southernmost point to its north-western arc by trees that climbed part way up stark, snow-capped mountains, it seemed idyllic to anyone sailing towards it, bettered only by the body of water at Triverne. The port town of Arlen occupied the west bank, its deepwater berths home to ocean going vessels, its fishing fleet sheltered in a shallow harbour, and its offshore anchorages served by craft fitted with rope-and-pulley assemblies.

Incoming sailors could see the whole town sweeping up a low rise, culminating in the castle whose white scrubbed stone shone in the morning light, flags from its four turrets snapping in the prevailing breeze. Today, though, the white would be muted. None in Balaia had seen the sun consistently for what seemed like an age, with lowering, rain-bearing cloud washing almost ceaselessly across the sky. The land had cooled dramatically and many species of bird had flown prematurely south, insects had died early or never hatched at all and farming communities were counting the cost of poor crops this harvest and the certainty of hunger next year.

Erienne stood near the prow of the *Elm*, her mind still a fog from the mana attack, her stamina yet to recover fully and her feelings mixed as they had been ever since she left Lyanna behind on Herendeneth.

At least she felt she was doing something to try and maintain the safety of her daughter; and she felt an undeniable thrill at the thought of seeing Denser very soon. But ever-increasing had been her longing to hold Lyanna again, to sit in the orchard watching her beautiful child play, or to read her a story from her favourite book. She had found tears on her cheeks every morning, sleep having breached her defences. And, for the last three days, with her mana abilities damaged, she had known another emotion. Fear.

Fear that she would never be able to cast properly again, a threatened isolation that would soon become terrifying and unbearable. And fear of what she would find in Arlen. If Ren'erei was right, the Black Wings were strong again and Selik was still alive. He had been the right-hand man of Travers, and had the same zealous insanity in his eyes. She had only encountered them once but it had been an encounter that had cost the lives of her firstborn twin sons.

She knew now that the ache for them would never pass. Some days it was less, others more, but always there. And it was another reason she had to do what she was doing now. No one was going to take another child from her again.

Erienne let the wind whip at her hair as she stood in heavy cloak and trousers, looking back along the *Ocean Elm*'s length. She felt a little better this morning. Better enough that when Ren'erei walked along the deck towards her, she didn't wish the elf gone.

As she approached, she looked hard at Erienne, trying to gauge her mood. She was wearing her brown and green cloak, laced leather trousers and brown shirt.

'How are you feeling?' Ren'erei asked, coming to lean with her back on the rail, arms folded, half-turned to see Erienne's face.

She shrugged. 'Not bad. Less foggy.' She made a scrunching gesture at the sides of her head.

'Is that good?' Ren'erei smiled.

'Yes, it's good. Mostly, I'm just glad we're nearly there. This voyage has seemed very long.'

Ren'erei nodded, her expression becoming sober. 'I can understand your impatience. But we have to be careful in Arlen. Denser's right, you should stay aboard. We'll find him.'

'I suppose so.'

'What is it?'

Erienne sighed. She wasn't used to feeling so helpless and it was something that did not aid her shortening temper.

'I'm irritated because I can't contact him and he, presumably can't contact me either. Gods in the sky, Ren'erei, we don't even know if he's there. And now you're having to search the streets and all that'll do is alert *them*.'

'The Black Wings?'

Erienne nodded, finding herself unable to speak the name. A sudden knot of anxiety twisted her stomach.

'They'll be nowhere near here.'

'No?' snapped Erienne, her anger flaring. 'How can you be so sure? Just ask Tryuun about them. When I was with The Raven we thought we'd destroyed them back before Dawnthief was cast. Gods burning, I swear I saw Selik die by my own hand. Yet you tell me he survived, and Tryuun's face is evidence enough.' She wiped a hand across her face, moving the stray hairs that blew about it. Taking a deep breath to calm herself, she stepped forward and covered Ren's hands with her own.

'These men are dangerous. They have mages working for them. I'm just imploring you to be careful. You're a good friend, Ren. Don't go getting careless. My daughter's at stake here.'

Ren'erei nodded. 'I'll never forget that. And I'll mind what you say. We'll find Denser, don't worry.'

Erienne's next words were cut off by a shout from the wheel deck. They turned to see the Captain pointing away to the east bank where the trees were slowly thinning to lowland plains on the approach to the lake's mouth. Ren'erei followed the lookout's arm, staring intently into the trees. Erienne could see nothing. They were over one hundred yards off the bank, right in the centre of the Arl's flow. To Erienne, the shadow under the canopy obscured whatever it was the lookout had seen.

'What is it?' she asked.

'Riders.' Ren'erei continued to stare, unmoving. 'Four of them. Scouts.'

Despite herself and her knowledge of these elves, she had to say it.

'I can't see a thing.'

Ren'erei turned to her, her eyes alive, her face brim with patience.

'Erienne, they are scouts because they ride horses with both short-sprint speed and long-ride stamina. They wear little armour and carry light weapons. But mostly, they're elves and they know we've seen them.'

'They're looking for us?'

'Who else?' Ren'erei's smile was forced.

'How?' Erienne felt suddenly exasperated, her fleeting good humour gone, her heart rate racing. 'And who? Who knows we're coming?'

'I expect we'll find out in Arlen,' replied Ren'erei. The elf looked back across the shore, tracking the riders Erienne couldn't even see.

She felt more helpless than ever and scared for all their lives. Their docking at Arlen was suddenly so much more risky and people, maybe even Black Wings but more likely Dordovans, would be after them, but there was support close by. She wanted Lyanna but Lyanna wasn't near.

Fortunately, The Raven were.

By next morning, with Arlen less than a day's ride away, The Unknown had managed to persuade the Lysternan guard that he posed no threat to Darrick and the two men rode side by side at the head of the column. For once, the wind wasn't blasting across Balaia and there were breaks in the cloud, allowing precious spears of undiluted sunlight to fleetingly caress the ground.

The mood throughout the cavalry was lighter following another drenching night spent huddled under leather and leaf bivouacs. Around them, the gentle undulating moorland that led inexorably down to Lake Arlen's west bank seemed less bleak and The Unknown felt some small relief, though Denser's scowl had not eased.

'Some prisoner you are,' said Darrick, picking up another confused gaze from one of his men.

'I'm sorry you even think of me that way,' replied The Unknown.

Darrick chewed his lip, unable to meet The Unknown's gaze for a moment.

'You have to believe me that it's for your own protection,' said Darrick. 'And I'm sorry too. For the necessity to take your weapons and for keeping Ilkar and Denser under mage guard. None of us like it.'

'Just orders, eh?' Try as he might, The Unknown couldn't work up any anger towards the General. He just had to understand what it was all about.

'I was advised that your reaching Arlen might be precipitate,' said Darrick carefully.

'Gods falling, really?' The Unknown couldn't help but smile. 'What did your adviser think we might do?'

'Get yourselves killed trying to get to Erienne, what else?'

'We aren't known for getting ourselves killed,' said The Unknown. 'And anyway, we expected you to be behind us. Hardly a threat if you're not in town, are you?'

Darrick turned in his saddle, frowning under his helmet.

'Unknown, I would never have ordered my men to fight The Raven. You misunderstand.'

'No, I don't. We're aware there may be a few Dordovans scouting Arlen, trying to pick up the mana trails. We just think we can avoid them.' The Unknown shrugged.

'A few? You've been out of touch too long. There are three hundred-plus there now, and more coming if I understand the Dordovan messaging right.'

The Unknown's heart skipped a beat. 'Three . . . What are you expecting to happen down there? I mean Erienne's hardly an army, is she?'

'It's not Erienne we're worried about. Or her elven guardians. You know as well as I do that Dordover and Lystern are not the only parties interested in securing the child.'

Even as Darrick was speaking, The Unknown was going cold all over.

'Dear Gods, I should have guessed, shouldn't I?'

'I beg your pardon?'

'I felt them a couple of days ago. I knew they were close. I can't believe I didn't make the connection.' He looked into Darrick's blank face. 'The Protectors. They're coming to Arlen, aren't they?'

Darrick nodded.

'How many of them?'

'We have to assume all of them,' said Darrick.

'Then they'll slaughter you. Three hundred plus your two hundred? You'll be throwing your life away, Darrick. Even with more support from wherever. You must see that.' The Unknown's pulse had quickened and he could see in Darrick's eyes that he didn't see at all.

'I've watched them fight. And we aren't Wesmen, Unknown. We have mage support. We can beat them, I'm sure of it.'

'Then you'll be killing my brothers. You understand I'll do everything I can to stop you.'

'I have my orders.'

'And I have my loyalties.' At last The Unknown could feel some anger. It was just sad it was in response to a threat against the Protectors.

He found Darrick's confidence both arrogant and ignorant. He had watched the Protectors, maybe, but he didn't understand their minds, their drive and their devotion, the things that made them so utterly different from mere soldiers. Tactics were great, but people feared

Protectors and Darrick's men would be no different. And Xetcsk would have sent mage support too, and plenty of it.

This was all getting completely out of hand.

'Why do you think Dordover are so keen to recapture Erienne?'

Darrick chuckled. 'Come on, Unknown, you don't have to ask me that. She's out of control. Just look around you. Her powers are destroying Balaia. I'm sure it isn't her fault but it does have to be stopped. I take it we're agreed on that point?'

'Yes,' said The Unknown.

'But . . .'

'But it was Dordover that awakened her. Erienne took Lyanna because they could no longer control her. She's gone to the Al-Drechar.'

'And you call this control?' Darrick waved his free hand about him. 'I've heard the stories and I've seen Greythorne and Thorne-wood. Look, Unknown, I'm really sorry. I have such sympathy for you, all of you. And I know that you think you're doing the right thing. So did I at first but I've seen and consulted too much. Erienne has made a mistake. Lyanna has to be under College control. It's the only way.'

The Unknown was in no doubt about Darrick's belief. The General was not given to frivolity, or to making rash statements.

'Is that what you believe Dordover will exert? Control? They mean to kill her, Darrick, and you're being used to deliver her to them. They won't murder her in cold blood but they'll see to it she dies. I know you don't want to let that happen.'

'And it won't. Not while I have a breath in my body,' said Darrick.

'Then look out for your own back, too.'

Darrick nodded and looked up at the sky. It was still flecked blue but rain-bearing cloud was again bubbling up from the east. Korina, Balaia's capital, would be suffering another storm already.

The General turned to his second.

'Izack, order slow to walk. We'll dismount in a mile.'

'Yes, sir.' Izack raised a flat palm above his head. 'Walking!' he shouted, the order relayed throughout the column. Darrick's well-drilled cavalry responded immediately.

'You know the Black Wings are in on this too,' said The Unknown as they moved more sedately through the moorland, purple heather blowing in waves across the gentle slopes.

Darrick gave him a sharp glance but then shrugged. 'I suppose I shouldn't be surprised. One sniff of a magical problem and they'll show up to stir trouble and twist the knife. All the more reason to get Erienne secure.'

'I'm with you there, at least.'

'You know, I hope that after all this has blown over, if you'll pardon the expression, we can still count each other as friends.'

The Unknown felt stung by the comment. 'Not if you deliver Lyanna to those who would see her die; and kill my brothers to do so. Now, if you'll permit, I'd like to return to the friends I do still have.'

Thraun's mind was ablaze and he knew the suspicious eyes of the pack were on him. He could sense their confusion, their fear and their anger, but he had no way to communicate what he felt deep within him. It was hard enough to come to terms with it himself. He first had to hope the pack would trust his judgement and neither turn on him or the man-packbrother.

And so, they travelled quickly across the land, following in the wake of all the men and horses, heading for a broad expanse of water and a settlement where, he assumed, would be the answers to the questions and an end to the wrong in the air.

He hadn't known whether man-packbrother would follow him but had kept the pack quiet as they had approached his camp. And they had waited downwind until he awoke, with no way to tell him his friends were gone, taken by other men, but anxious to stop him returning to where they had been sleeping because it was the wrong way to travel.

Man-packbrother had spoken to him then, much as he had done again as they travelled, his horse scared as was right, but under control. The pack would have to wait for their feast.

Thraun still had no idea what would happen next. His instinct merely drove him to see man-packbrother safely to the end of the journey. His feelings clashed painfully within him. Men weren't prey, they were threat and he was used to removing threat from the way of the pack. It had always been so. Yet this man-packbrother, like another he knew from a buried sadness, understood like few men did.

Thraun could see this and that was why he led the pack but why he was alone. Different.

Memories flashed in his mind again. Distant and shrouded. Two legs upright . . . a lessening of speed, power and instinct . . . scent trails denied him. The memories hurt and he growled to clear his mind. But since the time he had seen man-packbrother and his companions, such clarity was denied him.

Thraun turned his head, checking the pack and the rider behind them. He sniffed the air as he loped on, feeling that time was short.

Following the wolves down the trail of a hundred and more horses, Hirad had felt the release of a tension he hadn't known he harboured. Ilkar, Denser and The Unknown were alive. Ilkar had dropped one of his gloves, assuming Hirad would find it. They were certainly prisoners but alive, and that meant he could find and free them. And Thraun was still with him.

In his mind he knew it didn't all add up but he couldn't shake the notion that Thraun *knew* what he was doing. And it went without saying, Hirad trusted Thraun's instinct, wolf or human.

After all, Thraun was Raven too.

Chapter 19

The *Ocean Elm* was signalled into dock berth one in the middle of what had become an unusually calm afternoon. The portmaster had long since stopped sending out a pilot to help the elven ship reach safe berth. If any were capable of navigating the shallows – which in all honesty were simple when compared to the approach to Herendeneth – it was the crew of the *Elm*.

The ship moved serenely towards the berth, the Captain barking out a stream of orders, bringing the sails into furl until only the foresail drove her forwards. It would be another perfect docking.

'It's busy today,' remarked Ren'erei.

'Is it?' Erienne was scouring the dockside for evidence of her husband, indeed for any of The Raven.

'Yes.' Ren'erei shrugged. 'The docks are full. We're lucky to find a berth onshore.'

'So what happens now?'

'Well, if you'll allow, you go below and keep out of sight and try to gain contact with Denser if you are able. I'll go ashore and ask around, see what I can find out. Members of The Raven shouldn't be hard to find.'

'No,' agreed Erienne and she smiled. Being recognised was usually a boost to the ego but for her, right now, it was a risk. She flipped the hood of her cloak over her red-brown hair.

'Let's hope that will be enough.' Ren'erei smiled.

'We'll see.' She began to walk along the deck. Arlen and its people were scant yards away, the elegant elven vessel turning many a head as she understood it always did as it moved to tie up, crew swift and nimble, acting without error. She yearned for the ground beneath her feet – a security she never craved until it was denied her.

Ren'erei caught her arm. 'Erienne. I will find him and bring him to you as soon as I do. Trust me.'

'I do.' Erienne flung her arms around Ren's neck, crushing the elf to her. 'Thank you.' She found tears in her eyes, a welling of emotion she'd held pent up for the whole voyage. 'Please be quick.'

Ren'erei eased her away far enough to look into her eyes then leant forward and kissed her cheek.

'We'll be away from here on the morning tide and every pitch into a wave will bring you closer to Lyanna, and Denser will be at your side.'

The image filled Erienne with an elation that rushed through her body and sent those tears streaming down her cheeks even as a broad smile spread over her face. She kissed Ren'erei back and hurried below, hearing the tying-up orders sound across the deck. Just a day and they'd be resupplied and leaving for Herendeneth with The Raven on board, strong and invincible.

Erienne dropped her cloak over a chair and lay on her bunk, the first inklings of relaxation feeding across her mind.

Ren'erei walked quickly down the gangplank and on to the bustling dockside. It was just past midday and though the port was as busy as ever, the cranes creaking, the shouts of cratemen and netriders ringing out as they manoeuvred freight onto carts or into holds, there was an edge to the atmosphere.

Deciding to investigate, Ren'erei moved slowly along the water's edge, nodding at any she recognised but keeping her eyes and ears sharp, searching for the cause. With all four deepwater berths full, crates and boxes crowded the dock as she picked her way through workers hurrying to get goods to market or to onward transport into inland Balaia.

A netrider called out from above as he swung on a net filled with luggage trunks, looking for clear space before letting the tackleman lower it to the ground. Ren'erei waved acknowledgement and jogged on a few paces.

The elf moved effortlessly through the bustle, the wind blowing the nose-wrinkling smell of fish from the market behind her. A little further on, the Lakehome Inn caught her eye. At first glance, it just looked unusually quiet and still but there was far more to it than that. The doors were closed and windows shuttered and, outside, a ring of town guardsmen kept passers-by well away from the entrance.

Ren'erei moved closer, coming to the shoulder of a dock labourer who was standing with a knot of men and women looking at the blank face of the Inn.

'Trouble, was there?' she asked.

The labourer turned a salt-weathered red face to her. 'Just landed, is it?'

'That obvious?'

'Only explanation why you don't know, little elf. Town's been ablaze with it since sun-up. Earl's throwing the Black Wings out.'

Ren'erei must have blanched, or her face jumped a little, because next heartbeat, the man's face had hardened, his heavy brow creasing, his body tensed.

'Bothers you, does it?'

'That they're leaving, no. That's happy. That they're here at all, that bothers.'

'Scared, eh?' The hard face softened.

'Very. They don't like my kind.'

The man acknowledged the admission. 'Your business,' he said.

'Thank you.'

He nodded. 'I'll look for you.' He pointed to his eyes with splayed fingers. 'Go carefully.'

Ren'erei gave a small, respectful bow. 'Already in your debt. One thing. How many are there?'

'Black Wings?' The man shrugged. 'Thirty, forty. Long gone by sundown.'

'I hope so.' She caught the man's eye. ' Ren'erei.'

'Donetsk,' responded the man. 'Always on the dock.'

The ghost of a smile. 'Always at sea. We'll know you. One last thing. See The Raven, come to the *Ocean Elm*.' Ren'erei didn't wait for the response. She knew Donetsk would do exactly that should he see or hear of them. Dockers could be useful allies. There were always deals to be done and whispers to be heard but knowing the clipped patter made it possible. This time, though, Ren'erei wasn't worried about securing supplies at low cost. Security, muscle and discreet eyes were the goods of real value today.

The elf carried on along the dockside, assessing the readiness and flags of the other three ships at birth. All were ocean-going merchantmen as opposed to coastal vessels. None was less than one hundred feet long and while one was flying the flag of the much diminished Pontois barony, the other two were elven, hailing from Calaius.

All three were unloading or freighting normally and that was a relief to Ren'erei, who had considered the possibility that she might have been watching Black Wings preparing to board. She smiled. Not now. Arlen was a good man if sometimes a little overprotective towards his town. One thing was sure, the Black Wings wouldn't be granted re-entry.

With Donetsk able to put the word around the docks and Salt Quarter, where tenements and warehouses crowded, Ren'erei headed north to the Centenary Square market. The focal point of trade in all but the finest goods, the Centenary market was where she expected to hear if anyone as renowned as The Raven rode into town.

Ren'erei could not keep the thrill from her heart as she scouted the thronging market, ducking into every inn and eating house, not even sure what she expected to find. In her mind's eye, she saw herself walking into an inn, maybe, and seeing The Raven seated quietly round a table.

She was sure she'd recognise them though she'd never actually set eyes on them. Because, even though she spent most of her time at sea or on Herendeneth, The Raven were a living legend. The massive, shaven-headed warrior they called 'The Unknown'; the dark-robed and bearded Xeteskian, Denser; the black-haired, quiet and assured elf, Ilkar, and the thickset, powerful barbarian warrior, Hirad Coldheart. Maybe even Thraun-the-wolf. They surely couldn't be hard to spot.

But she found no sign of them in the market or its surrounds. They weren't in the Park of the Martyrs' Souls or riding down Market Approach. She supposed she shouldn't have been surprised but she couldn't shut out the disappointment. Erienne's first, and only as it turned out, contact with Denser suggested they wouldn't arrive until later that evening. She'd hoped anyway.

Ambling more slowly back through the market, she dropped words into the ears of those she knew she could rely upon to be circumspect if they found information, and made her way back to the docks.

By the Fish Market, she was ordered aside by a mounted town guardsman riding ahead of a knot of Arlen's soldiers and a column of other riders. Melting quickly into the mildly irritated crowds packing to either side of the street, she watched the Black Wings escorted up the hill and, presumably, out to the borders of Arlen. Staring at as many faces as possible, searching for the men who had tortured Tryuun, she bit back a shouted curse, leaving the jeers to the crowd. She felt a welling of hatred for these men, and the black rose-and-wings tattoos on their necks; and an utter contempt for everything they stood for. Tryuun would forever be scarred by their action and, while any of them lived, mages across the world would be at risk from the violent punishment they willingly gave out for the 'crime' of having magical ability.

Wishing death on them all, she watched their backs for a while before turning and immediately noticing a pair of tall, slim men walking a good forty yards behind the riders as the street began to move with normal traffic once again. For all the world, they looked like merchants headed for the silk market; however they were anything but.

Arlen wasn't a stupid man and mage scouts were just one more level of certainty that the Black Wings would not be back. A smile tugging at the corners of her mouth again as she walked back to the *Elm*, Ren'erei just wished they had been assassins instead.

Another thunderstorm was prematurely darkening the sky as Darrick's cavalry and its three prisoners approached Arlen from the north east. Communion with the Dordovan camp to the south of the town had left Darrick and the reporting mage a little puzzled and, once his scouts had returned with messages of cautious welcome from Earl Arlen, he decided to camp away from his allies of necessity and take his prisoners into the town.

The General was uneasy. The *Ocean Elm*, the elven vessel reportedly carrying Erienne, had been sighted sailing up the Arl in the early morning, yet she had not been boarded, nor even contacted by the Dordovan mage delegation. The reasons why were confusing to say the least, and seemed to shelter behind obscure port regulations and protocols. And again, it became clear during the Communion questioning that no one had spoken to the Harbour Master or any of Arlen's administrative officers.

It was equally clear that the irritated General would have to speak to the Earl himself. The actions of the Dordovans would be questioned later.

With ten guards in a loose circle around them, Darrick chose to ride with The Raven. He felt sick at the whole ridiculous affair and felt sorry for what he knew he was putting Denser through. The guilt he knew he couldn't fully admit was not helped by the venomous looks the tight-lipped Xeteskian shot him on the half-hour ride into the town.

'So, what's the deal?' asked The Unknown. 'Is there some problem with keeping us in the camp?'

'It's a military decision,' said Darrick stiffly. 'I don't want you getting hurt if there's trouble.'

'When,' grated Denser.

'Don't make this more difficult than it already is, please, Denser,' said Darrick, half turning in his saddle.

'Sure, no problem. I'd hate you to be in any way inconvenienced.'

'Look, I'm not enjoying this either,' said Darrick. 'But if it hadn't been me, it would have been somebody else and you'd be in chains.'

'I'm overcome by your kindness,' spat Denser.

Darrick turned all the way, left hand resting on the back of his saddle. 'Let me make one thing very clear, Denser of Xetesk. I am a soldier of Lystern and honoured to be so. In that capacity, I was ordered to bring about your capture and to deliver you to a secure holding point. This I will do. I don't have to like it, or even agree with it, I just have to do it. Right now, I am breaking every rule in the book regarding the transport of mage prisoners because I respect and trust you. Do not convince me I should act otherwise.'

He turned back in his saddle, a knot in his stomach. He hated what he said though he was glad his men had heard his words. It was a while before The Unknown spoke again.

'This secure place. The castle or the jail?'

Darrick raised his eyebrows. 'The jail, I'm afraid. It has a standing mage guard and I can leave some of my own men too.'

'You really are serious about this, aren't you?' said Ilkar, real disappointment in his voice.

Darrick didn't look round. He couldn't face the elf. 'I'm always serious.'

With the markets closed but the inns and eateries open, noisy and crowded, Arlen took on a very different aspect at night. Shore-leave sailors were intent on sinking as much ale and spirits as they could while whores turned brisk business as alcohol loosened purses, drowned promises to those back home and stoked loins with undeniable lust.

Trouble was a fact of life but the town guard patrolled in good numbers and serious problems were rare. So it was that Darrick delivered his charges reluctantly to a jailhouse that was so far empty of inebriates but stank eye-wateringly of those of previous nights.

'Don't let me down,' said Darrick, closing the grilled iron-clad wooden door.

'Can't think of any place I'd rather be,' muttered Denser.

'What do you mean?' asked The Unknown, coming to the grille.

'I mean I know you've done nothing wrong but you have to believe that I'm doing this to keep you alive.'

'We don't need your help, General,' said The Unknown. 'And if we want to get out, we will.'

'My men have orders to kill you,' said Darrick. 'Please don't make them carry those out. You have no weapons, no armour and I have mages tuned to the mana spectrum right outside this door. Stay where you are. I'll be back as soon as I can.'

'You're making a very grave mistake,' said Denser. 'I'm the only one who can save her. They'll kill her. And the blood will be on your hands and I will hunt you down.'

'If it turns out that way, I won't defend myself,' said Darrick. He turned and walked away, his doubts resurfacing and shored up not just by The Raven but by the apparent ineptitude of the Dordovans. Once he had spoken to the Earl, there would be much to discuss with the Dordovan lead mage, Gorstan.

The Unknown swung from the grille to the complete contempt of Denser.

'Plan working well is it? I must say, Unknown, this tactical ploy of yours is something else. Rescue Erienne by getting us locked up. Congratulations. You are responsible for the death of my daughter.' Denser had moved across the ten-foot-square cell as he spoke and now stood half a pace from the big warrior.

'Denser, I need you to let me think for a while, all right?' The Unknown faced the mage calmly, not wanting to go over the same arguments of the last two days.

'About what? Clever ways of getting them to shackle us to the walls?' Denser rattled one of the chains that hung at chest height all around the cell.

The Unknown looked past Denser to Ilkar. The elf had been very quiet since their capture and he knew what the Julatsan was wrestling with. He had always trusted The Unknown to make the right choice but even he had to be struggling to see what being locked in Arlen's jail could possibly do for them. The trouble was, The Unknown didn't know either. He had assumed first that they would remain with the cavalry, under guard in a tent in the camp. Even when they were riding to Arlen, he had been confident they'd be held in the castle and once there, he had no doubt he could persuade the Earl to release them. He was an old friend, after all.

But this. This was not in the plan. They had no weapons, no armour and no way of disguising magic from the guard outside. No way out. And the worst of it was that he had no answer for Denser. The Raven were caught.

'I know it looks bad now . . .' he began because he had to say something.

'*Bad?*' Denser grabbed the lapels of The Unknown's jacket. 'This place is about to be crawling with Dordovans and my wife has sailed right into the middle of them and she won't even know. They'll have her before she has time to blink and then we can start to count down the number of days my daughter has to live. Gods falling Unknown, we were her only hope. And what did you do? Lead us into bloody prison! Bad. Bugger me, but that's understating our problem more than just a little.'

The Unknown pushed him gently away. 'I'm sorry. I hadn't considered we'd be put here.'

'So what are we going to do?' asked Denser, the pleading back in his face, his anger gone as soon as it had come.

The Unknown shook his head. There was no use saying anything but the truth.

'I don't know.'

'Fantastic. I'll make myself comfortable, then.'

'You know, Denser, there's much more to this. You've always thought Dordover would kill her. Now you merely know the method. There's something else. I thought so outside Greythorne. I know so now. You've been rambling on about being the only one who can do something about this mess and now I want to know how. So let's hear it.' The Unknown loomed over Denser.

The Dark Mage stayed seated, looking up at the big warrior. 'Unknown, I don't know what you're talking about.'

The Unknown leaned in. 'Denser, you are an old and dear friend, and you are a mage of supreme talent. But this fist can still shatter your bearded jaw more quickly than you can cast. Now, you're hiding something, it's making you do and say stupid things, and I will find out whether you tell me or I divine it from examining your broken teeth.' The Unknown was not smiling.

Ilkar watched it all from his seat on the opposite side of the stinking cell, wondering how much intent lay behind the threat.

'Have we really been reduced to this?' he muttered. 'Sitting in cells, threatening each other?' No one answered him.

He could see Denser weighing up the threat. After a long pause,

Denser waved The Unknown back a little, reached inside his shirt and pulled out some folded pages.

'I translated more of the Prophecy in Xetesk,' he said.

Ilkar stood up. 'Just how many—'

'Six,' replied Denser. He shrugged. 'I'm sorry.'

'And are you going to tell us that your next little secret's nothing important too?'

Denser shook his head, his expression terribly sad. 'No, I'm not. I can save her Ilkar. I can save Lyanna. I can save us all. I really can.'

Ilkar exchanged glances with The Unknown, knowing they were thinking the same thing. They'd heard these words before he cast Dawnthief. Both of them grinned. Ilkar spoke.

'But that's great, isn't it?' he said. 'I don't understand why you're being so weird about it.'

'There's a side effect,' said Denser. Ilkar went cold all over. 'I will die.'

General Darrick had ridden back through Arlen with four of his guard, Denser's cold certainty that Dordover would kill Lyanna weighing heavily on him. Arriving at the castle, he had been ushered into a plush fire-lit drawing room and asked to wait, if he cared to. The Earl, he had been told, was at a supper engagement to celebrate the birth of the son of a merchant noble friend and would return before midnight.

After days in a cold wet saddle or shivering in a tent, Darrick couldn't resist the lure of soup, bread and a warm fire to sit by and, after ensuring his guard were fed, despatched one with orders for Izack, and settled in.

Fighting the desire to doze, he reflected that he had fully expected to arrive in Arlen to oversee the provisioning of ships for the voyage back to wherever Erienne had come from in the Ornouth Archipelago. In fact, he'd thought he might even be able to just step aboard and sit with Erienne and help her understand while the elven ship led the Dordovans and Lysternans to the prize they all prayed they could take and control to save Balaia.

But now it seemed the Dordovans had no urgency at all and he would have to organise the whole lot himself. Hardly auspicious evidence of inter-College co-operation.

Riding through the gates of Castle Arlen, he had seen the relaxation among the guards, the smiles of those who handled the horses and what verged on informality from the squire who led them into the keep. It was as if they'd won a great victory and had no idea of the scale of forces converging on them, coming closer with every heartbeat.

Darrick had expected the Earl to be in good spirits when he arrived back from his supper, but instead, Jasto had been cool, though his words were kind enough as he shook the General's hand.

'General Darrick, what a pleasant surprise.'

'My Lord Earl.'

'I've just had a mug of mulled wine delivered. Care to join me?'

Darrick smiled. 'Perhaps a little. All this talk of soup and hot wine, it sounds like winter's upon us.'

'Perhaps it is,' said Arlen, filling two silver goblets, handing one to Darrick and gesturing him to sit on one of the plush chairs that flanked the fire. 'This magic smells bad, so they tell me, and it's making my town cold and wet before its time. It's all about a girl, isn't it?'

'Yes,' said Darrick, interested to find out how much the Earl knew.

'Hmm. And it sounds like we've been lucky here so far. Just wind, rain and a little lightning. Spectacular, too.' He mouth twitched up at the corners. 'We've had hurricanes, the ground eating a town whole. Even Korina has not gone unscathed; the seas have risen and smashed the docks there. So tell me, what is it you are here to do?'

'Find the child,' said Darrick. 'Bring her to safety where she can be controlled before more damage is done to Balaia.'

'And is that what all those Dordovans are doing in the south?'

'Supposedly,' said Darrick. 'But they don't seem to have achieved much aside from erecting their tents.'

'And they've been here over two weeks.' Arlen took a long sip of his wine. 'Now, I've left them alone because they have been the souls of politeness whenever they have come here. They have arranged charter of the *Calaian Sun*, they have eaten and drunk with my people and said nothing about what they're doing. Strange then, their alliance with the Black Wings, who are nothing but mindless thugs I have had to expel. I understood the Colleges to be united in their hatred of these people.'

'I beg your pardon?' Darrick started, unsure he had heard the Earl correctly.

'And I'm even more surprised a man of your apparent honour and standing being linked with such an alliance. I thought Lystern above such mire,' continued Arlen.

'My Lord Earl, I must—'

Arlen raised a hand. 'This is my drawing room and I will speak until I am done. Now I understand you to have in the region of two hundred cavalry to the north west of my town. Take them home, General Darrick. They aren't needed here. I will not suffer College forces here any longer. The Black Wings are gone, your dubious allies are going to sail to Ornouth to find this child, and all will be put right.' He refilled his goblet.

Darrick rose, unable to keep seated. He couldn't believe what he had heard of the Dordovans.

'Earl Arlen, please,' he said, knowing his agitation was showing but not caring. 'The Black Wings. You are saying they are working with the Dordovans?'

It was such a bizarre question, he could barely credit it coming from his lips. Arlen looked at him for a long moment, confusion chasing itself across his face.

'You didn't know?' He pointed at Darrick. 'You didn't know.'

'No, and I'm afraid I cannot leave your town though I promise no harm will come to your people by the hand of a Lysternan,' said Darrick. 'There will be bloodshed and destruction here unless I stop it.'

'My dear General, you're being over-emotional. Ask anyone in the town what happened this morning. I snuffed out the situation. The Black Wings have been expelled, sent away with their tails between their legs. There is no one for you to fight.' He chuckled and shook his head.

Darrick fought to keep his temper. 'My Lord, there is a ship in your harbour. An elven vessel recently arrived.'

Arlen nodded. 'The *Ocean Elm*. Beautiful, isn't she?'

'You must give me permission to board her immediately.'

'Must?' Arlen raised his eyebrows. 'General Darrick, I am unused to having such demands made of me in my own drawing room.'

'Nevertheless, I stand by my request. Do I have your permission?'

'No, General, you don't.' Arlen rose to his feet. 'And until you can convince me it is a necessity for the security of Arlen, I shall continue to refuse.'

Darrick snapped, leaning across the table, his bulk throwing a shadow across the Earl. 'You want evidence of the need for security, then wait and it will come to you. But Erienne Malanvai, mother of the child who is causing all this destruction, is on that ship and she must be made safe. The only way to do that is to let me on board and have that vessel moved offshore immediately.'

'Step away, General, or I'll have my men take you to the cells I've let you borrow to keep friends of mine under lock and key. You seem so scared of them and perhaps I now know why. Want them kept from Frienne, do you? And what else are you scared of, the Black Wings? You really think they can get to her through me?'

But Darrick did not step away. Instead he grabbed the Earl by the collars of his expensive silk shirt, ripping it even as he dragged the man halfway across the table. 'The Raven are in jail because I fear for their lives, as I fear for yours,' he said, his voice rising in volume. 'And not from the Black Wings, damn you. Though they are far more dangerous than you seem to realise. You haven't been keeping up with the news from the east.' He shoved the Earl back and the older man grabbed for his chair and sat heavily, his face pale. Darrick found his hands were shaking and it wasn't just with anger. 'Xetesk is coming and unless that ship is gone, the Protectors will rip this town apart to get it.'

Chapter 20

Donetsk stumbled from the Bow Sprit ale-house in the Salt Quarter and began his meandering walk home. It had been a good night, the atmosphere in the Bow unusually light, with people still talking about the Earl's ejection of the Black Wings that morning.

He hated that scum and had followed their sorry procession all the way out of Arlen, before returning to the docks to complete a day's work that dragged on until at last he could get to the Bow for the first of many celebratory drinks.

Now, with midnight approaching, he had been ushered out as the doors closed, pausing only to hug the innkeeper who'd extended his credit another night. In the morning he'd remember the sympathy in his eyes and be irritated as always. For now, though, he needed a walk to help clear his head and bring the memories back to him.

The bad weather was coming back. He could feel a bite in the wind; beyond the mountains to the north, thunder rumbled and out to the south, way down the Arl, lightning flared across the horizon. But for now, the wind was fresh rather than chill and Donetsk decided to walk along the dockside, maybe take in the *Ocean Elm* at rest before going home to lie alone as he had done every night for the last twelve years. He had heard the whispers in the town, the muttering that magic was bringing the trouble, but he paid it little heed. If that was the case, the Colleges would see them safe. They would know what to do.

With his footsteps echoing off the warehouse walls in the quiet of the night, he took in the stark shapes of cranes, heard the gentle creak of timber on the water and smiled his brief smile.

He had been so proud. He had married a mage who wanted little more than to settle in Arlen, have children and operate her wonderful cleansing and healing charms on those that needed them. Their daughter was blessed too and when she was ten, he had cried tears of joy as they stepped into a covered wagon for the journey to Julatsa.

They didn't ever arrive. Robbers, the coachman had said but the truth had come to Donetsk later. Black Wings. Witch Hunters working against the survival of the next mage generation.

His smile disappeared as the depression rolled over him, as it always did in the dead of night and always would. No matter how much he worked or drank to forget, there would be a moment every day when it got to him.

Donetsk put a hand to his face and prayed to the sky that the Gods would care for their souls. There was nothing for him now. Not even revenge. He had once craved it but now it seemed unimportant because it would make him feel worse, just bring the pain closer. And the Gods knew that was the last thing he needed.

He stopped and leaned against an old mooring-post, strong but splintering. His heart was racing and for a moment he found it hard to catch his breath. He looked to the ground until it stopped swaying before him, breathed deeply and cursed his muddled, drunken mind that tossed the memories through him like bodies twisting on a flaming pyre. Slowly, he blinked back the tears, swallowed the sudden grief and stared ahead. The *Elm* was not far and, beyond it past the fish market, his home and bed. Empty but welcoming for all that.

Walking on, he opened his eyes wide and blew out his cheeks, letting the wind blow into his face. He yawned, looking forward to lying down until the dawn birds brought his aching head to reluctant wakefulness. Picking up his pace, he strode past the *Ocean Elm*, smiling and waving at the guard patrolling the deck. The elf signalled back. Donetsk couldn't tell whether he smiled too but the acknowledgement was enough. He liked elves, most of them. They had magic about them. He could feel it.

He yawned again, tasting the strong smell of fish in his mouth. Strong but secure somehow. He was nearly home. Donetsk walked around the corner of the market, out of sight of the dock and that was when he saw them, issuing from the night, all on foot, their steps slow and quiet, swords or daggers in their hands, metal flashing dully as it caught the remnants of moonlight. He looked hard, still approaching, confusion muddling his head. There were ten, a dozen, then twenty. First reaction was that they were town guard but a heartbeat later it was clear they were not.

Donetsk kept moving though he knew in the back of his mind it was a foolish act. He did it because they had not seen him but kept their eyes on a far larger prize. The *Ocean Elm*.

Black Wings. Black Wings walking the dockside when surely they had been expelled. Anger gripped him. An unquenchable force stemming from his longing for his long-dead family and a grievous insult to Arlen, the Earl and the town.

'Hey!' He started running, heedless of risk. He was Donetsk and the people of Arlen looked out for him.

Men looked up, stopped their movement. One in front spread his arms and they all straightened, falling completely quiet. He was cloaked and hooded, his gesture calming the rest and he made no move as Donetsk came forward.

'Get out!' he shouted, flailing his arms towards the road north. 'Get out!' He was breathless, running hard. 'Guard!' He looked around as he came but the street was empty but for him and them. His heart missed a beat. Too late to retreat now. He stumbled to a stop in front of them.

'You're not welcome here. You're expelled. Leave.'

'Come, come.' Drawled the hooded man. 'You're a little the worse for drink and don't know what you're saying. We're friends to everyone but those who deny the truth. Let some of my men escort you quietly home.'

Donetsk shook his head. 'No. You shouldn't be here.' He heaved in a breath and turned his head towards the castle. 'Gu—'

Pain, hot and intense, flared in his chest. He snapped his head back and the hooded man was so close he could feel his breath. The man put a hand around the back of his neck and pulled him closer. The pain spiralled. Donetsk grunted, feeling his strength flooding away.

'You cannot stand in the way of the righteous,' whispered the hooded man in his ear. 'You cannot be allowed to stand between us and the evil. Rest your soul now.'

Donetsk could feel his mouth moving though it felt numb and clumsy.

The man stepped back, withdrawing the long dagger. Donetsk slumped to his knees, absurdly aware of how dark his blood looked as it slicked the cobbles. He frowned then, as the darkness closed in, disappointed he hadn't made them understand what they'd taken from his life.

Ren'erei had returned to the *Ocean Elm* well before midnight, after a second fruitless search. She had heard no word that The Raven had arrived in Arlen, though a force of Lysternan cavalry were now camped to the north west and her anxiety was beginning to grow. The Captain was keen to leave no later than dawn the following morning, any later and they risked hitting the Arl estuary as the tide turned. Not normally any more than an irritation, with the winds as fickle as they had been since Lyanna's awakening began, it could present a real obstacle to escaping into the open ocean.

Erienne had been quite calm and Ren'erei drew strength from her total confidence in The Raven's certain arrival, late though it might be. But now, with her asleep and midnight upon them, her mind was unsettled again and she took a walk on deck, knowing deep inside that all was not right.

Outside, the night was quiet but the wind was starting to bite. She nipped up the ladder to the wheel deck where the dead-hours sentry was standing, elven eyes seeing far into the dark.

'All well, Tryuun?' she said as she recognised her brother.

Tryuun turned and shrugged. 'Well, Erienne's friends haven't shown up but apart from that, I've seen one drunk a little while ago and heard some shouting just now from over there.' He gestured towards the fish market, a low shape on the shore to their left. 'Probably arguing with someone over a woman or another drink, I expect.'

They both chuckled.

'And what about you, Ren'erei. Can't sleep?'

'No. I'm worried about them. The Raven, I mean. There's no word of them in Arlen, the Black Wings have been here and were only thrown out yesterday. There's an edge to the atmosphere.'

'Edge?'

Ren'erei held a hand out, fingers straight 'On one side, people who sense something's going to happen but they don't know why, and on the other, people who think all their troubles rode out of town with the Black Wings.'

'And what do you think?'

'I think we need to get away from here as fast as possible.' Ren'erei looked towards the fish market; there'd been a movement, probably the drunk or, if she was lucky, someone come to tell her The Raven had arrived. Maybe even the great men themselves.

'Do you—?' she pointed over to the market, wreathed in deep shadows but Tryuun was already drawing his slender elven blade.

'Yes. Ren, wake the ship. It's the Black Wings.'

Tryuun ran to the wheel while Ren'erei slid down the ladder to the main deck. Pushing open the doors aft, she heard the bell sound and Tryuun's voice rise in the call to arms.

'Awake! Awake! Weapons to the decks. Weapons to the decks.

Attack from shore. Awake, awake!' He would carry on until the first elves appeared from below.

Ren'erei sprinted down the narrow corridor, slapping her hands on doors as she ran for the captain's cabin.

'Up! Up! Black Wings attacking. Up!' Not pausing to knock, she entered the aft cabin. The Captain was already out of his bunk and pulling on breeches. Ren'erei unhooked his sword belt from its hook on the back of the door and threw it to him along with his leather jerkin.

'How many?'

'Maybe thirty,' said Ren'erei. 'Tryuun's topside. We haven't much time. They came out of the shadows by the fish market.'

'Get Erienne and get over the side. We'll hold them.'

Ren'erei hesitated.

'Go. She's all that's important.'

Ren'erei ran out. Two doors to the left was Erienne's cabin. She half-stifled a scream as Ren burst in, surprising her as she pulled a shirt over her head.

'Erienne it's me, it's all right.'

Her white face appeared out of the neck of the shirt, her movements to straighten it quick and nervous.

'What's going on?' she asked, her voice small. Ren'erei could see in her eyes she already knew.

'Black Wings attacking the ship. We have to get you off but I need you to remain calm,' she said though she could see it was already too late for that. Erienne was shaking at the very name and suddenly her fingers couldn't button the shirt at her neck.

'What, I—' she trailed off, staring at Ren, her eyes wide and confused, resembling nothing so much as an animal caught in a trap.

Ren'erei picked up her cloak. 'Come on. We have to leave now.'

'Hold on,' she said, her eyes flickering about her, wringing her hands then wiping them down her trousers. 'I need to—'

'Now!' snapped Ren'erei. She stepped forward and grabbed Erienne's arm. 'Be scared later. Now we have to go.'

'Don't let them touch me.'

'Not while I have a drop of blood in my body.' Ren half led, half pulled her into the corridor where the sound of pounding feet and shouted orders echoed through the ship.

Tryuun watched them coming as he rang the bell and shouted. There were well over the thirty he'd guessed when they had first appeared and they came well armed and carrying three long planks as well as grapples and ropes. There would be no time to set sail and cast off. This would go hand to hand. Inside, the fear churned his stomach and his ruined eye burned with remembered pain. But he couldn't let it show.

With the first crew dashing up from aft, he jumped down to the main deck.

'Go forward, make sure they heard,' he ordered the first elf before turning to the others. 'They have gangplanks, they'll have crossbows. We can hold them there, but I must have shields. And you—' he tagged another as he ran past '—bows. We must have bows now.'

The Black Wings ran on, breaking into two groups. The larger, carrying the planks and some with shields, came straight for the *Elm*. The second, smaller group detached and fell a few yards back, slowing.

'Crossbows!' yelled an elf standing on the wheel deck.

Tryuun looked to shore. So little time. He was disappointed by the sound drilling of the attack but had grudging respect for its organisation. He couldn't rely on any mistakes.

'Get those shields on deck!' he shouted. 'And where are my bows. Gods crying, let's move!'

'Ward!' Crossbow bolts flashed across the deck, most clearing the ship to splash into the water behind it, the odd one burying itself in deck or mast. They had been lucky this time.

Fore and aft, the doors slapped open and at last the whole of the *Elm*'s crew surged on to the deck. Bowmen ran to stations behind all three masts, seeking angles and cover while shields were brought up to the shore rail.

At a shout from the dock, the gangplank carriers moved forward, flanked by shield-bearing swordsmen. Another volley of bolts swept the deck, better focused with lower trajectory, four striking shields, another piercing the leg of a crewman. He dropped shrieking to the deck and was hauled away by two others.

One after the other, the planks were raised and dropped, two bouncing off the rail and sliding sideways, the third crashing right through and lodging fast between splintered struts.

'Get that rotten wood off my deck,' roared the skipper, barging his way to the rail. Elves stooped to shove the loose planks aside as the first elven arrows whipped in to the enemy, felling a crossbowman and two swordsmen. The Black Wings were already running up the third.

'Take them down!' ordered the captain. One plank was shoved off the side, the second was braced from the shore and the third was a disaster unfolding.

The Black Wings had nine crossbowmen standing. Their third volley hammered into the elves guarding the rail by the secure plank. Three went down clutching bolts in stomachs and legs, bones chipped, flesh punctured. Black Wing swordsmen poured up the gangplank, launching themselves into the shield cordon, their crossbowmen in two ranks releasing regular volleys at the crew of the *Elm*. It was a well-disciplined charge and even with the elven bows picking off the early runners, the Black Wings made the deck and the hand-to-hand fight commenced.

For Erienne, a blur of noise and shadowy figures, the smell of fear, and the excitement of action left her senses reeling. Her pulse was thumping in her neck, her throat felt full of bile and her mind full of visions of blood in a tower, of her murdered sons and of Selik's cruel smile. She shuddered and closed her eyes in a vain attempt to clear the memories.

Ren'erei went in front of her, shoving others aside as she pulled her on towards the deck. The shouts were louder but there was no ring of steel. Not yet. They burst into the chaotic spread of running feet, flailing limbs and the thrum of bow strings. A pool of blood was spreading across the deck.

Erienne let Ren'erei pull her right and they skirted the wheel deck, heading away from the fight to come and ran up a narrow gangway to the stern of the ship.

'Right,' she said, stopping and turning to her. 'Don't think about it, just get up on the rail and jump over the side. I'll be right behind you. The water's choppy but warm enough. We'll move along the *Elm* and into the next berth to another vessel. All right?'

Erienne looked at her, eyes completely uncomprehending. Below them, the water which rocked the ship was dark and menacing. She stared down into the blackness, seeing it move, writhing, waiting for her to leap into its clutches and suck her down.

She swallowed hard, fighting back a sweep of nausea. Her head swam.

'Isn't there a boat?' she asked, unable to grasp what she was being asked to do.

'No,' she said sharply. 'There isn't time. Come on, Erienne, please. We'll be fine. I won't let you go.'

The stern of the ship was high and, despite being below the wheel deck, the drop was still almost twenty feet. She could hear the water slapping against the hull and it sounded so distant. She could imagine only too well the cold as she hit its surface and the enveloping as she submerged. And then those hands, waiting to drag her down, to keep her kicking under the surface until her lungs exploded and she had to draw breath but take in only water. Then she would choke, try to gulp more, cough and scream but none would hear her and she would submit to the will of the sea, forever a prisoner of the depths.

'Erienne, what's wrong?' Ren'erei had grabbed her, spinning her shaking body around, the elf's strength surprising.

'I can't,' she managed, her breath ragged. 'I can't.'

From behind them, shouts rose and the unmistakable ring of swords clashing echoed into the night.

'You've got to,' urged Ren. 'If they take the ship, they'll take you. We cannot risk you.'

'But you'll throw me into the lake instead? No.' She turned away again and grabbed the rail, knuckles whitening.

'What are you scared of?' Ren'erei turned her around, gently this time. 'Please, Erienne. We must do this.'

'I won't be able to see what's beneath me,' she said, sure that Ren wouldn't understand her fear, would think it stupid. 'Please don't make me do this.'

The elf fell silent and Erienne could see her thinking hard. A frown creased her forehead and her eyes narrowed. She shook her head.

'I shouldn't do this but . . .'

Ren moved fast. Too fast for Erienne to react. The elf bent, picked her up just below the waist and levered her over the side.

The elven bows flexed again but the Black Wings were massing, ignoring their other planks to concentrate on the one that the crew could not shift. They had forced a wedge on the deck and the hand-to-hand fighting grew in intensity. The remaining crossbows fired, a bowman took a bolt clear through the chest, he fell, clutching at the metal, agonised cry unanswered by his friends who were fighting for their ship and their lives.

Tryuun took a blow comfortably on his shield and struck back, meeting solid defence. His opponent came again, punching forward with his shield and sweeping left to right with his blade. Tryuun swayed back, taking one reverse pace, easily evading the push. The enemy moved in but didn't strike again right away.

Tryuun looked left and right, the crew of the *Elm* was in a loose semi circle around the Black Wings, ten of whom had made the deck with more on the gangplank. A moment's confusion cleared. He knew what they wanted, and they didn't have enough elves to stop them.

Another volley of crossbow bolts and the last bowman fell. A shout rang up from the shore and the Black Wing swordsmen pressed forward but hardest of all to the right-hand side. Engaged in defence, Tryuun could do nothing as Black Wings smashed into the weakest part of their line. Pushing back his enemy, he winced as he watched a sword crash through the shoulder of an elf, blood fountaining into the sky, splattering the deck.

With the gap made, the Black Wings surged into the space, taking much of the deck while the rest of their number thundered up the gangplank and on to the ship. They would soon be surrounded. Tryuun called to the Captain and forged forward once again.

Ren'erei hurdled the rail immediately after, making barely a ripple as she landed in the water below. But Erienne hadn't fallen. Flailing her arms in panic, she'd caught the rail and hung over the stern of the ship, too scared to drop but unable to pull herself back on board the ship.

There was a roar from the other side of the wheel deck. Below her, Ren'erei called up, her voice, though soft, carrying easily.

'Come on, Erienne, we're losing the ship. You've got to do it now. There's nothing down here but water and safety.'

'I'm coming,' she said, aware her voice must sound feeble. Shutting out the images of the hell beneath the waves, the grasping hands and the world closing in as she drowned, she got ready to loosen her grip.

She felt the touch of steel on her neck and a strong hand gripping her arm.

'Let me save you,' drawled a voice that chilled her blood. 'In fact, I insist.'

She looked up, saw the face above her, and screamed.

Chapter 21

Darrick thundered into the Lysternan camp, shouting for Izack. The commander came running from the darkness. The General leapt from his horse.

'Izack, sound general alarm. I want this camp on horseback and ready to ride faster than you've ever done it before. Get a message to the Dordovans. Warn them away from the *Ocean Elm*. And if you can find our Dordovan mage guides, tell them they are no longer welcome to ride with us.'

'Sir?' Izack frowned.

'Later. We have to get to the *Elm*. There's going to be real trouble, I think.'

'Sir!' Izack turned and ran, Darrick watching him order a young soldier to the bell and snap out orders that had men running for the paddocks, had tent flaps flying and set the camp alive with the sounds of neighing and snorting horses, chinking metal and a rising tide of urgent shouts.

Darrick turned and ran for the paddocks for a fresh horse, one of hundreds of men for whom speed was everything.

The paddocks looked like chaos incarnate but Darrick knew different. All the horses were picketed according to precise instruction and every man could find his mount with the very minimum of fuss and delay. Closer to, Izack, who had somehow got there ahead of him, was bellowing orders.

'Mounted cavalry leave the paddock area and form up by squads at muster point one. One!' He held an arm aloft, fingers straight up, to indicate to those who couldn't hear him. 'Move Lystern, move!'

Darrick grinned. That would hurt the Dordovan mages, if they had heard it. The mages who shadowed them everywhere with a haughty air and who, he noted, were now conspicuous by their absence. If they had any remaining sense, they'd have left the camp already.

Dodging wheeling horses, the last saddles being hurriedly fixed and the flare of cloaks as riders swept up and over, Darrick ran on, his reserve mount held by his personal handler. The mare looked perfect in the torchlight, her coat shining, her head steady, bit and bridle polished. Like always. Nodding thanks, the General surged into the saddle, slipped his feet into the stirrups and kicked the horse on, vaulting the paddock fence and galloping to the muster point were he found Izack fretting.

'Not fast enough,' said the senior captain in whom Darrick had utter faith.

'Gods, Izack, I'm glad you don't command me. From a sleeping start, this has got to be some sort of record.'

'Doesn't change the fact we haven't the time to waste.'

Darrick watched his men streaming to the muster, the last already in sight. 'Bring them to order.'

'Listen up,' shouted Izack, both arms up and spread above his head. 'General speaking.' Instant hush fell on the riders.

'This is no charge across open ground to an enemy. Those of you who have ridden to battle with me in years past remember the thrill of the ride. This has to be different. We will be riding through tight streets, past the houses of innocents and there must be no injury to any of them.

'We will ride fast, but we will ride with care. We will keep weapons sheathed until we reach the dockside and the order to arm is issued.

'I don't know exactly what we will face on the docks but mind that those you thought of as allies may not be so. We ride to save a child from murderers. The innocent must survive. Lystern, ride on!'

With a roar, the cavalry kicked into action. They ate up the land to Arlen.

Hirad had turned north, leading the wolves away from the southern approaches to Arlen. This was no preordained plan. He'd wanted to be as near the docks as possible but what he had seen from a rise a couple of miles outside Arlen had shaken him.

Riding from a camp where fires still burned brightly and carrying lanterns and torches, hundreds of footmen and riders were streaming towards the small port. Dordovans, presumably. And to the west of them, running, indefatigable and closing very fast, a dark smudge issued across the wan moonlit countryside.

Silent, awesome, like a monstrous black blanket flowing through the lowlands, they came. They had no need of lanterns, they had no need of horses. Or rest. And when they arrived in Arlen all hell would break loose. The Protectors. Once set on their purpose, they would carry out their orders ruthlessly, putting down any that got in their way.

Hirad knew a man who might be able to stop them but didn't know where he was. Held somewhere. Perhaps with the Dordovans but he'd never get through there until it was too late. Heading a couple of miles to the north of Arlen, where more campfires burned, was the chance he'd have to take.

With Thraun and the pack trailing him, he rode into the periphery. The camp was all but deserted, with signs of a hasty exit in evidence. Tent flaps not secured, fires untended and dying down, weapon stands empty, some lying on their sides. He could see only two men, not so much guards as camp minders, standing by the central fire over which hung various steaming pots. Their spears were jammed into the ground and the duo warmed their hands over the flames as the wind whipped at their cloaks.

Knowing he couldn't hope to persuade Thraun to wait, he decided to ride straight in, trusting that the wolves wouldn't attack unless he did and knowing that the pack of five behind him was more likely to secure quick response.

The soldiers didn't see or hear him until very late, the wind stealing sound as it roared across the countryside, the harsh firelight making shadows heavy. When they did, their reactions were both comical and predictable, grabbing their spears but both moving back, open-mouthed at what they were seeing. They glanced at each other, weighing up what looked a hopeless situation, knowing they could not run nor hope to win a fight.

Hirad pulled up his horse and slid off, sensing rather than hearing Thraun move with him into the warmth of the fire. The soldiers said nothing, staring past him at the wolves.

'Impressive, aren't they?' he said, hand resting on his sword guard. 'But not dangerous. Not necessarily.'

'You want something?' ventured one.

'Good guess. The Raven. Where are they?'

Recognition flashed across both their faces, frowns deepening nevertheless.

'We were told you'd been killed,' said the second soldier, both of them young men. 'By wolves.' He gestured at Thraun.

'Whoever told you was wrong. Now, The Raven.'

'They were taken to Arlen. To the jail.'

Hirad nodded. The Raven jailed. An insult but one he had to admit he'd triggered. He swallowed rising anger.

'And Darrick? Come to that, all the cavalry? Assuming you're the Lysternans I think you are. This camp is too well pitched to be Dordovan.'

'There's trouble in Arlen.' They looked from one to another. Hirad understood. They were, after all, Darrick's men.

'Look, I know you have your orders but, no matter how it may seem, we all want the same thing in the end. Tell me. I'm not about to announce to the General where I got my information but it might just help me save a lot of your friends and I do not have the time to argue with you.'

There was a moment's hesitation before one shrugged and the other spoke.

'The cavalry have ridden to the docks. The General thinks there's been a betrayal. He's gone to secure the *Ocean Elm*.'

'And that's it?'

Both of them nodded but Hirad hardly waited to see. He turned and grabbed the reins of his horse, speaking as he swung into the saddle.

'Gods burning, but it's much worse than that. The Dordovans are coming in from the south and the Protectors are right behind them. If you can get a message to Darrick, do it. You know where I'm headed.' He kicked the horse's flanks. 'And thank you. Thraun, come on.' He pushed the horse to a gallop, the wolves following in his wake.

Ren'erei wanted to shout, wanted to let her know she'd seen and would do everything in her power to get her from Selik but knew she couldn't afford to. It would only cost her own freedom and perhaps her life.

The Black Wings had taken the *Elm* so quickly and Ren'erei cursed herself for Erienne's predicament. But she'd been so scared and it had seemed the only way. She listened to her cries as Selik dragged her back to the main deck and prayed Tryuun had survived to watch over her. Poor Tryuun, whose fear must be almost as great as Erienne's.

But Ren'erei had more pressing matters that demanded her attention. The water was cold and, whipped up by the fast strengthening wind, spray stung her face. Her leather was heavy on her body and her sword, though light and slung down her back for balance, merely added to her struggles to keep afloat as she trod water. She had to think fast, weighing up the two available options.

Though slightly overhung in the classic elven style, the stern of the *Ocean Elm* could be climbed if, like all the crew, you knew how. But what purpose that would serve was difficult to judge. She was hardly going to liberate the ship single-handed and, besides hiding herself and waiting for some vague opportunity, would otherwise only provide company for Erienne as just another prisoner.

So, Ren'erei struck out, away from the stern of the *Elm*, aiming to get to shore in the safe harbour occupied by the fishing fleet. At least there, she would be out of sight of the Black Wings and anyway, their plan was obvious. Erienne and the *Elm* were a means to reach their ultimate prize; Lyanna.

The question was, how much more did they know? Enough to take the *Elm* with such apparent ease was shocking enough but Ren'erei had to assume they had some knowledge of their destination, at least that it lay south. After all, the degeneration of the Al-Drechar's shield was the reason the *Elm* was here at all and a smart mage would be able to sense the interruptions in the mana flow.

Ren'erei swam a powerful front crawl, her economical strokes moving her smoothly through the choppy water. Ahead of her, the fishers' harbour loomed, a stone and wood structure that had provided placid waters for the relatively flimsy skiffs and smacks for as long as Arlen had been built. Even on the calm lake waters, the winds whipping round the mountains brought squalls and storms and, periodically, the fleet needed a place to hide.

She swam to the end of the man-made promontory and opted to swim to shore as opposed to walking along the shingle on the lee side of the harbour wall. This wind was no respecter of land conditions and its chill would cut her to the bone as soon as she emerged from the water. Indeed, it crossed her mind as she watched the pitching fishing vessels that many of their owners would be spending a sleepless night, praying to the Gods of the Seas that their boats were undamaged come dawn.

In the last fifty yards, Ren'erei's mind turned back to Erienne and the *Elm*. There was no way they would refuse passage to their captors; nor even delay them for too long – Lyanna's Night was upon her; and her and Balaia's fate lay in Erienne, Denser and Ilkar, at least, coming to Herendeneth quickly to provide support for the ailing and weakening Al-Drechar. But that same need for haste brought the Black Wings closer too, and their solution could not be allowed. The One had to survive.

But the Black Wings had a problem. They needed the elves to see them safely through the waters around Herendeneth and the elves wanted Erienne alive. That meant Selik wasn't going to be in total command, which gave them all a chance. So, the second option was the only one really open to Ren'erei. Find The Raven and take a ship to follow, if not beat, the *Ocean Elm* to Herendeneth. There, they would have to hope they had the strength to prevail.

But as she pulled herself ashore, shivering in the sudden cold of the windswept harbour side, Ren'erei heard elven orders barked across the echoing docks, heard the thundering of hooves coming closer with every heartbeat and saw moving lights approaching from the south-west. She ran north behind the fish market and towards Centenary Square, wondering if it wasn't all going to be taken out of her hands anyway. No matter, she had to try and that meant finding The Raven.

Erienne soon lost even the strength to scream and Selik had just stood, smiled his twisted smile and let her exhaust herself. Now, the fear, loathing and hopelessness swamped her, threatening to turn her legs boneless. There was a dreadful pain growing in her gut, a twisting agony of encroaching terror that blossomed and swept nausea through her whole body, leaving her shaking, tears streaming across her cheeks. Her throat was raw from the screams and she didn't resist as Selik pulled her back towards the unnatural quiet that had engulfed the *Elm*.

Selik walked ahead, strong arm on the neck of her shirt, fingers pushing at the skin of her throat, threat in every kneading movement. At the main deck, he thrust her forward into torchlight and the cheers of Black Wings soldiers. She stumbled but didn't fall, turning to take in everything she could.

Blood-spattered timbers, elves with heads bowed and under sword guard, bodies lying where they had fallen, some still moving and one nearby clutching at the base of a crossbow bolt buried high in his leg. His slim face was white and strained and his attempts to stop the steady bloodflow were watched dispassionately by the Black Wings. And there she stood, still unable to cast a spell to heal him because of the damage Lyanna had inflicted on her.

There were lights on other ships now as crews woke to the trouble in the docks and she hoped that they and those who must have heard in the town would come and help. It was pretty much all she had to cling on to. That and Ren'erei doing the right thing and not trying to get back on board without help.

Erienne dragged herself to face Selik, summoning up her last dregs of self-belief.

'You've got what you want. Now help these wounded before their deaths add to those already on your vile hands.'

Selik paced towards her, shaking his head. 'Tut, tut, Erienne. Hardly in a position to make demands, don't you think?'

'You want a crew to sail this ship, don't you?' Erienne could hear the words spilling from her mouth but didn't recognise the voice as hers. It quavered, with none of its usual confidence and strength. She could barely focus on Selik standing before her, his ruined face and laboured breathing testament to what she had done to him. Yet he lived, and the bile in her throat was all the more bitter that she hadn't killed him those years ago.

And in his eyes, she saw hate. Deep, brooding and cancerous hate. It came from him in waves. He had pursued her for more than six years, that much was now obvious; and safe in Dordover's College for much of that time she'd never given it a second thought. Why would she? Gods she'd *killed* him, surely? But there he stood, her nemesis, with complete power over her, and it was that which truly terrified her. Because it gave the Black Wings the ability to destroy her family and her life a second time, and the very thought set her heart lurching painfully in her chest. Because she could see no way to stop them. Stop him.

What choice did she have? He would never let her go now, and to refuse to show Selik the way would condemn Lyanna and perhaps Balaia to death, just as agreeing to do so would. She was trapped and the only option was to buy time while leading Lyanna's executioners directly to her. She swallowed hard, feeling close to collapse, her vision defocusing, threatening to unbalance her.

'Well?' she managed.

'I have no intention of letting them die, Erienne,' he said. He snapped his fingers at one of his men and waved him towards one of the stricken elves whose blood loss was surely critical. 'But far more efficient help, of a more, shall I say, mana-led nature, will soon be arriving.'

'What?' And it all crashed through Erienne's head once again. She was transported back to her time as a prisoner in Black Wings Castle. There she had as much as been told that traitor mages helped the Witch Hunters. She had felt sick at the thought then, now it just added to her overwhelming feeling of hopelessness.

Selik smiled, his slack mouth stretching unnaturally. 'Don't think of it as betrayal, lady mage, consider it help. After all, we all want an end to this mess which the uncontrolled magic of your daughter has placed us in.'

Erienne surged at him, fingers hooking to claw the skin from his hideous face, but he caught her easily.

'Don't you touch her,' she grated. 'Don't you lay a finger on her.'

'I? Erienne, you misunderstand me. I have no intention of touching a hair on her undoubtedly pretty head. Indeed no Black Wing will do so. Others know what is best for the mana creature you spawned and I am happy to leave it in their capable hands.' He pulled her very close, his fingers digging hard into her upper arms.

'Want to know why I'm still alive? Even after your spell froze my flesh? Your Raven friends dumped my body in the cellars to rot with my companions. They should have left me to burn in the tower, lying in the warm blood of your sons.'

At the mention of her boys, she hunched inwards, seeing their slaughter as if it were yesterday. Their sightless eyes, their torn throats and the red. The dark red that was everywhere.

'Well, I haven't finished with the Malanvai family just yet. There's one left I want. You. And now you are mine for as long as I choose to let you live. And when you are dead, I can live again without your cursed shadow over me. Think on it, Erienne Malanvai and savour your last days.'

He spun her around to face the ship. It was quiet and through her tear-fogged vision she could see every face staring at her. One thought thundered again and again through her mind. She was lost but Lyanna must survive.

'I pity you, Selik, still a lackey for others better than you,' she said through a choked throat. 'Because if you ever set foot where my daughter is living, the Al-Drechar will snuff you out as easily as you might squash a fly. Their power is like nothing you have even begun to conceive.'

Selik began pushing her towards the aft doors below.

'If that's what you believe. But my sources have seen the flares in the mana and say they are distressed in the extreme. And clearly, your precious Al-Drechar are not powerful enough to control your daughter. Still, I think it's time you and I had a private word about them.'

The aft doors were opened for them as he marched her over. She lifted her head and looked straight into the eyes of the Captain of the

Elm, whose humiliation was etched in his face. Behind him, a Black Wing held a sword to his throat. He pushed it aside.

'Harm her in any way and you will reach nowhere but the bottom of the Southern Ocean.'

'Don't presume to threaten me, elf. You are beaten.' Selik didn't stop moving.

'It's not a threat. Without us, you can't navigate your way and you know it. And if Erienne is harmed, we will die before taking you a league further. That is a promise.'

Now Selik stopped, thrusting Erienne towards a Black Wing. 'Take her below. Her own cabin if it's down there. Now you, elf. With you, I'll make this bargain. While that bitch is on this ship, no physical harm will come to her. But if you dare to speak to me like that again, I will bleed you in front of all your crew before feeding you to the sharks. And by my reckoning there'll still be enough of you left to sail. Understand?'

Erienne's last view was of Selik pushing the Captain in the chest, a contemptuous gesture for the proud elf that set her gorge rising. As she was ushered below, she heard his voice again.

'Now, ready your crew and this ship to sail on my order. When our guests arrive we will be leaving immediately. Ornouth is a long way, isn't it, Captain, and I do so hate delay.'

Erienne burst into tears. He knew so much but how did he know? And which College was it that would betray her? Entering her cabin to await Selik, she feared she already knew the answers.

Chapter 22

The Unknown sat with his face in his hands, trying not to believe what he was feeling. There was a closeness in his skull, a pressure he hadn't felt for years. He'd known they were marching before The Raven had been caught in the forest by Darrick but he hadn't dreamed they could make Arlen so fast. However, the Protectors should never be underestimated.

He snapped his head up. Ilkar was watching him.

'You all right, Unknown?'

'They're here,' he replied, rising.

'Who?' asked Denser from the opposite corner of the cell, only just visible in the light of the single guttering torch. He had been quiet since his admission, and their incarceration had gone on for hours now. Night was full and it seemed to The Unknown that he'd lost the will to act. It was as if he was beaten.

'The Protectors.' The Unknown strode over to the door and hammered on it with the heel of his palm. 'Hey. Get over here.' He continued the hammering until a middle-aged and scowling face appeared at the grille.

'Do you have to?' It was the night-watch jailer, a man who refused to give his name but was affable enough, given his prisoners' identity, and irritated by the intrusion of the Lysternan soldiers and mage seated just outside in the guardroom.

'Yes. Get me one of the others.'

'Not good enough for you, am I?'

'No, it's just not your problem. Or it shouldn't be. So, please . . .'

'Well, what is it? After all, I am in charge here.'

The Unknown grabbed one of the bars on the grille, the jailer flinching.

'There's going to be trouble in the town. Very soon.'

'Some sort of clairvoyant are you?'

'Some sort,' agreed The Unknown shortly. 'Look, I don't have time to debate this. Just get me one of the others.'

'Not going to try anything funny are you?' The jailer sucked his lip.

The Unknown snapped. 'Yes, I'm going to tell a few jokes. Gods, man, just get me a Lysternan. Now!' Another slap on the door which echoed through the jail.

The jailer backed off. 'I'm only doing this because you shouldn't be in here.'

'Thank you.' The Unknown watched him go. He felt a hand on his shoulder.

'Feeling better now?' asked Ilkar.

The Unknown turned his head, fighting down the smile that Ilkar's expression had prompted.

'This is serious. Darrick didn't believe what I said. I think he thinks he can talk to Xetesk, take on the Protectors if he has to, or take Erienne before they get here. But the fact we're still stuck in this stinking hole means he hasn't persuaded Arlen to let him board the ship yet. And now the Protectors are close.'

'How close?' asked Denser.

'I'm not sure,' said The Unknown. 'But near the town. They're in battle psyche, that's why I could sense them. It's loud.'

'Perhaps we should let them to do their job,' said Denser. 'Erienne'll be safer with them.'

'And never mind Lysternan casualties?' asked Ilkar. 'They're as much victims of Dordovan manipulation as we are. And that's not to mention innocents in Arlen.'

'Lystern has sided with Dordover,' replied Denser, his voice still coming out of the shadows.

'And what sort of choice do you really think they were given?' said Ilkar.

'We can't just sit here and let Darrick blunder into them,' said The Unknown. 'Well, I can't. You do what you like, Denser.'

'It'll be the best way to sort this out, I'm sure,' muttered the Xeteskian. 'The quickest way for me to get back to my wife.'

The Unknown ignored him and swung back to the door ready to shout but instead finding the mage standing there. He was a young man, a great talent according to Darrick. Tall, muscular and fit, as would be expected of one of the General's cavalrymen. Right now, he was looking more than a little scared.

'Been standing there long?' asked The Unknown.

'Long enough, I think. What will the General be blundering into again?'

'The Protectors,' said The Unknown. 'And you need to let us out right now.'

'Because you'll do what?'

'Perhaps stop a slaughter.' The Unknown watched the mage fail to take it in, and felt his temper fraying. 'Oh, not you too. Look, the Protectors are after Erienne as well, and they aren't going to be talked out of it by Darrick. And despite his admirable confidence and the equally admirable discipline of his cavalry, they will be massacred. Believe me.'

'We are already taking steps. The General is on his way to the docks now and our Dordovan allies are also on their way.'

'So he knows the Protectors' arrival is imminent, does he?'

The mage tried to smile. 'No, but we'll be fully in position by the time they arrive and ready to talk to their masters. We'll have retaken the ship and—' The mage stopped, biting his lip, but the slip had been made and he found himself immediately confronted by all three imprisoned Raven, The Unknown at their centre.

'What do you mean, "retaken"?' demanded Denser, his eyes full of fire once again. 'Who has the ship at the moment?'

'It's a temporary situation,' said the mage.

'Who?' The Unknown kicked the base of the door which shuddered ominously.

'We think . . .' The mage paused, weighing up the admission in his mind. 'A small force of Black Wings have—'

The Unknown silenced him with a look and waved a finger. Beside him, Ilkar swore.

'I bloody knew it,' said Denser. 'I bloody knew it.'

'Let us out. Right now,' said The Unknown, his voice dreadfully calm, belying the growing rage he felt inside. There, all was turmoil and in his head flashed visions of a three-way fight for the *Elm* which could only end one way; and he did not want Erienne's blood slicking Arlen Bay.

'Those bastards, those bastards.' Denser had walked away from the door and was pacing a tight circle. 'Oh dear Gods, they've got her again.'

The words went straight through The Unknown and his heart went out to Erienne, almost certainly in the hands of her worst nightmare for the second time.

'Please, Unknown.' Denser's voice behind him was little more than a desperate gasp, all its earlier vitriol gone. 'You have to get us out of here.'

The Unknown still held the dithering mage's gaze.

'Now you listen to me very carefully. On two counts now. Darrick doesn't know what he's dealing with and we do. The Black Wings won't let him just storm the ship. They'll kill Erienne before giving her up. Believe me, we've seen their handiwork before and it was Erienne's sons that were the victims.

'This is too big for him, and it's too big for you. So let us out, give me a blade and we can prevent this getting completely out of hand.'

'I can't do that,' said the mage. 'The General was very specific.'

'Damn his bloody specifics!' shouted The Unknown, fists pounding the timbers of the door with each word. 'They'll be the death of him. And you if you don't let us go.'

'I can't,' he said, his tone all but beseeching.

'Then we'll do it without you,' said The Unknown. 'This folly has gone on long enough.'

'We have orders to kill you if you attempt to break out.'

'Try it. Now get lost or unlock this door.' The Unknown turned away and beckoned Denser and Ilkar to him. But his words were lost as a howl split the air, followed by a cry and the clash of swords.

'Gods falling, what's that?' Denser said, startled from his misery.

The Unknown smiled. 'Be ready.'

'For what?' asked Ilkar.

'Just be ready.'

Hirad knew exactly where Arlen's jail was situated. He'd spent a night there years ago after a brawl in an inn off Centenary Square. He'd won the fight but the cell bed and stench hadn't been worth the bruising.

It was gone midnight when he galloped into the town past a guard who'd begun to protest before seeing the wolves trailing in his wake and leaping aside, yelling to his companions to get word to Arlen.

'You're already too late,' said Hirad to himself, his horse thundering past the Merchant Quarter on the way to the Salt Quarter. The streets were quiet; only the inebriates who'd left Centenary Square after closing were shambling around as he reined in at the jail house.

It was a squat stone building set between warehouses and, he knew, with cells overlooking a walled courtyard that doubled as paddock and exercise area for any longer-term prisoners of the two small cells.

There were three horses tethered outside, all pulling desperately at their reins, whinnies echoing, hooves clattering as they tried to escape the wolves suddenly coming at them.

Hirad didn't have time.

'Thraun!' he roared, jumping from his saddle and drawing his sword. It felt good in his hands. The wolf seemed to understand, howling to deflect the pack from their feast. They bunched around him, all eyes on the human.

'Time for some fun,' said the barbarian, striding to the door which opened as he approached. A guard appeared in the light that washed over the dirty cobblestones.

'One chance,' said Hirad. 'I need The Raven now.'

'I can't,' said the guard, raising his blade.

'As you wish.' Hirad swept his sword up and right as he ran forward, meeting a sturdy block in a shower of sparks. The guard fell back, a seasoned soldier by the looks.

'You don't have to die. Just give me The Raven.' Hirad backed up half a pace. 'We're on the same side.'

'I don't think so.' The man lunged forwards, Hirad ready to block. But Thraun leaped, bearing the man down, his head smacking off the stone, one of the wolf's paws thrashing at his neck.

Hirad breathed in deep and ran inside, confronting another three in the process of gathering weapons. Outside, the guard's screams had turned to pitiful gurgles.

'One down, let's not make it more.' Hirad heard the pad of paws behind him as Thraun and his pack came through the door. 'I can't control them if you attack.'

Another man ran round the corner.

'They're really . . .' His words died in his throat at the scene in the guard room.

'Angry?' suggested the barbarian, switching his sword between his hands. 'A bit like me unless you let my friends out of that cell right now.'

'I—' began the man but his gaze misted over. 'They're casting.'

Hirad dropped his blade and snatched a dagger from his belt, running across to the mage and grabbing him around the neck, metal point at his throat.

'I rather hoped they would,' he said. 'Door's going down is my guess. Let's not interfere, eh?'

The dagger point drew a bead of blood. Across the room, the remaining guards stood stock still, gazes shifting from Hirad to the wolves, scared by what they were seeing but not quite believing it.

The mage moved his hands, a minute gesture. It was enough. Hirad pressed the blade a little deeper.

'Don't. You aren't quick enough to beat me.'

Thraun growled deep in his throat. Hirad looked round. The pack were unsure. In front of them, three men held swords ready but made no move.

'Wait, Thraun,' said Hirad, with no idea if the big wolf understood him. If not, there'd be more blood.

From the cells came an unmistakable voice and the sound of splintering wood. A few heartbeats later, The Unknown appeared in the guard room, registering no surprise on taking in Hirad and the pack.

'Glad you stopped by,' he said.

Hirad nodded. 'All right. Drop your weapons. We need them.' He didn't let up pressure on the mage's neck.

There was hesitation. The Unknown hissed in breath and stepped smartly across, hooking a fist into the chin of the nearest guard. The blow took him completely unawares, sending him crashing into the other two, his sword clattering to the floor. The Unknown stopped, grabbed the blade and held it ready.

'Drop them now,' he growled. The other blades dropped. The Unknown moved forward and the two guards, one Lysternan and the jailer, backed off. Denser and Ilkar moved into the space and took the swords.

'Sorry,' said Hirad to the mage.

'Don't be,' he replied. 'I know the General was uncomfortable with all this.'

'Not for that, for this.'

He spun the mage to face him, reversed the dagger and snapped the end of the hilt into the mage's temple. The man crumpled.

'Can't have you casting, can we?' he said, cushioning the stunned body to the ground. He turned his attention to the guards. 'And you. I'm sorry for your friend outside but take it as a warning. Don't follow us.'

He took The Raven in; Denser looking at him as if seeing a ghost, Ilkar who couldn't suppress a smile and The Unknown carefully neutral. All three shifted gaze to the wolves and back.

'Yes, it's Thraun. Later, all right? We've got work to do.' He smiled. 'Raven! Raven with me!'

He led the run to the dockside.

*

Lights were on all over Arlen when the Earl was disturbed by a frantic knocking on his door. He had posted guards at the docks following General Darrick's rather dramatic departure but, as he had expected, had heard nothing.

'Yes, yes, dammit.' He heaved himself from his chair. His guard captain half-ran in, his face severe in the glow of the fire. 'What is it?'

'The Black Wings have stormed the *Ocean Elm*, the Lysternans have just ridden down a guard post and the Dordovans are riding too. Our dock's going to be a battleground.'

'Not while I'm Earl,' said Arlen. 'You know what to do. Block every exit into the town. Seal off the docks and get my bloody dresser out of his bed and down to the armoury.'

'Already done, my Lord.'

Arlen's grin was mirthless. 'Then I'll be joining you all the sooner.'

The guard captain ran out, his footsteps clattering on the marbled floor. Arlen walked to a window and pulled the drapes aside. He could see nothing at the dockside but the lights everywhere told him his town was awake and not just the nightly revellers in Centenary Square.

'Damn this magic,' he muttered. 'Damn it all the way to hell.'

Darrick rode at the head of the muted charge, already feeling guilty about the Arlen guards he'd injured or killed while riding through the northern approach to the town. The cavalry clattered across the market square, scattering drunks and late-night walkers back into the bars and inns where music sounded and light still burned brightly. They galloped dead south past shipping offices and the Lakehome Inn before turning hard right for the *Elm*'s berth.

Every ship in the docks was ablaze with light, the *Elm* no exception. Darrick could see elves on the rigging and heard orders drifting on the wind. The first spots of rain were beginning to fall. It promised to be a very unpleasant night.

He reined in at the *Elm*, the cavalry filling the dockside behind him.

'*Ocean Elm*!' he shouted. 'I would speak with your Captain.'

All action on the ship had ceased at the arrival of the cavalry, only for a barked order sending the elves scurrying again. A man moved to the port rail and leaned on it.

'General Darrick, what a pleasant surprise.'

'Who are you?' demanded Darrick.

'An ally,' came the reply. 'I'm afraid the ship's Captain is rather busy at the moment but I'm actually in charge. I am Selik, Captain of the Black Wings.'

'Then you are no ally,' spat Darrick.

'I think your Dordovan friends might disagree with you, General.'

'I have no Dordovan friends,' said Darrick. 'And neither do you.'

'I beg to differ,' said Selik, shrugging. 'But it's immaterial. You can ask them yourself shortly. Can I help you in any other way?'

Darrick paused a moment, aware that every ear was listening and, like him, none believed what they were hearing. He wished he hadn't left without the Dordovan mages. At least they could have been questioned. The scum on the deck of the *Elm*, though, was not going to give any straight answers.

'I require you to deliver Erienne Malanvai to me immediately. I then demand that you leave this ship before there is more bloodshed. I have over two hundred cavalry and thirty mages. We will take the ship if we have to.'

'And as you so accurately point out, I have Erienne Malanvai. Your next move could result in unwanted death,' said Selik. 'I suggest you don't make it.'

'You won't kill her,' said Darrick. 'She's your only card.'

'Attack me if that's what you believe,' replied Selik. 'Quite a risk, though, I'd say.'

Darrick turned to Izack. 'Deploy the cavalry. Mounted. No one gets near this ship. If it attempts to leave, burn the sails.' He looked back to Selik.

'You are unwelcome, Selik. And you will never make open waters. Be mindful before you raise sail.'

'Your warning is obviously appreciated,' said Selik. 'But I feel it to be a waste of your breath.' The man turned from the rail.

Darrick dismounted and led his horse towards the Lakehome Inn to watch and think. Izack marshalled the cavalry, and in short order, the entire column formed a semi-circle, four deep, interspersed with mages. Shields were cast and the offensive mage force sat at the centre of the formation, spells prepared, waiting.

Already to the east, he could hear hooves on stone and he wondered whether Selik would not be proved right. Reluctantly, he remounted and trotted his horse to the western end of the Lysternan formation. Snapping his fingers, he waved over an elven cavalryman.

'What can you see?'

'Several hundred riders in Dordovan colours. Our escort mages are among them, riding close to the head of the column.'

'Really.' Darrick's jaw set. He held up an arm. Hush fell in the ranks.

'Guard. These are not necessarily friendly faces. Look to me. Look to Commander Izack. Once again, guard.'

His voice carried clear to the *Ocean Elm* too. He studied the ship. Somewhere on board, Erienne was captive. The elves moved about, seemingly unhindered, but the Black Wings watched their every move. This would have to be played out with great care. He could still scarcely believe there was a link between the Dordovans and the Witch Hunters but the evidence was growing. Selik had to be buying time, readying for sail. If he got clear, the problems would mount.

'How far?' he asked, not turning his head. He could see the torches but the distance was hard to judge.

'They'll be here imminently. A three-wide column. Not tight. You wouldn't have been happy, sir.'

Darrick looked across to the elf. 'I'm sure I wouldn't.'

'That's not a compliment, sir, merely the way it is,' said the elf, suddenly nervous. 'It may point to a lack of discipline in the column.'

'Point taken. Let's wait and see, eh?'

'Yes sir.'

The Dordovan mounted force emerged from the shadows, sweeping around the fish market. Darrick could see what the elf meant.

'Remind Izack of your name,' said the General. 'I'll be asking for it later.'

'Yes sir.'

Seeing the Lysternan defence, the Dordovan cavalry reined in. At their head was a man Darrick didn't recognise. He was a mage, not a soldier.

'General Darrick,' said the mage, his tone not matching his smile.

'For the second time tonight, I am at a loss. I would have your name.'

'Gorstan,' replied the mage. 'Aide to Vuldaroq, Tower Lord.'

'I have the ship under guard,' said Darrick. 'Odd that you've been here this long and not seen the Black Wing threat. I would have expected you at the dockside sooner.'

Gorstan's smile was feeble. 'There is no threat, General Darrick. A meeting of minds, if not ethics. Call it an alliance of temporary convenience and necessity.'

There it was. Darrick sat stunned in the saddle, his hopes that Arlen had been mistaken lying in tatters; and behind him, even his disciplined cavalry whispered and moved in their saddles. He held up a hand to silence them. He could take the Dordovans, but in their wake the Protectors were coming, and Xetesk wanted the child too. He couldn't afford the bloodshed among his own men, nor the confusion.

And in the jail languished the men he knew he should have listened to all along. You could trust The Raven like you couldn't College hierarchy and men were about to pay with their lives for his lack of faith in his old friends.

Darrick flicked the reins of his horse and walked it forward, signalling for Gorstan to do the same. The two met in the ten yards of space between the cavalry forces. Darrick kept his voice deliberately low.

'Tell me you haven't sanctioned the Black Wing action.'

'Each to their own strengths, General. The Black Wings said they were adept at ship-taking and it appears they were right. No Dordovans were harmed and we have Erienne.'

'You have delivered one of your own to the Witch Hunters. It makes you no better than them.' Darrick squeezed the reins he held, determined not to move a hand in angry gesture, a sign he considered weak in front of his cavalry.

Gorstan shifted a little in his saddle.

'General, there are times when we must ally with the devils amongst us to obstruct a greater ill. We are facing such today and Balaia will thank us for our actions.'

'Erienne is a Dordovan,' spat Darrick.

'She is a maverick who made her choice when she deserted the College and damned us all,' said Gorstan. 'Are you blind to that?'

'No, I am not, but neither do I think that she, of all people, should be exposed to the Black Wings.'

'Your compassion will be your undoing,' said Gorstan.

'And your unholy alliance will be yours.'

Gorstan paused. 'I take it you are still in support of the accord between the elders of our respective Colleges.'

The pulse beat hard in Darrick's neck. Every moment of his training bade him simply to nod his head and ignore the consequences, foisting all blame and guilt on those who gave the orders. It was the way of the career soldier. Normally.

'They kill what they do not understand,' said Darrick.

Gorstan shrugged. 'Sometimes, it is the only way.'

Darrick could almost see Vuldaroq's fat face nodding his agreement. Even alliance with Xetesk seemed a preferable plan to what he was presented with now. He drew a long breath, acutely aware of the effect of his next utterance.

'I cannot and will not speak for those under my charge but no, I do not offer my support. Neither do I offer my blessing or my belief in the outcome justifying the means. Your actions sicken me to the pit of my stomach and I have nothing but contempt for Dordover and for any in Lystern who were party to this abomination.'

Gorstan merely smiled. 'I do believe that is treason, General Darrick.'

'So be it.'

'Vuldaroq said you were trouble.'

'I think the term you're looking for is honourable. A quality apparently in very short supply.'

'I—'

'Be quiet, Dordovan. I am tired of your bleating. I will now announce my intentions to my cavalry. They will act on their own wills. You and I will have no further contact. Indeed, if we meet again, your life is forfeit.'

'Honour.' Gorstan chuckled. 'You would see Balaia fall for it. Fool. Why do you think Lystern is so weak?'

Darrick burned to say something more, to drag the mage from his horse and punch him until his sneers were bubbles of blood and bile in a toothless mouth. But he knew he couldn't.

'Like I said, no further contact.' He wheeled his mount and walked it back to his men.

Chapter 23

Aeb strode easily at the side of the mounted lead mage, Sytkan. The Protectors were resting after running through the day and into the night, after word from Arlen of the Black Wings' expulsion earlier in the day. The suspicion had been that trouble would flare later, probably under the cover of darkness, and the Protectors, at the time still more than thirty miles from the town over rough terrain, had been forced to make up a lot of time. There had been no further Communion.

A couple of miles outside the town, they had picked up the Dordovans; foot-soldiers trailing their horse-borne comrades by half a mile and steadily losing ground. Forward scouts reported a force of two hundred foot plus one hundred and fifty cavalry and mounted mages in all. The foot-soldiers were undefended.

Sytkan had immediately called for rest pace but had requested that Aeb order battle psyche, priming the Protectors for the potential fight.

There was a decision to be made. Aeb understood there were political considerations but did not respect the reluctance to order battle. Dordover had announced its intentions days before on the borders of the Xeteskian mage lands. The foot-soldiers were a threat to the success of the overall mission. Protectors were bred to remove threat.

'Opinion, Aeb,' said Sytkan.

'Engagement outside Arlen is more efficient,' said Aeb. 'There is more room for deployment, a reduction in the capacity of the enemy to flee effectively and minimal risk to innocents.'

'You can surround them?'

'Yes, my mage.' Aeb betrayed no reaction though the tactic was clearly the most obvious to employ. It would make the battle swift. They outnumbered the enemy by almost three to two.

'But can we justify the attack?' asked Sytkan. 'Opinion, Aeb?'

'They are Dordovans moving to join their cavalry. They pose a greater threat if they do so. Here they are weak.'

'That is not justification,' said the mage.

'They are the enemy,' said Aeb.

'Yes, they are.'

Aeb waited for the order. Behind him were the vanguard, now separated by less than a hundred yards from thirty more mounted mages and three hundred and fourteen Protectors. It had to come soon. Flanking the Dordovans would take a little time and the lights of the town were now plainly visible.

'Will you need magical assistance?' asked Sytkan.

'Unnecessary. Containment is easier with weapons alone.'

'You think they'll scatter under magical assault?'

'We would,' affirmed Aeb.

'Attack at will.'

'Yes, my mage.' Aeb didn't break his stride as he issued the orders.

Flanking attack. First centile right, second centile left, third centile form crescent for rear attack. Encirclement desired, balance to protect our Given. Silent running. Execute.

Aeb broke into a run, leaving the remainder of the vanguard plus designated brothers to guard the mages. Soon, he was joined by three brothers, the first centile tracking right away from the path, their pace even and matched by those to the left. The crescent following would form a little further along the track, lining three deep and closing with the rear of the flanking columns.

The ground was flat and open and despite the dark, the noise the Dordovans would be creating and the relative silence of the Protectors, Aeb only expected to overhaul a third of the enemy column before being seen. It would be enough.

The Protectors ate up the ground, Aeb's centile on a slight rise to the path, those of the left on a down slope. Weapons were strapped across their backs on snap fastenings and made little sound as they sped along the trail. Aeb could already see the figures of the Dordovans ahead, their torches bouncing as they moved, their formation tight, five broad, and their pace quick. But they were not expecting trouble behind them. The forward Protector scouts had reported no dropped tail guard for the marchers and no vanguard ahead. Both fatal mistakes.

Slowing, front of first and second centiles approaching the tail, pulsed Aeb. *Prepare the sweep on my word.*

He could hear the enemy now. Chatter in the ranks, not a Xeteskian failing. But these men believed they were already victorious and their discipline was the worse for it.

Running in deep gloom perhaps forty yards from the enemy, Aeb bade the brothers scan them for signs they had seen the attack coming in. As it was, a quarter of the way up the column an elven voice rose in alarm.

'Left flank, left flank. I've got runners at thirty-plus yards. Check right.'

A voice answered almost immediately.

'Runners right flank.'

Even as the Dordovan column slowed and the night came alive with the sound of swords whipping from scabbards, Aeb pulsed the command to break. The flanking centiles sprinted forwards, angling in towards the front of the column.

The Protectors were silent, snapping axes and blades from their backs as they came, and Aeb heard their name taken up throughout the enemy ranks and could see the fear in their faces.

Archers.

Bowmen sent a flight of arrows skywards. They were too few and too inaccurate to cause problems and only one found a home in the arm of a brother. He discarded his axe, another closed up to protect his injured side, and he pulsed that he would continue.

Centile rear, close. We meet the left. Attack spread, double rank.

Aeb curved around, seeing the brothers from the left centile cruising in to close the trap. Like a wave breaking at angles to the shore, the Protectors' flank lines formed and attacked the Dordovans, Aeb straightening his run and smashing into the bemused enemy's front, their panic already spreading.

First pace in, Aeb chopped his axe left to right across the body of his opponent, feeling the blade bite flesh as it beat the guard which had been placed to anticipate an overhead. Beside him, Xye blocked a blow on his axe and drove his blade through, straight and waist-high, stabbing it clear through the enemy's body, making light of the chain-and-leather armour.

In front of Aeb, the enemy still stood and somehow struck out in an upward arc. Aeb swayed back and flat-bladed his axe into the man's face before driving his sword up between the victim's legs, splitting his groin and showering blood five feet in every direction.

Rear centile engaged. Back line breached.

Upper right block axe, Xye. Control, sword low, strike forward.

Xye complied. A man died.

Aeb felt the calm detachment of imminent victory. Pulsing commands left and right, he brought the Protectors in, allowing any wounded, and there were precious few, to fall back as the ring tightened. Seeing they were trapped, the Dordovan voices rose further, their blows came in harder and wilder, and their defensive formation buckled and heaved. Although noise flowed around and over Aeb, he concentrated on the pulsed messages in his mind, leaving the desperation to those he faced.

He buried his axe in the neck of a Dordovan, the man grasping at the weapon as he fell. Aeb let it go, retaining his balance and blocking high with his blade as directed by the brother behind him. He turned his attention on the astonished enemy, smashed a fist into his mouth and nose, knocking him back before reversing his blade across his chest.

The sword screamed against chain mail ringlets, sending sparks flying and knocking the wind out of the man. He was in no state to defend the next strike which tore out his throat, spattering gore on Aeb's mask. He shook his head to clear the drips over his eye slits.

No one lives. No one goes home, he pulsed.

We will be victorious. We are one.

The Protectors drove on, their weapons flashing dully under the clouded sky as their enemy's torches sputtered to extinction on the muddy ground. The screams of the hapless Dordovans diminished as they fell. One threw down his weapon in a gesture of surrender. Xye beheaded him in the next heartbeat.

And so it was over. Aeb's final Dordovan took a blow through his gut and he and half a dozen comrades breathed their last.

We are one.

We are victorious.

Report, pulsed Aeb.

Three Protectors were down. Twenty-one had cuts, of which twelve would not fight again that night. Aeb felt a surge of annoyance. Somewhere, their discipline had failed them.

No, pulsed Xye. *The cornered fight like two men. Desperation breeds strength in the dying.*

Then we assumed too much. Learn, brothers, learn.

We are one.

Aeb retrieved his axe and cleaned the blades of both his weapons on the clothes of the fallen, before handing them to Xye to replace in their back mounts, a favour he reciprocated. Stooping and tearing a length of cleaner cloth from a Dordovan shirt, he wiped over his mask and shoulders, turning to greet the approaching Sytkan.

'I would say congratulations but it seems a heartless statement in the face of such slaughter.'

'We are victorious,' said Aeb.

'So I can see,' said Sytkan, surveying the carnage with obvious disgust. 'Surely they tried to surrender at some stage. Report.'

'Prisoners are a threat,' said Aeb.

'And that's it?'

'We have no capacity to hold prisoners,' said Aeb.

The mage sighed. 'No, I suppose not. Retrieve any masks and have any wounded report to a mage. Leave any that can't run and form up. The battle is not over. Problems?'

'None. We will return this way?'

'Of course. Let's go, Aeb.'

The Protector chosen issued the orders and soon the army ran on into Arlen.

Darrick turned his mount and faced his cavalry, aware that whatever he said would carry to Selik too. It couldn't be helped. His men stood expectant, quiet, their horses calm, flanks steaming in the pale light of the lanterns and torches on ship and in hand. Earl Arlen would doubtless be here before long but it wasn't him Darrick feared. It was the Protectors. He hadn't let it show but The Unknown's words had struck home. He didn't want to be seen as a coward. He nodded to Izack.

'General speaking!' shouted the commander. The silence became deeper. Darrick saw Selik saunter back on to the deck of the *Ocean Elm*.

'I am surprised, disappointed and disgusted to confirm that the Dordovans behind me are in full support of the Black Wings on the ship to my right.' He paused as a ripple ran through the company. He held up a hand and continued.

'As you are aware, our Council has agreed to support the Dordovan Council in its efforts to secure the child and return her to safe keeping. But clearly the desire has changed and instead the Dordovans have willingly delivered the child's mother, a Dordovan herself, into the hands of the Witch Hunters.

'We are not, therefore, being invited to retake the ship, and indeed our task has become one of defence of the vessel and its current incumbents.' Another pause but this time there was no sound. Izack would know what was coming. For many of the rest it was a hammer blow.

'I cannot speak for any of you on this because it is for the individual consciences of you all. You know what is happening to Balaia; the elements batter us and it is magic that drives them. We all accept that this must stop but the method is apparently not so clear.

'Here you face Dordover. Nominally our ally. Approaching are the Protectors, and Xetesk too has designs that we are, again nominally, opposed to.

'I say again, look to your morals and your consciences, think of your families and all that is important to you before deciding your actions. For myself, I cannot and will not countenance or support the scum aboard that vessel. I therefore resign my commission, my Generalship and my command of this cavalry and withdraw my support for the actions of the Lystenan and Dordovan Colleges. This makes me a traitor. Any of you that would arrest me now, I will make no protest. If not, I take my own path. Izack, you're in charge.'

Darrick put his heels to his horse and rode from the growing tumult, the tears already rolling down his cheeks.

'You up to this, Unknown?' asked Hirad as they ran for the dockside.

'What?' The Unknown frowned.

'You know, dodgy sword, no armour. Hope you're feeling quick.'

'I'll get by. Just you mind your new pets.'

Hirad smiled. The wolves loped easily along beside him, while The Unknown ran the other side, with the two mages a pair behind them. The Raven could see the dock ahead as they came alongside the timber yard.

'I'll let Thraun know you called him that.'

'Fluent in wolfish, are you?' The Unknown grimaced suddenly and put a hand to his head. 'Gods, it's started.'

'Protectors?'

'Like echoes of war in my head. They're fighting,' affirmed The Unknown.

'Must be outside the town or we'd be hearing it. Go right at the dockside,' said Hirad.

The Unknown nodded and led The Raven around the corner. The wind was harsh and cold off the lake and the rain, which had begun falling as little more than a blown mist, was now heavy and well set. The Unknown had to be cold but he didn't show it. Hirad was feeling the chill across his face and wasn't looking forward to the sweat freezing on his body when they stopped. If they stopped.

No, when they stopped. In front of them was a mass of cavalry no further than a hundred yards distant. They were fanned out in front of what had to be the *Ocean Elm* and beyond them, dozens more torches flickering in the downpour indicated another force they couldn't really make out.

'That's Darrick's lot in front of us,' said The Unknown as they dived into shadow in the lee of the timber yard as much for shelter as obscurement.

'Is he *defending* that ship?' asked Hirad, peering out.

'Either that or stopping anyone else getting on,' said Ilkar. 'I can see him. He's addressing his men and judging by their reactions, they're not liking what they're hearing.'

Hirad watched Thraun and the pack. Initially, they'd run on but turned as The Raven stopped and now Thraun was padding in a loose circle around the pack, all of whom were on their feet, eyes fixed on the mass of horseflesh ahead of them.

'So what now? The wolves are getting edgy.'

'I can't understand why you brought them, Hirad,' said Denser.

'Tell you what, Xetesk-man, *you* tell them not to come and see how far you get.'

'Quiet, you two,' said The Unknown. 'Save your bickering for later. We have to get to Darrick and warn him what's coming in. Let the Dordovans take the hit as I suspect they already have outside the town. Trouble is, I think that's Dordovan cavalry behind him and I think they'll be even less pleased to see us.'

'Never mind that,' said Denser. 'Erienne's on that ship and we need to get her off it.'

'Hence speak to the man whose cavalry is standing all around it.'

'Bugger that, Unknown,' snapped Denser. 'We don't need muscle on that scale, we need this.' He tapped the side of his head. 'Some well-positioned spells to panic them, Ilkar and I fly in, grab her and get out under smoke and night.'

The Unknown turned and looked Denser square in the face. 'That's why I make the plans. You're talking suicide. Do you really think the Black Wings aren't expecting something? Gods, there are probably sixty mages on the dock not counting you two. You don't know where she's being held or anything about their strength. We can't afford to precipitate anything that will get her harmed.'

'They are already harming her,' said Denser.

'Killed, then. If we are to attack it must be a surprise. We don't know enough. That's why I want to talk to Darrick. Look, Denser, I understand your desperation and we all want Erienne out of there as quickly as possible but now is not the time for folly. Now if you can think of a way to get us to Darrick without—'

'No need,' said Ilkar. 'He's coming this way. Alone.'

Even Thraun stopped his circling to stare.

Chapter 24

Ren'erei had ducked back behind a raised wooden jetty as riders had thundered past. She had watched, shivering violently, as a short exchange with Selik led to a deployment of the cavalry in what for all the world looked like a defensive formation. The riders weren't Black Wings, they were a College force of some sort. It scarcely mattered, merely adding to her confusion. She pulled herself up and ran hunched along the dockside until she was out of sight behind the fish market.

Moving silently along the wall, she made to jump some sacks of rubbish before seeing the white of flesh. She stopped and stooped. The man was dead, face down in the stinking sludge that filled the guttering designed to take fish offal back into the harbour. It was not a place to lie, dead or alive.

Ren'erei couldn't leave the man there and rolled him over to get a grip under his arms.

'Oh no,' she breathed. It was Donetsk. Grimly, she hefted the heavy body and dragged it slowly from the filth, Donetsk's steel-capped boots scraping over the cobbles, and pulled him on to the shingle slope that led back into the fishers' harbour. Better he be found somewhere clean, come the morning.

Tidying the man's coat, Ren'erei noted the single knife wound in his chest, the lack of any wounds on his face, neck or hands and reflected that he'd not been ready for the attack. There'd been no fight at all. Ren'erei placed two fingers over the wound and uttered a short prayer for peace in the next life. All small gestures, she knew, but the man deserved something as his body chilled and stiffened.

More horses were coming. The noise grew quickly from the east and Ren'erei flattened herself by Donetsk's body to watch. The sound of hooves, clashing metal and men's voices echoed around the buildings and in the wan light thrown by torches, dark shadows grew as they neared. She recognised the insignia of the Dordovan College as the cavalry galloped by and heard them come to a stop by the *Ocean Elm*, though whether it was to converse with or confront the others she didn't know. She couldn't afford to wait and find out.

The cold wind would have mostly dried her by now but the rain fell instead. She looked up into the heavy sky, its clouds washing past in violent ill-humour, occasional flashes deep within its banks hinting at worse to come, and prayed for Lyanna's Awakening.

She was at a loss. She picked herself up and ran around the back of the fish market, heading for Centenary Square. There were lights on in almost every house, people woken by the hundreds of horsemen who had descended on the docks. In the Square, others would still be drinking in the late-night taverns. If The Raven were in the town, that would be the place she'd find out.

The Unknown Warrior stepped in front of Darrick's horse as the General broke into a trot towards their position. Hirad was kneeling by Thraun, an arm over the big wolf's neck, half in restraint, half in comfort. The pack was clearly nervous and aggressive because of it. They'd let him lead them but now he'd stopped and they weren't satisfied. Whatever it was they were after, Hirad hadn't led them to it. Not yet.

In front of The Raven, Darrick reined in and immediately dismounted, his horse bucking and twisting. He let go the reins and it bolted away, galloping up a side street and into the dark.

'Gods, I'm glad to see you,' he said.

'I wish we could say the same,' said The Unknown. 'I don't like being locked up.'

'Clearly.' Darrick's smile was grim. 'Look, we can't talk here. They'll be watching,' he said, indicating behind him.

'So?' demanded The Unknown.

'So I've just resigned my commission. Deserted, I think the term is.'

'I beg your pardon?' Hirad spoke and Darrick looked over, seeing him for the first time.

'Gods falling, what the hell is all that?'

'That's Hirad and the wolves you so confidently said killed him,' said Ilkar.

'Useful as jail-breakers, as it turns out,' said Hirad.

'I see.' Hirad watched Darrick get hold of himself. 'Let's get out of sight. I think I can help.'

'You'd better,' said Denser.

The Raven moved. Hirad rose and Thraun followed him with his gaze.

'I can't explain,' said Hirad. 'We're doing everything we can. I just don't know what you want. We're trying to get to Erienne.'

At the mention of the name, Thraun growled. The pack followed The Raven under the eaves of the timber yard, a chorus of voices rising behind them.

'So talk,' said Denser.

'I should have listened to you,' said Darrick. 'I'm sorry.'

'Never mind that just now,' said The Unknown. 'We've got big problems and you're not making sense.'

'I know. Look, don't question this, just accept it. The Dordovans have made a pact with the Black Wings. I can't do the same so I've left, deserted. My men have to make their own decisions and I think a good proportion, while loyal to me, won't worry about the Black Wing alliance. They want to save their families and their homes like we all do, and this alliance represents the quickest and most obvious way to the child.'

'They have no idea!' exploded Denser. 'These bastards will rip her beating heart out.'

'I know,' said Darrick. 'Gods, I know that now. But we can't try and take Erienne here. They'll kill her and hope to get to Lyanna another way, I'm sure of it. Look, I don't know much of what Dordover is planning but I do know they've chartered that vessel as support.' He pointed the opposite way to the far end berth, where a large ocean going ship lay tied up, lights and movement on its deck. 'It'll be provisioned and ready to sail, I'm sure. After all, the Dordovans have been here two weeks at least.'

'So we take that ship and follow the *Elm*?' said Hirad.

'I can't see another option,' said Darrick. 'Not immediately. At least this way, we can see how things unfold.'

The Unknown was nodding. 'I concur. Right, we need a plan fast. I don't think the Dordovans will wait until morning.'

'Well, you're the expert, Unknown,' said Denser.

'And you're still extremely funny,' returned Hirad.

'It's just that I don't see what the point of following them is,' said Denser.

'It's not a question of preference,' said The Unknown. 'We just don't have the opportunity in Arlen. The island, or even being out at sea, will provide that as long as we're ready to go immediately.'

Denser shook his head and was about to speak but the bloom of a spell rose over the harbour yard, its detonation clattering around the docks an instant later. The roar of men and the stamp of hooves followed as cavalry was turned in a hurry. Orders were yelled into the cacophony and the thunder of approaching battle filled the air.

The Unknown looked at Hirad and nodded.

The Protectors had arrived in Arlen.

Ren'erei arrived in Centenary Square to find it alive with Arlen's guards. The Earl himself sat astride a large dark brown stallion and he was addressing a growing mob.

'. . . a peaceful town and sometimes, perversely, we have to fight to keep it that way. Our docks are invaded. All there that we do not recognise are unwelcome and must be expelled. My guard are with me and any of you who feel able are welcome to add to those numbers.'

Ren'erei shook her head. Preaching to the drunk. It was an easy sell if violence was promised and the roar that greeted his words was testament to it. The elf saw some men hurrying towards the docks in ones and twos, doubtless sailors anxious to reach the relative safety of their ships.

She scanned the crowd for The Raven but the blur of faces confused her eyes. The Earl was shouting other orders and his guards were forming up, the mob at their heels, anxious for action. Another shake of the head. Two dozen drunk men and not many more guards against trained mounted cavalry. She only hoped Arlen could talk his way out of a fight when it came to it.

Behind Ren'erei, the light of a spell tore at the night, bringing a brief fiery glow to the sky. A dull thud reverberated into the square and, following it, the muted roar of hundreds of voices raised in anger. In that instant, the mob developed a single mind and streamed towards the southern end of the market, Arlen and the guards at their centre, all pretence at order gone.

Ren'erei moved back smoothly and watched them go, grabbing at the arm of a guard sensibly bringing up the rear. The man looked round, face set, angry and determined.

'The Raven,' said Ren'erei. 'Where are The Raven?'

The guard laughed. 'Where any friends of magic should be right now, elf. Under lock and key. Join us if you want to save your ships.' And then he was gone, running with the rest.

Ren'erei sighed and set off for the jail, fearing a slaughter.

*

Thraun howled and the pack leaped away around the corner and back on to the dockside, heedless of Hirad's shouts for them to stop.

'Raven with me!' ordered The Unknown.

Swords unsheathed, Ilkar and Denser preparing spells, The Raven moved swiftly on to the dock. The rain was heavier than ever, pounding the street and their faces as they came, a scene of complete bedlam unfolding before them.

A warehouse by the fish market was ablaze and, beyond the *Ocean Elm*, heavy fighting could be heard between Protectors and Dordovans. A good proportion of the Lysternans stood off but many joined the struggle, seeing an enemy in Xetesk that they could hate, despite the fear of what they faced.

Running on, Hirad saw the pack disappear into the torch and fire-lit mayhem, saw horses rearing and heard Thraun's unmistakable howl. What they thought they were doing he had no idea but at least they'd found an outlet for their pent-up aggression. He was just glad he wasn't in their way.

'Shield up,' said Ilkar as they ran.

'Orbs prepared and ready,' said Denser.

There were shapes in the air, moving against the flaming backdrop of the burning warehouse.

'Mages airborne,' confirmed Ilkar, voice quiet but carrying.

'The *Elm*'s putting to sea,' said The Unknown. 'Look.'

The foresail was running up the mast, the fore and aft lines were chopped and, with a grating that must have distressed the captain, the ship pivoted against the berth wall while the foresail filled with wind enough to drive it away from shore. The airborne mages circled high as the *Elm* got underway.

'How many can you count, Ilkar?' asked The Unknown. The Raven had stopped again, unwilling to join the battle in front of them, which raged just to the side of the Lakehome Inn, from where patrons were streaming back towards the centre of Arlen.

'Ten, maybe more,' said Ilkar. 'It's hard to be certain.'

There was another flash, FlameOrbs spattered down into the centre of the uncertain Lysternan cavalry, scattering horses and riders. HotRain fell away to the east and, despite the wet, smoke and steam were already rising from the soaking roof of the fish market. The pungent smell of burning fish offal and oil washed across the dock on the wind.

A detachment of Dordovan cavalry broke from the back of the

fighting, punching through the Lysternans and riding up the left-hand side of the inn in the direction of Centenary Square.

'That's a bluff,' said Darrick. 'They'll be coming back to the other end of the docks.'

'We need more muscle if we're going to take the other ship,' said The Unknown.

'Any ideas?' asked Hirad.

'Yes. Darrick, get to the ship, see if there's anything you can do. Denser, go with him. Ilkar, Hirad, with me. We're going to get some Protectors.'

'And that's why you make the plans, is it?' said Denser.

'Just do it.' The Unknown turned to Hirad. 'Let's go.'

Running in, Hirad could see the battle unfold before him. The Lysternans were in a state of leaderless near-panic. The loss of Darrick had been a catastrophic blow and though the stand-in commander, a man Hirad recognised as Izack, barked order after order, it was clear they didn't know whether to run or fight. As a result, the unit was disintegrating and only spell shields kept them from disaster. If the Protectors reached them, it would be a massacre.

Beyond the milling Lysternan cavalry, the Dordovans had organised a tight defence across the narrow battlefront that existed between the fish market, the burning warehouse and the harbour's edge. After the initial surge, Dordovan mages had forced the Protectors back with a series of ForceCones and others would be shielding the cavalry from missile and spell attack.

Inevitably, the Protectors sought another route and they could be seen streaming away into the town to circle back while the Dordovans set up similar blocks to the east of the fish market and around the Lakehome Inn.

Meanwhile, Xeteskian attack mages had turned their attention to the boundary buildings. The first fall of HotRain had hit the market roof accidentally, but now Hirad watched FlameOrbs crashing again and again on to the timber and slate roof. They boiled off the rain and set drying wood alight, flames licking into the night from ten or more places along its length.

'Into the town,' yelled The Unknown, and he took them up the right of the Lakehome Inn, away from the immediate din. Hirad could see the pack spooking horses as they nipped in and out of the Lysternans, Thraun pausing to stare at the disappearing *Ocean Elm* before running back in to the mass.

In front of The Raven trio as they left the docks, a throng was approaching them, a mounted man at its head. Arlen.

'Oh, that's a mistake,' said The Unknown.

He ducked into an alley that ran past the rear of the inn but too late to escape attention. Several men slowed and looked in, choosing to make the Raven their first targets. The Unknown and Hirad stood side by side, the big man's blade tapping on the cobbles, metronomic.

'Don't do it,' The Unknown warned the men, not Arlen guardsmen but townsmen high on alcohol and adrenalin.

'The Earl wants your type out of here,' slurred one.

'We can't do that right now,' said Hirad. 'Just move on, or better still go home. It isn't safe here.'

'This is our town,' said another behind the front pair. 'We say what goes, not you.' A murmur of assent was followed by a concerted move forward.

Hirad could count six, all big but none of them natural swordsmen. He regretted what was about to happen. The Unknown's sword still tapped its beat, the barbarian switched his grip twice for effect, but the aggressors were too far gone to notice the skill it demanded.

Behind them, Ilkar sighed.

'What is it?' Hirad didn't look round.

'I—' The elf broke off momentarily. 'Gods. Just grab the two in front of you now. It's all you can do.'

The Raven never questioned Ilkar. Whatever he felt, it had to be big. Far too quickly for the men in front to react effectively. Hirad and The Unknown Warrior reached out and grabbed the collars of the men before them, hauling each off balance and dragging them under the shield, their blades flailing uselessly. Hirad jabbed the pommel of his sword into the jaw of his opponent to quiet him but his struggle was short-lived.

HellFire smashed into the inn, the columns of superheated flame seeking the souls of the living. But there were many columns and few still inside the building. And even as the fire gorged itself on souls and wood, blasting every window outwards in a spray of glass shivers, those loose columns sought and found the nearest victims to their cast destination.

Flame raged over Ilkar's spell shield, turning Hirad's world into a dome of sheet orange, white and yellow while the Arlen townsmen screamed in terror. But beyond, the cries were of death as the HellFire plunged into defenceless bodies, seared flesh spattering the walls, burning corpses flying like dolls about the alley and beyond in the street.

At The Raven's side, the Lakehome Inn was ablaze, flame gouting from empty window frames and rents in the slate roof.

'Ilkar?' asked The Unknown.

'Yes. Go, go!'

The Unknown shook the man in his grasp.

'Go back to your homes and look to your families. This is too big for you.' He thrust the man away, Hirad doing likewise, the two stumbling off through the carnage.

'Raven! Raven with me!'

Chapter 25

Thraun knew where she was and he called the pack to him, though he knew they were scared enough to flee. They ran through the prey, howling and nipping as they went, sending the scared animals jumping and turning against the wishes of their masters. The pack dodged the sharps in the hands of the humans easily, darting between the legs of the prey and beneath their sweating bodies.

But again, there would be no feasting. Because the air smelled bad and the flame around them made it worse. The answer to it was the woman with the mist around her soul, whom Thraun knew and had seen with the infant before his meeting with man-packbrother. She was on the floating land that moved with the wind and it was her name man-packbrother had spoken. Thraun could not reproduce the sound but inside he understood, and knew he had brought the pack close to the answers they sought.

Yet this close, they were to be cheated. At the edge of the land, there was a gap too large to leap and with every beat of his heart, it grew larger. The wind blew hard and strong and drove the floating land far from his grasp. He howled and barked for it to return, turning around and around in his frustration, but the wind only blew harder, the rain stinging his eyes and nose and soaking his fur. And more of the great white leaves blossomed on the trees of the floating land to catch the wind and the woman disappeared into the night.

He howled another time, called the pack to him and fled away, looking again for man-packbrother.

The Raven had no time to help Arlen. The Earl and his men had run into something way beyond their capacity to control. A glance down the street behind them showed the *Ocean Elm* deploying more sail as she cruised into the lake. And in the sky above, the circling Dordovan mages swept across the flame-filled night, one landing on her deck.

Sprinting up towards Centenary Square, Hirad could hear the detachment of Dordovan cavalry ahead of them, probably skirting the square itself to avoid contact before riding down past the jail and back to the dock. To their left, more hoofbeats and running feet.

Just to the south of the market and at the end of a row of offices, The Unknown stopped and held out an arm to stop Hirad and Ilkar running by him. He was facing better than seventy Protectors in a defensive ring around six horse-borne mages. It was clear the mages would have run him down but the Protectors had instantly slowed at the sight of The Unknown, and Hirad could feel the awe sweep out from them.

'I need forty Protectors and as many mages as you can spare from whatever plan you're operating,' said The Unknown. His sword was before him, point down and still.

'And who the hell do you think you are – Lord of the Mount?' demanded one mage, the irritation in his voice mixed with a certain respect.

'No, I think I'm the Unknown Warrior and that we are The Raven and we all want Lyanna saved from Dordover.'

The mage nodded. 'In truth, I recognised you. You think you have a better chance of achieving our goal your way?' Now the respect overrode the ire.

'The *Ocean Elm* is gone. Our only chance is to get a ship ourselves. We know of one provisioned and ready but Dordovan cavalry are riding to it now. I need the Protectors to get aboard and to help in any future fight. And I need the rest of you to keep the main Dordovan and Lysternan forces busy. I need your answer now.'

The mage nodded again. 'Take thirty. I can spare no mages. I am Sytkan. Have Denser signal me when you have the ship.'

The Unknown smiled. 'Thank you, Sytkan. You might just have saved the One child.' He pointed. 'Aeb. Bring our brothers.' He didn't wait for them but turned and, with Hirad and Ilkar, ran for the docks once again.

Erienne heard the sounds of battle but could see nothing, her tiny window looking backwards into the night. She prayed her College had come for her. She prayed harder that the next time the door opened, Denser would be framed in it. She felt the bump as the stern of the *Elm* ground against the berth wall, the timbers protesting. She heard the orders shouted out by the captain, reluctance in every syllable, and she felt the rocking as the ship gained clear water and got underway. And finally, when the door opened and Selik entered, she wept.

'Well, well, well,' said Selik, ignoring her tears. 'Such excitement, it seems a pity to leave it behind.'

'Get out, Selik. You are filth and I don't need to see you until you come to kill me.' She used the cuffs of her shirt to wipe at her eyes.

'Unfortunately for you, this is my ship and I go where I please,' said Selik before lightening his tone. 'I spoke to your old friend General Darrick just now. It seems he's unhappy to see the forces of good in charge of this ship.'

Erienne was interested in spite of herself but didn't raise her head. 'Well, he's not a murderer, is he?'

'No. But a man whose principles get in the way of expediency.'

'What do you mean?' Erienne felt confused and alone. They were sailing to Lyanna yet the journey only promised her death at the hands of her betrayers and she was exchanging irrelevancies with the Black Wing, Selik.

'He has deserted rather than help his Dordovan allies further.'

'Good for him. They've proved little better than you,' said Erienne, the taste of bile back in her throat. 'Is there anything else?'

'Actually there is. I wanted to introduce you to those I promised would be arriving. And I do so like to make good on my promises.'

'You know something, Selik, you sound just like your dead friend Travers.'

'I'll take that as a compliment. He was a great man.'

'Don't.'

Selik's smile was forced. 'Don't forget to whom you belong. Now, I'm forgetting my manners.'

Erienne saw him come in and saw the smile on his face, the half-open arms and the benign expression. Then, the rushing in her head fogged her vision and she sat heavily on her bed, hands pressing on the blanket either side of her to keep her upright. She looked again, forcing herself to focus.

'You,' was all she could find to say.

The Raven ran ahead of him but Aeb's eyes never left the figure of Sol, The Unknown Warrior. The Protectors ran with him, and only him, and Aeb experienced a feeling of which he had only a vague recollection. It burned through him and in the tank, all the souls shared. But it was he and the brothers by him who felt it the most strongly and, though alien, it was most welcome.

Joy.

*

There were lanterns lit along the length of the ship Darrick indicated as the one provisioned and ready for boarding. It was called *Calaian Sun* and its deck was ringed with its crew, staring down the dock to where the stand-off was being played out in front of the fierce fires now burning and hissing into the rain-drenched sky. Whipped up by the wind, great sheets of flame scoured the dark, threatening nearby buildings so far undamaged by spell attack.

HotRain fell in a steady stream over the dockside, cast by Lystern, Dordovan and Xeteskian alike and the flaring on the shields that now covered every horse and rider completed the magical tapestry.

As Darrick watched, HellFire struck the Lakehome Inn and in the screaming death that followed, men flooded out of a side road and threw themselves at the Lysternan cavalry. Surprised, the Lysternans responded, beating back the attack with a half charge before it became evident that spare mages had blocked the road with ForceCones.

'See what you can do with the crew. I've got to prepare,' said Denser.

'Certainly,' said Darrick.

'And Darrick.'

'Yes.'

'Thank you.'

Darrick frowned. 'What for?'

'For putting my family's lives above politics.'

'Eventually.' Darrick turned away.

Denser eyed the buildings opposite. There were three warehouses end on to the dock, each with a passage between, wide enough for four or five horses abreast. Knowing he couldn't hope to cast a ForceCone with anywhere near enough strength to cover the possible entry points, he opted for something more of a hindrance and prayed The Unknown brought the Protectors on very soon. He knelt to give himself balance against the wind, closed his eyes and, ignoring the rain that lashed into his face and the growing smell of burning wood and hot metal, began his preparation.

Ditching the shield for the run to the docks, Ilkar had paused to cast ShadowWings and was lost in the sky above Hirad, searching for the Dordovan cavalry. In the absence of information, The Unknown was leading them back past the timber yard, giving them quickest sight of the docks and the target ship.

The rain made the stone cobbles slick, water ran down the guttering in torrents and mud brought in by the rains and the hooves of every horse was sluicing down the streets, adding to the treachery underfoot. More than once, Hirad slipped on the surface, only to find the hand of a Protector steadying him almost before he realised he'd lost his balance. He wanted to be angry that they assumed he needed help to run in the rain but found himself instead amazed at their quickness of thought and action.

He glanced up into the fire-stained night to see Ilkar swooping towards them. He flew beside them as he spoke.

'Denser and Darrick are at the ship. Denser's preparing something. The Dordovans will be on them in a few moments, they're riding down the side of a warehouse a couple of streets from here. There's no movement from the ship but the crew's all on deck. This is going to be close.'

'We'll need a shield when we hit them,' said Hirad.

'With you all the way.' Ilkar flew ahead, landing fifty yards away to disperse the wings and prepare the shield.

The Unknown upped the pace, Hirad feeling the Protectors ease along while he suddenly felt every one of his thirty-nine years.

'I could do without this,' he said, gasping slightly.

'Too much good living with the Kaan,' said The Unknown.

'Let me do the jokes, all right?' said Hirad.

They rounded the corner, Ilkar now beside them, and in moments, the docks were awash with chaos.

For a few paces, it looked as if the impossible would happen and they'd beat the Dordovans to the ship but when they were seventy yards from Denser and Darrick, the General yelled something inaudible and the Xeteskian mage brought his fists together in front of his face before bringing them down in a punching motion.

The warehouses close to the berth shuddered, were still and then shuddered again. The stone of the docks rippled by the timbered buildings and loose wood tumbled off the roofs. There was another momentary pause, in which Hirad saw the first Dordovan horse gallop on to the dockside, before huge wedges of stone thrust out of the earth in a dozen and more places, cascading cobbles, flags, mud and water in all directions.

The centremost of the three warehouses buckled at its front as one of the rock wedges shattered supporting timbers. The wall bulged outwards and the roof slipped sideways into the road, and above the sudden roar of noise, the sound of terrified horses rose briefly as riders tried to control bucking and twisting mounts desperate to avoid the avalanche of wood from above and the rock from below.

'Good old Denser,' said Hirad. But it was only a temporary hold. Already, horses were picking their way around the still shifting stone and splintered timbers, and though the EarthHammer would have caused casualties, the Dordovan cavalry came on.

'Let's go, let's go.' said Hirad, sprinting forwards as the first horseman closed on Denser.

'Aeb!' called The Unknown. 'Take left, Hirad takes right. I need an angled wedge.'

'Yes,' came the reply.

'And speak freely. Do what you have to do,' added The Unknown.

'Yes.'

The first horseman didn't even get close to Denser. The mage backed up in response to Darrick's shout and the General swept his sword high and fast into the rider's ribcage, clipping the horse's head on the way up and severing an ear. The rider collapsed out of the saddle, his mount whinnying in pain as it ran blindly past, a threat to no one but itself.

Hirad ran on. The main body of the Dordovan cavalry detachment was picking its way out on to the docks now, an initial move to the ship halted by an urgent shout. Quickly wheeling, the cavalry formed a line that moved towards the onrushing Protectors headed by The Raven. Over the heads of the horses came FlameOrbs, splashing off Ilkar's shield, the mage ensconced in the middle of a three-deep line.

The horses hadn't the space to make speed for a full charge and, as they closed, the animals faltered, shying away from the solid wall of men who showed them no fear.

The Unknown slowed a little, tapped his blade twice on the stone and smashed it through the neck of the first horse. It came down in a tumble of limbs and a spray of blood that was washed away by the rain. The sky was lit by lightning that flashed through the tumbling cloud, thunder rumbling and echoing as it fired.

Beside The Unknown, Aeb, his axe unhitched, sword still across his back, batted the cheek of a horse with a flat blade, sweeping up in the same movement to bury the edge in the stomach of the rider who was lifted bodily from the saddle and thrown backwards under the hooves of the horse behind.

Hirad stepped smartly inside the flailing fore-hoofs of a rearing horse and ducked the sweep of a sword, placing his above his head to catch any downward strike. He hated fighting cavalry. Space was tight, blows came from all angles and horses moved unpredictably in the press, making crushing a real risk. But after him came the Protectors and he knew that, for once, he could ignore the threat from behind, confident that Xetesk's killing machines would watch his back.

In between two tall horses, he jabbed right with an elbow and flashed his sword left, clashing with the rider's axe. Moving to a one-handed grip, he glanced right and grabbed for that rider's jerkin, pulling him off balance and dragging his sword flat to catch the return blow from the axeman left.

Unexpectedly, the grabbed rider fell and Hirad ignored him as he hit the ground, snatching his sword back and hacking it into the axeman's unprotected leg before letting himself drop, his knees connecting with the chest of the man he'd pulled down. He heard and felt ribs snap and a blow to the throat with the pommel of his sword ended the enemy's struggles.

Around him was a mass of flailing legs. He moved to a crouch and then up, hearing the cries of a dying man behind him, and struck forward once more, seeing, to his, left, The Unknown's blade savage through the midriff of a Dordovan and Aeb's axe fall on another's neck.

The cavalry were losing their shape. Their commander yelled for a break and those that could wheeled and rode away from the fight, the Protectors letting them go, riderless horses following on. Fourteen Dordovans lay dead as did one Protector. The Unknown had a gash on his left arm.

'Unknown, all right?' asked Hirad as they reformed.

'Bloody sword. Terrible balance. No wonder Arlen was never good as a fighting town. Their weaponsmith needs stringing up.' He put a hand to the wound and looked at the slick of blood, quickly diluted by rain, that came away. 'They've ruined my shirt, the bastards.'

Hirad smiled. 'We need to focus on the next charge. I—' There was a roar from behind and the rush of hooves. Hirad looked back. Dordover and Lystern were coming. 'Shit. Trouble.'

'Understatement,' said The Unknown. 'Aeb! Rear defence. Tight form. We can't allow them amongst us this time.'

'It will be done.'

The Protectors moved immediately. From three ranks, they stepped up or back, each one hefting a single weapon, presenting a solid line to the Dordovan and Lysternan cavalries coming at them.

From Hirad's direction HotRain fell on the Dordovans, flaring on shields and blowing on to the ruined warehouses nearby. It was Denser's work but largely ineffective this time. The horsemen turned and charged.

'Be ready,' said The Unknown, his sword blade tapping.

'You know it,' said Hirad. The hooves clashed off the stone, the fires behind him lit the blades of the attackers in stark relief. Hirad roared to clear his head and looked for his first target.

Xye watched the crush of opposing forces with the detached analysis afforded a Protector through the sifting of every stimulus by the entire brethren in the Soul Tank. It allowed him to assess immediately, act with supreme confidence and authority, and minimise the chances of damage to any Protector or Given. He had the unfailing support of every brother and his courage was eternally undimmed.

He stood in the centre of the line, his back eight paces from those of Sol and Aeb, looking back towards the fires that had engulfed the fish market, the inn, and the timber yard and now threatened the foundry and warehousing nearby. The fires denied the night and shed a garish glare over the entire dockside, lighting the charging horses and their riders in the colours of hell.

Xye considered the enemy had taken an ill-conceived gamble based on panic, not tactics. The mixed Dordovan and Lysternan forces drove hard along the dockside, the latter unsure, the former desperate to destroy the line threatening their comrades. But behind them, the mages had dropped their barricades and the Given mages launched FlameOrbs, HotRain and IceWind across the cavalries as the Protectors, unhindered by ForceCones, surged after them.

And into the mêlée came more that Xye couldn't place. Men on foot, directed by a single man on horseback; and through the maelstrom of thoughts and pulses, Xye picked up a thread that warned of the howling of wolves. Animals to be spared.

Strength and courage. Fracture the charge. Help comes from behind. We are one.

Xye knew the brethren could not lose.

'Head up, Hirad,' said The Unknown, his sword point still tapping the slick stone at his feet. 'Go centre, go low. I'll take the rider.'

'Got you.'

The Unknown took the short blade in both hands now and watched the Dordovans as they came. It was not a full charge. Both horses and riders were nervous at the enemy they faced, their usual confidence undermined by the lack of fear in their foe.

'Ilkar, how're you doing.'

'Debating offence,' came the reply.

'When they hit us, not before.'

'Any moment now, then.'

The Unknown heard the grim humour in Ilkar's tone. This was not a good situation. The front rank of the cavalry was on them, formation wide enough to allow weapons clear path. The thunder of hooves, the shouts of the men and the snorts of the horses clamoured all around, in front and behind, counterpointed by the total lack of movement or sound from the Protectors.

The Unknown ceased tapping his blade, paced forward, raised it high and crashed it into the centre rider, seeing from the corner of his eye, Hirad dropping to a crouch to power up under the horse's neck. The rider was ready but it wasn't enough; his one-handed block hadn't the strength to counter The Unknown's massive swing. His blade was knocked aside, leaving his chest and neck open to the Raven man's blade which sliced through exposed flesh and screamed across his chainmail chest guard. Blood fountained into the air and as his horse collapsed from Hirad's strike the man toppled lifeless from his saddle.

Turning to face his next opponent, The Unknown was struck in the back of the shoulder. He half-turned, guard up but there was no threat, just the head of a Dordovan bouncing to the floor.

The second rank of cavalry bulldozed through where the first had failed, forcing back Protector and Raven alike. The Unknown fielded blows on his blade from left and right, feeling the press of horseflesh around him and craning his neck to look for an opening. He heard Hirad curse, and saw the flash of a blade. A horse screamed. The Unknown struck right, biting into a rider's armour. Winded, the man turned to wheel away, but his dying mount wouldn't respond and he merely lurched in the saddle. The Unknown snatched his foot from its stirrup and pitched him to the ground for Hirad to finish.

'Ilkar! Now's a good time for something.'

The mage didn't respond immediately, then.

'Shield down. Crouch, Raven.'

The Unknown complied and Ilkar's spell thudded over his head, a ForceCone which smashed into the remnants of the front rank, driving back horses into those behind and stripping riders from saddles.

A loose horse, caught as it reared, flailed its hooves, catching The Unknown a glancing blow on his shoulder and on to his chin. He sprawled over the wet stone, seeing stars, sword knocked from his grasp and gasping from the sudden pain. Rolling immediately on to his left-hand side, he saw the Dordovans regrouping and heard Hirad shouting his name. He was in front of the line and vulnerable, his sword a couple of paces away. He dragged himself to a crouch, pain spearing through his shoulder and up into his neck. He crawled forward quickly and grabbed the blade, standing ready to back up.

'Unknown, left. Left!' Hirad's desperate shout cut through him. He swung left, raising his sword instinctively in his right hand.

The horse had come from nowhere, riding across the line, and as he made to jump right to avoid it, the Dordovan cavalryman leaned out and swung his axe hard and low, smashing it into The Unknown's unprotected hip.

He felt the agony, he knew he was falling and he felt the smack of stone on his face.

Chapter 26

The pack bunched in terror as explosions thundered around them. Nearby, one of the human buildings was engulfed in flame and sounds like trees falling, the screams of men and the howling, evil wind fractured their collective spirit. They ran.

Thraun could see where they were going, to shadow and quiet, but knew it was the wrong way. No answers there, nor safety. That was only to be found with man-packbrother. But it was long before he could stop the pack, let alone make them obey him.

He barked and half-howled, urging them to slow their blind run and, one by one, they did, drawing into the shelter of a narrow passageway between the high human-built walls. Here, the sounds of destruction were muted and the scents of burning, blood and death were overpowered by those of rotting vegetation and stagnant mud churned up by the rains.

What filled Thraun's ears now were the harsh pants of the pack and what filled his eyes were their lolling tongues, their eyes white and wide and their ears flat against their heads. He knew they shouldn't be here, in the centre of the world of men. He understood their fear of the fire that fell around them, of the stench of burning and the screams of men dying and buildings falling, but knew he couldn't allow it to dominate them.

So he stood while they crouched in surrender. He watched while their breathing returned to an even pace and depth and he waited until all of them looked to him for support and the whines in their throats disappeared. And all the while the noises he made in his mouth and chest soothed them and gave them strength.

Part of him wanted to take them back out to the forests and the surviving pups and bitches but they were so close now. Man-packbrother and the others would find the woman and the answers would be there for them. He yearned for the forest but more than that, he yearned to stand with man-packbrother. To help the humans. It was not a feeling that was easy to accept but it was there and could not be denied.

It was something he wished he could express to the pack but there were no sounds or expressions to convey it. He knew they didn't understand why they were here, just that their pack leader was and they trusted him to be right. And so they would follow him again, back to the fires, the pain and the bad scent that covered everything. But they would return by another route and try to avoid the worst of the burning wood, to where man-packbrother had run with the strange humans whose faces were wood and who had nothing where their souls should be. He feared these humans. They were blank.

Thraun nuzzled each one of the pack in turn, feeling their soaking fur against his muzzle and easing their remaining fear. He would be with them. He would protect them. Now was the time to act. Yet they were so reluctant to go, cowering still in the dark, their eyes fearful. But he needed them with him, to give him strength.

He made to move back out into the horror but they wouldn't follow him. He padded back to them, standing above them where they crouched, heads low to the ground. They couldn't stay here and he struggled to make them understand that. Hiding in the dark was not the way of the wolf. The pack hunted, the pack ran free.

He growled, demanding they get up, requiring their obedience. He was the dominant male and they had to obey him. And slowly, their respect and fear of him overcame the need to escape what lay beyond the dark alleyway. Heads still hung, limbs still shivering, they rose.

The pack were ready again and he led them out of the dark place and back into the firelight and noise, the scent of the evil gale assailing his nostrils, the sounds of clashing metal and the cries of humans becoming loud again in his ears.

Howling to give them strength, he ran in front of them, searching the air for the scent of man-packbrother. Thraun knew where he had run to and as they closed on the place where the land met the water once again, he knew he would turn away from the terror the pack had suffered.

But the conflict had moved.

All along the waterside, the human dwellings burned, their heat crackling the air and making the rain steam as it fell, fizzing in the air. He couldn't see man-packbrother but knew he was there. What he could see were prey and the humans that rode them.

With a bark, he led the pack to attack, leaping and closing his fangs around the throat of a prey, feeling the warm gush of blood and its anguished movements as it sought to shake him off. The rider called

out and swung his sharp which stung as it bounced from Thraun's
impervious hide.

Thraun dropped from the neck of the prey and, in the same move,
sprang to take the human, giant paws thumping into his chest and
bearing him to the ground where the weak creature fought uselessly
while Thraun tore at his throat.

The mingled blood tasted good but there was no time to feast on
prey and human flesh was not to his liking. He lifted his head and saw
the pack surrounding their prey, which reared, pawing the empty air
while its rider clung to stay on. He watched as one circled to a flank
and drove into the rear legs. The beast collapsed, its cry of pain loud,
its rider tumbling to the ground, momentarily and fatally helpless.

With the human dead, Thraun barked them to him and looked for
the next target. The riders and prey were aware of them now, and
more turned to fend them off while the clashing and shouting
continued behind them.

Thraun's heart froze as he saw a man with mist over his soul
staring at them. He had no sharp and was all the more terrible for it.
Thraun made to dart forward but was blocked by one of the pack.
Barking to scatter them, he ran at the man, leaping as globes of fire
erupted from his hands, sailed over Thraun's head and landed behind
him. With his jaws clamped on the man's face and his paws raking his
chest, he heard the awful yelps and whines of the pack.

He bit down to finish the human, turned and ran, pulling up short
when he saw them. They hadn't scattered as he had asked, the
proximity of prey and blood had been too much. And now three
were down and one staggering. All were ablaze, all in agony, all
dying. Thraun looked on helplessly as the unnatural fires ate at their
fur and flesh, stole their voices and stopped their bodies. At the last,
one found Thraun's eyes and as the wolf's gaze dimmed, he read the
message in them.

Betrayal, wrong death.

Thraun sat by the burning carcasses and howled, heedless of the
enemy around him and not caring whether he was attacked or not.
He had let them down. The pack were gone and it was his instincts
that had cost them their lives. He had failed them just as he had
failed—

A stab of long buried memory flashed through his desperate mind.
Of a small human. Another man-packbrother, covered in white, his
eyes closed, his chest not moving.

Confused, Thraun had neither the strength for revenge or flight. So

he lay where he was, last guardian of the dead pack, and watched the
prey and riders flow around him as if through eyes that saw slowly.
    And with every heartbeat a word, a word, gained in intensity and
dominion. Deep inside, he knew he could not ignore it.
    Remember.

Arlen turned this way and that in his saddle as he sought some way to
enforce order. He and his men had spilled on to the dockside past
raging fires and collapsed buildings to encounter a battle in full flow.
College cavalry were set against Protectors, the violence of the
fighting shocking as it flowed over the cobbles of his docks. Men
roared, horses screamed, and spells crashed on all sides, flaring over
shields or pouring their might over helpless victims.

The eye-watering odours of scorched wood and flesh filled the air
through the pouring rain. Swords clashed together or against amour,
the ringing echoing in all directions, and in the firelight great slicks of
rain-diluted blood ran towards the sea, men and horses splashing
through them as they engaged their enemies.

In the harbour, the *Ocean Elm* was sailing clear, sails full, driving
her on to the lake while to his left, another battle near the *Calaian Sun*
was taking place in front of tumbled and splintered warehouses and
the flames that swept a hundred feet into the night sky. The noise was
deafening, the sight appalling and Arlen had no idea how to stop it.

Around him, his townspeople had faltered, their energy draining
away as they saw death surround them. Some of them had run away
and Arlen couldn't blame them for doing so. Only his guards had
formed up in proper defence and they had been attacked on two sides,
some falling prey to Protectors beating a path back to the centre of
the town, others by Dordovans determined to stop them. Eventually,
he had withdrawn and now the survivors looked to him for help.

One of the men he'd sent to assess the spread of fighting through
the town sprinted up to him, gasping for breath.

'Report,' said Arlen.

'It's everywhere,' said the youngster, not more than twenty years of
age and scared half to death. 'There're fires burning right through to
the jail and into the Salt Quarter. One side of Centenary Square is
ablaze with fire carried on the wind and there's fighting in a dozen
pockets.' He stopped, breathing hard. 'Protectors are marauding all
through the town and the Dordovan mages are casting at them
from rooftops and windows. Our people are on the run. There are
hundreds heading north to the castle but I don't think they'll stop

there. It's like the whole place is falling down. What will we do, my Lord?'

The young man looked at him, pleading.

Arlen wanted to yell at him that he didn't know. That nothing they did could stop the fight which raged out of control, as did the fires that ate the buildings. There were too many of them. Hundreds fought on the docks and through the town and he had less than thirty scared men at his disposal. There was nothing they could do but he had to force them into some sort of action. They had to be doing something.

'Listen men!' he shouted. 'Get off the docks. We'll set up a safe zone in the square. Give somewhere for our people to run, then stage them back to the castle. Forget these bastards, let them kill themselves. Let's save our own. Go!'

He turned his horse and led his men away, guilt lying like a lead weight across his shoulders. He'd saved a few for now but the awful realisation was that he'd lost control of his town. He wondered how many of them would realise it too when the relief of escape from the dock wore off. If the Protectors and Dordovans wanted to destroy Arlen, there was nothing he could do to stop them.

'Unknown!' roared Hirad. 'No!'

He launched himself at the cavalryman who had struck down his friend. Five paces and a jump that gave him the perfect angle to strike. The Dordovan was wheeling his horse and presented his body as a target. Hirad was in the air as he brought his sword through right to left, cleaving the man's head from his neck, his body toppling back, blood spraying into the rain-drenched sky.

Hirad ignored the horse and dashed to stand astride The Unknown's body, not daring to look down in case he saw the big man was dead. He had already seen it once before and twice would be too much.

'Aeb! Protectors!' he shouted. 'Help me!'

But they already were, pouring into a frontal attack while those behind stayed the rear advance. Dual weapons scorching through the air, the Protectors stormed into the cavalry, axes carving into horse flesh, swords blocking desperate swings before savaging into the riders.

Dordovans came at Hirad, hoping for an easy target; a man relatively defenceless as he attempted to help a downed friend. The first lost his left leg as Hirad swayed under a roundhouse blow, the second had his horse killed under him. After that, the Protectors were with him, Aeb to his left, forming a circle of steel that gave The Unknown sanctuary.

'Ilkar, check him!' he called as he blocked a sword thrust aside, caught the rider's arm and pulled him from his horse, where Aeb crashed his axe through the unprotected stomach.

'Right behind you, Hirad. Keep going,' said Ilkar

Hirad's heart was thudding wildly as he fought to keep perspective. Every sinew begged him to dive into the cavalry headlong, let his blood instinct take over and see how many he could bring down before they killed him. But he denied the urge, forcing himself to remember the man he was defending.

'He's still alive but it's bad. I need Denser, Hirad. Quickly.'

'Leave it to me,' said Hirad, his body awash with sudden vital energy. 'Aeb, we have to break them now. Front and rear.'

'Yes, I understand. We will move with you.'

Hirad nodded, looked up and saw the Dordovans organising for another run. Twenty bodies were scattered on the ground and, forming more barriers, horses, dead and in distress, lay on the dock. It would be a broken charge and Hirad determined to use that to his advantage.

Along the line, the Protectors waited, silent and unmoving. Their casualties were light but couldn't be ignored. The time was now.

'Come on!' Hirad sprang away, running full tilt at the Dordovan horsemen, and hearing the footfalls of the Protectors as they made their progress. A shout went up from the cavalry, who began to move, riders struggling with horses unwilling to ride into the face of the masked killers Hirad led. Their heads down, they could smell the blood of the dead and dying and their hooves were uncertain on the crowded, slick ground.

Hirad raced on. Running straight at a cavalryman, Hirad saw the man heft his blade. He hurdled the body of a still-twitching horse, landed and rolled to the left, coming to his haunches behind the rider. He was up, spinning and jabbing into the rider's kidney before he could turn his horse.

Turning again, Hirad took in the Protectors, a perfect picture of organised savagery. Arranged two and three to an opponent, horse and rider were attacked simultaneously, giving the cavalrymen nowhere to turn, no meaningful defence and no clear target. No chance at all.

With no immediate opponent, Hirad watched, for a few mesmerised heartbeats, a trio of Protectors in action. One crouched and sank his axe into the horse's hindquarters, another slashed his sword into the animal's neck while the third fielded the rider's desperate swing on his axe before slashing through a disembowelling strike with his blade.

It was over before Hirad had drawn second breath and reminded him of nothing more than a pack of wolves.

Thraun.

Dimly, Hirad recalled howling as he stood over The Unknown's body. With the Protectors occupying the Dordovans, Hirad did a full circle, searching for evidence of the pack, but could see nothing. To the west along the dock towards the berth vacated by the *Ocean Elm*, the Dordovan and Lysternan cavalry had scattered, pockets being hunted down by Protector groups run by mounted mages.

Towards the target ship, the scene was of carnage all over the ground. Protectors had swiftly beaten away any lingering resistance and were already checking every body, crouching to finish off any that were still breathing. Otherwise, the dock was empty and that was very bad. Hirad came to himself with a jolt and knew why The Unknown was lying so close to death. The Raven had allowed themselves to be split and scattered. Something they had sworn never to do.

Thraun would have to look after himself.

'Denser!' shouted Hirad. 'Darrick! Where are you?'

His voice was whipped from him by the wind and further diminished by the steady rain that pattered stone, timber and water, and the crackle of flames from the still raging fires spreading towards Centenary Square fanned by the gale.

'Denser!' Hirad swung around. 'I need you now!' He looked at the target ship, frowning. It was very still on board. The crew that had lined its rails had gone. All that was left were the lanterns swinging wildly and illuminating the empty deck.

Hirad marched towards the ship.

'Denser!' he roared a third time. 'Please! The Unknown's hurt. Denser!' Gods, where was he? He turned and began to walk back to Ilkar and The Unknown. 'Ilkar how're we doing.'

'Not well, Hirad. Find him quickly.'

'D—' There was movement on the ship. A door opened and a figure emerged. Denser. 'Get down here now.'

'What's up?' Denser surveyed the docks, the scattered cavalry and the Protectors who chased them, and raised his eyebrows.

'Gods, you must have cloth in your ears. It's The Unknown, he's hurt. Ilkar needs you.' Hirad pointed to where the elf knelt over the prone form, his face white in the firelight. 'Quickly.'

Denser nodded, cast, and flew from the ship on ShadowWings. Hirad watched him fly through the smoke that blew overhead like low cloud over Arlen. He began to trot back towards the Big Man, not pausing to wonder why Denser was aboard, or where Darrick was. For the moment, it didn't really matter.

The fighting had all but finished on the dockside but he could hear the sounds of violence further back into the town as the Protectors sought the last of the Dordovans. Hirad could see what were probably some of Arlen's guards, wandering aimlessly around the bodies or staring at the fires that heated the chill of the night. The rain hadn't eased at all and the wind howled its force onshore.

Hirad felt drained. It was a long time since he'd run and fought like that and, though the battle had been quick, it had been intense. But more, he'd seen The Unknown cut down and he could see by Ilkar's urgent gestures as Denser landed that the injury was bad. Probably fatal if spells couldn't help him.

Hirad sheathed his sword and slowed to a walk.

'Hirad!' It was Aeb. The Protector was striding towards him, weapons on his back mounts.

'What is it?'

'Come with me.'

Hirad glanced over at Ilkar and Denser, both men still, concentrating as they cast. There was nothing he could do. He shrugged. 'Lead on.'

Aeb turned on his heel. As he approached a smouldering mass of black, two other Protectors rose from next to it and withdrew.

Hirad frowned and looked harder, quickening his pace, the smoking bodies resolving themselves as wolves, rain hissing on seared flesh.

'I don't believe it,' he muttered but Aeb restrained him with a hand.

'You can do nothing for them. But you can for the shapechanger.'

Hirad stared into Aeb's blank mask.

'Say that again?'

'The shapechanger.' Aeb pointed to a form which Hirad had assumed was just another body, white face staring at the sky.

'Gods falling.' Hirad ran, sliding to a stop and dropping to his knees, heedless as he splashed down into blood and water.

Beneath the cloak, the figure was hunched in foetal position. Protectors had lain another cloak beneath him and had tucked the loose edges in to keep the chill from his body.

A mass of brown-flecked blond hair flowed from the exposed head and the face was covered in a fine fur perhaps half an inch long, with only his nose and closed eyes hairless. His skin seemed old, somehow, his ears long and more elven than human. Hirad laid a hand on the quivering body and bowed his head. Thraun.

'Never thought we'd see you again, old friend,' he whispered. 'Gods, how you must be suffering.'

The barbarian considered for a moment and looked up to Aeb, who was staring over at The Unknown, his Protector's stillness broken by an uncharacteristic repetitive clenching and unclenching of a fist.

'If anyone can save him, it's Denser and Ilkar,' said Hirad.

'We have failed him.'

Hirad nodded, a sweep of guilt washing through him. 'We all have.'

Yet again Hirad scanned the dockside, its cranes smashed, its warehouses gutted and its walkways and paths swathed in death. It was not a place for sick men.

'We need to move them both,' he said.

'Arlen has medical facilities.'

'And they'll be full if they aren't destroyed,' said Hirad. 'No. Thraun can't be cured like that and besides, they're both Raven. I won't leave them here.'

'I understand.'

The barbarian looked at the ship. It was still quiet. Unnaturally so. What had Denser done? And then, of course, it clicked.

'Help me with Thraun and bring your brothers. It's time to get aboard that ship.'

Aeb said nothing, just nodded and crouched. He picked up the cloak-wrapped Thraun and set him gently over his right shoulder, standing with the slightest hint of effort.

'Are you all right with him?'

Aeb nodded and began walking.

'Are you sure?' Thraun was a big man.

'Yes,' agreed Aeb. 'Xye will help carry Sol.'

Hirad trotted over to Ilkar and Denser, vaguely registering the sound of horses' hoofs which still echoed through the town above the noise of the gale and fires.

'Can you . . . ?' He gestured uselessly at the prone form, seeing for the first time the horrible injury just below The Unknown's waist, where the Dordovan axe had smashed his hip.

'He'll live,' said Denser, his breathing deep as if he'd run ten miles. 'But I doubt he'll walk again.'

'But he can't be—' He broke off, cocking his head. There were hoofs getting louder, much louder and quickly. He turned towards the sound and out of a pall of smoke between two ruined warehouses charged a single rider, Dordovan. He was heading for the *Calaian Sun* but swung around when he saw Aeb, yelled in anger and rode for the Protector instead.

Hirad started to run but it was obvious he wasn't going to make it in time and that Aeb was stranded, Thraun quite literally a dead weight. Other Protectors were running too but they would all arrive after the event. Aeb stopped, knelt carefully and slid his charge to the ground, cushioning his head, though he must have known the action would cost him his life. But then, Hirad realised, perhaps death was a release for his soul.

Closing in, the rider raised his blade, straightened suddenly and clutched at a crossbow bolt in his neck before pitching from the saddle. With no direction, the horse veered sideways, avoiding the kneeling Protector and galloping straight on along the dock. Aeb looked briefly at his erstwhile attacker, hefted Thraun again and walked on, other Protectors now around him.

Hirad turned on his way to the downed Dordovan. 'Ilkar, this place isn't safe. We need to get him on board.'

'On board?' Ilkar's weary voice wafted back.

Hirad heard Denser say something he couldn't catch.

'Oh,' said Ilkar. 'All right, we're coming.'

Hirad smiled. Xye was standing by them and the barbarian turned his attention to the cavalryman. He was twitching as he died, his blood pumping sluggishly over the stone. The bolt had taken him a couple of inches below his ear.

The barbarian nodded and looked back along the likely angle of fire.

'Show yourself,' he called, not expecting anything.

Immediately, a figure emerged from the shadows, arms wide, the crossbow dropping to the ground. The elf moved fluidly, the grace identifying the race well before Hirad could make out the shape of the face and ears.

'It was a good shot.' Hirad raised a hand and the elf stopped.

'I was aiming for his eye,' said the elf, the voice female. 'Damn Black Wing crossbow. Badly calibrated.'

'Thank you for missing so well, in that case,' said Hirad. 'I need your name and what you're doing here. You're not Arlen's, are you?'

'No.' The elf smiled but there was no humour. 'I am Ren'erei. I am of the Guild Of Drech and I've just lost Erienne to my worst enemy. We came looking for you, Hirad Coldheart. You, Denser and The Raven.'

Hirad stepped forward and offered a hand which Ren'erei took.

'I think you'd better come and meet the others.'

It was like someone had thrown a lever and it was all over. One moment, the cursed Protectors were running amok in his town, hunting and slaughtering cavalrymen from Dordover and the next, they had reformed into an orderly line and trotted out of the town, leaving their dead maskless, their mages not turning their heads once at the devastation they had left behind.

That, they had left for Earl Arlen to face. The thought of what was on his docks was too horrific to even contemplate and now, with the rain still lashing down and the rumbling of thunder promising no respite, he was standing in a circle of hell.

Centenary Square was ringed by fire and echoed to the sounds of the wounded and the terrified. Arlen's horse lay dead at his feet, his arm was broken and his face bloodied and bruised. Behind him, he knew, more fires raged than he could hope to contain and now he had ordered the pulling down of some more buildings in an attempt to stem the tide of flame driving north towards the castle.

Everywhere he looked, his townsfolk drifted by like ghosts, staring open-mouthed at the ruin that had become of their lives. College men and mages had invaded his town and, in less than an hour, had reduced it to a burned out shell.

Darrick had been right; the Protectors were to be feared. But he had not made his case strongly enough. They were not human. Nothing could be that savage. The demons that controlled them had seen to that. And the mages that rode with them were worse. These were men in possession of their own souls yet he had seen them unleash such horror in the name of magic and so many innocent people had died frozen or in flame, with blood gushing from ears or eyes. He had seen them firing buildings to frighten horses, he had seen hail drive horizontally across streets to rip man and beast to shreds and he had seen fire like rain fall from the sky to spread panic and more agony.

'Why here?' he muttered. 'Why my town?'

Arlen's sword dropped from his fingers and he sagged to the ground in the middle of his square, wishing for the night to be eternal so he wouldn't have to look on the ashes of the morning.

How dare they visit such destruction? What presumption that they could take his land as a battle ground for their squabbles? He put his head in his hands and wept, his energy gone, his humiliation complete.

But at least he knew where to lay the blame.

Magic had started the rot in Balaia and magic had sparked the battle that had destroyed everything he had worked for all of his life. There would be a reckoning. Not today, not tomorrow, but there would be a reckoning. And the wielders of magic would be made to suffer for what they so easily wrought and with such contempt.

Perhaps that bastard Selik and his Black Wings were right after all. The Colleges had assumed superiority for too long and they had to be shot from their pompous towers.

Sitting in the mud with rain lashing down from an unnatural sky and his town burning around him, Earl Arlen swore to himself that he would take the first shot.

Chapter 27

Darrick and Denser had captured the crew of the *Calaian Sun*, Denser flying in, carrying the heavy former General the mercifully short distance, and sweeping into the centre of the main deck.

Posing as the first of the Dordovans due to board, the pair had made easy enough progress to the wheel deck and it had been with some apology that Darrick had put his sword to the Captain's neck and invited him to usher his crew into the hold. All the while, Denser stood behind him, the origins of a FlameOrb spell visible between his palms for extra emphasis.

Now, with a gangplank lowered temporarily to allow The Raven and twenty-eight Protectors aboard, the crew had been released to make ready for sail, muttering and scowling as they came.

With The Unknown and Thraun both laid out in cabins, the remainder of The Raven, plus Darrick and Ren'erei, sat around the captain's table. The Captain himself, a brown-haired, tall and muscular elf named Jevin, sat at the head of the table, taking his time to comprehend what he had heard.

The only one of them he had really listened to was Ren'erei and the two had held several quick conversations in an elven dialect that Hirad noticed even Ilkar didn't understand. The barbarian warmed to the elf who had saved Aeb and Thraun. She was earnest and committed and had smoothed the angry elven crew by her very presence and a few obviously well-chosen words.

'And this ridiculous weather pattern is down to this one girl?' Jevin held up a forefinger.

'Yes,' said Denser.

'And you say that she is of the Al-Drechar?' He raised his eyebrows.

'Yes,' said Denser.

'Then why aren't the elves protecting her? She is so important.'

'They are,' said Ren'erei. 'But the Guild isn't big enough in numbers and we had to have more support. Erienne needed Denser and The Raven and that has meant we could bring Protectors to help us against the Dordovans.'

'They are Xeteskian,' said Jevin. 'Their agenda is no less selfish than the Dordovans.'

'Except in one vital area,' said Denser. 'We won't kill her, we want her to live and her talents to come to fruition.'

' "We" being Xetesk in this instance,' said Ilkar. 'We're The Raven and we aren't working for Xetesk. It just so happens our desires meet in some areas.'

Jevin nodded. 'It appears I am invaded by the lesser of two evils.'

'Will you help us?' asked Ilkar.

'I'm preparing for sail,' snapped Jevin. 'What more would you like?'

'That isn't what he meant,' said Denser, his voice calm. 'I'm sorry for what we've put you through. What we want is for you to help us willingly. You'll be paid, we'll see to that, but more than that, you'll be stopping Dordover committing a crime against Balaia. And you'll be helping to save my daughter.'

At last, Jevin smiled. 'The pay had better be good.'

'Double what the Dordovans promised,' said Hirad.

'That will serve,' said Jevin. 'And if I'm honest, I've always wanted to meet The Raven. I had imagined it a little differently but there you are. My conditions are these. You will let me sail this ship my way. I know the route to Ornouth and will ask for advice only when I need it and will not risk her keel under any circumstances. You will stand down the Protectors immediately and we will only then leave the dock.

'You are my guests here and not my captors. As such you will follow the rules of my ship which my first mate will explain to you when we are underway. I will assemble my crew and explain our position. Are there any questions?'

Heads shook all around the table.

'Then we have a deal.' He reached out a hand which Hirad, in the absence of The Unknown, shook.

The door to the Captain's cabin opened, Aeb stooped his huge frame inside.

'There is a man asking for you, General Darrick. One of your cavalry.'

Darrick rose quickly. 'I'll see to it. Denser, I think you'd better get the Protectors off the deck to let this ship get away.'

'Yes, I suppose I'd better,' said Denser.

The Raven followed Darrick out of the cabin, along a short corridor, up a flight of slatted wooden steps and on to the deck. Half a dozen riders stood under the light of a pair of torches. Hirad recognised Izack at their head.

'Commander Izack,' said Darrick, standing by the rail. 'Is this the arresting party?'

Izack chuckled. 'No, sir, it most certainly isn't. We've brought The Raven's weapons and armour and have come to offer our services.'

'The first, I will accept with gratitude, the second, I must refuse though I am touched by your loyalty.' He held up a hand as Izack made to say something more. 'Izack, you're a fine soldier and a good friend and it's because of both of those qualities that I don't want you mixed up in this, tempting though it is to have a man of such stature by me.

'I have committed a crime against Lystern, though I know you and I don't see it that way. I'm on the run and Lystern will need good men like you to shore up her defences.'

'Defences?' asked Izack.

'There will be trouble between the Colleges, Izack. Whoever gains the child, there will be trouble. I have made my choice and I'll be fighting my battle in the Ornouth Archipelago. You must go home and start to prepare. Make Heryst listen. He's a good man if misguided at times and the Dordovans cannot be trusted as he thought. What do you say?'

'If you ask it, General, I will do it.'

'Thank you, Izack.' Darrick relaxed a little and leaned on the rail. 'Take care of yourself. Lystern will need you in the times to come.'

Izack nodded. 'What will I do when they ask me about your actions here tonight?'

'Tell them the truth.' Darrick straightened again. 'Good luck, Izack. We'll meet again.'

'I hope so, sir. Good luck to you.'

He wheeled his horse and led his men away, leaving a tied bundle on the dock. Hirad could see the hilt of The Unknown's two-handed sword protruding from it and prayed he'd hear the point tapping its rhythm again.

All pretence at maintaining the shield had long since gone and Ephemere knew that their enemies would be coming. It was just a question of whether help came sooner. Like a volcanic eruption, and just as obvious to a watching mage, the tortured mana surged from Lyanna's mind. The devastation it caused worsened by the hour.

When they weren't with Lyanna, and only one of them could be at a time now, the drain was so great, they slept, or ate the broth that the Guild elves made. They tried to smile, but Ephemere could see the exaggerated care they took with every action and heard the soft lies about how well they were bearing up.

Ephemere sat in the dining room, the pipe of Lemiir in her hand. In an adjacent anteroom, Myriell sat with Lyanna. There was no sense in leaving her in her own bedroom, she couldn't know the difference in her current state, and it was just that little bit easier for her dying watchers.

The old Al-Drechar's face cracked into a vague smile as she drew deeply on the pipe, feeling the herbal smoke smooth the edges off the pain she experienced every waking moment. So many hours they'd spent here, the four of them, arguing, talking, chiding and hoping. It was only now she realised how happy those times had been.

The smile faded. It had been five days since she had passed more than a few words of encouragement to Aviana on her way out and wished restful sleep to Myriell on her way in to Lyanna. She hadn't seen Cleress at all in that time. And with every passing day, they got weaker and weaker and Lyanna's Night showed no signs of passing.

The only encouragement they could draw was that it had moved to another stage but even that development meant more misery. Where Lyanna's mind's random usage of her enormous talent would have previously brought such trouble to her homeland of Balaia, now that net had widened and encompassed Herendeneth too. It showed greater understanding and a modicum more control and direction by the child's unconscious, but its result was a battering of the whole archipelago under what was often a clear blue sky.

No longer were the winds irritated spats delivered by Lyanna as she dreamed; now the lightning crackled and fell to earth in an endless stream; the waves pounded the shores and swept up to within scant yards of the house; the wind thundered ceaselessly at shutters, windows and walls and, when the clouds did roll across, the rain was incredibly heavy, washing off the higher ground in rivers and pouring through the house on its way back to the sea.

The smells of damp wood, ruined rugs and soaking timbers were constant reminders of the mastery of the elements over the Al-Drechar's domain. Ephemere sighed. How naïve they had been. Hundreds of years old yet they had still fallen into the trap of overestimating their own abilities and, worse, underestimating the destructive power of Lyanna's untrained but awakened mind. Her only consolation was that, even had they known, there was little they could have done, but at least they would have begun a little better prepared.

And that would have made dying more comfortable.

The ancient elf took one more draw on the pipe and set it down on its stand, where it would be refilled and lit for Myriell in a few moments. She opened her eyes, not having remembered exactly when she closed them and saw two Guild elves standing to her left, waiting. With a pang of sorrow, she realised she couldn't remember their names and could only nod to indicate it was time.

The young elf males eased her chair back and with one to each arm, helped her to her feet. With agonised slowness, she dragged one foot in front of the other, determined not to let them carry her as they already had Aviana on three occasions. It was stupid, she knew, but sometimes the petty competitiveness was all that kept her going.

One of the elves opened the door to the makeshift bedroom and they moved into the gentle lantern light. To the left, the curtained window was open a crack on to a sheltered corner and though the wind buffeted the island, only a fresh breeze wafted into the room. Soon it would be light but the curtains would remain closed. It was better for concentration that way.

Lyanna lay on her back on the bed they'd brought in for her. She hadn't opened her eyes for six days now, subsiding not long after Erienne went to find Denser and The Raven. Her favourite doll and a glass of water lay on a table at her bedside, symbols of hope and belief that she would come through her Night. But they'd changed the untouched water time and again and the doll was gathering dust.

The elves helped Ephemere to the bed and she sat on its edge, leaning forward to smooth Lyanna's hair. Her face was cool and dry at the moment but another of the convulsions, when her whole body was wracked with spasms, tormented by phantoms the Al-Drechar could do nothing to diminish, would not be far away.

The Guild elves were tireless. Bathing her daily, changing soiled sheets, feeding her soup through her unconsciousness, encouraging her swallow reflex by stroking her neck.

'Poor child,' whispered Ephemere. She kissed Lyanna's forehead and indicated she wanted to move.

She was helped to a two-seater sofa and sat beside Myriell, indicating the elves could withdraw. She heard the soft click as the door closed, steeled herself for a moment and uttered a prayer that she would survive to feel the touch of Aviana's mind when her sister came to relieve her. For now, it was she who would relieve Myriell. She tuned herself to the mana spectrum and faced the tempest.

As she dived towards Lyanna's mind and the shield that Myriell maintained around it, the gales outside became as puffs of air on her cheek in comparison. It made the rain and thunder seem like distant, comforting echoes and it made the power of the lightning like the flicker of a single, guttering candle.

Ephemere imagined her face stretched taut by the force of the mana storm, her hair straight behind her and tears forced from her eyes. Directionless but focused, the streams entwined and whipped by, like an endless, white striated tunnel of deep dark brown, shot through with flashes of yellow, orange, green and black-tinged blue, with Ephemere falling towards its core.

But she wasn't entirely helpless. The tunnel had a light, dim but pulsing. Myriell's mind. Ephemere fought to reach it, pushing a bulb of protective mana in front of her, deflecting the roaring, howling Night Child magic from destroying her as she went.

She craved the warmth of contact and it drove her on until she found it, melding seamlessly with her sister and feeling the joy of touch reciprocated. Ephemere could sense the exhaustion in Myriell but, stronger than that, the determination not to fail Lyanna. She moved her consciousness to take some of the strain from Myriell, breathing hard as the mind shield placed around Lyanna bucked and threatened to tear itself apart. She imposed her will, driving energy into the mana shape until it stabilised. Only then did she turn any attention to her sister.

'I am here, Myra,' she said.

'I thought you'd never come,' answered Myriell.

'Go and sleep now.'

'Be careful, Ephy. It isn't getting any easier.'

'I know, Myra,' said Ephemere. 'I know.'

'I love you, Ephy,' said Myriell as she began to disengage.

'Always,' said Ephemere.

And Myriell was gone and the isolation clamped down on Ephemere, sending her heart into palpitations and leaving her momentarily short of breath. Beneath the delicate mind shield, Lyanna cried out in pain, her thoughts confused and scared.

For all that Ephemere felt alone, for Lyanna it was far, far worse. Such a small child and now separated not just from her mother, but from her senses too, living in a pitch black world of night where uncontained mana battered ceaselessly at her fragile mind.

Lyanna's mind was like a magnet, dragging in magical essence in enormous quantities but quite unable to mould it or understand what it was she unleashed. While she lay in her Night, her mind experimented, fought to control what it craved and threw out random mana shapes with staggering power because that control was denied it. For her to survive, she would have to learn.

For Ephemere and all the Al-Drechar, their only focus was to defend her from that which she couldn't yet control or manipulate. Collapsing shapes posed a great threat as they unravelled and they had to be first deflected from where they might wreak havoc, and then given an outlet. It meant suffering blow after blow of half-formed magic, each one chipping away at the strength of their minds. Any shape fully formed had to be allowed free rein despite the resultant devastation in Balaia and now, Ornouth. But it had to be endured. For the succession of the One, it had to be endured.

Ephemere cried. It happened with the beginning of every shift. She felt Lyanna's moans as they modulated through the mana, the only human emotion in the elemental tumult she created. She couldn't respond, couldn't put her arms around an entity that was not there to embrace and wasn't there to be comforted.

All she could do was deflect the dangerous magical energy that Lyanna provoked. And with every slamming of a bolt against her shield, she weakened, but with every breath she took, her resolve hardened.

But none of it was why she cried.

She knew she had to suffer whatever the Night Child threw at her but her tears were because she didn't know if Erienne would return in time.

And if she didn't, the world was already dead and all her pain would have been wasted.

Erienne was momentarily confused, genuinely refusing to believe her eyes. Though Selik had intimated he was assisted by mages, never in her worst nightmare had she contemplated being before the man who had walked through her cabin door. She shook her head, shuddering at what it all meant. This was no rogue Dordovan mage, this was the High Secretary of the College. A man steeped in respect and the ethics of her College. A man she had known all her life and had thought she knew and could trust.

'Erienne, please don't judge me too quickly.'

Berian's words made her feel sick. She was glad she was sitting down or she'd have fallen. Emotions and thoughts crowded her mind. She had no idea how to react or what to say. All she knew was that the revulsion she felt at Berian's presence, and the magnitude of the betrayal that presence represented, was overwhelming. She swayed and turned her head away.

'Don't talk to me,' she rasped, tasting bile in her mouth. 'Don't even look at me. You revolt me.'

'Please, Erienne,' said Berian. 'We had to find you. We worry for you and Lyanna.'

'How dare you lie to me!' Erienne's eyes blazed, her rage growing. 'You're standing next to the murderer of my children. Dordovan children. How could you!'

Berian gave Selik a sideways glance. 'But they knew where to find you again,' he said gently. 'And we would see you come to no further harm.'

'Liar!' Erienne flew across the cabin, landing one punch on Berian's face before Selik dragged her away and threw her back on the bed.

'Calm yourself,' he drawled.

'Calm?' she screamed. 'Great Gods burning, I've delivered myself and my child to hell.' She jabbed a finger at Berian. 'And you, you bastard betrayer. You're dead. I swear it. You've betrayed everything and joined with Witch Hunters to find your own and kill them.'

She slumped, her head dropping to her chest, her rage extinguished. Helplessness swept through her and tears fell down her cheeks. Everything she'd believed in was in ashes at her feet.

'How could you?' she whispered.

'Because your daughter is a danger to Balaia,' said Berian, all hint of gentleness gone from his voice. 'And she is a herald of doom for Dordover. Did you really think we'd stand by and let you bring her to the One uncontested? She must be controlled by Dordover to ensure our College survives. It is you who are the betrayer, Erienne Malanvai. I would save my College. You would see it fall.'

Erienne shook her head. 'No,' she managed through her weeping. 'No, you don't understand.'

'Yes, Erienne, I do,' said Berian. 'I understand only too well.'

She heard footsteps receding and her door close and lock.

Erienne had never considered the circumstances of her death until now. Never wondered if she'd know it was imminent, what she might say, how she might react, how she might feel. But here it was, only worse. Because she wasn't dying alone. She was sealing the fate of her daughter at the same time.

She felt detached, looking in from afar. Her life had taken on dual qualities of utter certainty and dreamlike unreality. There were many things she knew. Selik wouldn't touch her until they reached Herendeneth. The Raven, if they survived, would be chasing her. She'd been betrayed by Dordover. And Berian, of all mages, was travelling with her, helping to organise her death. But her grasp of time seemed vague. She felt the ship move, knew they were in the channel heading down towards the Bay of Arlen, but somehow couldn't connect it with her reality. None of it should be happening and there were parts of her that still believed that she would come to and find Denser watching over her.

She had tried to cast, of course. It was one way to reconnect herself with everything she knew. But though her faculties were recovering, she hadn't the stamina to attempt complex shapes and, even if she could, a Dordovan spell shield covered her cabin, leaving her completely cut off.

She poured a goblet of water, walked to the back of her cabin and looked out of the small window. Through the rain, she could see the red smudge in the skies above Arlen, indicating the fires that still raged there. She held on to the window ledge as the ship rolled, water spilling over her hand. The wind was gusting very strong and though making headway, the *Ocean Elm* was surely under limited sail. She wouldn't know. Selik wouldn't let her out on deck.

She sat on the bed, draining the goblet and placing it on her small table. Another roll and it fell to the floor, clinking dully on the timbers. She left it there. Trying to ignore the conditions outside, the rain that drilled into the glass of the window and the wind that washed over them, howling as it came, Erienne set her mind to what, if anything, she could do.

It wasn't a long list. The most obvious route was magic but she had only just begun to probe the shield placed around her. It was strong, probably the work of three Dordovan betrayers and she had no doubt that it was being monitored closely for signs she was testing its structure. If she found weakness, she'd have to be ready to exploit it immediately.

On the physical plane, there were two escape routes, neither viable. The door to her cabin was kept locked and two guards stood outside it. She hadn't even considered attacking them despite the fact that they stood inside the spell shield. After all, where would it get her?

The window had been nailed shut and, even if she could force it, the drop to the water would result only in her death from drowning.

Yet suicide was an option she couldn't ignore. If she died, the *Ocean Elm*'s crew would no longer have the incentive to complete their journey. But it would only buy the Al-Drechar a little time. With the defences around Herendeneth in terminal decline, the location of the island wouldn't stay hidden for ever – if indeed it still was – and, despite the treacherous waters, Lyanna would be found eventually.

The ship lurched again and shuddered as it plunged into a wave. She recognised the sideways movement and knew they were approaching the mouth of the Arl. She'd learned enough to understand that the tidal forces in the bay made passage uncomfortable as high or low water approached and, fanned by gale force winds, the waves would be very difficult. She could only imagine what the open sea would be like.

Inside she felt like collapsing. Like giving up her will and letting what was to come wash over her. But in her heart beat belief. Belief that Lyanna, her beautiful girl, must live and that somehow she would be helped, rescued.

She clung to that belief because it was all she had. It would take them seven days at least to reach Herendeneth and so she put herself in someone else's hands. Not Dordover's, not her husband's but something potentially more powerful than all the forces ranged against her. And she knew that the whole would never give up while one of them had the strength to help.

The Raven.

Chapter 28

It had begun days ago but no one had taken any notice, not really. Despite the floods, there had been no one killed, indeed not many injuries at all. They had heard the stories from the undefended farmsteads, the coastal towns and the lakeside villages as refugees had poured in. But here in Korina, they had always thought themselves impervious to real damage. Now the refugees were flooding out, not in.

Diera ran from her room, the screaming Jonas clutched to her chest as her window blew inwards, the force of the blast shaking the whole inn to its foundations. And this was worse than a mere hurricane. The force of the wind had slammed the shutters so hard, they'd snapped in, tearing frame and glass from the sturdy brick walls as they came.

Hurrying down the stairs, she came upon a scene of panic in the bar as The Rookery's drinkers tried to escape the roaring tempest scouring the market square. Half of the front of the inn had been torn away, books and papers flashed through the air, tables slid and tipped, the fire blew in all directions showering hot embers and over the ringing sound of the smashing of glass, the cries of terror and pain rose like spectres.

'The cellar, the cellar!' someone was bawling in her ear while pulling at her arm. She turned. It was Tomas, his face white, forehead cut and blood pouring into one eye. He pointed to one of the doors behind the bar, then pushed past her and out into the wreckage of his inn, kneeling by a man whose legs had been crushed by a falling beam. She watched, mute, as Tomas spoke words to the trapped man, nodded and cut his thigh deeply above the artery, holding him as his life blood flowed on to the floor and he died.

Screams filtered in from the outside. People ran past, heading west, glancing over their shoulders and running harder. A great roaring filled the air, a deafening painful sound that beat at the ears. Diera pushed Jonas' head into her chest and covered his exposed ear with her free hand.

'Tomas!' she screamed. 'Tomas!'

The roaring took on a deeper intensity. A cart flew by the torn front of the inn and smashed into a wall nearby, timbers and springs scattering. The remaining people inside ducked again, clinging on to whatever they could. Tomas was shouting at them but they couldn't hear him.

He crawled, hand over hand, back to the bar, grabbed her and pushed her to the cellar door. He wrenched it open and she stumbled down the lantern-lit stairs, hearing the door shudder shut behind them.

In the sudden relative quiet, she could hear her own breathing, her baby's whimpers and Tomas' cursing. Below them, the space was crammed with people. She saw Maris and Rhob hugging each other, and many others she only dimly recognised, their fear written in their expressions, their limbs quivering with exertion, and those that could still stand tending those that could not.

Above them, a terrible rending sound was followed by a thunderous impact that shivered beams and shook dust into the air in clouds.

'It's the inn,' gasped Tomas. 'Gone. Gone.'

Diera saw agony in his slim, blood-smeared face.

'What can we do?' she asked.

He turned to her and put a hand on her cheek, stroking gently with his fingers.

'Pray,' he said. 'Pray this cellar roof holds. Pray the floods don't reach here. Pray you see tomorrow's sun and that your husband finds a way to end all of this before we are all killed.'

Diera looked at him. She understood it was all down to magic. The word had spread through the city days ago. One part of her wanted to demand what one man could possibly do. But another, deeper and more spiritual part knew they all had to believe in something.

And Tomas chose to believe in Sol.

Diera rocked her crying child against her chest, finding comfort in sharing the same belief. After all, he'd never let Balaia down yet.

The *Calaian Sun* struggled to make real headway. The winds that had taken the *Ocean Elm* out of sight had backed and now blew straight up the Arl to the lake.

With the night full and dark and the destroyed town behind them, The Raven, in dry clothes provided by the crew, had time to take stock while Jevin, their reluctant skipper, deployed as much sail as he dared and tried to read the difficult conditions. He had already reported the likelihood of having to short tack the length of the river and warned The Raven that if the *Elm* had been lucky, they would enter open water as much as half a day behind.

While Darrick organised food and drink from the galley, Hirad, Ilkar and Denser stood between the narrow twin beds on which lay The Unknown and Thraun. Hirad felt helpless. He replayed over and over what had happened, searching for any ways he could have helped. He found none.

And so the rock of The Raven lay unconscious under a WarmHeal, alive but badly damaged. Hirad wiped the corners of his eyes with his right thumb and forefinger, and felt a hand squeeze his shoulder.

'It wasn't your fault,' said Ilkar. 'I cast the ForceCone.'

Hirad looked at the elf. 'It's not that. There's no blame to anyone. I just thought that there would be more you could do.'

'If Erienne, were here, we could. She's a BodyCast master.'

'But I thought . . .' Hirad gestured uselessly.

'WarmHeal can only do so much. Knitting tissue, promoting muscle growth and sealing fractures. He needs more than that. Much more,' said Ilkar.

'So what's the situation?' Hirad hadn't even wanted to ask the question, as if not knowing would make things better.

'The axe has smashed his hip and cracked his pelvis,' said Denser. 'And that's apart from the mess it's made of his tendons, muscle, skin . . . We were able to fuse the pelvis and that will knit. But the hip is crushed and there are shards of bone everywhere. We aren't physicians, Hirad, and we don't have the skill to reforge in the way a BodyCast can.'

Hirad shook his head, grasping for a conclusion. Both mages were looking studiously away from him.

'So, will he walk?'

Ilkar nodded. 'After a fashion. The joint will stiffen and he'll be in constant pain. He'll limp heavily but he'll walk.' The elf shrugged.

'Oh Gods,' said Hirad, the ramifications obvious. 'He won't be able to fight.'

'With a two-handed sword, no,' said Ilkar. 'He won't have the balance or the strength in that leg. But he'll get by with a long sword if someone shadows his left side.'

'He's lucky to be alive at all,' added Denser. 'He's lost a massive amount of blood.'

Hirad looked down at the big man. The mages would keep him asleep on the rolling ship for days, perhaps the whole voyage. And when he awoke, it would be as a cripple, the power and grace that were his trademark gone forever. Except there still had to be something that could be done. Hirad wasn't about to give it up.

'Could Erienne help him?' he asked.

'If she got to him before the muscle grew back around the joint and the bones fused completely, yes,' said Denser. 'But so what?'

'How long before it's too late?'

'Well, we can retard the healing a little, I suppose, but the spells are already doing their work,' said Ilkar. 'Three days perhaps?' He glanced at Denser, who shrugged and nodded.

'Then we'd better get her off that ship, hadn't we?'

For a while, all Hirad could hear was the sound of the ship ploughing through the rough river waters, the sails snapping on the masts and the timbers creaking and settling. And all he could see were Ilkar's and Denser's stunned expressions.

'What?' he demanded, his hands spread, palms up.

'Well I think we're both just waiting to hear how you propose to achieve this miracle,' said Ilkar.

'It's simple,' said Hirad, the plan crystallising in his head. 'Captain Jevin catches up with *Elm*, we fly across under cover of darkness, rage below the decks, grab Erienne and fly out. We can bring Protectors too. They can hold ShadowWings, can't they?'

'Yes, but—' began Denser.

'But what?'

'When I suggested something similar back in Arlen, I was shouted down.'

'That was different,' said Hirad.

'Oh well, that clears it all up, thanks,' said Denser, beginning to turn away. Hirad clamped a hand on his shoulder and hauled him around.

'I'd do it for you,' he said. 'I'd do it for any of us. This time it's The Unknown.' He glared into Denser's face. 'Take a good look at him, Denser. He left his wife and child behind to help you find yours. He didn't even question it. And see what it's cost him.

'Now we will help him. I won't see him a cripple. He's Raven.'

'So is Erienne,' muttered Denser.

'And we're getting her too. The time wasn't right then. They were ready for attack back in Arlen. They won't be now.'

Denser regarded him solemnly for a time before his mouth turned up into a wry smile.

'You're right. We'll probably die, but you're right.'

'Good!' Hirad clapped him on the shoulder. 'Now, you need to commune with Sytkan in Arlen so he knows who of the Protectors we have on board, before punishment is invoked. Then see if you can get to Erienne, Ilkar, with me. We'll talk to Ren'erei, see what we can persuade Jevin to do. Then you can talk to me about Thraun.'

He turned and opened the door but Denser's voice stopped him.

'Hirad?'

'What?'

'I'm sorry. In the forest, you know . . .'

Hirad shrugged, finding in Denser's face a genuine sorrow. He shrugged.

'Me too. But it worked out didn't it? If we hadn't scrapped, I'd have been captured by Darrick too. So let's forget it, eh? Now let's get your wife, fix The Unknown and save your daughter. Then maybe we can work out how to send the Kaan home and I'll forgive you anything. Get communing.'

'I'll be in here,' said Denser.

Hirad nodded and led Ilkar out of the cabin.

The small Protector force was quartered in the forward hold where the Dordovans had been due to billet themselves for the uncomfortable crossing of the Southern Ocean. Twenty-four had survived more or less unscathed. None that were too injured to fight after the journey had come aboard.

They stood in a circle, hands clasped in front of them, masked heads bowed, swaying with the motion of the ship. The silence of their contemplation was matched far away in Xetesk, where the Soul Tank, deep in the catacombs, was dormant. Every surviving Protector grieved for the souls that had departed but celebrated their freedom from thrall.

Every death lessened the whole but every released soul gave hope. For Aeb, it was a confusion of emotion, suppressed for the most part but finding voice in the silence. He knew it was the same for them all. They craved the companionship of the tank while hating the forces that had put them there, ripping their living souls from their bodies and inserting the linkage that kept them alive. The DemonChain.

Every Protector wanted freedom from the DemonChain. None wanted to lose his brothers in so doing. Sol was the only living example and in him were all the dangers of freedom. The brotherhood could feel him and he, them. But they could not connect. He was, and would always be, one of them but outside of the net of support they shared. Yet he stood as an icon of hope, and they revered him.

'We are one,' said Aeb, his voice filling the hold, speaking rather than pulsing as was their right when not in battle psyche.

'We are one,' the Protectors intoned.

'Sol lies grievously injured, his condition closed to us as is his soul. We move away from our Given. I have requested that we be assigned to Denser, the Dawnthief Master. It will be an honour we will celebrate in the Soul Tank with our brothers.

'Prepare yourselves, near ones. Hone your blades, bathe your wounds, harden your minds. Our enemies would destroy that which would make Xetesk dominant. We will protect.

'We are one.'

'We are one.'

'By the lore of the Chain, and to the mercy of the Life beyond Brotherhood, I call upon He who guides us to watch us wherever we may be. We are one,' said Aeb.

'We are one,' they responded.

Another short contemplation followed. Aeb returned to pulsing now action was demanded.

Xye, we must have hot water. The elves may have cloth and balm. Ren 'erei has the ear of the Captain.

It will be done.

Aeb looked around the circle. He could feel the tiredness there. They had been running for days and now, after the fight, they had no Given to channel recuperative energies along the DemonChain.

Sit, brothers and let the air play on your faces. Fin, the door. Brothers, let the dark hide us.

Fin moved to the hatch and slid it shut. It would open only for Xye. One by one, the lanterns were hooded, and as the blackness became complete, Aeb heard the unbuckling of straps as he pulled at his own.

His mask came away and the blessed air played across his raw face. Smooth though the ebony was, sweating skin broke beneath it. He lowered his head, not daring even to catch the glint of a brother's eye. To do so when unmasked brought bad luck and death in the next conflict.

It was the way things were.

'So what have we got?' asked Hirad.

The Raven plus Ren'erei and Darrick were sat around the

Captain's table while topside Jevin was talking to his first mate and navigator.

'Good news and bad news,' said Denser, first to respond. 'Sytkan has passed the Right of Giving for the twenty-four Protectors on board to me. I'll talk to them later but suffice to say that you'll be able to use them as you need to on Herendeneth. They'll be speaking freely and will be as untethered as Protectors can be.'

'Meaning?' asked Ilkar.

'They won't wait to engage in pre-emptive offence if the opportunity arises, they will inform you if they believe you are not making best use of them and they will be in automatic charge of their own formations unless otherwise directed.'

'So the bad?' Hirad drank a mouthful of tea. On plates across the table were hard cheese, bread and dried meat. The galley hadn't been forthcoming with vegetables.

'Balaia is a mess. Politically, it's degenerated into something approaching inter-College warfare. There are skirmishes across the mage lands though so far Arlen's the only non-mage place hit.' Denser paused for breath. 'But that's nothing to the elements. Sytkan's talk with Xetesk revealed reports of tornados in Korina, volcanic activity in the Blackthorne and Balan mountains, more hurricanes to the north and flooding all the way along the Southern Force.

'Balaia's all but run out of time.'

'And Erienne?' prompted Hirad.

'Hold on,' said Denser. 'I haven't finished the other bad news yet. Sytkan also reported that a Dordovan fleet has sailed from Gyernath in the last couple of days.'

'How big and when?' asked Darrick.

Denser shrugged and poured a fresh mug of tea. The ship rolled slightly, the mug sliding against the raised lip of the table but not spilling.

'Details are sketchy. Gyernath itself has seen flooding,' he said. 'Sytkan will try to contact me in the next two or three days if he finds more information.'

'Can we call on more reserve?' asked Hirad.

'That's something else Sytkan is trying to find out,' said Denser.

'It'll make no difference,' said Darrick. 'Unless my intelligence is badly astray, there are no significant Xeteskian forces within ten days of any southern port and Korina is out of action completely. That's excepting the Protector army, of course, and even if they ran back to

Arlen and took ship there, they wouldn't be able to leave for a day or they'd starve at sea.'

'And who do you think it is in charge of the Dordovans?' asked Denser.

'Vuldaroq,' said Darrick immediately. 'That fat idiot was due in Arlen days ago but never arrived. I have a feeling he might have run into trouble in the mage lands.'

'So it's us against however many,' said Hirad. 'I just hope this island is defensible.'

'There is only one landing point on Herendeneth. The island was chosen with great care,' said Ren'erei.

'It's not something we can worry about now,' said Ilkar. 'What about Erienne?'

'She's being shielded,' said Denser. 'I suppose we should have expected that. I can't get through – not without alerting the shielding mages.' He looked down into his mug.

'You all right, Xetesk man?' asked Hirad, still reeling from the news he'd been given of Denser's fate.

It was only now, sitting in the relative calm of the *Calaian Sun*'s Captain's room that the reality was sinking in. Ilkar had told Hirad almost casually that saving Lyanna would cost Denser his life but he could see now that the Julatsan was already grieving. And now he could contemplate it, the fact sat as an ache in Hirad's stomach and wreathed his heart.

He felt a great guilt for how he'd treated Denser in the forest outside Greythorne. All the time, he knew he was going to die and had said nothing. He wasn't sure whether that was bravery or stupidity. The Raven would support him now they knew but he could have enjoyed that support for longer.

For all Denser was a difficult man at times, Hirad didn't want to be without him in the world. It made their arguments and silences over the last few years seem so stupid. But at the time, he'd always thought Denser would be there. Now he knew different and the thought broke him in two.

Denser looked up, smiling sadly. 'I need her near me, Hirad. We haven't got much time left together.'

'I know, Denser, and I'm sorry,' said Hirad. 'We'll get her back for you.'

'If anyone can, The Raven can,' said Darrick.

'I haven't quite forgotten it's because of you we're in this particular mess,' said Denser, though there was no anger in his voice.

Darrick said nothing, merely nodded and dropped his gaze.

'Moving swiftly on,' said Ilkar. 'What did the captain say, Ren?'

'He said he'd talk to his crew. He said he'd look at the conditions. He didn't promise anything.'

'Well he's going to have to,' said Hirad. 'I'm not interested in excuses.'

'Can I say something?' asked Ren'erei.

'Of course,' said Ilkar.

'I know the captain of the *Ocean Elm* very well. I know he'll do everything he can to delay progress without it seeming obvious. There are a lot of tricks he can employ. You must trust Jevin, please. He's an experienced captain and he'll go as fast as he can. But you can't expect him to sacrifice his ship and crew for the sake of speed.'

'But he must take some risks,' said Hirad. 'We've only got three days.'

'He's aware of all this,' said Ren.

'He can always be made more aware,' returned Hirad.

'Don't threaten him,' said Ren. 'That's not the way.'

Hirad pushed his mug and plate away and leant forwards.

'Ren, let me tell you the way,' he said. 'We are all very pleased you're with us. And we respect both your knowledge and what you've already done for The Raven and particularly Erienne.

'But we *are* The Raven, and we've succeeded by always doing whatever it takes. That will not change because Jevin is a bit sensitive, all right?'

Ren'erei opened her mouth to reply but Ilkar placed a hand on her arm.

'Don't,' he said, managing to smile. 'I'll explain later.'

'Tell you what,' said Denser. 'I'll tell you now, elsewhere. I want to hear all about my wife and daughter.'

Ren'erei smiled. 'I would like that.'

Hirad watched them go, avoiding Ilkar's eyes and choosing to refill his mug and plate instead. Outside, the force of the wind had dropped, or perhaps it had backed again since the ship's progress was distinctly smoother.

'Excellent tact, Hirad, well done,' said Ilkar, when the door had closed.

'What?'

'You and your "we are The Raven" lecture. Doesn't work any more. All you've done is irritate her and we need her on our side.'

'She needed to know how it is with us.'

'Belligerence in the face of desperation is not how it is with us,' said Ilkar sharply. 'Doing what it takes is right but there are ways and ways.'

'And you think I took the wrong way.'

'Strangely, yes.' Ilkar sighed. 'Still, it's not like you've become different overnight, is it?'

Hirad smiled, knowing the gentle chiding was over. 'No. Sorry, Ilks, it's just that this isn't how it's supposed to be.'

'What do you mean?'

'Us. The Raven. Gods burning, Ilkar, we're a complete mess. The Unknown's crippled, Erienne's a captive, there's Thraun . . . But the worst of it is that Denser's about to sacrifice his life and there's nothing we can do. It's wrong.'

Ilkar pursed his lips. 'I know. But we can still win this thing.'

'It won't feel like winning. Denser will be dead.' He shrugged, the words he'd just spoken sounding strange, like they came from someone else's mouth.

'It won't be like death, though,' said Ilkar, his words hollow but reflecting his sincere hope. 'A part of him will survive inside Lyanna.'

'He'll be gone,' said Hirad. 'That's all I understand.'

They fell silent, listening to the creaking of the ship, the sounds of feet overhead and the muted rush of the wind. Hirad felt tired. He hadn't slept properly for days. His body ached, his lower back and shoulders particularly. It hadn't always been like this but days of sleeping rough in the barely sheltered open, and eating only what he could catch or pick had brought home to him the reality of his age. He had come off the peak of his fitness and that meant long fights would be a struggle. Grudgingly, he had to admit that their enforced inactivity might be a blessing though his mind would continue to churn.

To his left, Darrick had maintained a studious silence for much of the discussion, contenting himself by listening and, by and large, avoiding Denser's potentially caustic tongue. Hirad smiled inwardly. The capture of Erienne hadn't even been his fault.

'Hey, Darrick, cheer up,' said the barbarian.

'If you don't mind, I don't think I will,' said Darrick, not lifting his head.

'We know it's not all your fault, all this mess. So does Denser, when he thinks about it.'

'But it is,' said Darrick. 'I should have listened to my heart before I ever rode to Arlen. If I'd let you go, you'd be on the *Elm* and sailing now. The Unknown wouldn't be injured. I'm a fool and I could have stopped the worst of it. I should have refused to take you.'

'I don't think so,' said Ilkar. 'Any hint of insubordination and you'd have been replaced.'

'Can we talk about something else?' Darrick's tone was sharper than he probably intended. His mouth tugged up just a little. 'What about Thraun?'

It had been Hirad's next burning question. Thraun. More extraordinary than anything he had seen for a very long time. He nodded and looked across expectantly at Ilkar. The Julatsan sucked his lip and sat back in his chair.

'He's in a bad state too. He's been a wolf a long time now. Too long to be returning to human form, that's clear. You've both seen the hair on his face; well, it's all over his body. But that's the simple part. He's lying like an animal. His arms are locked straight, his legs likewise but bent in at the knee. His musculature is unbalanced, his feet still have claws and his heart is far too large. And those are just the effects we could detect easily.

'The point is that he may look more like a human but, frankly, he's not. Not yet, anyway. Now we're hoping that his physique and organs will revert further but we don't know they will.'

'Can you keep him alive?' asked Hirad.

'That's no problem. All we have to consider is what sort of life it's going to be. Gods falling, but his mind'll be a complete shambles. How much of his human psyche and memories he's retained is anyone's guess. He's going to need a lot of help.'

'Then we'd better make sure that some of us stay alive to give it,' said Hirad.

'That we had,' agreed Ilkar.

'It's unbelievable isn't it?' said Hirad. 'Thraun back amongst us. Like it was always meant to be that way.'

'What do you mean?' asked Ilkar.

'For weeks now, we've been reforming The Raven very slowly and in a lot of ways it feels like we never went away. But I never thought we'd see Thraun again and he followed us from Thornewood, he must have done. And now he's changed back. Hard to credit, isn't it?'

'You said it,' said Ilkar. 'If only I could offer you good news about him. Or any of us for that matter.'

'No,' said Hirad, and his momentary lightness disappeared. 'So what's to do now?'

'Well, I don't know about you, Hirad, but it's the middle of the night and I'm shattered,' said Ilkar.

Hirad nodded. Despite the movement of the ship, he felt he could sleep anywhere. The very thought made him yawn broadly.

'I see you concur,' said Ilkar.

'Yep,' Hirad said, rising and stretching. 'C'mon General, you too.'

'Good idea.'

As Ilkar passed by him at the door, Hirad grinned, a sudden thought striking him. He grabbed on to the chance to change the mood.

'Tell you what, Ilks, that Ren'erei. Not bad-looking, eh?'

Ilkar stared at him. 'Not bad,' he agreed.

'You could be in there. Y'know, good-looking elf like you, famous, head mage in Julatsa. Could make the trip south more entertaining for you.'

Ilkar shook his head. 'Only you, Hirad Coldheart,' he said. 'In a situation like this, only you could think of sex.'

Hirad shrugged and moved along the corridor to their cabin and bunks.

'Sweet dreams, Ilkar.'

Chapter 29

Throughout the next day, the *Calaian Sun* struggled against strong winds whipping up the sea into a swell that reached almost thirty feet at its peak. Carrying more sail that he should, Jevin didn't leave the wheel deck all day, his eyes searching the lightning-lit, roiling dark cloud for clues, scrutinising the sails for trouble, or worrying at the wind which had precious little direction.

Ren'erei had been with him much of the time, cajoling and encouraging. Darrick was lost in his own thoughts, a lone figure on deck or lying on his bunk in the forward area originally set aside for the Dordovan command. Of the Protectors, there was little sign. The Xeteskians stayed in the hold, only one ever appearing to ask for food or hot water. For them it was a time of rest.

It was the middle of the afternoon. Hirad gripped the forward rail with one hand, his other arm supporting Ilkar who was leaning out again over the side of the ship, retching, his body shaking with exertion, his face wet from spray and sweat. It had been a miserable day for the Julatsan but the worry wasn't his immediate condition. The elf had already voiced his concerns about the effect this would be having on his mana stamina and on his ability to concentrate and cast effectively. And they couldn't do without him if they were to stand any chance of rescuing Erienne.

For Hirad, it was just one more problem on a mounting list. His idea that Ilkar and Denser would be able to assign ShadowWings to Protectors had already been dismissed. Even without Ilkar's seasickness, the drain from keeping Thraun and The Unknown alive and asleep was high. At best estimates, the two mages could cast their own wings for the journeys to and from the *Ocean Elm* and cast limited shield or offensive spells during the rescue attempt. But that was it. They were left relying on Erienne and what condition she was in was anyone's guess. Hirad wasn't getting his hopes up.

The *Sun* pitched into another wave, the impact shuddering through her hull and sending a wash of spray over the foredeck and soaking them once again. Despite the constant drenching, it was where Ilkar said he felt most comfortable, though that was clearly a relative term.

Hirad stared at the sky. On the far horizon, lightning sheeted across the heavens, illuminating the black of the clouds and the angry, white-flecked, dark grey of the ocean. Above them, the thick, unbroken ceiling of cloud stormed by at frightening pace, driven by a wind which, had it come down to sea level, would have driven them straight to the bottom of the sea. There was no longer any land in sight behind them and he felt a shiver of anxiety down his back because there was no certainty they would see any ever again.

The barbarian could understand the superstitions of the sailors all too easily. He had been sceptical of them at first but now the desire to have something to hang on to that settled the mind was one with which he could sympathise.

All over the ship, the signs were there. Every cabin had a shrine to one of the Gods of the sea or the skies. Figurines, dried flowers, candles and tiny models of boats floating in water-filled, carved wooden bowls were common. And by the head of every crew bunk, prayers were carved into the wood, or pinned up, painted in garish reds and yellows. Not one of the crew was without a talisman, either fish or bird and always metal, around his neck.

But the most curious superstition surrounded the cat. Hirad knew ships commonly kept a cat on board to kill rats and mice but on this ship at least, it went much further. The animal had a luxurious basket, plenty of meat and biscuit and a bowl of water was always full. One of the crew, he had been told, was duty-bound each day to see it safe, examine it for splinters, sing it songs of the sea and place it in its basket at the start of the first night watch. Naturally, being a cat, it would sleep elsewhere but the tradition could not be ignored. Whatever kept them happy was fine with Hirad.

Ilkar straightened a little and turned his dripping, ashen-white face to Hirad.

'Let's go back, I've got to lie down.'

'Jevin said it was worse if you stayed below deck,' said Hirad.

'He also said I'd get my sea legs by tomorrow and I don't think that's possible either. Help me below.' He gagged suddenly again and spat bile over the side which whipped away.

'Come on then, walk on my inside.'

Hirad kept a hand on the rail and the other arm around Ilkar as the two friends walked slowly to the fore cabins. As he opened the doors, he heard a shout and turned to see Ren'erei hailing them from the wheel deck. She made a shrug and pointed, presumably at Ilkar. Hirad shook his head, indicated himself and pointed back at the wheel deck. Ren waved her understanding.

Ilkar and Hirad were sharing a tiny cabin which looked out over the port side of the ship. Ilkar had the bottom bunk and Hirad helped him take off his cloak, lie down and then wiped his face with a towel. The ship rolled and pitched. Hirad stumbled.

'Oh Gods, I wish I was dead,' groaned Ilkar.

'Just try and sleep. I'll see if there's anything that can help you.'

'A knife in the heart should do the trick,' said Ilkar, closing his eyes briefly and putting his hands over his face.

Hirad patted his shoulder. 'I'll bring one for you. See you later.'

'Get the Captain to find us a millpond, would you?'

Hirad chuckled. 'Keep it up, Ilks.'

He closed the door and walked back up on to the deck. Funny. He'd hardly ever been aboard ship either but felt absolutely fine. Balance wasn't difficult except when the ship drove down into a wave and he'd slept long, eaten a good breakfast and, in complete contrast to Ilkar, felt more refreshed than he had in days. Climbing the ladder to the wheel deck, he wondered if he hadn't missed his calling.

Captain Jevin and Ren'erei stood behind the helmsman, all three elves looking alternately at the flag riding atop the main mast and at the compass to the right of the wheel. Jevin's face was set severe and he barely nodded acknowledgement as Hirad came to stand by them.

'How're we doing?' he asked, his voice raised above the roaring of the wind. Rain started to fall again, heavy and punishing. He drew his furs closer.

'Well, we'll be faster than the *Elm*,' said Jevin.

'How come?'

'Because they are a smaller vessel, less broad and long. Their skipper'll be running minimal sail in these conditions. She wasn't built for this.' He turned to look at Hirad. 'Mind you, neither were we.'

'Will we catch her?' asked Hirad.

Jevin licked a finger and held it up as if testing the wind. He scowled. 'Gods, man, how the hell should I know? I don't know how far they are ahead, in which direction they are going and how fast they are travelling. It's all guesswork. This weather should not be possible. The wind comes from three directions, the swell ignores them all and I'm trusting my compass but don't know whether I should. I know we're heading south but that's about it.'

Hirad nodded. It had been a daft question.

'Sorry,' he said. 'Please do everything you can. So many lives depend on you.'

Ren looked at him in some surprise but there was a smile on her lips. She touched his arm and mouthed her thanks.

'My crew are brave and I am too young to die this voyage,' said Jevin, his voice a little softer. 'Best you tend to your sick and leave the wheel deck for sailors.'

Hirad turned to go but the Captain hadn't finished.

'Go to the galley. Ask the duty cook for some Lemiir powder. Tell him I sent you or he won't give it you. Dissolve it in water. That should soothe Ilkar's head and stomach. Help him sleep.'

'Thank you.'

Jevin nodded curtly and turned back to the sails.

Night was coming again, though the day of lowering cloud, buffeting wind and sometimes torrential rain had been so dark it would hardly seem to make a great difference.

On the *Ocean Elm*, the skipper patted his helmsman on the shoulder. It was a small gesture but the elf knew what it meant. He nudged the wheel very slightly, bringing the ship four degrees into the wind. With the pitching and yawing of the vessel in the storm, there was no way Selik would discern the change in direction nor the reduction in speed. He was no sailor.

Indeed, the skipper could see him now, clutching at the starboard rail, his face feeding on the wind, his stomach hopefully churning. He had already seen the man vomit half a dozen times as the storm worsened. He would be weakened and inattentive. It was a pity that some of the mages with him were not. Particularly the old one.

Berian, his name was, and he spent altogether too much time peering over the skipper's shoulder. It was he who had determined the course and he whom the skipper watched for before indicating that course could change. There was something dangerous about this Dordovan. He knew a good deal about the sea and watched the compass closely when on the wheel deck, waiting for it to settle between pitches before nodding acknowledgement that all was well.

But he had not been there through the early hours of the morning and his deputy had no idea what he was looking at. They had strayed far off course in that time and bought any pursuit precious hours. The skipper had not started looking back yet. Perhaps on the third day he would but even that might arouse suspicion.

He knew there would be pursuit. He had great faith in Ren'erei and her capacity to get aboard another elven ship. He prayed The Raven would be with her but the battle he had left behind on the docks of Arlen left those hopes severely dented. He needed to know that, as he approached Herendeneth, he wouldn't be leaving the Al-Drechar helpless. If another ship followed, and could match them through the tortuous waters of Ornouth, they still had a chance.

Below him, on the main deck, Erienne had been allowed a brief walk in the fresh air. He had managed to catch her eye as she was ushered back below by a mage guard and had smiled in what he hoped was encouragement. But she had the air of the condemned and he found it hard to disagree with her mood.

'Captain?' His helmsman indicated the starboard rail. Three mages were talking with Selik and, among them, Berian gestured behind him more than once at the wheel deck. It was an angry conversation and the skipper bit his lip.

'Come back to heading, lad,' he said, his lips barely moving. 'And keep yourself calm.'

The helmsman nodded, waited for the next pitch and edged the wheel away from the wind. The skipper felt the take on the sails, which were as light as he could argue, drive through the timbers at his feet. The four men left the rail and headed for the helm.

'Keep looking forward,' whispered the skipper, his face down looking at the compass.

'Aye, skipper.'

Footsteps rattled on the ladder and thumped across the wheel deck. The Captain was shoved aside and managed to assume an air of indignant surprise as he found Selik's sword resting on his chest.

'What have we done now, oversweetened your tea?' he asked, looking past the Black Wing at the mages who gathered around the compass.

Selik backhanded him across the cheek and he stepped back, rolling with the blow.

'You are testing my patience, elf,' drawled Selik. 'Berian?'

'Our direction is correct,' replied the old mage.

'But it wasn't always the way, was it Captain?' Selik pushed the point of his blade a little closer, the skipper aware that a sudden roll could end his life.

'Maintaining exact direction is impossible in these conditions,' he said. 'We are doing the best we can.'

Another slap. 'Liar.' Selik's good eye burned into the skipper's face.

'You think you're being clever, elf, but I have better men with me. They can see our destination through the mana trails, they can divine our position by light, wind and magic and they can sense an elf toying with the lives of his crew while he delays our purpose.'

The Captain said nothing. Selik drew back.

'Now we don't know exactly what you have cost us. We suspect it to be a good deal of time. And for every cost, there must be payment.' Selik moved his sword point higher where it wavered in front of the skipper's neck.

'I could take the payment from you but I fear your crew might not accept your death. Fortunately, there are ample substitutes.'

He spun and drove his blade through the helmsman's neck; the young elf stiffened, gurgled and collapsed as Selik dragged the sword clear. The elf twitched as he lay dying on the deck, his blood flooding from the awful wound.

The Captain felt a surge of sickness and a greater one of fury. He made to spring forwards but found Selik's sword point at his stomach once again.

'That's one step closer to your own death,' he said.

Selik didn't smile. 'You know, somehow I doubt it. The righteous are rewarded, the evil are cast down. It has always been the way. Now I suggest you take care of the wheel before we lose our course again. I'll have my men dispose of this body. After all, we can't afford the time for your ridiculous rituals, now can we?'

Selik strode to the ladder, the Captain's eyes following his every step. He wished for a wave to take him, for a slip to send him tumbling to the deck. Looking down now on the body of his fresh-faced young helmsman and seeing the renewed rain washing the blood from around his feet, the skipper mouthed a prayer to commend the elf's soul to the gods of the sea and gripped the bloodied wheel, his body on fire with hate.

Hirad was on deck early on the third day, scouring the way ahead for any sign of the *Ocean Elm*. He knew he wouldn't see anything before the elven lookouts but he had to do something. Denser and a marginally recovered Ilkar were tending The Unknown and Thraun, Ren was with Jevin as always and Darrick, well, Darrick was in a place of misery of his own invention. It was unlike the General but Hirad let him wallow. The time for bringing them together was not yet, and maybe not ever. Only when Erienne was on board would Hirad feel that there was a Raven to lead.

The weather had steadily worsened throughout the second day and Jevin had been forced to furl in some sail to retain control of his ship. It was frustrating but Hirad comforted himself in the knowledge that the *Elm* would be suffering the same and he trusted Jevin's assertion that they would still be travelling faster. But would it be fast enough?

Even if they sighted them now, would they be able to make up enough ground for a ShadowWing flight that night? Hirad thumped the rail and looked up into the rain and dark cloud, shivering. He had been cold for a day, the energy from his sleep gradually worn away by a growing sense of helplessness. The Unknown was relying on them to save him from being a crippled warrior the rest of his life. And there was nothing Hirad could do. Not until—

'Ship forward!' The shout came clear down from the crow's nest in the main mast. 'Ship forward!'

Hirad looked but could see nothing. He heard Jevin shouting up from the wheel deck but his elvish was lost on the barbarian as was the answering call. Hirad half ran back along the length of the ship and hurried up the ladder.

'Careful, Hirad, more haste less speed on a pitching deck,' said Ren'erei.

'Yeah, yeah. Captain?'

'It's a definite sighting. We can't yet tell if it's the *Elm* but it's travelling across our starboard bow.'

'Meaning?'

'If it is them, they've been off course. Probably deliberately,' said Ren.

'Can we catch them?' asked Hirad.

'There's no doubt of it,' said Jevin. 'It's more a question of when.'

'By nightfall. We have to be close enough by nightfall.'

Jevin stared hard at him. 'I am aware of our timetable. And I will do everything that I can that keeps this ship afloat. Do you understand?'

Hirad cast his gaze skywards. 'Yes, but—'

'But nothing, Hirad Coldheart,' said Jevin. 'Now, as I've mentioned before, kindly leave the wheel deck to the sailors. Why don't you prepare your plan, or eat something or whatever. Get Ilkar some more Lemiir.'

'Just get off your deck, eh?' said Hirad.

Jevin at last smiled. 'Now you're getting it,' he said.

Hirad turned and headed down the ladder, hearing Jevin's voice ring out across the ship.

'Bo'sun! I need more sail forward. Let's run this bitch of a storm! Let's show these ignorant humans what sailing really means!'

The barbarian shook his head, laughing as he strode across the main deck to the forward cabins and heading for the galley. The cook handed him his Lemiir wordlessly and he let himself quietly into the cabin where both mages sat watching the sleeping forms of The Unknown and Thraun. The cabin was stuffy despite the part-open window and the stale air mixed with the smells of urine and strong soap to make an unpalatable mix.

He poured water into a tankard and added the Lemiir powder, swirling it once and handing it to Ilkar.

'Surprised you can stand the smell in here,' he said.

'No choice really,' said Ilkar, accepting the tankard and continuing to mix its contents. 'Thanks. It's good stuff this. I wonder why I didn't get it earlier.'

'I have a feeling it's both expensive and in short supply,' said Hirad. 'Lucky you're an elf or I reckon Jevin'd let you suffer.'

'Believe me, I'm still suffering,' said Ilkar. He drained the tankard in one swallow, screwing up his face in disgust. 'It's good but it tastes rank and sweet at the same time. It's like swallowing sugared tree bark.'

'So, are you fit to cast?' asked Hirad. Denser looked around and Hirad grinned broadly at him, clapping him on the shoulder. 'Because we've just sighted a ship ahead.'

'Is it the *Elm*?' Denser brightened, a light growing in his dull eyes.

'How many other single ships do you reckon are round here?' said Hirad.

'Precious few,' said Denser, nodding his head vigorously. 'So, Ilkar, what's the verdict?'

'Well we've got all day. I'll rest up, if you don't mind, but so long as it's simple stuff, I should be all right. Just don't ask me to frame a MindMelt.'

'ShadowWings?' asked Denser.

'Borderline but probably,' replied Ilkar.

'You'd better be able to,' said Hirad. 'Because I'm coming with you.'

'Has it occurred to you, Hirad, that these are not the conditions for carrying someone of your bulk any distance at all?' said Ilkar. 'Sorry, but this is going to be just me and Denser alone.'

Hirad shook his head. 'No, it isn't, because I've had an idea.'

Chapter 30

By the time darkness had fallen, Hirad could see the *Ocean Elm* through the murk of the rain and low cloud. The wind had abated just a little, the swell had settled and Jevin had ordered the bo'sun to deploy as much sail as he dared, knowing the skipper of the *Elm* would dally as long as he could.

But as the night began to obscure their quarry, it was clear they still had a long way to go and, at current speeds, would not catch them for another day at least. As the sea softened, the sleeker *Elm* could pull away from the wider merchantman on which The Raven travelled, and Hirad found himself hoping for another storm. In the middle of the night his prayers were answered but far more violently than he'd wanted.

Taking a rest along with Denser and Ilkar to prepare for their attack, he was flung awake in pitch dark as the ship rolled sickeningly, almost throwing him from his bunk. Ilkar, lying on the edge of his, wasn't so lucky and tumbled to the floor, cursing. The thundering of feet and the echoes of shouted orders floated down.

'Doesn't sound good,' said Hirad, just about seeing Ilkar's outline and dropping to the floor to help him up.

'What time of night is it?'

'Gone midnight, I think,' said Hirad. 'How's your stomach?'

'Bearable,' said Ilkar. 'We should have been woken before now—'

They were thrown together as another wave struck the ship broadside, shaking figures out of the shrine and throwing their blankets off their bunks.

'Let's get topside, then,' said Hirad. 'You get Denser and meet me on the wheel deck. I hope we've closed enough on the *Elm* for you.'

'So do I.'

They half ran, half stumbled from the cabin, Hirad feeling his way back to the doors to the main deck, Ilkar going next door to fetch Denser. The Unknown and Thraun would just have to be all right for the time being. Besides, Darrick was sitting with them and the spells would keep them asleep.

On deck, there was bedlam. Jevin and the bo'sun were screaming orders at the crew. Above on the main mast, one sail was torn in half, its shreds flapping in the gale. All around, the seas were huge and Hirad could see the helmsman fighting to turn the ship head-on to the worst of the swell. Rain hammered down on to the deck and, up in the rigging, elves grappled with sail, trying to furl enough to give them back control.

Hirad raced for the wheel deck, making it out in the gloom. There were no lights anywhere on board. They wanted to remain hidden and the elves didn't need them anyway. Halfway up the ladder, another wave struck the forward port side, water pouring across the deck. Hirad lost grip with one hand but clung on with the other, smacking backwards into the wood above the aft hatch.

As the ship righted, he swung himself back onto the ladder and scrambled up the last few rungs.

'What the hell happened?' he shouted, not releasing his grip on the deck rail. The ship lurching, thundering down into a trough.

'It came from nowhere,' answered Jevin. 'Are you ready?'

'Why, how close are we?' The rain became hail, drumming on to the decks and thudding painfully on their heads. Hirad dragged his furs up onto his skull.

'On the sea, more than a day, still. For you on your wings, I don't know. But we'll get barely closer tonight. If the *Elm* has any sense, she'll have hove to by now, trying to ride it out. I'm dropping all but topsail. Either that or we'll founder.'

Hirad nodded. 'Thank you for all your efforts,' he said.

'Perhaps there'll be bonus pay in this.'

'Count on it,' said Hirad.

Ilkar and Denser were heading up the ladder. Ilkar looked pale but better than he had on the first day, the Lemiir buying him the time to rest and eat what he could keep down. Denser had a savage light in his eyes, a determination edged with desperation. Hirad had seen it before. It would make him powerful, but changeable.

'This is it,' said Hirad, voice barely less than a shout. 'Jevin says we'll get no closer tonight and The Unknown can't wait any longer.'

'Can you see the *Elm*?' Denser asked Ilkar. The Julatsan peered forward, the hail like a sheet in front of them. Hirad could barely see the prow of their ship. Beyond, it was just raging darkness. The wind howled across the open sea.

'No. We'll just have to fly high and hope.'

'Terrific.'

'Stay close to me,' said Ilkar. 'I'm your eyes.'

Denser beckoned them both close and put an arm around each shoulder.

'We'll need wings trimmed for speed, not mass, so I'll be unstable with Hirad hanging off me. Don't you take your eyes off me for long because, if he falls, you'll be getting him. And remember, Ren said Erienne's cabin was aft. We'll have to assume she's not been moved.'

'If she has, this could be a very long night,' said Hirad.

They broke. Hirad fetched a length of rope he'd had tied round his waist all night. Ilkar tied one end around his left wrist and then he lay flat on the deck while the elf attached the other end to Denser's left ankle. One thing Hirad couldn't risk was fouling Denser's wings.

'Just you get there safe, all right?' said Ilkar.

'Tell him that, he's driving,' said Hirad. 'Have you two got enough weapons? This could be a good night for knives, I think.'

'We're sorted out. Ready?'

'Of course not.'

Ilkar clapped him on the back. 'Then let's go.'

Hirad readied himself. Denser stood with his legs apart enough for Hirad to put his head through them and hang on to both his calves. 'I can't believe I'm doing this,' he muttered.

The hail came down harder. He heard a shout from Denser and a heartbeat later he was airborne and yelling his fear into the teeth of a gale.

'So kill me then!' roared the skipper. 'Kill any one you like. Because if we raise any more sail we'll all die anyway.' He shoved Selik away from him, the Black Wing steadying himself quickly and coming back, dagger still drawn.

'And what the hell good is that handkerchief you've got fluttering up there going to do for us, eh?' He renewed his grip on the skipper's throat, three of his men in attendance should the elf try to fight him.

The fury of the storm had taken them all by surprise, boiling up from the south under cloud so low they felt they could almost touch it. The skipper had called all hands to the deck and they'd swarmed up the rigging to furl sail as waves crashed across his deck, hurling two Black Wings and a member of his crew into the water to drown in the merciless ocean. Another of his crew had fallen from the rigging and he too would die, his body broken.

But Selik had stormed up to the wheel deck, demanding he go faster. Faster? They were lucky to be still afloat at all.

'I'll tell you what it'll do, you ignorant fool,' spat the skipper. 'It'll give us just enough manoeuvrability to keep our head to the wind so we can survive this thing. I take it you do want to survive?'

'Your tone will get you very badly hurt.'

Jevin grabbed Selik's hand and dragged the dagger towards his own throat.

'Then do it now, Black Wing, because I am past caring.'

Selik stared at him, jerked his hand away and backed off a pace, letting go the skipper's throat. He nodded.

'And what about them behind us?' he demanded, pointing over the skipper's shoulder into the filthy night.

'If their captain has any sense, he'll be doing exactly what I'm doing,' said the skipper. 'They won't catch us, Selik, more's the pity. And even should they, what can they achieve? They can't get through Ornouth in a ship that large.' The skipper was telling the absolute truth. The draft of the ship they'd glimpsed was far too deep to ride the reefs into Herendeneth. Fortunately, a ship that large also had single-masted landing skiffs to offload cargo from deep water. Something Selik was probably unaware of. If Ren was aboard, she'd know when to advise dropping anchor. And he'd sign her any way he could.

'Unfortunately for the civilised world,' said the skipper, 'I know what I'm doing.'

Selik huffed. A contemptuous sound. 'Civilised. Yet you embrace the evil of magic. Elves. Little better than animals in your home continent, I've heard.'

'Go away, Selik, and let me do my job or you'll be drinking sea water.'

'I will have you, elf,' said Selik as he turned and gestured his men away. 'Yours is a life borrowing heavily from the death.'

The skipper said nothing as Selik left the deck but his mind was ablaze with revenge. But he allowed himself a small inward smile. The Black Wing fools had demanded light on deck as soon as night fell so they might walk in greater safety on the pitching deck. The ship would be visible for miles once the rain abated.

'Come on, Ren. Come on.'

The journey to the *Ocean Elm* was pure torture for Hirad. Clinging on to Denser's legs while the hail lashed into his face and drained his strength, the barbarian could see practically nothing ahead of him. Every now and again, Ilkar would flash into view but apart from that, all he knew was that when he could see the waves and feel the spray on his legs, Denser was too low.

They were heading in the right direction, that much he did know. Ilkar had sighted the ship soon after leaving the deck of the *Calaian Sun* and hovered in close to tell Denser. But how far away they were, he couldn't begin to guess and, as the wind and rain began to chill him, sending aches through his arms and inexorably numbing his fingers even through his gloves, it was close to being too far.

A sudden gust drove them downwards hard and fast, Hirad yelling as his boots skimmed the top of a wave. Denser jerked back up quickly, too quickly for Hirad's cold hands and his grip was torn away and he swung like a human pendulum from the mage's left ankle, a couple of feet of rope all that separated him from drowning.

The sudden shift of weight unbalanced Denser completely and he plunged seawards, Hirad looking up to see him fighting for height and direction even as he was plunged into the sea. The cold flashed through his body and he gasped in shock. Water washed over his head and Denser, under the heavy drag, was all but catapulted into the wave in front of him, veering up and away at the last heartbeat, hauling the drenched Hirad with him.

The barbarian looked up again. Denser was shouting something but he couldn't hear it. The cold ate at him. They lurched sickeningly as Hirad swung back and forth, he trying to climb the rope that must be causing Denser agony, and the mage wrestling with his balance as he fought to keep them both from the ocean.

Hirad tried to swing his right arm round but couldn't get any momentum. The rope was cutting into his wrist and he grabbed onto it with his fingers, trying to relieve the pressure, praying now that they'd reach the *Elm* before Denser's boot came off. He tried again to get his other hand round but again fell short as the wind buffeted and blew him round and round in dizzying circles. He felt sick now, the cold muddying his mind, the hail and seawater blinding him, the blood running down his arm from the rope-torn skin of his wrist.

With a thumping of air, Ilkar flew to catch him, driving upwards in one movement and hovering until Hirad found his grip again.

'Thanks,' gasped Hirad. 'Thank you.'

'We're almost there.' And then he was gone.

They changed direction, flying low over the waves and coming up to the rear of the vessel. There were no lights here as there were along its flanks and, confident that no elf who saw them would betray them, they flew in very close, below the level of the deck.

Here, despite the pitching of the ship, there was blessed relief from the storm and Hirad's pounding heart started to calm. Denser took them slowly upwards, Hirad bringing his knees up to his chest to clear the rail. Once down, he lay flat to allow Denser to land and heard the light step of Ilkar come by his head. His hands were too numb to untie the rope. Happily, Ilkar's weren't and, with it off his wrist, he could refasten it around his waist for later and survey the damage to his arm.

'That's going to hurt later,' he said. 'Your ankle all right, Denser?'

'It'll last,' whispered Denser. 'What's next?'

'We listen,' said Hirad.

They listened to the shrieking of the wind, the odd word that came to them on the gale and the protesting of the ship's timbers. It told them nothing of who was on deck, or how many, but after their silence it was at least obvious that there were no patrols. At least, not to the stern.

'If this is anything like the *Sun*, we'll have to get in through the aft doors,' said Denser.

'Very risky,' said Ilkar.

'Well, besides blowing a hole in the wood about here, I reckon that's our only choice,' said Denser.

'And we have to exit that way anyhow,' said Hirad. 'Or you won't be able to deploy wings unless you can cast underwater.'

'Then let's not waste any more time,' said Ilkar.

Hirad nodded and drew two daggers, one for his right hand, one to be gripped in his teeth, leaving his long sword in its scabbard on his back. With Ilkar and then Denser in his wake, he edged down the port rail towards the main deck, keeping low, the pitching of the ship a constant threat. The wood beneath his feet was slick with water and the hail was turning to rain, mixed in with spray from the sea. His hands were cold, the ache in his left wrist growing as he gripped the rail.

Flattening himself along the wall behind him, he moved on slowly, letting more and more of the deck reveal itself. They were still in deep shadow but under the light of a few swinging lanterns he could see three Black Wing guards near the bow of the ship, their arms clutching the foremast for balance. Another was halfway up the port rail and he had to assume there would be more, probably starboard and on the wheel deck beneath which they were currently crouched.

He turned to Ilkar. 'Got enough stamina for CloakedWalk?'

'That, a shield and another set of wings, no more,' whispered Ilkar.

'We've got to know more about the situation in front of the aft doors.'

Ilkar nodded. 'Just hope I don't connect with the shield covering Erienne.' He framed the shape for the spell, moved forwards and disappeared.

'Denser, you all right?'

The Xeteskian nodded. 'Just let's get her away from here before I lose it.'

'Revenge later, all right?'

Denser grunted, his eyes fixed forwards.

They waited in the shadows. The Black Wings barely moved though elves did, checking lines, climbing rigging and passing round hot drinks to their captors. Drifting down from above them in a momentary pause in the wind, Hirad could hear elven voices. He wondered what they were thinking and whether, with Erienne gone, their lives would be worth much to Selik. Perhaps he should go with Denser's desire and try to kill all the Black Wings.

The slightest of rustling by Hirad and Ilkar reappeared.

'Right, I've retained the Cloak so this better be fast. There's a Dordovan on the wheel deck, along with two elves, and another one talking to a pair of Black Wings on the opposite side to us. We might be hidden from them, we might not. Our problems are the guards ahead who are looking back towards us and the one on the rail just here. They're bound to see us so we won't have much time.'

'Time for what?' asked Denser.

'Just go with this because it's our only chance. When I Cloak again, follow me at a run after a count of twelve. That gives me time to open the door on my way past. You run in, I follow and bolt it from the inside and we take it from there. We'll be up against swords and magic but they won't be expecting us. All right?'

'That's why The Unknown makes the plans,' said Denser, a wry smile on his face. 'Let's get it over with.'

Ilkar nodded and disappeared again. Hirad counted out loud and deliberately, using the numbers to keep calm himself for the fight. This could be no Rage, it would be too tight.

'. . . eleven, twelve. Go!'

He stood and ran for the corner of the deck, the ship pitching into a wave as he arrived, sending him sliding forwards into the light. There was a shout from ahead and he saw the Black Wings coming.

Forgetting them, he turned and headed for the aft door which swung open as he approached it, a slight shimmering in the air telling of Ilkar on the edge of losing concentration.

'Run, Denser!' he pounded to the opening and jumped through it, coming to a crouch, head up, and looking down the corridor.

Two guards flanked a door about ten yards ahead and by them, two mages were seated. The guards looked round as he hit the floor, unsure for a second. Hirad wasn't. He ran forwards, a cry ripping from his lips and threw a dagger as he approached, taking one of the guards in the shoulder as he turned. The man fell back, the other dragging his sword from its scabbard and stepping to block the corridor.

'Denser, mages ahead,' warned Hirad.

'Yes,' said a voice behind him.

The guard stabbed forwards, the corridor too narrow for a swing, Hirad stepping back smartly. The Black Wing came on, another stab, but this time Hirad flattened himself against a corridor wall, the blade missing him.

'Now, Denser!' he shouted, bringing his fist down on the guard's sword arm and lashing forwards with his dagger, ripping through the man's clothing and scoring his chest. He found purchase on the sword arm and dragged the man forwards and off balance, reversing the dagger across his face as he came. Into the clear space ran Denser, while behind him, the aft door shut and a bolt slid across.

'Ilkar, help him,' called Hirad. But, as he smashed his fist into the guard's face again, he saw the Xeteskian needed no help, pouncing on the wounded guard and stabbing him through the chest. The barbarian lashed a kick into his victim's stomach and as he fell, stamped down on his neck. They all heard it snap beneath his foot.

The two mages, coming round after deep concentration from the shield they had held over Erienne, were easy prey. Denser and Ilkar took one each, showing no mercy for the Dordovan betrayers. Denser said something to the mage he killed but Hirad couldn't hear it.

Not waiting for them, Hirad kicked open the door and strode in, dagger ready. Erienne was crushed into a corner of her bunk, her mouth dropping open at the sight of him.

'Hirad! How—'

'No time, Erienne. Get prepared with ShadowWings. We have to get off here quick or not at all.'

Denser and Ilkar ran in.

'They're at the hatch,' said the elf as Denser stormed across the floor and picked Erienne up into a feverish hug and a kiss.

'And they'll be through it in a moment. Ideas?' He drew his sword, keeping the dagger in his left hand. 'Denser, put her down. Time for that later.'

'Killjoy.'

'Ideas!' he repeated.

A door was wrenched open nearby. Hirad stepped up to the corridor. As the guard's face edged round, he backhanded his dagger straight into it, taking the man through the eye. He jerked the blade clear, the Black Wing falling without a sound.

'Wrong place, wrong time. Ilkar?'

There was a heavy thud on the aft doors.

'They'll be ready with spell so we need a shield. Denser can take that. I'll prepare a ForceCone. We have to drive them back to give us space to run aft, assuming that's where we're going.'

'Agreed,' said Hirad. 'Everyone ready?'

'I'll HardShield,' said Erienne, feeling a surge of exultation at having back her power to cast. 'They've got crossbows.'

After a pause, Hirad nodded. 'Good, thanks. But keep the ShadowWings shape in mind. All of you, for that matter.'

They moved back into the corridor, Ilkar ahead with his Force-Cone ready, Denser and Erienne with their respective shields cast and Hirad bringing up the rear. Where one guard could have come from, there could easily be others. Ahead of them, the door still held. At the other end of the passage, a door opened. A man stepped out, a crossbow in either hand.

'That's far enough,' he slurred.

'Keep going,' said Hirad to the others over his shoulder. 'I can take him.'

'Come on, you're not going anywhere. I've got thirty men and a dozen mages on this ship. Good try, but it's over.'

'Selik, delighted to see what a mess Erienne made of you. Shame you survived.'

'Hirad Coldheart, isn't it? Yes. A lone swordsman. Give her up and I'll let you live.'

They were nearing the doors. Another heavy blow and they creaked, the bolt part giving way. Nails squealing as they were forced clear.

'Ready,' said Ilkar. 'Concentrate.'

'Die then,' said Selik.

He fired the crossbows together, the bolts flashing towards Hirad and bouncing off the HardShield, one burying itself in the wall by his head, the other clattering away across the floor.

'Oh dear,' said Hirad as Selik backed off. 'One lone swordsman. Three mages. No Raven is ever alone. Your turn.'

Hirad stepped back along the passage as Selik retreated towards his cabin, dropping the crossbows and reaching for his sword. In the same moment, the aft doors burst inwards.

'Hirad, get back under the damn shield,' hissed Erienne, her voice taut with concentration.

The barbarian paced back smartly, seeing Selik's eyes widen. The Black Wing dived left and out of sight, into his cabin and an IceWind roared along the corridor. The air froze all around them, white enveloping the spell shield, the supercooled mana whistling through the gaps between shield and wood. The spell dragged at the timbers, covering them in a thick film of ice and pounded into Selik's cabin, scouring through where his head had been and forging huge deep blue corners of frost on roof and floor. The shield held.

'Good work, Denser,' said Ilkar. 'Let's move, they're readying to cast again.'

Hirad sensed the ForceCone deploy, carefully and under total control, and The Raven started on up the corridor.

'Selik,' said Hirad. 'I can get Selik.'

'No. We have to go now,' said Ilkar. 'Ready Raven?'

'Ready.'

'Heading left at the deck, keep those shields up. Run!'

Selik appeared at the frozen cabin door, sword in hand. Hirad waved, turned and ran, shouting over his shoulder.

'Bye bye, Selik.' Til next time. Push that Cone, Ilkar, there's trouble at my back!'

The elf released the Cone, flinging it full spread at the casting mages and Black Wings, punching them from their arc by the door.

'Ilkar sword, guard stern to starboard. Denser, Erienne, hang on to those shields. I've got the rear.'

The Raven burst on to the deck, Ilkar sprinting left, slithering on the greasy, wet timbers. Behind him came Denser, hand-in-hand with Erienne, daggers drawn, and finally Hirad, Selik at his back, the Black Wings dragging themselves to their feet in front of him.

The ship rolled and Hirad fell to his right, tumbling on to his back and around onto his knees, dagger sprung from his grasp and sliding away. Scrambling back to his feet, he raced back towards the port side. Selik's head appeared at the aft doors. Hirad cursed, sword in his wrong hand to strike and instead lashed out with his left fist, catching the Black Wing leader on the side of the face, and hearing Selik's head connect with the door frame as he ran past.

'Yes!'

Steps behind him spurred him on, and ahead a Black Wing ran down the side of the wheel deck after the mages. Hirad slid into the rail to brake himself and charged after the soldier, striking overhead with his blade and slicing deep into the man's exposed neck and back. He pitched forwards, sword flying out of his hands and flipping just over Erienne's head and out into the raging ocean, his flailing hands catching her and dragging her over.

Denser slowed.

'Go!' yelled Hirad. 'I'll bring her.'

He kicked and hauled the body of the dying Black Wing aside, grabbed the elbow of the scrabbling Erienne and pulled her towards the stern.

'Shield down,' she said. 'Shield down.'

To illustrate, a crossbow bolt hissed past and thudded into the rail. Hirad ducked reflexively.

'Gods. Go!' He pushed her ahead of him. 'Go!'

Erienne turned the corner, Hirad right behind. As he slid to turn, a crossbow bolt tore into the flesh of his calf, the impact throwing him from his feet and he fell, hammering into the rail which cracked under the impact. He heard a cheer behind him and hauled himself out of immediate sight.

'Fuck it!' he said.

'Hirad,' said Erienne, turning back.

'No time,' he grated, dragging himself to his feet. 'Keep away from those windows. Denser, Erienne, get your ShadowWings sorted and go. Ilkar, what have you got?' The pain screamed through Hirad's leg as he applied weight to it, feeling the blood flooding into his boot. The bolt was lodged, which was a blessing and hadn't struck his bone, which was close to a miracle. He hefted his sword.

'Unknown numbers running towards us this way,' said Ilkar. 'I'll keep them busy.'

In front of Hirad, the first Black Wings were coming down the port rail towards them. He hefted his sword, changing to his left hand for a better angle and waited, knowing every bought moment was vital.

'I can cast Orbs,' said Denser.

'No, Xetesk-man, get Erienne off this bloody ship!' snapped Hirad. 'Go before I pitch you over myself. We'll be right behind you.'

'You'd better be,' said Denser.

'Fly!' The first Black Wing paced around the corner, sword swinging round at shoulder height. Hirad blocked it aside then swept his blade back left to right, the man swaying backwards to dodge the blow, bringing his sword back in front of him and stabbing forwards. Hirad blocked easily and backhanded the man across the face with his right fist and lunged forwards, pain flaring from his calf and spearing up through his back. He took the man in the midriff, skewering through his leather armour. He felt the sword grate against the Black Wing's spine and wrenched it clear, the body collapsing to the deck.

'Ilkar, how are you doing!' Hirad thrust forward, seeing a crossbow edge around the corner. His blade ground along the stock of the weapon and smashed though the sight, burying itself in the eye of the Black Wing who screamed and fell, finger flexing on the trigger, the bolt scoring Hirad's leather as it passed.

'Holding them back,' said Ilkar, out of breath. 'Just.'

'Keep going, watch for crossbows.'

He glanced over his shoulder. Erienne and Denser were gone.

'Time to leave, Ilkar.'

'How?'

Hirad crouched, waiting, his wound throbbing badly. The next attacker was more cautious. The barbarian listened closely, hearing a boot slide along a timber. And again. Gripping a stay with his left hand and ignoring the billowing agony from his calf, he leant out and struck low, his sword thrashing into the man's ankle, biting through boot and into bone. The Black Wing howled and fell back. More bolts whistled by, missing comfortably.

Hirad swung back. It had to be now. He limped down the stern rail. Ilkar was struggling.

'Behind you,' he said, approaching. 'Duck on my word.'

Ilkar fielded a blow to the stomach and pushed the man away but he was strong and snatched his sword back, whipping it round and over his head.

'Now!'

Ilkar ducked. Hirad's sword powered round, blocking the downward strike and sending the guard off balance. Hirad stepped over Ilkar and thumped a fist into the man's face. He staggered back a pace.

'ShadowWings and go, Ilkar!'

'They'll come from behind us, Hirad.'

'I'll hold them. Go.'

'No.'

Hirad slashed again, the Black Wing blocking but only just.

'Trust me, and don't lose sight of me. Now get lost.'

He stepped up and crashed his sword through the enemy's neck. The man teetered and pivoted over the rail.

'Fish food,' growled Hirad. 'Who's next?'

Behind him, he heard Ilkar deploy the wings and leave the deck.

'Hirad, they're on you,' he shouted.

Hirad put his back against the wall of the aft cabins. Black Wings were filtering down the rail from his right. He could see crossbowmen behind him.

'Don't you lose me, Ilkar!' he yelled into the night, praying that the elf was watching him.

'Drop your weapon!' ordered a Black Wing.

Hirad smiled. 'I don't think so,' he said.

He stepped forwards and dived over the rail, sword ahead of him, and splashed into the sea.

The freezing water enveloped him, the waves huge and dark surrounding him. He broke surface briefly, kicking his legs, feeling his injured calf protesting as the salt edged in. He scoured the sky but could see nothing. The *Ocean Elm* moved gently away from him and he was lifted by another wave. The wind roared in his ears, he could feel more hail lashing down and he felt heavy. Very heavy.

He knew he should let go his sword and try to shed his leather but something inside him refused. He submerged again, water piling over on him, the storm singling him out as its next victim. He kicked again, feeling the air on his face and grabbing in another lungful.

'Ilkar!' he shouted into the gale.

He scrabbled at his back, sinking again, fighting to get his sword into his scabbard, knowing it was stupid, knowing he could afford to lose it, but having to free both his hands. He was going down but he refused to die. And there it was, like the feel of silk on the body of a woman, his sword slipping down into the leather. He swam for the surface, breaking clear and shouting again for his friend.

He looked up and there was Ilkar, diving out of the night with the hail.

'Grab my legs. Don't you let go.'

Ilkar hovered above him, trying to get close enough as the wind buffeted him and the waves splashed over his legs. Hirad grabbed and missed, kicked his legs and grabbed again, this time, catching hold with one hand.

'Go!' he shouted and Ilkar started to rise. He swung with his left arm and caught the toe of Ilkar's boot as the mage climbed high above the waves.

Hanging on for his life he climbed up Ilkar's legs inch by tortuous inch, stopping only when he had his head jammed just above the elf's knees and his arms locked around his calfs. He could see other shapes around him. Denser and Erienne.

He took a look back towards the ship, searching for pursuit from the Dordovan mages but knew that they'd have been lost to sight almost instantly. They were clear and no one who left the deck would have any real idea where to fly to find them.

'We did it!' he yelled. 'We bloody did it!'

Whooping his joy he hung on for the flight back to the *Calaian Sun*.

Chapter 31

The skipper of the *Ocean Elm* felt a deep satisfaction. His ship was not his own, too many of his crew had been murdered and he was trying to ride out the worst storm he'd ever experienced in the Southern Ocean, but he felt a sense of overriding peace.

He'd just witnessed a rescue that should have had no chance of success but for the fact that it had been carried out by The Raven. The man he had seen laying out Selik with a single punch had simply not believed he could fail.

And, in the midst of it all, on a ship occupied by Black Wings, he and his crew were free. With Erienne gone, they could choose their fate. And choose it, they would. Tryuun had seen The Raven mages clear the ship, pluck the warrior from the sea and disappear into the night, the crossbowmen and Dordovan mages having no targets to aim at as the blackness swallowed them up. And seven more Black Wings were dead. As the hail thundered down on to his thick leather skullcap, it was turning into a wonderful night.

But better was coming up the ladder to the wheel deck. The skipper was alone there at the moment, having sent his new helmsman from what could easily be harm's way in the aftermath of the rescue. For himself, though, he felt no threat to his life and he smiled broadly as Selik dragged himself to the top of the ladder and limped towards him, a bruise growing on one side of his jaw and a lump the size of an egg dominating his temple on the other.

'Need a hand?' he asked, sparing Selik a quick glance and half smile.

Selik pushed an angry face into his.

'Don't forget who is running this ship,' he spat.

'No,' said the skipper. 'The Guild of Drech have always done so. All you had to do was guard one woman and you failed even to do that. How does it feel?'

Selik grabbed the neck of his coat. 'Your taunting will get you killed, elf, slowly. You and your crew. Remember who has all the weapons and all the magic.'

The skipper sobered but he couldn't keep the smile from his face entirely. 'I won't.'

'Now you will keep this ship heading for Ornouth. Any deviation and your crew will suffer.'

The skipper laughed. 'Oh, Black Wing, how little you understand. I have no intention of sailing anywhere else. Ornouth is where we belong. You will be the strangers there. And now Erienne is gone, the deal is different. Before I was taking you there to kill. Now, I'm taking you there to die.'

Though her mind still recoiled from memories of the Black Wings, Erienne worked through the rest of the night, her enforced rest from magic leaving her stamina strong. She was desperate for the warm embrace of Denser but there was one man who needed her more.

The Unknown Warrior's hip bone had shattered like a vase dropped on stone. Bone splinters had invaded flesh and muscle, tendon and ligament were slashed and dying, and the joint was a lattice of cracks that would hold no weight and allow no movement. The pain, even through his spell-induced sleep, must have been terrible.

Tears had fallen from her eyes as she probed the appalling damage with mind and gentle fingers. She would have said there was nothing to be done, not even with a BodyCast but the look in Hirad's eyes as he asked her if she could help would live with her forever. He had come to rescue her and she could not let him down. He wouldn't even have the bolt removed from his calf until she had said she would try. He had kissed her then, his rough face against her cheek. It had been a display of emotion she thought beyond him but that was an unfair assessment. The barbarian hid his feelings beneath his tough warrior skin when he could, but they ran as deep as any man's. Perhaps deeper than most.

She created the shape of the BodyCast, a spell of tremendous versatility but so difficult to control. It was heat-driven, it covered her hands in a beautiful warmth and, as she probed The Unknown's hip again, tendrils snaked away to soothe infected flesh at her bidding while she concentrated on the main problem.

Using the mana to free each splinter in turn, she moved them back towards the top of the thigh bone, arranged in front of her as pieces in a child's puzzle. She used the spell to examine them, define their edges and divine where they had come from. And any that were too small, she teased out to drop on to the bloodied sheet, hoping the bone would grow again in time.

But time was something in short supply. She was keenly aware that there was more fighting to come. Dordovans would soon find their way to Herendeneth and she needed The Unknown to be standing with The Raven when they did.

She bent to her task, the BodyCast forging, reforming, knitting and healing. It was slow, painstaking and desperately draining, using the hair-thin filaments of mana to guide shards and splinters back into position, to encase the cracks in his joint and to bring nerve endings and muscles back to bond.

It wouldn't be perfect, that much was obvious. Perhaps if she'd been there immediately after he'd been struck it would have been different but now, too much time had passed and the body had its own imperfect ways of rebuilding itself. And some of those she could not undo. Too much of the bone was crushed useless to make her BodyCast anything more than a best fit. Some things magic could not reverse.

The Unknown would never be quite the same again. How he adapted would be up to him.

Hirad joined Ren, Ilkar and Jevin on the wheel deck well after the sun had passed its zenith on the next day. He could still feel the pain of the bolt but Denser had done a good job with a low strength WarmHeal and the elves had soothing balms that caressed the flesh and numbed the pain. He'd be all right by the time they landed.

The ferocity of the storm the night before had diminished and the pitching and yawing of the *Calaian Sun* was calm by comparison. Above them, the cloud had thinned, allowing occasional watery sunlight between squally showers of rain.

Jevin had ordered full sail and they were moving well across the ocean, trailing the *Ocean Elm* by several hours though Hirad could still make out its shape on the southern horizon.

'Why is he still going south?' asked Hirad.

'Because he's showing us the way,' said Ren. 'And when we can't sail any further in, he'll let us know if he can and we'll have to take to the boats.'

'And if he doesn't let us know?' asked Hirad.

'I won't let this ship run aground,' said Ren.

'And neither will I,' growled Jevin.

'How long do we have to go?' asked Ilkar.

'Three days, maybe a little more. We lost time last night,' said Ren.

'Think I might sleep the rest of the way, then,' said Hirad, smiling.

'You deserve to,' said Ilkar.

'You too, Ilks. Good fun, though, wasn't it?'

Ilkar stared at him for a moment. 'No, it wasn't. Unless you consider searching black, heavy seas for a fool in the dead of night, after a scrap on a ship miles from nowhere, good fun. What the hell were you doing in the water anyway? I almost had you and you sank, messing about with your scabbard.'

'I was sheathing my sword.'

'Oh, how stupid of me not to realise. Why didn't you just drop the bloody thing? You could have drowned,' said Ilkar. His voice softened and he punched Hirad on the arm. 'I thought you had. Don't take that sort of risk. I don't want to lose you like that.'

'I'm not losing that sword until I've driven it through Selik,' said Hirad.

'Think you'll get the chance?' asked Ren.

'I know it,' said Hirad.

The window in the bedroom blew in and Aviana screamed, her anguish echoing through the minds of all the Al-Drechar. Myriell had been dressing, preparing to take over as the dawn broke but now they were all awake, thrust to consciousness by a cry for help that went on and on.

Myriell called for her helpers and they ran into her room.

'Get me there now. Carry me and run. Bring the others.'

'Yes, Myriell,' said one. The two picked her up in an armchair lift and hurried from the room, calling others from their beds.

The wind howled along the passages, driven by Lyanna's mind, blasting into their faces. To their right an enormous crashing resounded in the air and across the orchard the west wing of the house shuddered and dropped, the roof caving in, wooden beams splitting, brickwork shattering and tumbling, the vibrations rocking the ground beneath their feet.

'Dear Gods, she's broken free. Faster, faster!' urged Myriell.

The Guild elves ran on though the ballroom and into the dining room, not pausing on their way to Lyanna's makeshift bedroom. They set Myriell down and opened the door into a howling gale. Aviana lay on the ground, Lyanna was upright, her hair twisting about her head, her doll clutched in her outstretched hands and her eyes open but seeing nothing.

'Get the others here!' shouted Myriell.

She moved into the room, sat on the edge of the bed and clutched the little girl to her, attuning her mind and eyes to the mana spectrum and seeing the horror laid out for her there.

Surrounding Aviana was a mass of dark grey, pulsing over her mind, attacking relentlessly, pushed there by what force Myriell couldn't begin to guess. Something malevolent lurked deep in Lyanna and it had to be found and destroyed. The girl's mind was encased in orange, flecked with dark brown. She appeared to be channelling perfectly, dragging in the random fuel of magic, creating vortex shapes and casting them out in a stream of destruction.

Myriell formed a light mind net and moved it gingerly towards Lyanna, hoping to separate her from the force attacking the helpless Aviana. She dimly heard movement behind her, knew her sister was helping, and pushed on. She got nowhere near. The moment Lyanna sensed her, coils of orange mana lashed out from the whole, slapping away the mind net and dragging in its mana energy. Myriell dispersed it moments before the unravelling reached her own damaged mind and snapped out of the spectrum, her head thumping, her vision ragged at the edges.

Lyanna pushed against her and Myriell released her. The child was looking at her intently, recognition in her eyes. Myriell almost shouted and then Lyanna spoke.

'Hello Myra. Why are you keeping me in the dark place?' It was the child's voice but it was laced with foreboding and echoed through the room on the back of the gale.

'Oh, Lyanna, we aren't keeping you there, your mind has taken you there and we are guarding it to stop you being hurt.'

'But I don't want to be in the dark any more,' said Lyanna, clutching her doll close and stroking its head.

Myriell frowned. Her Night wasn't over. There was no calmness in the mana. Her control only went as far as stopping hurt to her own mind. What she released she had no way of understanding or controlling. She should still be under, learning, modulating and accepting.

'But you know you can't stop the wind in your mind, don't you? I know being in the dark place is lonely but it will help you to be happy.'

But Lyanna shook her head. 'No. Ana wanted me to stay and I didn't and something from me hurt her.' Tears rolled down her cheeks. 'I don't want to hurt anyone. So I don't want you to be with me in my mind any more.'

Myriell looked round. Ephemere was deep in concentration around Aviana's too-still form but Cleress was watching her and could only shrug in mute incomprehension.

'And anyway,' continued Lyanna, 'Mummy's coming soon and I have to brush my hair.'

She swung her legs out of the bed, then dropped to the floor and walked out into the dining room, the doll in one hand. Myriell watched her go.

'Clerry?' she pleaded.

'I don't know, Myra. I think we've lost her.'

Deep in the Southern Ocean, two hundred of miles off Balaia's southern coast the seabed cracked and moved, sending pressures to the surface the like of which hadn't been felt for a thousand years. They surged upwards, creating a single, mountain-high wave backed by many lesser waves, minions in the wake of majesty.

The wave rushed northwards, an unstoppable force a dozen miles wide. It moved effortlessly across the ocean, its noise thunderous, its energy undiminishing. Beneath it, water shifted on the sea bed, creatures large and small fled behind it and swam from its influence as it stormed on, looking for a place to break. That place was Gyernath. It towered over the land as it came, like a predatory animal preparing to strike down at its prey.

The port had sea defences, the finest of any port in Balaia. They were built to deflect the ferocity of the waves the winter gales threw up and to channel the floods from the town's streets and outlying fields. They were the pride of the port's council leaders. But no defences could hope to counter a wave a hundred and fifty feet high and a half mile deep.

By the time they had begun to run, it was already too late for the townspeople. And by the time the last ship had been dashed against the ground at the top of Drovers Way, almost a mile inland, there was nobody left at all.

The *Calaian Sun* drove on through the steadily calming waters of the Southern Ocean, two days out from the first islands of the Ornouth Archipelago. The mood on board had lightened considerably. Blue sky had been seen through breaks in the clouds, the winds had become steady and dependable from the west and the hail was a distant, painful memory. They were keeping pace with the *Ocean Elm*, Jevin convinced that the skipper was dragging his heels, and the break in the elemental battering gave rise to real hope that the Al-Drechar had exerted real control over Lyanna.

Hirad lay alone in the cabin he and Ilkar shared, the elf up top and actually enjoying a sea voyage for the first time. Hirad was happy for him. He was happy for them all. Erienne's BodyCast had done as well as it could, she had said, and The Unknown could now be allowed to waken naturally. How he reacted would tell them what work still needed to be done and what he would just have to live with. Hirad prayed for a miracle.

As for Thraun, well, he remained under magically-induced sleep. Ilkar said he had lost some of the hair and that his clawed feet were resembling toes again but within, the picture was not so hopeful. He was another reason why the Al-Drechar must survive. They were all hoping, though none of them would say it, that the ancient elven mages could help because there was precious little else The Raven could do for their friend.

And that left Denser and Erienne. They'd barely been out of their cabin since Erienne had finished her casting. Hirad knew she'd have had to rest well but even so, there was just so much you could catch up on without becoming exhausted.

He caught himself smiling and quashed it. Of course, for Denser, there was no time, not really. In the moments they'd been on deck together, wrapped in embrace, he'd seen joy in the Xeteskian's eyes but a distance that meant he hadn't told her. Hirad could understand that. It would shatter her happiness and she'd been through so much already. But he had to break the news, and do so before they landed.

He put his hands behind his head and felt the tug on his mind immediately. He closed his eyes and breathed deep, speaking with his mind as he had been taught.

'Great Kaan, I thought you had forgotten me,' he said.

'And you me,' said Sha-Kaan. 'I sensed you were at rest. Is that so?'

'It is, and I feel better for the warmth of your thoughts within me,' said Hirad.

'And the distance you are from the chill of the mountain,' said Sha-Kaan. A feeling of fleeting mirth ran through him. The Great Kaan had made a joke. Something had to be wrong.

'You're learning some humour, I see,' said Hirad.

'It is the only thing left to us while we wait for death or redemption,' rumbled the dragon.

'Tell me,' said Hirad.

'Our condition worsens. Hyn-Kaan has difficulty flying, I tire too quickly and we have all lost our fire. Even that which we held in reserve is gone, leached from us by this cursed land of yours. It kills us more quickly every day. The Kaan asked me to contact you for news. It needs to be good.'

'And it is, mostly,' said Hirad, taken aback by the rapid deterioration Sha-Kaan described. 'We have Erienne and we are two days from the Al-Drechar. We fear more trouble from the Dordovan College but we will make them safe. And the child too. The elements have stopped attacking us, at least for now, but that could change. I only hope they can help you.'

'It is our last chance, Hirad Coldheart,' said Sha-Kaan. 'We are too long away from our Brood, the living air of Beshara and the healing streams of the Klenes in interdimensional space.'

'And the hunters?' Hirad hardly dared ask.

He felt Sha-Kaan sigh, a weary sound booming about his mind. 'They are everywhere, it seems. News of your departure has reached the wrong ears and they come in greater numbers. We have killed when we must but they are not deterred. Help us, Hirad Coldheart.'

Hirad punched the wall by his head. All the hurricanes, tempests and floods. And only the innocent seemed to have died.

'I will, Great Kaan,' he said. 'I will call you when we reach them.'

'Make it soon,' said the old dragon. 'Or one of these hunters will claim their prize before long.'

And he was gone.

Needing air, Hirad jumped off the bunk and walked out on to the deck, coming to stand by the starboard rail and look out over the benign seas, so beautiful when they were blue. He scratched his head and puffed out his cheeks, willing the ship to go faster. He heard someone walking up to him.

'Something wrong?' asked Ilkar.

'The usual,' said Hirad.

'The Kaan,' said Ilkar.

Hirad nodded. 'I don't know what to—'

But Ilkar wasn't listening to him. The elf stared out and ahead of them, then ran towards the bow of the ship, leaning out, peering into the distance and the empty horizon beyond the *Ocean Elm*. Hirad caught him up.

'What is it, Ilkar,' he asked.

Ilkar shook his head. 'Gods drowning, Hirad. There's so many of them.'

'So many of what?'

A shout echoed down from the crow's nest.

'Them,' said Ilkar, pointing way out to sea.

Hirad strained his eyes, seeing tiny shapes in the haze at the edge of his vision. They were sails. He counted seven. There could have been more but the distance confused his eyes.

'Who?' he asked through he knew the answer.

'Dordovans,' said Ilkar. 'It's the whole damned Dordovan fleet.'

Hirad didn't wait, he couldn't afford to. He returned to his cabin. They needed help and, with or without fire, there was only one source.

The Kaan.

Denser kissed Erienne's breasts gently, his tongue flickering at her nipples while his hand caressed her side and right thigh. She giggled and lifted his head, looking deep into his eyes.

'I've been fantasising about this,' he said.

'But not practising, I trust,' she replied, drawing him forward to kiss his lips. 'I wonder what you'd be like with a smooth chin?'

Denser scratched at his beard. 'Younger,' he said. 'Definitely younger.' But Erienne could see him struggling to smile.

'What is it, love?' she asked. 'Don't look so sombre. We're nearly there.'

'Yes, I know.' He looked away and watched his hand run down her stomach to rest on her pubis. Erienne felt a warmth rushing through her but took his hand away in any case.

'So what is it?' she asked. 'No answer, no fun.'

He stared at her face and she could see his eyes roving, taking in everything from her crown to the point of her chin. He nodded.

'All right. It had better be now.'

He rolled out of bed and she watched him pull on his shirt and loin cloth, her heart suddenly beating anxiously, her mind rushed with a thousand uneasy thoughts.

'Denser?'

'Put your shirt on and look at this.'

She cast around for and found her shirt, rearranging it to slip it over her head while she watched him open a cabinet and pull out some parchment. He handed her a page.

'Seen this before?' he asked, coming to sit beside her and stroke her hair.

She pulled her shirt over her waist and sat on the tails, covering herself. She unfolded the page and gasped.

'Where did you get this?'

'Your library,' he said. 'There are others but this is the one you have to see now.'

She looked hard into his eyes and saw terrible sorrow there. Her heart lurched and thudded painfully. She realised she was scared.

'But it's Lore. Lower Lore, I grant you, but Dordovan all the same.'

'It's part of the Tinjata Prophecy,' he said.

Erienne shook her head. 'I don't recognise it.'

'I know you don't. They hide it from people they don't want to see it and refuse to offer the translation to others.'

'People like you,' she said.

'Yes, so I stole it. I had to know.' He grimaced and swallowed and she put a hand to his face, trying to comfort him for a pain she didn't understand. 'And now I do.'

He handed her a second sheet. She took it and read it. It was a translation. Short, filled with gaps, but for all that, very explicit. She began to tremble, the parchment shaking in her hand. She had a lump in her throat and her stomach twisted. She looked at the prophecy, then back at the translation, searching word by word for an error.

'No, no, no,' she whispered, her eyes scanning feverishly, finger following lines of text.

And there was one. Basic but commonplace in untrained translation.

'Oh Denser,' she said. 'It's wrong. Whoever did it translated it wrong.'

'Where . . . how?'

He grabbed the parchments from her, she didn't know why. So she pointed at a single word in the Lore.

'They got the gender wrong,' she said, dragging in her last breath before the tears came. 'That doesn't mean Father. It means Mother.'

Chapter 32

For one brief day, as they closed on the Dordovan fleet heading in from the west, Denser and Erienne hoped it might not come to the death of either of them. The clouds carried on thinning, the sun warmed them from a patched blue sky and the winds were exactly as strong as Jevin expected for this part of the Southern Ocean.

They had cried long together, bolting the door of their cabin and refusing any refreshment but their own company. Once they'd regained control and could bear not to clutch each other, Erienne had scoured the pages of the prophecy Denser had brought for some clue that their reading of it was wrong. But there was nothing, and Tinjata knew his signs only too well.

In the early evening of the sixth day, Denser lay with an arm around Erienne's shoulders, stroking her right arm with the tips of his fingers. The love they had made was tearful and tender, sensuous and quiet, each delighting in the other's body, knowing the other's pleasure by the sound of a sigh or a groan. No words were necessary then and they weren't now as they basked in the afterglow, the sun still streaming through the window from low on the horizon.

Soon, it would be time for dinner with The Raven, and to watch the sunset, glorious and red, firing its energies across the darkening sky under the remaining cloud. But for now they lay silent, staring at the ceiling above them, their bodies warm and the silence beautiful. Denser breathed in deep, Erienne's scent filling his nostrils. Maybe. Maybe her sacrifice wouldn't be necessary.

He knew he should worry about the Dordovans, who could reach the Ornouth Archipelago in front of them, but somehow he was certain they would fail. All that consumed him was the burgeoning hope that Lyanna's Night was over. If the weather held, if calm returned to Balaia and the Southern Ocean, it could really only mean one thing. That Lyanna had learned the control that was vital to her and Balaian survival. And if that was so, Erienne wouldn't have to die.

A shadow passed in front of the sun. Denser craned his head to the window to watch it pass. The shadow deepened and he frowned.

'Sundown's early tonight,' he said, propping himself on one elbow and looking down at Erienne.

'No it isn't,' she whispered, and there were tears standing in her eyes. 'It's started again.'

'No, love,' he said, but he already knew it was true.

The temperature was falling, the ship was shifting against its forward motion. There was a swell rising and a storm coming.

'We knew it couldn't last,' she said. 'Didn't we?'

He nodded. There were no words, not now.

Above them, he heard orders rattling across the decks and the sound of hurrying feet. He heard the slap of limp canvas and felt the ship turning. There was a knock on the door, urgent and insistent.

'Sorry, you two, but you've got to see this. I'll meet you on deck.' Ilkar's voice was apologetic but determined and Denser listened to his footsteps receding and the sounds of sudden tension from above before turning back to his wife.

'Well?'

'We should go,' said Erienne. 'No sense in wallowing in our self-pity at the moment.' She sat up and kissed him fervently and managed a half-smile as she drew away. 'There's plenty of time for that later. The Unknown'll be waking soon. I shouldn't miss that. There could be more work to do.' She pushed him away and swung her legs out of the narrow bed and rummaged on the floor for her clothes.

'I love you, Erienne,' said Denser.

Erienne swallowed a sob. 'Remember that you do.'

They dressed quickly and, after a long embrace, walked up to the deck. Pushing open the forward hatch, the gusting wind felt strong in their faces. The ship was beginning to pitch sharply.

'Here we go again,' muttered Denser.

He led Erienne by the hand out into the fast fading light and looked around for Ilkar. He was there, standing by the port rail, which was lined with people. Hirad, Ren'erei, Darrick, one of the Protectors and half the crew of the *Calaian Sun*. They hurried over, Ilkar seeing them and stepping back so they could see clearly.

A light was arrowing out from sea to sky over at the Ornouth Archipelago, the first islands of which would soon be visible. It was a vast column, green-edged yellow, shot through with orange, brown and a dismal black. It disappeared up into the sky and where it touched them, the clouds spun around it, thickening and expanding.

They already covered the horizon and blotted out the sun and with every heartbeat they fled across the ocean towards Balaia. Inside them, lightning flared and smudges in a dozen places told of rain falling in torrents. Beneath them came the wind, and below the wind was driven the sea, white-capped and murderous. The swell was growing, already at ten feet. The ship still made headway but Jevin had already furled all but topsail and foresail, and soon he would be forced to take in more.

'Oh dear Gods,' said Denser. 'Look at what our daughter is doing to us all.'

Erienne's arm was around his waist and it tightened. He looked at her, saw her eyes reflecting the pain he felt and he squeezed her trembling shoulders and turned her away.

'I think we should eat now, before it gets too rough,' he said to Ilkar as they passed him. The elf nodded.

'I'll sort it, don't you worry about it.'

The forward hatch slid back as they approached it and a very familiar shaven-headed figure came halfway out, spotting them and beckoning them over. He was clutching a sheet around his waist.

'Any idea where my clothes are?' he said.

'Unknown, it's good to see you,' said Erienne.

'And you, Erienne. And it'll be even better when I catch up on what the hell has been going on and have some food. I am bloody famished.'

The gale roared into the Choul in the early hours of the morning. It was some time before dawn and the night was black, the cloud unyielding and the rain unceasing. Sha-Kaan brought the Brood to wakefulness, their dulling eyes regarding him in irritation.

'We are doing nothing here but dying,' said Sha-Kaan. 'Hirad Coldheart is right. We must help them.'

'It is not our way to help but to be helped,' said Nos-Kaan. 'We are the Kaan.'

'And this is not Beshara, and here we do not rule,' said Sha. 'So we will help my Dragonene. He, at least, has stayed true and deserves our help. Without him, we would already have perished. Unfurl your wings, young Kaan, and we will fly. But beware. The hunters are everywhere.'

'Yes, Great Kaan,' said Nos and Hyn.

'I will lead.'

Sha-Kaan moved along the Choul to find himself some space and stretched his wings. It was becoming a painful exercise, alleviated only by the thrill of the hunt for prey. But even that was beginning to pall. Sha-Kaan was already an old dragon when he was first marooned in Balaia. The unhelpful conditions merely brought his death closer. But there was still hope. The Al-Drechar could help. They had both the knowledge and the power. While they lived, so would he.

He opened his great mouth, sucking in the air and opening the muscles above his flame ducts, feeling the chill rush around the emptiness of the sacs. He wondered how much more confident the hunters would be if they knew the dragons were dry. Not so terrifying then, he supposed. Then again, he considered as he examined his claws and felt the tips of his huge fangs with his tongue, then again . . .

Sha-Kaan snaked his neck around to see his Brood pair working their tired wing muscles and stretching the drying, cracking membrane. But they were ready and would not fail him.

'Come, Kaan. We will fly high and fast. Let the Skies keep us.'

'Skies keep us,' the Kaan intoned.

Sha-Kaan walked along to the entrance, his keen eyes piercing the gloom, seeing nothing but flat dark rock, trees bent double under the gale and the teeming rain.

'Balaia,' he growled. 'Sooner left, better my scales.'

With a roar, he spread his wings and leapt into the air, beating upwards. Nos and Hyn-Kaan following. Sha-Kaan rose to the peak which housed their Choul and circled, waiting for his Brood to join him.

There was movement below. He barked a warning and an order to climb faster. He could see metal glinting in a thick area of brush. There was a dull thud which he could pick out above the wind whistling around the peak. A long shaft rose very quickly and Hyn-Kaan squealed as it pierced his left wing, the metal tip ripping through the membrane and the shaft dragging the hole larger as it passed, continuing on into the sky before falling back to the earth.

Sha-Kaan roared and dived on the brush. The humans had already scattered to hiding places but one had not been quick enough. The Great Kaan snatched him in his jaws and bore him back into the air, the puny body writhing pitifully against his grip. Above the peak of the Choul mountain, he bent his neck round and grabbed the human in a fore-claw, bringing him close to his eye.

'Fall. Like you wished on my Kaan.'

Sha-Kaan flung the screaming figure away to his death, not bothering to watch his impact. He turned and beat his wings, driving to where Nos and Hyn circled. Hyn was pained but the wound was not critical.

'And you still want to help the humans?' pulsed Nos.

'They are not all alike,' said Sha-Kaan. 'Hyn-Kaan, return to the Choul if you cannot fly the distance we must travel.'

'When we reach the upper skies and can glide, I will match your speed. Do not ask me to stay, Great Kaan.'

'Then follow me. This is the flight to our fate.'

Roaring into the wind and thunder, he drove up into the cloud, searching for the calmer air of the heights.

Erienne woke earlier than Denser, with the wan light of dawn edging through the window. In truth she had hardly slept. The ship had plunged in all directions during the storm, which still raged outside and, since Jevin had ordered them all below shortly after dinner, she had been lying here in the dark, her husband close.

It was strange. Funny almost. On the *Ocean Elm*, she had become accustomed to her impending death but hated why it had to happen. Now, with her death just as certain, she felt calm and had felt close to euphoria during the night. There was a reason. The perpetuation of the One and the life of her child. And no matter how much she would miss Lyanna and all those she loved, she knew that her death would mean something to the whole of Balaia. Perhaps bring a new dawn in the days of magic.

There had been a moment for both of them during their despair of the last couple of days, and neither she nor Denser would deny it, a moment when they considered the death of Lyanna as preferable to their own irrevocable parting. It was an option that would save Balaia and they would not have been human had they not considered it, however fleetingly. But as this day came, the thought seemed almost laughable.

Erienne turned in the small bed and rested her head on Denser's chest, running her hands through the hair on his chest and listening to his even breathing and the gentle beating of his heart. Outside, the wind battered the ship and drove it on towards her doom. If it all went according to plan, she would be dead in about two days' time. A strange thought but one she felt she could cope with. After all, there was a great deal to be done before she could indulge Balaia with her passing.

She smiled and rubbed her head against Denser. At least one more success was walking about the ship again. He was limping, as he would forever, but The Unknown Warrior would regain the strength in his left leg again. She wasn't sure he'd be able to fight effectively with a two-handed blade, and that was an anxiety to come for him, but he would fight and eventually, he would run. Standing and fighting was about it for now. She hoped he was satisfied.

Bizarrely, she felt as if some form of status quo had been reached. Her arrival back with The Raven had certainly cheered Darrick who had, by all accounts, been brooding the whole voyage so far. Only Thraun was a continuing problem. She had been shocked to see him, let alone see the state of his body. She hadn't said it but she feared he'd be better off dead.

Anyway, enough of all that.

She angled her head up and saw only beard. She reached up and scratched at his chin. Denser's hand flapped in his sleep and he blew through slack lips as if trying to dislodge a fly. So she poked his cheek. Still he failed to wake. There was no way she was going to lie here awake alone while the ship pitched and rocked. She slid her hand under the sheet and grabbed his penis. He grunted. She massaged it gently. He murmured. That was more like it but he still gave every impression of being dead to the world. It was the hand that whipped across and cupped her breast that finally gave him away.

'Good morning,' she said.

'It is now,' said Denser.

Lyanna walked through the orchard, her shoes crunching on broken glass. She was unhappy. The old ladies didn't talk to her much. They hadn't since she had woken. And Mummy wasn't back yet, though she had felt her close while she was still in the dark place the sprites had told her she would go too.

So she had come to see the sprites. To play with them again. But they weren't dancing on the trees like she remembered. And the trees weren't all standing straight like she remembered. Some of them were broken and all the sprites were lying on the ground, most of them bunched in the corners of the orchard. Just like leaves in autumn.

Lyanna walked over to a corner and crouched down, weaving her hand through the drift of leaves that had been sprites. There was no life there. They were all dead.

She stood, sobbing quietly. All her friends were gone except the old ladies and she didn't think they liked her. She ran back towards the door. It had no glass in it any more. She wondered what had happened. Perhaps one of the elves would tell her. Maybe Ren was there even if Mummy wasn't.

'Ren!' she called, walking back into the house. It was all wet underfoot. 'Ephy!' Her voice echoed in the corridor. She started to cry.

She didn't understand. When she had gone to the dark place, everything had been fine and the sun had been shining. Now she had come back, it was all different. It was cold and all the pictures had fallen down and everything was wet and the house was quiet.

'Myraaaa!' she wailed.

There was no sound. The sky was all black. All except the light she sent into the air to guide Mummy home. That was something the wind in her mind had taught her. But she didn't know why all the cloud tried to make the light go dim. So she'd tried to send the cloud away, only there was so much of it.

'Myra!' she shouted.

No one could hear her. That wasn't right. The wind spoke to her. She could make them wake up and make them come to listen to her so she could understand why it was so cold and wet.

Lyanna turned and wandered back towards her room.

The rumbling in the earth had already started. That would make them wake up.

Hirad and Ilkar were in their favourite place in the bow of the ship again, but this time Ilkar wasn't vomiting over the side and Hirad didn't have to keep him upright. It was mid-morning, the storm had abated slightly, the swell had lessened and though Jevin had deployed enough sail since dawn to drive them on, they would not outrun the Dordovan fleet. The seven ships flying the orange College colours were coming up on the starboard bow, close enough now to make out the shapes of people moving about on deck. They were all heading for the same channel into the archipelago but while the *Ocean Elm* would make the Ornouth Archipelago ahead of them, the *Calaian Sun* would not.

The Dordovans had to be halted and the Kaan were overdue. Ilkar and Hirad were scanning the sky. Looking for some sign in the dark cloud, Hirad spoke to alleviate the tension he felt.

'They were at it again all morning,' he said.

'You're just jealous.'

'No,' said Hirad defensively. 'I just wonder where they get their energy from.'

'Maybe from the fact that they haven't got much more time,' said Ilkar.

'I know that, but even so—'

'Hirad, can we talk about something else? Like where your dragons are or something?' Ilkar turned his head slightly to narrow his eyes at Hirad. 'I thought perhaps our rather difficult circumstances might be of more import to you than your friends' sexual energy.'

'They'll be here, don't worry about it,' said Hirad.

'Are you sure they can find us in all this?' Ilkar gestured at the dense rain-bearing cloud.

'They don't need to see, they can find us by following the signature of my mind,' said Hirad, mildly irritated. 'You know that.'

'I pity anyone following your mind at the moment,' muttered Ilkar. 'Full of filth.'

Thunder rumbled overhead. Inside the roiling mass, lightning flashed incessantly. Thunder sounded again and suddenly the clouds disgorged a flood of rain. It drummed on the deck, rattled into the sails and drove into their faces.

Hirad turned his face away for a modicum of shelter.

'Gods falling! This is unbelievable,' he said.

He and Ilkar hurried back along the foredeck, the rain lashing down heavier and heavier. They raced across the main deck, the water pouring down their necks soaking their clothes, heading for the aft hatch and the galley, suddenly in need of a hot drink and the warmth of a cook stove.

At the hatch they met Darrick, who was staring intently into the sky, seemingly oblivious to the downpour. He smiled at them.

'Refreshing, isn't it?

'Bloody soldiers,' said Hirad. 'Always got to prove how tough they are.'

'Not really,' said Darrick. 'I was just wondering what was causing this, all of a sudden.'

'Well, while you're wondering, would you mind stepping aside?' Ilkar waved him left.

Darrick obliged. 'I thought it must be something in the cloud triggering the lightning. Probably them.'

He pointed along the length of the ship. Hirad turned, his head already filling with thoughts of welcome. The Kaan had broken through the cloud and were powering away towards the Dordovan fleet.

I take it, this is the group of ships you want us to deal with, pulsed Sha-Kaan.

Yes, Great Kaan. The orange colours. Seven of them. Be careful of magic.

Be careful of wreckage. More mirth. Sha-Kaan was mellowing in his old age, not that that would be any comfort to the Dordovans. Hirad ran back to the bow, the rain forgotten, and yelled the Kaan on.

Chapter 33

The Kaan flew from the clouds in a chevron, Sha-Kaan at its head, Nos and Hyn on the flanks. They glided fast over the fleet, seeing the humans below panicked and rushing for the sails, for the places below decks or for any cover they could find. Sha could sense the mages below, there were many of them. Hirad Coldheart was right, they presented serious danger.

Passing the lead vessel, they gained height and banked, turning to attack.

Break their formation. Take the masts if you can. Spells will come, pulsed Sha-Kaan.

They dived, roaring into the rain-sodden air, each targeting a ship, seeing the fleet begin to break up as wheels were swung, rudders bit into the ocean and the vessels turned and scattered. Much too slow.

Sha-Kaan came in low and across the bow of his target, wings beating back to slow him, great talons biting into the deck as he landed, his weight causing the ship to bounce and slew. Water poured over the bows, a torrent streaming for the holds, weighing it down.

His neck lashed forwards and his jaws bit at the mast in front of him, the wood splintering. Another bite and it fell, bringing down sail and line. He pushed away from the ship, seeing a group of men running along the deck towards him. Mages. They sprawled as the aft of the ship smacked back into the water. With a lazy beat of his wings, he angled towards them, lashing out with his jaws, dragging his hind claws along the deck and sweeping with his tail, not caring with what he connected.

Behind him, the raised foredeck was shattered and men lay where they had been hit, or crawled away, limbs broken. Sha-Kaan swept back up into the sky, high above the range of any spell, and looked down at what he had done. One mast was down, the humans were terrified and the dragging sail hindered their progress. It was not enough.

He came in again, higher this time, coming across the ship

broadside. Feeling the first edges of pain from individual spells as he closed, he braked sharply, brought his hind claws around and grabbed the main mast, feeling the wood compress under his talons. Unable to get a grip to wrench the mast clear, he used his momentum, beat his wings hard, and slowly, slowly, the ship began to tip.

More spells crashed into his back, intense heat and harsh cold eating into his drying scales. He barked in pain, shifted his weight and the mast snapped beneath his enormous bulk. He tumbled towards the sea, letting go the part of the mast he held in his claws and diving straight into the water to quell the magical fires, depriving them of the air they needed before surfacing and racing again for the heights. He was surprised by the severity of the damage he had suffered and pulsed new warnings to the Brood. He looked back as he climbed, feeling the weakening in his scales where the spells had struck. The mast had broken through the deck and ripped its way down the hull to below the water line. The ship was sinking. Time for a fresh target.

Sha-Kaan circled, calling the Brood to him. Below, two ships were going down but the one targeted by Hyn-Kaan was still afloat and as Hyn climbed, Sha could see the damage to his already wounded wing was severe.

'Hyn, the battle is over for you. You can land on one of the islands. You must rest.'

'No, Sha, not unless you order it. I can still fly.'

Sha-Kaan sighed. 'I will order nothing of you. But I wish to see you live. They will be better prepared this time and we still have much work to do. Do not risk yourself.'

'We may all live to see Beshara again,' pulsed Hyn-Kaan. 'But not unless these enemies are stopped.'

Sha-Kaan agreed. 'We have broken the fleet, their direction is lost. One ship at a time. Nos, the masts, I will take the helm and rear mast. Hyn, seek the rudder then swim clear. Follow me.'

For the third time, Sha-Kaan dived, his Brood at his sides once more. He bellowed his approach, choosing an undamaged vessel that was coming about to regain its original heading. Spells soared out. Orbs of flame hissing and spitting by, and gouts of intense cold that caught his wingtips and froze vein and oil where they struck. He switched direction, presented his back to the mages and swung in hard left, jaws sweeping across the wheel deck, taking wheel, helmsman and compass with him, spitting out what lodged as he made for open sea again.

Behind him, a loud impact on water told of Hyn-Kaan entering the ocean and a series of rending cracks signalled a mast toppling. More flame caught on his back as he flew away. The pain was deep, grinding into his scales and flesh and every beat of his wings pulled at his wounds. Their time in Balaia had made their hides and scales far more vulnerable than he could have imagined. Perhaps the humans would have to complete the battle for Herendeneth alone after all.

Vuldaroq watched the dragons attack, his words about not under-estimating The Raven repeating like bile in his mind. His mood had turned from victorious joy to near desperation in a few scant hours, his careful plans scattered like his surviving ships.

Once it had been clear that the Protector army was driving towards Arlen, he'd left the town to rot, choosing to take ship at Gyernath with a much larger force than he'd originally planned, following his skirmish with Sytkan.

Readying the standing College fleet, bringing the crews to Gyernath and provisioning for the long voyage had delayed him by several days. But the relayed news that Erienne had been taken in Arlen vindicated his decision; and he'd already envisaged sailing to destroy the Al-Drechar and the Malanvai child, shown the way by the mother herself. It had been beautiful irony and he'd confessed grudging admiration for the efficiency of Selik and his Black Wings. Another decision proved correct.

Selik, of course, would not be returning to Balaia. Those who murdered Dordovan mages in cold blood suffered a similar fate themselves.

But slowly, it had all begun to unravel. The fool Gorstan had failed to take ship at Arlen. The battle had gone the wrong way. Worse, The Raven had stolen the vessel. And they hadn't settled merely to the chase; unbelievably they had managed to steal Erienne from beneath Selik's idiot nose.

Even that, though, shouldn't have been too bad because in the sky now was a new beacon that only the blind could miss. Navigating the legendary treacherous shallows would be difficult but then that was what the long boats and masted skiffs were for.

Yet now The Raven had called on their pets and his fleet had been badly hit. However, the dragons were not as invincible as Vuldaroq had believed. They had no fire, that much was plain. And their bodies had proved vulnerable to spells. They just needed to be correctly focused.

Vuldaroq stood waiting with thirty mages. Their preparations had been fortunately unbroken, the ship unmolested as yet but heading away from the desired direction. But there would come a time and Vuldaroq had bade those ships closest to be ready as he was.

And the chance would come very soon.

The Dordovan Tower Lord watched the three dragons tearing the heart from the *Chaser*, saw the masts fall, the wheel deck disappear in a hail of splinters and the ship savaged in the water as the third beast tore at its rudder.

It was an unequal struggle with each of the dragons being as big as the ship. They were a staggering size and bulk, toying with it like a plaything. And when they had wrecked it, they'd turn to another. Vuldaroq would not let that happen.

He pointed to the thrashing waters at the stern of the *Chaser*.

'There. The most injured one,' he said to the ranks of mages behind him. 'On my command.'

The dragon bit and tore, the hull sluicing back and forth. With a wrench, the rudder came clear and the boiling waters calmed. The dragon had dived.

'Wait,' said Vuldaroq. He scanned the sea in front of them, the heavy waters, white-capped and angry still as the storm pounded away. Yet there they were. Ripples at odds with the seas, moving away from the crippled *Chaser*. 'Wait.'

The dragon broke the surface forty yards distant, scales glinting wet, wings powering its body out of the water, its belly exposed for a few precious moments.

'Aim high. High. Now!'

He jerked down an arm though they wouldn't have been watching. The IceWind, the single product of all thirty mages, howled away.

The dragon climbed fast but not fast enough, the spell catching it on the lower belly and along the length of its tail. An unearthly screaming wail tore from its mouth, a sound that rose above the roar of the wind and the crashing of the waves.

Vuldaroq watched it still climb but its tail could no longer balance it and the IceWind gouged into its flesh. Slower and slower, the wings beat. It angled its head down on its slayers, long neck curling down, tipping its body over. Its eyes glinted, another bellow, answered by the others, escaped its mouth and it fell from the sky.

He'd been disoriented under water and had surfaced too near the enemy, and now Hyn-Kaan couldn't drag in his breath. Where the spell had struck, his whole lower body was numb, alien to him; his scales were cracked with cold and his flesh burned like it was on fire.

He called to the Kaan and entreated the Skies to keep him though he could never now return to Beshara. It was to be a lonely death, far from the Brood ancients, far from peace. His great body shuddered, his mouth gaped and his wings swept at the air but drove him no further. Hyn-Kaan's energy was spent, his mind registered the slowing beating of his heart and the deep cold spreading up to his chest.

He sucked another breath into his tortured lungs. In his final moment of clarity, he knew there was one more thing he could do.

The cheer from the deck was cut short.

'Oh dear Gods,' muttered Vuldaroq. He rounded on the mages. 'ForceCones now. Linked spread. I want that reptile bounced. Do it!'

Feverish muttering rose from the deck, the mages kneeling for stability as they prepared. The dragon barrelled on in, neck out-stretched but wobbling, wings beginning to ripple but determinedly spread, its angle steep but true. It would hit the ship. They only had a few heartbeats.

He felt a movement in the mana. ForceCones flashed out, invisible barriers anchored by the casting mages, a desperate attempt to deflect the beast as it hurtled right at them.

Hyn-Kaan struck the wall of ForceCones, his massive bulk slapping them away, catapulting mages from the deck or crushing their bodies into the rails.

'Run!'

Anyone that could already was, fore or aft, scattering from the point of impact. Men jumped into the sea and the helm spun the wheel, the ship lumbering into a turn.

Too late.

The dying dragon smashed head first into the vessel, catching it square, just below the level of the main deck. The impact was enormous, echoing out over the ocean. The huge body slammed in amidships, breaking its neck and driving its shoulders straight through the hull. The ship shuddered, whipping sideways and down, pitching some men into the turbulent sea and knocking every other over.

Wood and timbers exploded up and out, the main mast was chopped at its root to slap on to the ruins of the deck and bounce into the water. The dragons' wings tore rents in the weakened hull, buckling back as they went, the frozen tail shattering as it struck.

Its back broken, the ship collapsed in on itself, Hyn-Kaan's body coming to rest amidships, dead weight dragging the vessel down.

Above the noise of splitting timbers and rushing water swallowing the ship, the screams of the injured and trapped, doomed and pleading for help, was a wailing cacophony, smothered by the ocean that sucked them all down.

Slipping away on the ShadowWings he had prepared as he ran, Vuldaroq flew close to the waves to a sister ship, shaking and terrified, fearing what might fall next from the storm-filled sky.

Sha-Kaan's bellow of rage and grief tore the silence that followed. He and Nos-Kaan sliced through the heavy skies, entering the water where Hyn-Kaan and the ship had gone, wings tucked in, bodies like great bolts, seeking their lost brother.

And he was dead when they found him, tangled in rope and wreckage, his carcass slipping gently deeper. His head, with eyes glazed, pointed skywards as he went, his slack, broken neck graceful with the support of the sea which bore him down so carefully.

Sha-Kaan turned, pulsed Nos to follow him and drove back up to the surface, breaking into the air, his wings thrashing, his mind ablaze, his brother lost after so much hardship on Balaia, his life taken by man. There would have to be revenge.

But as he soared up to just beneath the clouds, neck coiling round, his head searching for the next enemy, one man saved him from himself and his anger.

No, Sha-Kaan, said a voice in his mind. *They'll kill you.*

And he looked down again, saw the massed mages on the decks of the surviving ships and knew that Hirad Coldheart was right.

The *Calaian Sun* ploughed on, riding through the wreckage that was strewn across the sea. Sail cloth, baggage, broken timbers, ropes and lines. Bodies. Dozens of bodies. All rippling on the swell, the rain still pounding down.

The Kaan had scattered the Dordovan fleet. Only three ships still sailed and they were all angling away from the battle, north and west. Two mortally damaged vessels subsided into the ocean, their surviving crew frantically lowering any boats they had left and leaping into the sea. A third was also in serious trouble, its sails and mast fragments dragging in the water, its deck tilted at a crazy angle while waves crashed across it, battering the helpless crew.

They could be seen hacking and pulling at line, mast and sail, trying to shift the dead weight that dragged them over. And, with no control over direction, they sat broadside to the swell which was inexorably destroying them.

But Hirad didn't really take it all in. He had watched Hyn-Kaan's death plunge and had seen the surviving but severely wounded dragons dive after him. Now he tracked them high in the sky as they flicked in and out of the cloud layer. His heart was heavy. He had bade them come to The Raven's aid. And now Hyn-Kaan was dead and neither Sha nor Nos would survive a further spell attack.

Fly to Herendeneth, pulsed Hirad. *Rest.*

We will stay above you for now, came the reply. *No enemy will fly to attack you. When darkness comes we will find a hiding place. The spells burn us still. We had no defence. We weaken with every beat of our wings.*

I am sorry, Great Kaan.

Skies save me, Hirad Coldheart. Your land has brought us to this, not you. The air is bad, the food does not sustain us and we cannot renew ourselves. Good luck in what lies ahead.

Thank you, Great Kaan. You have made it possible for us to win this.

But Sha-Kaan's mind had closed to him. Hirad knew they would be gliding in the upper skies, resting on the wind until they had to land when darkness came.

Hirad looked again at the ocean. The Kaan had done their work. Whether it would be enough, only time would tell. Small sails were up and long boats were struggling to make headway as crews abandoned crippled vessels. Some of them headed for sister ships. Others, lost in the swell with the soldiers and mages they carried, might make it to shore. The Raven had the Protectors and they were worth five of any warrior. If they could force battle in tight confines, they could win.

But mages were what The Raven lacked. Dordover must have sixty-plus left alive. Maybe more. The Raven had three, and whatever the Al-Drechar could summon up. Very little, if Erienne's assessment of their deteriorating condition was anywhere near accurate. Even before any mage battle, though, they had to establish what it was they had to defend. And they had to get there with enough time to make preparations.

There was work to be done. Hirad turned from the bow rail and walked back down the ship. He waved Darrick over from where he was standing near the forward doors.

'Get The Raven together. We need to talk. Make sure The Unknown is there and include yourself and Ren'erei. Captain's room. I'll be there in a moment.'

'No problem,' said Darrick.

Hirad carried on to the wheel deck, pulling himself up the ladder. Jevin nodded as he approached.

'An extraordinary display. They're majestic creatures,' said Jevin. 'We have an edge.'

'But it's slight and we'll lose it unless we push on now,' said Hirad. 'This is the time to risk everything if you believe in what we're doing. Can you make this thing go faster?'

The skipper of the *Ocean Elm* noted the progress of the *Calaian Sun* with pleasure and saw more sail than was wise billow on her masts. Every eye had been astern as the dragons attacked the Dordovan fleet. Every heart had beat double time with fear at the awesome, alien sights and sounds. Every eye had widened and hardly a breath had been drawn.

The skipper had heard there were dragons on Balaia, marooned after the Wesmen wars. And he knew they were linked in some way with The Raven. He had not considered his ship under threat and had passed that message around his crew but had not seen the necessity to extend his thoughts to the Black Wings and Dordovans on board. Watching their panic, hasty spell preparation and taut faces as they lined the deck had given him brief satisfaction. More stamina wasted, more nerves frayed. It could only be good.

He had never thought to see dragons and the sight of their extraordinary size and power had been breathtaking. The death of one and the obvious and possibly mortal wounding of the other two had been regrettable but their action had turned the tables. And now he could ensure that Ren, if it was her on the *Sun* as he assumed, would reach Herendeneth first.

She knew the channels well, and knew the route that had to be taken. What she didn't know was exactly where the *Calaian Sun*'s draft would make passage impossible. The skipper would show her in the only way he thought likely to work.

The rain was just beginning to ease but the mountainous seas were unabating. He ordered a trimming of the sails to slow them just a little, sighted on the beacon that dominated the southern skies, prayed the Al-Drechar still lived, and patted his helmsman on the shoulder.

'Keep her steady, lad,' he said. 'Keep her steady.'

Chapter 34

There had been anxious moments through the night. The rest of the afternoon had passed under heavy clouds, strong winds and occasional sudden downpours mixed with the ever-present sounds of rolling thunder and lightning flashing in the storm fronts.

They were several hours ahead of the Dordovans as night fell and perhaps one behind the *Ocean Elm* and though any sensible captain would have ordered a dropping of the anchor as they entered the channel of the first islands of the Ornouth Archipelago, that was an option not open to Jevin.

The *Elm* was not slowing and Jevin could not afford to lose sight of the sleek, fast elven vessel. Neither could he let the chasing Dordovans catch them. And so his crew had a sleepless night, those not directly engaged in sailing the ship being on watch port, starboard, fore, and aft. Plumb lines were swung and dropped to give an indication of depth under the swell, which was subsiding as they reached relatively sheltered waters, and the lookouts kept up a constant commentary on conditions all around them.

Ren had stayed on the wheel deck throughout the night, advising Jevin on safe channels and calming his nerves as the ship sailed perilously close to rock walls to find the best depth, running in the wake of the *Ocean Elm*.

After the meeting had broken up and the mages had retired to bed to rest and maintain mana stamina levels, Hirad, The Unknown and Darrick had stayed in the Captain's room, mulling over defensive tactics and the strength of their forces. The remains of a meal lay on the table still and the three men picked at the scraps, washing it down with a light wine diluted with water.

The Unknown was preoccupied, his left leg stretched out in front of him, his hand constantly massaging the hip, a grimace on his face.

'I think it's time you told us how it really is,' said Hirad. 'We'll have to work it into our formation.'

'I want Aeb on my left,' said The Unknown. 'Aside from that, no special treatment, all right? We can't afford it.'

'You're not getting off that easily. Tell me how it feels.'

'Stiff and weak,' said The Unknown. 'I've had no time to build the muscle so what's there now is what Erienne patched up. It's locked up on me more than once and though Erienne says that'll pass, I don't have the freedom I need.' He chewed a lip. 'It's not going to be very easy to fight.'

'So?'

'So I'm not going to use the double-hander, I won't have the strength to brace it through any kind of swing. The elves have got some spare blades on board. Not exactly what I'm used to but what choice do we have? I'll use a dagger in my left hand, I suppose.' He shook his head. 'Sorry, Hirad. Looks like I'll be a bit of a liability.'

Hirad raised his eyebrows. Darrick couldn't stifle a laugh.

'Liability?' said the General. 'It may reduce you to the status of better-than-most rather than absolutely-everyone but that's about it.'

'Still, there's little we can do about that now,' said Hirad. 'Tell me, Unknown, what do you think are the biggest problems after what we've been hearing from Ren and Erienne?'

The Unknown blew out his cheeks. 'Well, they aren't going to all run up the path from the landing point, are they? Never mind the wards we think may be in place, they can fly and carry swordsmen short distances so we're going to have to expect attack from anywhere. If we can't block some of the potential entry points to this house, we stand to get swamped. Mind you, if we can't shield the house against a mage barrage, none of that will matter.'

'You think they'll do that?' asked Hirad.

'I would,' said Darrick. 'It doesn't risk any of their men and it could get them what they want quickly.'

'Anything we can do to stop that happening?' asked Hirad.

'Well that depends on how many Protectors you're prepared to risk outside the house,' said Darrick. 'I suspect that the Dordovans will expect us to be in a tight defensive formation wherever we are. They know we only have one ship and that means there's a finite number that can be ranged against them.'

'Don't forget they have no idea what resistance to expect from the island itself,' said The Unknown.

'Agreed, but they'll realise soon enough that there is no meaningful force already there when they start to advance,' said Darrick. 'If we can hide Protectors outside of the house, they could attack mage groups while they're casting. The success of that will depend on the number of swordsmen they've brought and the risk they think we pose.'

'How many would you take from the house defence?' asked Hirad.

'Eight, no more. But it's so dependent on terrain. They must be invisible from above as well as at ground level. I just think it's something we should consider.' The General poured water into his goblet.

'Anything else?' Hirad was looking at The Unknown. 'I know we can't be certain of anything but we aren't going to have time to scratch our heads when we arrive.'

'We aren't blessed with many options,' said The Unknown. 'We shouldn't split our force unless we really have to but Darrick's idea could prove successful if we can guarantee surprise. So much depends on the health or otherwise of the Al-Drechar. We don't want The Raven's mages wasting their stamina on shielding the house but it could come to that. And if it does, we're going to have to think on our feet about how to keep the swordsmen out.'

The Unknown breathed heavily and stood up, wincing as he flexed his knee and hip.

'I've got to rest. I'm going for a stroll round the deck first to try and loosen this up. Anyone else?'

'Yes, why not?' said Hirad.

Darrick nodded and smiled. 'I'll leave you two to it. I fancy rolling off my bunk a few times while I try and sleep.'

'See you at dawn, then,' said Hirad. 'And try not to wake up too bruised, eh?' Hirad turned to The Unknown. 'Come on, old man, let's get those creaking bones up top.'

'See this fist? It still works, you know. I'm not so crocked I can't take you on, Coldheart,' said The Unknown.

'You'll have to catch me first.'

The two friends headed for the deck.

Dawn saw the *Calaian Sun* slowing. Wind howled around the islands of the Ornouth, sawing at the trees that covered the slopes, and forcing Jevin to reduce sail. Ahead of them, the *Elm* had done the same and no doubt when they encountered the vicious swirling gusts, the Dordovans would follow suit.

They were sailing down a wide channel between two of the larger islands in the inner group, the clouds lower than they'd ever seen them, obscuring the hills and mountain peaks, and sweeping into valleys, thick, fast-moving and heavy with yet more rain. The only respite was in the swell, which hadn't the power of the open sea and though waves crashed against exposed shores, spray flying in the wind, the narrowing channels were quieter.

Ren stood on the wheel deck as she had throughout the night, her eyes never far from the stern of the *Ocean Elm*, waiting for a sign that they should take to their boats. Every hour they could stay aboard would make their job that little bit more comfortable and she estimated they had a day's sailing ahead of them, travelling as slowly as they were. Though more tricky to handle in these conditions, the masted skiffs could probably travel more quickly.

Lining the decks were the off-duty crew, The Raven and the Protectors. No one was below decks apart from the cook and even he was required topside whenever he could leave his pots safely. Jevin was clearly nervous, wanting everyone ready to react should they run aground and beside the plumb-liners shouting out depths scant feet below their keel, teams of Protectors stood ready to lower boats, with elven crew standing by to direct.

Herendeneth was dead ahead. The beacon struck through the gloom of the grey morning, beautiful but disturbing, a demonstration of magical power that Ren knew was nothing to do with the Al-Drechar's will and everything to do with their diminishing ability to shield Lyanna. Ren feared what she would find when they reached land.

The ship shuddered suddenly, slowing dramatically. A grinding sound travelled all the way down the keel beneath their feet, agonisingly slow, its volume amplified as it reverberated through the ship's timbers. Eyes scanned the seas, the plumb liners shook their heads. The vibration went on.

'Hold her steady,' said Jevin, his voice taut, his hands gripping the rail in front of him, his knuckles whitening.

Beside him, Ren waited for the sound to become the ripping, splintering one she knew he would be dreading. For an age, they dragged across the sea bed, sometimes heavily, sometimes almost lifting away on the slight swell. But there was no splitting of timbers and no rushing of water into a breach and the grinding sound ultimately faded and stopped altogether.

Jevin turned to Ren'erei, his face pale, breathing hard.

'Sand,' he said, his voice low. 'But maybe not next time. How much further?'

'Not far,' said Ren, though she didn't know and could feel herself shaking. 'We'll be all right, they won't let us down.'

'Assuming the skipper's still alive,' said Jevin. 'I'm not putting my crew through this much longer. Nor my ship. What sort of sign are you looking for, exactly?'

Ren was about to shrug but glanced back at the *Elm* and a smile lifted her features.

'That one,' she said pointing. 'That's it.'

Selik stormed up to the wheel deck, two henchman right behind him.

'You had better have sound reason to change the direction of this ship,' he grated, pushing the skipper away from his helmsman.

'You've seen the channels and you've heard the depths being shouted out,' said the skipper smoothly. 'And dead ahead is not the route to the destination for this ship.'

'You're lying,' said Selik. 'I can see it in your slanted elven eyes. Get this ship back on course. Do you think I am blind?'

'No, but unless you have better information on the depth of the channel I've just turned from than I have, I suggest you leave me to do my job. After all, why would I lead you astray? I'm happy to be taking you to the island. I'm looking forward to burying you there.'

Selik leant away, considering. 'You must think me stupid,' he said quietly. 'How long before we turn again.'

'Half a day,' said the skipper. 'It depends on the wind. If you don't believe me, then kill me and take the ship yourself.'

Selik's eyes glinted coldly.

'That's a sign?' asked Jevin.

'Yes,' said Ren. 'Because the route is straight ahead. There's no turn to the landing point until we clear the next island.'

Jevin nodded. 'I bow to your knowledge. Now, what do you want me to do?'

'If you can, sail up to the point where they've turned. Then bring the ship around and we'll launch the boats we need and go. You can either follow the *Elm* and find calm water to hide in or go back. There's no other way out to the ocean that I know of. You'll have to decide for yourself.'

'And what is to port up ahead?'

'Island upon island. You can't reach Herendeneth that way but you can make safe harbour in a lagoon a day's sailing away. You'll know it when you see it. You'll be hidden and you can rest. But keep hard to the starboard shore. The land shelf is very steep right off the coast of the islands there. The port side is littered with reefs just under the surface.'

Another nod from Jevin. 'And what of the *Elm*?'

'I don't know,' said Ren, worry gnawing at her. 'I guess he'll try and lead the Black Wings as far away as he can. He's a very brave elf.'

'I'll do what I can.'

'Thank you.'

Sweat was mingling with the rain and salt spray by the time the *Calaian Sun* had crept along the channel to the point where the *Elm* had turned. The ship hove to and started to come about to port, ready to follow the other elven ship away from Herendeneth.

The deck was filled with men and elves, weapons, small sails and crates of foodstuffs. Protectors clustered round davits that were brought up from the hold and locked into place. They hefted the long boats up and on to the pulleys and lowered them away into the sheltered seas on the lee of the ship, scrambling quickly down the nets and taking up oars, their gear stowed forward and aft under sheeting.

There were two long boats Jevin had been prepared to let go and the Protectors shared themselves out between them. Darrick and Ren would also travel, one to a boat. Thraun too, though still kept asleep, was leaving the ship on a long boat. Hirad would hear no dissension.

'If we're all to die, it will be together and Thraun must be where the Al-Drechar can work on him,' he had said.

The Raven would sail in a masted skiff. These three craft were the most Jevin could allow them. He would not leave himself and his crew with no means of escape should they founder.

Elves swarmed down to the skiff and raised the mast, leaving the sail furled but ready, and helped down The Unknown, who was struggling to climb the scrambling nets, tears forced from his eyes by the pain of his hip. He refused to sit, determining to hang on to the mast for support while they sailed. Hirad exchanged an anxious glance with Ilkar as they watched him before climbing down themselves. The two of them sat forward, Ilkar's face pale at the very thought of a trip in a small boat, while Denser held the tiller, unable to keep a brief smile from his face. Erienne sat by him.

'That old familiar feeling,' he said.

'If you'll recall, the Triverne Inlet was like a pond compared to this,' said Ilkar. 'And your steering still made it feel like rough seas. I can't believe we're letting you helm again.'

'I didn't see any other volunteers,' said Denser. He looked across at

Erienne. She was looking towards Herendeneth, her arms about her stomach, her shoulders tensed.

'We'll be there soon, love,' said Denser.

'I know,' said Erienne, half turning to look at him. 'I've missed her so much but . . .' She broke off and swallowed.

'There's always hope,' said Denser, though he felt none.

'No there isn't,' said Erienne. 'Just get us there safely. And quickly.'

Hirad pushed them from the side of the ship and, with a wave and shouts of thanks for the watching crew, they steered away, The Unknown hauling up the sail which filled and drove them after the Protectors.

The skipper of the *Ocean Elm* had seen them well before the shout went up. He walked aft across the wheel deck and leaned over to see a Dordovan mage peering into the gloom of late morning. Selik was hurrying along the walkway.

'Damn,' muttered the skipper. He walked back to the helmsman and stood by him. 'Leave the deck. If Selik's mage has seen them, he'll be up here to kill me. You know what to do.'

'Aye, Captain.'

'Remember, the One must survive and the Al-Drechar are important above all other feelings. We've done everything we can.'

The skipper hurried him to the ladder, took the wheel himself and looked determinedly forward. Below him, the helmsman scurried across the deck to talk to the bo'sun and first mate. The pair looked up at him, nodded slightly and set about their tasks.

The skipper heard the sound of running feet. His heart rate increased and he gripped the wheel. Hands slapped on the ladder and Selik's head appeared, the look on his face giving the skipper the answer to his question. Behind him, two mages and a henchman. Selik strode across and grabbed the skipper by the throat, marching him backwards, a dagger in his free hand, his ruined face contorted in rage.

'Tell me now,' he said. He looked over his shoulder. 'You, take the wheel, just keep it where it is. For now.' Selik brought his dagger up, its point scant inches from the skipper's right eye. 'Talk.'

'You didn't even bother to really question me, did you?' said the skipper. 'In your arrogance, you thought I'd simply roll over and let you plunder the most sacred things in my life. Well, my work is done now. You have lost Erienne and I have led those most able to stop you to the correct path, while we sail in an entirely different direction.

And all the time, the world turns a little further and your hopes of murder recede.'

Selik looked at him, his mouth hanging open, a line of spittle dripping from the slack, nerveless left-hand side. He even stepped away a little, though the dagger point remained steady.

'But the forces of right must not be denied,' he whispered, a fervour creeping into his eyes. 'You have betrayed every living thing in Balaia.'

The skipper could see the hate beginning to grow, could feel the tightening of the hand at his throat and the wobble of the dagger in front of him, its unfocused point shimmering. He knew he didn't have long.

'You're too late, Selik. Erienne will be united with her child and together they will destroy you and everything you stand for. If that is what I am betraying, then I will die content. So push home your dagger, Black Wing, you cannot threaten or hurt me any more.'

Selik looked over his shoulder. Under full sail and in calm waters sheltered from the storms, the *Elm* drove on at exhilarating speed. To where, the skipper didn't know and cared less. Eventually, the sea bed would rise to meet the keel of the ship but the skipper knew he wouldn't live to see it.

The dagger point came closer still. The skipper didn't flinch.

'And of course, if I do kill you, your crew will refuse to sail. I am not such a fool as you believe,' said Selik.

The skipper laughed. 'Look behind you, Selik. They have refused already. You have lost and I have won.'

Selik swung the skipper around so that he could look along the line of the ship. The elven crew were still there in the rigging and near the lines and stays. Even mops and buckets still rested on the deck and plumb lines lay in coils. But the crew were motionless. All of them. Waiting.

'Turn this bastard ship around!' roared Selik. 'Or your beloved captain dies.' Not one of them moved.

'Your man has the wheel,' said the skipper smoothly.

Selik sneered. 'Yes. He does. Turn us into the centre of this channel.'

'But—'

'Do it now! How hard can it be. Turn the wheel.' The skipper watched as the Black Wing soldier turned the wheel. The *Ocean Elm* began to come about, jibing across the wind, sails snapping briefly into a run before starting to pick up the new tack. They needed trimming to make the most of the direction. He didn't have to turn to know what his crew were doing now. Every one of them was moving from his post to come to stand below the wheel deck, or as near as their captors would allow.

'Get back to your work!' shouted Selik.

'No one may turn this vessel without the permission of the captain,' said the skipper quietly. 'They will not lift a finger to your order.'

But Selik was looking at the sails filling as the ship turned further and the sneer returned. 'But it doesn't look like I need you anyway, does it, dear captain? And I'm sure your crew won't let themselves drown because of some obscure rule of the sea, will they? You, of course, will not get the chance to find out.'

And as the dagger punched upwards and his head roared with brief pain before the end, the skipper knew Selik would soon be joining him, embraced by the Gods of the Sea.

They would make their own judgement and exact their retribution.

Chapter 35

The going was occasionally tricky but never particularly dangerous. While the Protectors drove on, oars biting into the choppy waters, a picture of precision synchronisation, The Raven, sail full, skimmed quickly down the channel, soon leaving the long boats in their wake.

With soaring cliffs to the left, lost in the low cloud, and a jagged series of smaller rock islands to the right, the wind whistled across the skiff, forcing The Raven to sit to starboard to balance the pull of the sail.

One hand on the main sheet, the other gripping the tiller, Denser sailed under the watchful but approving eye of The Unknown who still stood, hand on mast or mainstay.

Denser's heart raced, his mind a fog of excitement and sorrow. Their speed was a joy, rushing them towards Lyanna, the daughter he hadn't seen in too long but who would cost him the life of Erienne. He looked at her. She sat on his right, one hand clasping the gunwale, the other on his shoulder. She was staring at him from under the hood of her cloak.

He smiled at her and her hand gripped his shoulder a little more firmly, massaging it through his heavy cloak. He nodded, unable to say anything. They'd been inseparable these last few days and had known a closeness, a oneness, that they had never experienced before.

It had been borne partly of desperation of course but there was far more to it than that. The sense that what they had to do was right and that though they would be parted forever, the love they knew would live in on Lyanna. Denser was sure already, though, that he would never get over losing Erienne.

But they were cried out now. What could or should have been was unimportant. Dreams and plans could not be made. Now, there was reality to deal with, and Denser had to focus on saving his daughter so that his wife could die for her.

He looked away again, adjusting the tiller slightly and edging out the main sheet as the latest gust grew stronger. Not far now.

The Raven had their first sight of Herendeneth as the afternoon began to drift towards dusk. It looked at first sight a blank wall of unapproachable rock, but all over its grey face, green poked out as if through part-open doors, fronds cut off unnaturally though the remnants waved in the wind.

Erienne drew sharp breath. 'The illusion's breaking up everywhere. They'll be able to see the house from above, I'm certain of it.'

'We need to know the situation,' said The Unknown.

'Why don't you fly up there and take a look round now, love?' suggested Denser. 'Let them know we're coming, spend a little time with Lyanna before we have to get busy.'

Erienne beamed. 'What a lovely idea.'

'I am known for them occasionally,' said Denser.

Erienne half-stood and flung her arms around the Xeteskian, kissing him passionately.

'Disgusting display,' said Hirad, mouth wide in a grin.

'Certainly is,' said Denser, disengaging himself and pulling the tiller back towards him from where Erienne had pushed it with her body.

She steadied herself, prepared the spell and took to the air, hovering behind and above Denser, and leaning down to kiss the top of his head.

'Don't be too long,' she said.

He reached up and cupped her face in one hand. 'I'll see what I can do.'

She flew away south, keeping low and out of the worst of the wind that blew hard above the cliff line, soon becoming a small dot in the dull sky. Denser watched her go, jealous that anyone should have the benefit of her love bar him. Even his daughter.

'Tell you what,' said The Unknown, looking down on an increasingly green Ilkar. 'Fancy a look behind us, Ilkar? We need to know if there's anyone coming after us and how far they are away.'

Ilkar nodded. 'Anything to get off this rickety assortment of bobbing logs.'

'Don't get too close,' said Hirad.

'Don't worry,' said Ilkar pointing at his eyes. 'These are very good.'

Jevin sailed down the right of the channel as Ren had advised. His lookouts kept watch fore and aft and when the shout came and the sign was relayed from the crow's nest, he wasn't surprised. But the sight saddened him.

There she came, emerging from the periphery of his vision in the lowering dark afternoon, the *Ocean Elm* slewing from side to side like some giant drunkard. At her helm, someone with no notion of the rudder in relation to the wheel, the strength or direction of the wind or the inertia of the beautiful vessel. It was no elf that steered and in that moment he and his crew mourned the dead on their sister ship.

Jevin acknowledged their passing and led a prayer to the Gods of the Seas and the winds to keep their souls safe in the bosom of the ocean. And then he watched and waited for the inevitable.

He shook his head time and again as he watched the *Elm*'s progress. Saw her wander this way and that under full sail. No one stood ready in the rigging, no one swung lines. Not one of them would be ready and in that he would take some satisfaction. Perhaps most of them would drown and spend eternity in a twilight of pain, just too far from the surface to draw breath. He wished for it.

He briefly feared collision but in truth, the fools on the *Elm* could not steer well enough to orchestrate any such thing. He wondered whether they had paused to question why he travelled under such little sail, content to amble while his crew took soundings from every part of his ship. He wondered whether they had even seen him at all.

So he watched, and when it happened he heaved a sigh. Beauty destroyed. The sight came to him before the sound. Perhaps only a mile distant, the *Elm* slowed suddenly as if the hand of a God had grabbed her prow. She rose up, still driving forward, then toppled sideways, still coming, the holes in her hull awful and mortal. It was a horrible sight.

The sound came a heartbeat later, a rending, tearing, grinding sound. The death wail of a helpless ship. He imagined . . . he hoped, he could hear the screams of those onboard as they pitched into the merciless sea or were dashed against rock and timber. The water around her boiled as she foundered, sinking quickly.

'Bows ready!' he ordered.

A dozen crewmen lined the port quarter, arrows nocked, ready to draw and fire.

They came like he knew they would. Cowards too scared for their own skins even to attempt the launch of a boat. And while their surviving ship-bound companions made desperate attempts to save themselves, the mages flew. He tracked them, his gaze skipping across the sky, one carrying another like Denser had done Hirad.

'Don't let them close,' warned Jevin. 'None of them will touch my deck while they still breathe.'

Strings were drawn, longbows bent, arms strained. Jevin waited while they approached, aiming to fly along the channel, presumably in the hope of finding their Dordovan friends. Jevin found that, although they presented no danger to his ship, he couldn't let them fly free from what they had done to the *Elm* or her crew.

'Shoot them down.'

The volley of a dozen arrows flashed away into the sky. Five dropped screaming, their magical wings gone, the sea closing over their thrashing limbs, the gods helping them to hell. Three remained, including the carrier, wheeling away. More arrows nocked, the thrum of bow strings again, the sight of the black shafts whipping out after their prey.

Another mage fell and the carried man cried out. Jevin couldn't quite make out where the arrow had struck. He trusted the wound would bring him a slow death. Perhaps a lung. He nodded.

'Stow the weapons!' he called. 'Lookouts to port. Let's see if any elves survived.'

But the looks on the faces of his crew told him that they felt what he knew already.

Ilkar flew back towards the skiff which carried The Raven. He'd seen all he needed to see. He let the wind blow full into his face and felt the first drops of new rain start to fall. At least he'd soon be on solid ground.

Although he hadn't actually been seasick after the first couple of days on the *Calaian Sun*, knowing he could avoid vomiting didn't make him any happier about sailing and he had no intention of landing on the boat.

He came alongside, matching speed and flying next to The Unknown just as the intensity of the rain increased and began to sting in the blustery wind.

'How's it looking?' asked The Unknown.

'Well, there are three Dordovan ships still coming,' said Ilkar. 'They won't make it all the way down this channel by nightfall, they're going too slowly, but they'll make it to where we left our ship.'

'Hmm.' The Unknown stared back, gauging distances. 'We can expect attack after dark, then,' he said at length. 'They can sail skiffs down here in darkness, particularly if there are any elves in the crews. They can also send mages in by air. Pity we can't shut off that bloody beacon.'

'We don't know we can't,' said Ilkar.

'No indeed,' replied The Unknown. 'Well, seeing as you're clearly not about to get back in with us, why don't you go and see what you can do?'

'The thought had more than crossed my mind,' said Ilkar. 'I'd take one of you with me but I think I'd better conserve stamina.'

'See you in a couple of hours, then,' said The Unknown.

'Any sign of the Kaan?' asked Hirad.

Ilkar shook his head. 'No. Nor Jevin, nor the *Elm*. Not from where I was, anyway. Sorry.'

Glad to be heading for cover, Ilkar shot away towards Herendeneth.

Erienne's pulse was thudding in her throat by the time she neared Herendeneth. She had been away for less than fifteen days but so much had changed. So much had been damaged.

The Raven's long view of the cliffs was more shocking close to. The illusion was decaying almost before her eyes. It swirled, fragmented and reformed indistinctly, almost mosaic-like at the weakest but still existing points. Elsewhere, it had gone altogether as the extraordinarily complex mana structure unravelled and destabilised. There would come a critical point where it collapsed completely but that hardly mattered now.

The fact was that to anyone the carefully laid illusory mask of angry-looking rock was compromised; and what lay behind it, beyond the harsh reality of the nestling reefs, was an eminently habitable island with a canopy of trees, partly covering verdant steppes up to a central dormant volcanic peak.

From above, it was yet more obvious. Erienne flew in at a height of around a hundred feet and could make out the house, gardens and graves immediately. Coming in closer, the damage to the house made her gasp.

The whole west wing was gone; so much rubble and splintered wood collapsed into a tear in the ground that ran away up the slope behind eating into the beauty and sanctity of the steppes, scarring them forever.

The gentle streams, pools and falls had become fast-flowing rivers, and where they had burst their banks water rushed up to and surely into the house at four points she could see at a glance. Holes speckled the roof in too many places to count and littering the ground was the debris of storms. Glass, wood, slate and stone. All carelessly smashed.

But what dominated the house was the beacon of visible mana light that Lyanna, it had to be Lyanna, had created. It stood silent and stunning, shot through with the colours of the four Colleges, a deep calm brown and flares of black, a gentle swirl in its make up that spiralled faster as it rose.

High above her, the cloud mass spun about it, rolling with thunder and crackling with lightning. There was a pale mist clinging to the underside of the cloud and around the column, spreading out across the island and beyond, coating everything beneath it in a cool, fine rain.

Erienne took a brief pass around the light, which came from the centre of the orchard, and as she flew down to land, saw a sight that gladdened her pounding, nervous heart. A little girl had run from the ruins of the main doors and was staring up at her, eyes hooded with one hand, waving vaguely with the other.

Lyanna.

Erienne called out and curved in steeply, a strong backward beat of her wings stalling her so she could step off the air. She dismissed the spell as she crouched, pulling Lyanna to her in an embrace she had thought she would never enjoy again. She held it for a long while, the little girl clinging back, one of Erienne's hands moving up to stroke the hair at the back of her head.

'Lyanna, Lyanna,' she whispered, the lump in her throat threatening to break her voice, the tears falling down her face. She sniffed. 'Oh my darling, how good it is to be with you again. Tell me everything. Have you missed Mummy? I've missed you, my sweet. What have you been doing? Do you remember very much? Mmm?'

She pulled away to look at Lyanna and saw a quizzical look on her face.

'What is it darling?' she said, tracing a finger down the outline of her jaw. 'What's wrong?'

Lyanna frowned. 'You know what I've been doing. I've been in the dark place. The ladies kept me there and that's why you went. Because you thought I wouldn't know. But I did and I made a light for you to help you come back. Why did you go?' Her voice began to tremble.

Erienne resisted the urge to hug her again. 'Oh, sweet, you know why I went. You waved me from the beach, didn't you? Don't you remember? I went to get some help for us because the Al-Drechar were getting so tired. I went to get Daddy.'

Lyanna considered for a moment and nodded. 'Yes, but I didn't want to be in the dark place and the old ladies made me stay until I made them let me wake up.'

Erienne's heart missed a beat. A suddenly shaky hand swept hair away from Lyanna's forehead. 'What do you mean?' she asked.

'I hurt Ana.' Lyanna's chin was wobbling. 'I don't know what happened. Please don't be angry Mummy, I didn't mean it. I was scared.' She started to cry and Erienne held her close, rocking her and shushing gently into her ear.

'Of course I'm not angry.' Erienne looked around her, the wreckage so much easier to understand. She feared for the state of Aviana's mind, if indeed the mage was still alive. But sorry as she was for Aviana, that wasn't the real problem. If Lyanna was telling the truth, it presumably meant that her Night wasn't actually over. That her acceptance and control of the mana would not be complete. And that she could relapse any time, unshielded, wreaking untold damage to herself and Balaia.

She steeled herself and tried to keep her voice light and friendly. She couldn't afford Lyanna to see how scared she was.

'And how do you feel, darling?' she asked.

Lyanna smiled a little smile. 'All right. My head hurts and I think I made the light a bit bigger than I should. The wind is still in there and the ladies said they'd help me stop it and they didn't.'

Erienne pushed herself to her feet and held out a hand which Lyanna took.

'Shall we go and see where the Al-Drechar are?'

'I don't think they like me,' said Lyanna. 'They don't talk to me any more.'

'Oh I'm sure that's not true,' admonished Erienne gently. 'Come on, I'll show you they're still your friends.'

'Then can we go and watch for Daddy?' asked Lyanna. 'I've got a special place where I stand to look. I looked for you every day.'

'Thank you, darling,' said Erienne. 'That helped me come back sooner.'

Reluctantly, Lyanna allowed herself to be led back into the house. Erienne walked over the soaking timbers, passed shattered, flapping windows, smashed vases, broken pictures and torn tapestries and drapes, trying not to react. Lyanna didn't seem to notice any of it and chattered away about her friends in the orchard and the nice soup she had for lunch.

She slowed as they approached the Al-Drechar's rooms. Already anxious that the only sound in the house was the wind whistling through the empty frames and holes in the roof, Erienne feared the worst when she pulled open the doors to their corridor. No one stood guard, no one was waiting. She didn't even need to look in their rooms to know they were empty.

Erienne picked up Lyanna and hurried along to the ballroom, hoping against hope that they were all seated around the dining room table, smoking the pipe. Lyanna looked back over her shoulder as she ran. She didn't resist being carried but shifted uncomfortably as Erienne pulled open the doors to the ballroom and stood staring at the great chandeliers lying like ancient, whitened animal skeletons on the cracked floor.

'Who's that man, Mummy?'

Erienne spun around, Lyanna turning in her arms so as not to lose sight.

'Ilkar, thank the Gods. Lyanna, this is one of Mummy and Daddy's friends. He's going to help us. Are you going to say hello?'

Lyanna shook her head and turned it half away.

'Never mind,' said Ilkar as he jogged up. 'Gods falling, Erienne, but this place is a mess. What the hell happened?'

Erienne nodded her head at her daughter. 'Guess,' she said. 'Look, I can't find anyone. There should be Guild elves all over the place, there are four Al-Drechar as well and the place feels like a morgue. Come with me a moment, will you? I've got the creeps.'

Ilkar smiled. 'Which way?'

In answer, Erienne walked on through the ballroom to the dining room, their footsteps echoing wetly around the open space. There was a hole in the roof the size of a cart and the decorative plaster had fallen down in chunks to scatter and blow to the sides of the room. She barely noticed, trying not to break into a run as she neared her last hope.

She grasped the handle with her free hand and pushed the door inwards.

'Oh no,' she said, stumbling to a stop and putting a hand to her nose and mouth. In her arms, Lyanna squirmed and made a revolted noise.

Ilkar came to her shoulder and Erienne could hear him fighting not to gag.

'Erienne, take Lyanna away. I'll see what I can do in here.' His strong arms turned her to face him. 'Look, Denser is only an hour or two away. We need you to try and persuade Lyanna to take the beacon down. The Dordovans aren't that far away and that thing will bring them in like moths to a lantern.'

Erienne nodded, swallowing back the sobs that threatened to overcome her.

'Please don't let them all be dead,' she said. 'Please.'

'I'll do everything I can,' said Ilkar softly. 'Now go. Get outside and get some fresh air.'

Erienne ran back through the ballroom, desperation welling up inside her.

Ilkar looked into the dining room and could see what had driven them to come here. It was dry. Probably the only room in the house that was. There was a fireplace opposite which still put out residual heat and the windows had been battened shut, shutters over fractured glass.

The dining room table had been pushed most of the way to the left and in the centre of the room, four beds, all occupied; at least one of which had to contain a corpse. He walked into the room, the stench almost overpowering. His eyes watered and he gagged suddenly.

He had to get some air through. Hurrying to a door to his right, he pushed it open and found another bedroom, its single small window torn from its frame. He took in a huge deep breath, wedged the door open with a sofa and walked quickly over to another door which swung on creaky hinges, letting him into some kitchens. He was halfway back with a chair to wedge open the swing door when he stopped, straightening and frowning.

He put down the wooden kitchen chair and walked back to the ovens. They were hot, flames flickering inside the grills. There was no food ready for preparation and no water ready to place on the hot plates but unless he was mistaken the ovens had been fired up recently, the flames were bright, and the grates looked full.

'Hello?' he called, walking across the kitchen towards a pair of doors opposite the entrance to the dining room. 'Hello?'

He drew his sword and put a hand on the leftmost door, pushing it open. A cold store. Empty of life. He let the door swing back and paced right, turning the handle of the other door which swung in. He took half a pace back.

'What, by all the Gods, do you think you're doing?' he asked in low, plain elvish, not believing what he was seeing.

A male voice came out of the mass of huddled bodies; he could count six and there might be more.

'Waiting for the end. Praying for deliverance.'
'From who?'
'Lyanna.'

Chapter 36

Ilkar persuaded the group of elves to leave their hiding place and move into the kitchen. He had been forced to explain exactly who he was and what he was doing here before any of them would so much as look at him, let alone do his bidding. There were eight of them. He hadn't seen the two small children. While one of the young elf males put on water for hot drinks, Ilkar sat the others down, all the time mindful that in the next room, the Al-Drechar were dead and dying. He had to get these people moving.

'I'm finding it hard to understand what's going on,' he said, addressing himself to a couple who seemed the most willing to speak. They were an old pair, had probably been with the Guild two hundred years or so and yet their confidence had been completely shattered.

'You haven't been here,' said Arrin, the husband. His wrinkled face held piercing blue-green eyes and his hair, once black, was thin, grey and straggled. 'It's all happened so quickly.'

'But what? You're the Guild of Drech,' said Ilkar.

'And no power of this magnitude has ever visited us,' said Arrin's wife, Nerane, a slim elf, hair long and silver grey, tied back in a pony tail. 'Or become as uncontrolled.'

'Ah,' said Ilkar. He'd had visions of Lyanna terrorising them somehow, a malign force bent on their destruction.

'She's just a little girl,' said Arrin. 'And that's the problem. She doesn't understand what she's doing. She should still be enduring her Night under the Al-Drechar's shields.'

'But she's come through it, obviously,' said Ilkar.

The water began to steam on the hot plate. An elf moved to fill some mugs. He looked weary, like he'd been awake three days. Perhaps he had.

'No,' said Arrin. 'She broke the shield three days ago. She walks, talks and eats but she has no real concept of acceptance or control, though her subconscious is more than capable of shaping mana. And she certainly has no idea what her mind is creating. Or destroying, to be more accurate.'

'I'm not sure I get this,' said Ilkar. He looked up as a mug of leaf tea was placed at his right-hand. 'Thank you.'

'It's like this,' said Arrin, sipping at his drink. 'Her Night has been different to that of other mages. She's too young to accept the forces within her and assume responsible control without damaging herself and others. So there's an element of the mana controlling her. Every feeling or reaction she has carries an echo of expression in the mana she's holding.

'When she's angry, lightning strikes the island; when she's sad, it rains; when she's happy, the sun shines. Simple metaphors. Just as you might expect of a five-year-old.'

'In a perverse way, I suppose so,' agreed Ilkar. 'There's a "but" in here somewhere, isn't there?'

Nerane nodded, almost smiling. 'There are a couple. Most predictably, the mana events are more violent as the depth of the emotion increases. But with one or two exceptions, we can deal with those. Our main problem is that her subconscious shapes mana in very dangerous ways in order for her to get her way. She manipulates it and us and her anger, for instance, hasn't just been limited to lightning since she awoke.'

Ilkar nodded. 'Mental attacks?' he suggested.

'Yes. If her target is an individual. But you've seen the west wing of the house. That was a tantrum that manifested itself as an earthquake which cost the lives of seventeen Guild elves. We're all that's left,' Arrin said, looking away to his companions. Nerane put an arm around his shoulders.

'I'm sorry,' said Ilkar.

Nerane shrugged, a gesture expressing her despair. 'And right now she's using the Al-Drechar as a conduit for that beacon she's placed in the orchard though she doesn't know it, of course. We don't dare ask her to remove it. That makes her so angry.'

'And you were hiding from her just now?' said Ilkar.

'Yes,' said Nerane. 'It's silly, I know, to be so scared of such a small child but she can't deal with being told no and she wanted to wake Ephemere. When we wouldn't let her into the room, she flew into a rage and brought down half the roof in the ballroom. That was yesterday. We're lucky she hates the kitchen or I don't think we'd be here.'

None of them would catch Ilkar's eye, their embarrassment was acute. But he didn't blame them or think any less of them. Non-mages had absolutely no defence against magic and there was little else they could do but hide. Responsibility was a critical element in a mage's training. Lyanna had a great deal to learn.

'And none of you have been through that door since?' He indicated behind him.

'No,' said Arrin. 'We know Aviana's dead. She's been gone for two days but Lyanna didn't want us to move her.'

'All right,' said Ilkar, holding up a hand. 'Now look, there's things we really have to do now. Lyanna is with Erienne and out of the house. You have to get the dead mage out of there and tend to the ones still alive. Then you have to show me the state of this house. I've got more friends coming, about thirty, but there are Dordovans coming too and they want Lyanna dead. You have to help me make sure that doesn't happen. What do you think?' Ilkar felt like he was addressing children. 'Please, you have to trust us. Erienne will persuade Lyanna to disperse the beacon and maybe the Al-Drechar can recover. I need to know if they'll be able to help at all.'

Arrin frowned. 'Why would they want her dead?'

Ilkar sighed. 'What you've experienced here has been visited on Balaia for seventy days and more. Thousands are dead, so many more homeless and the country is coming apart. Some think Lyanna's death is a way to stop that. Erienne and Denser think there's another way.

'So, will you help?'

'You don't even have to ask,' said Arrin. 'We are the Guild Of Drech. We are pledged to the cause of the One.' He turned to take in the surviving Guild. 'You've heard what needs doing. Finish your drinks, then two of you attend to Aviana. Two more to check Ephy, Myra and Clerry. Another two to begin a meal for thirty – see what you can find, and bake bread if it's all we have. I will go with Ilkar to view the house.'

Murmurs of assent ran around the table. Ilkar nodded and smiled. 'Thank you,' he said.

'No, thank you,' said Arrin. 'Your coming has saved us all.'

Ilkar raised his eyebrows. 'Not yet, my friends, not yet.'

Erienne let Lyanna lead her away from the house, away from the stench of death and into the fresh, wind-blown air of Herendeneth. The light misty rain swirled in the sky but it was warm, though not humid, and the sun was trying to break through rapidly thinning cloud.

Lyanna was content and she skipped occasionally as she urged her mother along the path that led to the hidden landing point.

'Daddy won't know which way to go,' she'd said and Erienne realised with a jolt that she was absolutely right; there was no obvious entrance to the small landing beach.

Most of the trees along the gently sloping and stepped pathway had blown down, some having been dragged or cut from where they had obstructed the path. Most though, had been pushed into the arms of those around them, and every gust sounded with the ominous creaking of trunks gradually slipping their grip.

Just before the path made a right turn to lead down to the beach, Lyanna led Erienne towards a steepish rock scramble of about twenty feet. She could hear waves below and the wind picking at the exposed shore.

'I'll show you, Mummy,' said Lyanna, slipping her hand from Erienne's and trotting to the rocks, which she climbed with considerable agility and surprising confidence.

'Who showed you this?' asked Erienne, standing anxiously below her and ready to catch her if she fell.

'No one,' said Lyanna, slightly breathless as she clambered, her little body straining to reach hand and footholds.

Erienne went cold. Who had been looking out for her child? She felt a twist of anger. She'd left Lyanna in the care of people who'd claimed she was too precious to leave anywhere else in the world. But they hadn't stopped her climbing rocks apparently unsupervised. One slip. Just one.

'Didn't anyone watch you?' asked Erienne.

'I wouldn't let them,' said Lyanna. She reached safe ground and stood. 'See, Mummy, it's easy. Now you try.'

Erienne had no choice. She shrugged and started to scramble, finding it a good deal simpler than she had anticipated, her reach and strength making light of the climb. Lyanna watched her, the smile broadening on her face.

'You're clever, Mummy,' she said when they stood together.

'Not like you, my sweet,' said Erienne. 'It's difficult for little girls.'

Lyanna preened briefly. 'Come on,' she said.

They walked a few steps across an uneven, pock-marked surface and found themselves staring out at the sea. To their right, the rock outcrop fell away to the landing beach, and to their left on to the unforgiving stone shores. Directly ahead, they looked over the reefs and into the channel that led ultimately to the Southern Ocean.

The rain had ceased for a while and the sun finally broke through the clouds. Away in the middle distance, the blue-grey sea, backed by stark black rock, had a splash of colour. A sail.

'Do you see the boat, Lyanna?' Erienne pointed.

Lyanna nodded. 'Will Daddy be here soon?'

'Yes, he will,' said Erienne, an arm around Lyanna's shoulders as she crouched. 'And all our friends who will help us.'

'Like the elf man inside?'

'That's right.' Ilkar's words echoed in Erienne's ears and the memory of the dining room returned to send a shiver through her body.

She sat down on the damp rock, her legs stretched out, her feet hanging just over the edge.

'Now, Lyanna, I need to explain something to you. Sit down, darling, there's a good girl.'

Lyanna sat on Erienne's lap and looked up at her. Her eyes held a depth that Erienne found disquieting. They removed the innocence from her otherwise perfect face.

'There are bad people coming here,' said Erienne. 'And they would hurt us if they could. Take us away from here.'

'I know,' said Lyanna simply. 'We would all die. Me and you and the old ladies.'

Erienne was quiet for a moment, digesting what she'd heard. Lyanna was only five years old, for god's sake. Too young to understand the concept of death, let alone accept it so readily.

'But we can stop them,' said Erienne. 'And you can help.'

Lyanna brightened. 'Can I?'

'Yes, it's easy. Your light that helped me find you. You should take it away or the bad people will find you as well.'

Lyanna thought about it a moment, her bottom teeth chewing at her top lip.

'And Daddy can find his way, even if you take the light away now,' urged Erienne.

'When I can see him. Then I'll let them go,' said Lyanna.

'Who?'

'The old ladies. They are helping me.'

And so Erienne understood the Al-Drechar's stillness. She prayed Denser got that boat here quickly. Lyanna understood on so many levels but they were uneven and unconnected. It made talking to her a challenge and understanding what she knew about her own capabilities impossible.

'Perhaps you should let them rest now. We're all here with you. We won't let you go.'

She hugged the little girl to her body, opening her self to the joy of the feeling and knowing it couldn't go on for much longer. Lyanna looked away to where Denser's sail grew slowly larger.

'He'll be here soon,' she said.

'Yes, he will,' said Erienne.

She relaxed with her child in her arms and tried to forget how little time they had left together.

By the time The Raven arrived, Ilkar had seen the Guild elves remove the body of Aviana, wrap her in light cotton and place her in the otherwise empty cold store. There had been no talk of burial. That was a ceremony which would have to wait and Ilkar feared that many more would be joining her below the ground when this was all over.

His tour around the house had left him depressed at its ruin and at the prospects of defending it. He hoped that The Raven's warriors would have more idea how to plug the gaps than he had.

He was seated in the kitchen, nursing another mug of tea when the Al-Drechar awoke. A wave of excitement and relief swept over the Guild elves and he was soon ushered into the dining room where the Al-Drechar had been made comfortable.

Walking in, Ilkar was faced by one of the old elven women sitting propped up in her bed, a long pipe in her mouth. It was an incongruous sight but he recognised the smell of the smoke immediately and understood.

'Lemiir,' he said as he approached. It was rare that Ilkar felt overawed but, walking towards the Al-Drechar, that was exactly how he did feel. He was in the presence of history, of great power and of living myth. It increased his pulse and made his throat go dry.

'It is a wonderful infusion but also has great restorative powers when taken in the bowl of a pipe,' said the Al-Drechar, her voice rough and deep.

Ilkar was ushered into a chair near the bed of the Al-Drechar. He looked into the taut, fleshless face framed by her long white hair and was captivated by her glittering, piercing eyes. In beds flanking her, the other two were watching him, both tended by Guild elves but not sitting up, their faces drained and sallow.

'I am Ephemere,' she said. 'To my left is Cleress and to my right, Myriell. It is a great regret that you did not arrive soon enough to meet our dear sister, Aviana. For her we will grieve but not just now, I fear.'

'No,' said Ilkar. 'I'm sorry for your loss. I am Ilkar, mage of The Raven and Julatsa. I take it since you're awake that Erienne has persuaded Lyanna to disperse her beacon.'

'Yes. She is a girl of staggering talent. It's a great shame we weren't strong enough to keep her shielded in her Night for longer. I'm afraid she has no idea of the consequences to others around her of what she does.'

'So I understand,' said Ilkar. 'I'm sorry to rush you but I need to apprise you of our current situation and I also have to understand the condition of you and your sisters.'

Ephemere raised a brittle smile. 'I suspect neither of us have much good news.'

'No,' agreed Ilkar. 'I'm afraid there was a great deal of trouble in Arlen when we tried to meet Erienne and now there is a significant force not far behind us. Along with The Raven, we have brought twenty-four Xeteskian Protectors to help us. But the Dordovans outnumber us, we don't know by how much, and they could be attacking us tonight. They'll kill everyone here unless they are stopped.'

'How interesting where the College alliances fall. I am not surprised that Xetesk seeks to aid us, or that the Dordovans seek to destroy us. Fear and ignorance are powerful forces. But you, Ilkar of Julatsa, where do your loyalties lie?'

'As a Julatsan I'm worried about the return of the One magic,' said Ilkar. 'It is a threat, however small that threat appears as I sit here. But Erienne and Denser are my friends. They are Raven and I will do anything I can to help them.'

'And you are an elf, Ilkar. Honour and respect are part of your make-up.'

Ilkar nodded. 'But you. How are you now you've awoken?'

'I take it this house is in something of a state?' asked Ephemere as if she hadn't heard his question.

'That's a considerable understatement,' said Ilkar. 'And that's why I have to know what you're capable of. The Dordovans will attack us with magic and we must have the house shielded. We can't hope to plug all the gaps effectively but at least we can stop the magic hurting us.'

'It's a question I can't answer now,' said Ephemere. 'We've been so drained by Lyanna's demands for so long now. We're old and our powers of recuperation are limited these days. Keeping her in her Night was hard enough but she has used our reserves for her extraordinary light. We will dress, eat, exercise in our orchard if there's anything left of it, and tell you later. But don't expect too much, please.'

Ilkar rose, feeling the meeting was over. He felt awkward in their presence, like a boy mage before a great master. 'I'm sorry to press but The Raven musters just three mages and the Dordovans could have twenty times that. The situation is severe.'

'Before you go, tell me two things. What of the crew of the *Ocean Elm* and Ren'erei?'

'Ren'erei is with us and safe,' said Ilkar. 'But the crew were taken by the Black Wing Witch Hunters and I fear for them, I'm sorry.' He shrugged. 'And there's something else?'

'I could be mistaken but while I was asleep I felt the touch of ancient minds seeking us out. Powerful minds. It's been a long time since I sensed Kaan dragons.'

Ilkar nodded. 'You weren't mistaken. Three Kaan helped us during our voyage here. One was killed by Dordovan magic and the other two are badly hurt. Too badly to help us any further. They're resting in the archipelago somewhere.'

'Hmm, their minds were quiet, almost resigned. You must tell me later how they came to be here. Perhaps we can help them.'

'With their health, I'm sure you can, but they need more. The path to their dimension is lost and they are marooned on Balaia. That's why they and Hirad Coldheart have come here. Hirad is Sha-Kaan's Dragnonene.'

'Sha-Kaan is here?' gasped Ephemere. 'Such magnificence. I must speak to this Hirad.'

Ilkar raised his eyebrows and suppressed a smile. That was one conversation he didn't want to miss. He turned to go, the door to the ballroom being opened by Arrin.

'Ilkar?' It was Ephemere. He turned. 'I would so love to see Erienne and Lyanna. Please, could you tell them we are ready for them?'

'Naturally.'

'Poor Erienne.'

Ilkar frowned. 'How do you mean?'

'I think you know. I can see the sadness in your face too. We had hoped that it wouldn't come to this but we are so weary. We don't have the strength and I'm afraid there will be no other way.'

Ilkar walked away across the wreckage of the ballroom, a hope he didn't know he had harboured, extinguished within him.

Chapter 37

Hirad strode through the partially collapsed entrance of the house, happy to be on dry land again. Behind him, Denser was enjoying his reunion with Lyanna. The Unknown, his hip painful after the uncomfortable journey from the *Calaian Sun*, was taking his time, limping up the path.

With glass crunching underfoot, Hirad wandered into a big, damp-smelling entrance hall, saw to his right collapsed beams and doorways and so headed left.

'Ilkar?' He walked up a long, soaking corridor, counted the doors off on his left and looked right out on to an orchard. Drifts of leaves lay in sheltered areas and away across the ranks of damaged trees he could see hints of the demolition job that had been done on other parts of the house. Above him, water dripped through holes in the ceiling and large splinters of wood were scattered along the length of the corridor.

A door opened ahead. Ilkar came out and walked down to him.

'Hirad, we're in trouble.'

'Glad you noticed.'

'No, not all this. The Al-Drechar. One of them is dead, the other three not far off. If they can't shield even part of this place . . .'

'Right,' said Hirad. 'Have you been around the house?'

'Yes and it's not good. I'll show you when The Unknown and Darrick get here. How far are the Protectors behind?' asked Ilkar.

'An hour, The Unknown says.'

'How is he?'

Hirad scratched his head and looked over his shoulder. 'Is there some food anywhere? I'm starving.'

'Sure.'

Ilkar took Hirad to the kitchen and sat him down with some soup and a mug of tea. The gorgeous smell of baking bread filled the room.

'Bread's still in, sorry,' said Ilkar. 'Now, The Unknown. And no stalling.'

'Well, it's not good. He wouldn't sit down the whole journey and now he's walking up the path like an old man. I thought Erienne was supposed to have sorted him out. Doesn't look much like it to me.'

'Bloody hell, Hirad,' said Ilkar sharply. 'Seven days ago he was practically dead. Now he's up and walking about. What more do you want? She's rebuilt his hip, knitted back muscle and tendon but she's not a miracle worker. The job isn't anywhere near finished yet and he'll never be the same as he was. There was too much damage. Right now, he needs gentle exercise and plenty of rest and he's not going to get either. What you've got now is the best you're going to get for the fight to come, so deal with it. The question is, can he? That's what I'm asking.'

'Hmm.' Hirad ate his soup. It was a tasty thick vegetable broth, filling enough that he hardly missed the bread. 'I know what you're saying. I just want him to be the warrior we all know and he's not. Not at the moment.'

'And up here?' Ilkar tapped his head.

Hirad shrugged. 'He wants to believe that he can fight like before but it's pretty obvious he won't be able to. I think it'll affect his confidence and that's why he's asked for Aeb to be on his left. I mean, Darrick's a more than capable fighter but he's no Protector, is he?'

'Yes,' said Ilkar. 'The question is, what are we going to do about it?'

'Not let on that we're worried about him, for a start.'

A door to the kitchen from the ballroom swung open and The Unknown limped in.

'Then you'd better keep your voices down or he'll hear you,' he said. Ilkar closed his eyes.

Darrick stood looking at the collapsed west wing from outside in the orchard. The Al-Drechar were tottering about behind him in the company of Erienne, Lyanna, Ren'erei and the Guild elves. There were no grounds for confidence there and precious little more in front of him.

With the light fading fast and prospects for an attack growing as night took over, he'd come straight from his long boat to survey the house. To his surprise The Raven had put the defensive decisions in his hands while they discussed what to do about the Dordovan mages. He knew it was a mark of their respect for his ability but even so, they were The Raven. He couldn't deny the pride he felt.

Having established that there was nowhere else to hide or protect anyone on the island, he'd turned his attention to defending the house. Already, Protectors were blocking rear entrances to the main building and the three standing wings; and more were assessing the main entrance.

Signalling Aeb to come with him, he walked down the orchard towards the front of the house, taking in the tumbled brick, slate and wood and the teetering roof where it sat on unsound foundations. Much of the huge wing had slipped into a crack in the ground but beyond the immediate devastation, there were walls still standing. The two men walked through the warped wooden doors into the main entrance hall, took in the work on the entrance and stopped by a series of doors into the west wing.

'Here,' said Darrick. 'All this needs to come down. I don't want there to be any way they can come in this side. Send some to the far end and do the same there as necessary. Our main problem will then be entry through the orchard, through the three eastern wings and through the ballroom roof, if they find the hole. And there, of course,' said Darrick, pointing at the main entrance. 'Gods but this place isn't going to be easy.'

'It will be done,' said Aeb.

They walked across the hall and up the corridor with the orchard on their right. There were three pairs of double doors, one leading into each of the wings which Erienne had described as insect legs from above. The first housed what were now little-used rooms, the middle, the Al-Drechar, and the last one the Guild quarters. That latter had passages into the ballroom, kitchens and store rooms. There were also return ways to the other wings. It was a warren of passages that troubled Darrick.

'We could bring the ceilings down,' said Aeb.

'But it doesn't necessarily stop access. These structures are sound enough, unlike the opposite side. They can come in through any window, any hole. And we have to assume we will win. We can't demolish the place unless we have to.' He looked into the impassive mask of Aeb. The Protector's eyes gave not a flicker, his shoulders not a shrug.

'Victory first, living later,' he said.

They were walking along the central corridor of the first wing. Doors led left and right to suites of rooms, dining areas, bathing facilities, indoor fountains, and roofed rock pools. Though the area had been soaked by flood water and rain that washed in through

broken roof tiles and shattered windows, the structure didn't appear
to be weakened.

'I understand your thoughts but we have a responsibility to those
we eventually leave behind,' replied Darrick. That said, every turn
they took increased his sense of desperation. Less than thirty warriors
to defend a house that could have housed hundreds.

They walked through a service passage that linked the ends of all
three wings, finishing in the Guild wing. They took a quick look at
the passages to the kitchens and beyond, assessed the entrances into
the wing from outside and returned to the service passage.

'This,' said Darrick. 'This has to be blocked in two places. We can't
afford free movement through here.'

'Even our best efforts will not stop them forever.'

'I know,' said Darrick. 'It's a question of driving them to where we
want them to come, then withdrawing to the next dead point if we
have to. It could be a very long day.'

Aeb nodded. 'They will all have to die.'

Spread among the masted skiffs and overcrowded long boats, the
Dordovans made slow but steady going towards the island. The sun
had gone down but a pale light still filtered across the sky from the
moon, reflecting off the sea. The weather had calmed and, with cloud
cover light and broken, Vuldaroq felt that at last things were
beginning to go the right way.

But looking back over his shoulder, his eyes enhanced to banish the
encroaching gloom, he'd have had to take his courage in both hands
to say so. Etched on the dimming horizon was the outline of the lead
ship, its masts canted at a crazy angle, spars dipping in the water. He
could still recall the awful sound of grinding wood on stone, the
tearing out of the hull and the rush of water as it washed through the
crippled vessel.

The remaining two ships had come about in a hurry, their captains
roaring orders across the sudden panic of their decks, their wheels
dragged round to force tight turns to starboard, the gusting wind
driving them on, the fear of what lay beneath the water sawing at
nerves. The dread vibration underfoot that would become a shuddering stop and a pitching of the deck that would signify disaster.

Casualties had been light but the entire force of soldiers and mages
had been forced into the flotilla of skiffs and long boats. They had
carried all the surviving small craft from the original fleet of seven,
leaving space for something just short of one hundred and fifty

bodies. It was enough, but Vuldaroq could already see the tiredness in the warriors who would be forced to row much of the night to make the island, and his mages were taking turns to fly alongside the overloaded boats, draining them of vital stamina.

Even so, he was confident now. They would make the island well before dawn and set up a camp to give them some rest at least before first light saw them destroy the pitiful resistance that The Raven and their handful of Protectors would offer. The dragons were gone and he hoped they presented no real threat anyway. They were damaged and susceptible to focused mass casting and, without their fire, had to come close to inflict losses.

He turned his gaze forward again and could just make out the island in the distance. The extraordinary mana light column had gone but it had served its purpose for them all and with elves on the tillers of every boat, he had no fear of them driving too close to the shore or of making a wrong turn.

Still, there were preparations to be made. He signalled one of the mages who flew alongside his boat.

'It's time for our esteemed assassins to do a little work,' he said. 'I need to know the layout of any landing points, positioning of guards, buildings and any entry points. I want to know the type of terrain, the potential direction for our attacks and I want to know whether there are any other forces there bar the ones we already know about.'

'Yes, my Lord,' said the mage, a young man with scared eyes. 'How many do you want to despatch.'

'All of them,' said Vuldaroq. 'And tell them not to engage unless their lives are directly threatened. Tell them to fly in below the level of the headland and to Cloak the moment they hit dry land. I don't want The Raven even knowing they've been there.'

'Of course, my Lord.'

'Excellent. Be about it then and take a rest yourself, you're looking a little tense,' said Vuldaroq, smoothing his robes.

'Thank you, my Lord.'

The mage flew away to one of the trailing long boats, Vuldaroq watching him go. He smiled and prodded the leg of the man in front of him with his foot.

'Feeling any better?' he asked. 'You know you really should stick to the land. Neither sailing nor flying are really your province, are they?'

Selik turned a scowling, white face towards him.

'Just see this bucket gets me there, Dordovan,' he slurred. 'And keep your smart mouth closed.'

Vuldaroq's smile faded and he leant in close but made sure his crew could hear him.

'You want to be a little careful how you speak. Look about you, Selik. All this potential for accidents.' Vuldaroq tutted and patted him gently on the shoulder. 'Hmm . . . So many Dordovans. Only one Black Wing.'

'I thought you were the master tactician,' said Hirad into another tense silence in the kitchen. The Raven, Ren, Darrick and Aeb were seated around the table, empty bowls in front of them. In the dining room, Lyanna was asleep and watched over by Arrin while other Guild elves tended to the Al-Drechar who were asleep once again. In the store room where Ilkar had found the elves, they'd set up a bed for Thraun. It was much less than ideal but it kept him close and at least it was dry.

Outside, the weather was closing in again. The wind was picking up and rain squalls thrashed at the house. It was an oddly comforting sound, following on the heels of a few hours of calm conditions which did far more to help the following Dordovans than it did the defenders. It had escaped no one's attention that the changes in the elements coincided with Lyanna's time with her mother and father followed by her sullen acceptance that she had to try and rest.

With night all but full and Protectors patrolling the house and hidden near the landing beach, tempers had become frayed as the enormity of the task was relayed to them by Darrick.

'Hirad, you could try and be a little more constructive,' said Ilkar.

'But he's just told us that this house is practically undefendable,' said Hirad, pointing at Darrick.

'No,' said Darrick patiently. 'What I said was, it wasn't built to keep people out. It's a welcoming place, open and friendly. It's not a fortress and it would take us days to make it into one. What I'm suggesting is, in my opinion, the only possibility that can lead to success. If you have others, please let's hear them.'

'You're the tactics man, you tell me,' snapped Hirad.

'I have told you,' said Darrick quietly.

'Well tell it to me again in a way that makes me think it isn't just going to be drawn-out suicide.'

The Unknown shifted in his seat, the scraping noise of his chair entirely deliberate.

'Night has fallen,' he said, his voice utterly commanding. 'We know spies or assassins are going to be crawling all over this house any time now. So let me ask you this, Hirad. Do you have an alternative suggestion?'

'No, but—'

'Then shut up. Because we have to agree on positions, then we have to get a few hours rotating rest and then we have to fight all day. If we aren't cohesive, we'll be slaughtered very quickly and I have no intention of wasting Erienne's great work on my leg. Despite your worries, I intend to have more blood on my sword tomorrow than the rest of you put together.

'And speaking of Erienne, I want her and Denser in a private room guarded by Protectors so they can enjoy what is probably their last night together. You are shortening that night.' He glared at Hirad until the barbarian leant back, sighing extravagantly and staring into space.

Ilkar watched it all like he had watched it a hundred times before. And he knew what Hirad was doing. So did The Unknown. Just making sure they would do it right. It was just that he was not very good at expressing his concerns.

'I want us to win this,' said Hirad. 'And I'm sorry, Erienne and Denser, but I don't want this to be your last night because it means we're all dead tomorrow.' He pushed away his chair, grabbed his mug and walked over to the water pot, his boots slapping on the stone.

'You know he's right, don't you?' said Denser from where he sat at one end of the table, with Erienne's head on his shoulder and his arm about her waist.

'But we've argued this for an hour and there is no better way,' said The Unknown.

'And he still needs a little more instruction on tactful conversation,' said Ilkar.

That broke the mood, even Hirad chuckling as he refilled his mug. Only Aeb, there because he needed to relay any decisions to his brothers instantly, sat unmoved by everything.

'Again, then,' said The Unknown, inviting Darrick to take them once more over the hastily drawn map that was weighted down on the table with various pieces of crockery.

'Ready, Hirad?' asked Darrick.

'Yes, General, sir,' said Hirad.

'Come on, let's concentrate,' said The Unknown. 'This is it, now.'

'All right,' said Darrick. 'As I mentioned earlier, we are not establishing our core defensive position until just before dawn. I don't want any more information than is absolutely necessary getting back to the Dordovans. We're assuming that they will know the position of the house, its entrances and might infiltrate the building itself, possibly through the orchard. However, Aeb has stationed Protector pairs at every critical entrance and the Al-Drechar have a shifting shield which should detect Cloaked incursion.'

He cleared his throat and leaned over the map.

'Right, as you know, it is here in the kitchen that we are setting core defence at daybreak. It's right for a number of reasons. It's dry and warm for those we're protecting and from every entrance in, we have a clear field of vision. The only direct way to the outside from here was fortunately blocked when the west wing collapsed and the ventilation windows' – he pointed up to a line of six horizontal hinged half-lights along the wall opposite the door to the ballroom – 'are therefore our only truly weak point. Erienne is going to set a ward along the width of the windows before turning in tonight and it should have enough play to last the battle. Am I right?'

'Yes,' said Erienne, lifting her head from Denser's shoulder and brushing hair from her face. 'It's an explosive trap, focused outwards to reduce the chance of harming anyone in here. The noise will also act as an alarm.'

'I should mention that we're going to black out these windows to stop any passing flying mage looking in,' said Darrick.

'You can see them happening by on their way somewhere else, can't you?' said Ilkar, his eyes full of humour.

'Of course,' said Denser, picking it up. 'Many's the time I've been out for a flight and come across a desperate last stand by pure chance.'

Darrick rapped the table for attention. 'But returning to more mundane matters like living through tomorrow, here's how the rest of it will work. I've established three defensive areas based on where I feel the Dordovans will attack. Firstly, the main entrance, the three side wings and the orchard. This is the widest and outwardly the most difficult to defend. However, access to the house itself is limited and fighting will be focused.

'Should we be breached, the first fallback position is the ballroom with its doorways from the corridors bounding the wings and orchard. The last is the dining room and kitchen area but I anticipate holding them at the ballroom at the very least. Everyone understand so far?'

There were a series of nods around the table.

'The orchard presents a way to cut us off at the main entrance,' said Aeb.

'It does indeed but there can't be a large incursion into it unless the main entrance or wing areas are breached,' said Darrick. He pointed at the west wing. 'Because of the collapse of the west wing and the barricades we've added to ensure it is sealed, the only undefended way into the orchard is from above. That means mages only, unless they are carrying soldiers. Whatever, it reduces the possible numbers and makes them vulnerable. Ren has agreed to station herself out there with the three Guild elves able to use bows most effectively. And we have Jevin to thank for providing us with such.'

Hirad had leaned in and Ilkar watched his growing enthusiasm as, at last, he saw the logic behind Darrick's plan and could see it working.

'So who goes where, then?' asked Hirad.

'Five Protectors will stay in the kitchen at all times,' said Darrick. 'The Raven plus Aeb plus six other Protectors will take the front entrance. We can expect spell and sword attack there. It is the widest front and needs the best shielding. Two more Protectors will provide rolling guard in the dining room and ballroom. I don't anticipate attack through the ballroom roof but I refuse to be surprised by one. A single clever mage is all they would need through there. Similarly, the dining room. We've effectively blocked the way in from the small anteroom with heavy cabinets, bramble and rock. Similarly, the dining room windows and doors are both WardLocked and blocked by a great deal of furniture. Also, as you've seen, access to that part of the rear of the house has been made very difficult by one of Lyanna's tantrums.' He smiled at Erienne and Denser.

'We've brought our child up well,' said Denser. 'Even her tantrums are properly directed.'

'Finally, I and the remaining ten Protectors will guard the wing doors, act as a reserve and keep watching brief over the orchard,' said Darrick. 'Any questions?'

There was silence while they all digested the plan.

'Communication will be vital, which is why I've split the Protectors. I know they're better in one group but this time I think we have to use their other main advantage.'

'We agree,' said Aeb. 'We will be victorious.'

'We are one,' whispered The Unknown.

Ilkar chose to ignore the remark though it sent a shiver through him. All this time and The Unknown still felt compelled to react as a Protector.

'All this goes into effect after the Dordovans' inevitable spell barrage?' he asked.

'It was the first thing I considered in the defence but it doesn't affect our defensive areas unless our shield is breached in a critical area,' said Darrick. 'The Al-Drechar think they can raise a strong enough shield but it will have limited coverage. No bombardment will be too long because they have finite resources but you can expect it to be fierce and focused. I've asked them to cover kitchen, dining room, ballroom, corridors and front entrance if they can. There will be some protection for the wings but the area I've described is big enough to keep them guessing and make them cautious.'

'Any other questions?' asked The Unknown. Heads shook. 'Right. Erienne, get that ward up then get away with Denser. Ilkar, bed now. Likewise you, Hirad and Ren. Darrick and I are taking first watch, the Protectors will rotate themselves. I don't need to tell you to be vigilant and if the Al-Drechar call, then jump. Right, let's get to it.'

But The Raven didn't leave immediately. In an unspoken act, they'd all remained seated while the others withdrew, a deep silence covering the kitchen. For some time, they sat with heads bowed, contemplating what was to come and what it meant to them all, but more particularly, to Denser and Erienne.

'It's difficult, isn't it?' said Erienne. They all looked up at her, still with her head on Denser's shoulder. 'We've spent time coming to terms with it over the past few days but for you it's very different and we've neglected you. I'm sorry.'

'Come off it, Erienne,' said Ilkar. 'You have nothing to be sorry about. What you're about to do is something for which mere words of thanks are totally inadequate. It's a sacrifice so few will ever know of but everyone will benefit from. And I can do nothing but express my admiration on behalf of the whole of Balaia. You're dying to try and save countless numbers. It's extraordinary. Just extraordinary.'

He stopped, voice catching. Denser smiled.

'Thank you,' he said.

'But there's more and we all feel it,' said The Unknown. 'Erienne, you're our friend. You're Raven. And ultimately, we can't save you. That hurts more than anything.' Hirad and Ilkar were both nodding. 'We've been through so much, all of us. And though we've lost people before, this is harder than them all.'

Hirad felt their eyes on him. He shrugged and stood up and walked round to her. 'I don't have any words. All I know is that we should say goodbye now because there might not be time in the morning.'

He held his arms wide and Erienne launched herself into them, clasping him close, he crushing her as he returned the embrace. Her tears were flowing now and Ilkar could see Hirad fighting against his own. They stayed that way a long time before he released her. She rubbed a hand against his stubble.

'Great lump,' she said. 'You don't need words.'

'C'mon,' said Denser. 'It's time for bed.'

Erienne turned to The Unknown and Ilkar in turn, hanging in their embraces and sharing whispered goodbyes with the Big Man. When she stepped away from Ilkar, she looked deep into his eyes.

'I know you don't agree with the One,' she said softly. 'But look after my little girl, won't you?'

'Her and Denser, both,' said Ilkar. 'I promise.'

They watched Denser and Erienne leave the kitchen arm in arm before Ilkar spoke again.

'Come with me you two. There's something I want you to see.'

They followed him to the store room where Thraun was sleeping, his body shuddering sporadically beneath the warm covers. They gathered over him, seeing the face of the man they thought they'd lost emerging from his wolven side. It was a slow process.

'What's wrong?' asked Hirad.

'Nothing,' said Ilkar. 'I just wanted to remind you both of something. Although we can't save Erienne, we can save Thraun. He's Raven too.'

'Gods but I've never stopped to think about it,' said The Unknown. 'Ever since I woke up, we've been so busy . . . It's unbelievable, isn't it? Him being back, I mean.'

He straightened and Ilkar and Hirad turned to face him.

'Just think about it a moment,' he continued. 'What must have been going through his mind as a wolf. Compelled to do things he couldn't really comprehend but that he knew were right. And he lost his family doing it.'

'So he turned to us again,' said Hirad quietly.

'Yes,' said The Unknown. 'Us. Think how he was when Will died. He'll blame himself for the pack too.'

'He's going to take some saving isn't he?' said Hirad.

'But we'll be there,' said Ilkar. 'Together or apart, we've proved these last few weeks. The Raven is always there.'

Hirad smiled and Ilkar could see that for the barbarian, there had never been any doubt of it.

The mage assassin swept in low over the island. His companions had landed and moved Cloaked up a path from a hidden landing site not visible from sea level. He had chosen to risk being seen but considered the risk low. Beneath him, he could see and sense a decaying illusion and, ducking through its periphery, saw the sprawling mass of the severely damaged rambling mansion.

In its centre, trees. Around its edges, cleared ground and at its rear, a water-filled rockfall that had been arrested only by the house itself.

There was great power here and something innate told him not to fly any lower. They would be looking for him. Probably on the mana spectrum as well as by sight. So he circled just below the illusion seeing no light or movement. To a casual observer, the house was deserted. Indeed, there was a part of him that wondered if it wasn't. But there was nowhere else to be on the island.

He swept back over the house one more time, logged possible access points in his mind and flew away back to the flotilla, trusting his sect mages to remain undetected as they carried out more detailed inspection of the terrain.

It wouldn't be an easy fight but they would win. They had to. Dordovan magic depended on it.

Chapter 38

Sometime in the night, Lyanna had found them and crept in between them without waking either of them. But there she was when Erienne awoke, arms flung out to the sides and occupying far more of the bed than a small five-year-old should. Denser had moved all the way to the right-hand side and was in danger of falling off the edge while Erienne had moved her body into a curve to accommodate the little girl.

It was an idyllic moment and tears fled briefly down Erienne's cheeks before she steeled herself, drying her face and moving down in the bed. She propped her head on one hand and stroked Lyanna's cheeks. There was movement in the house despite the fact it was still dark and Erienne guessed it would soon be time to get up.

Their room was the first in the Guild wing and despite a little damp it had been comfortable enough. Outside, two Protectors had stood vigil and the windows were shuttered and locked, one of Denser's alarm wards placed across the frame. They hadn't been disturbed.

Lyanna opened her eyes and smiled blearily at her mother.

'Good morning, beautiful,' whispered Erienne.

'It's still dark, Mummy.'

'I know, but there's going to be lots of danger here today and I do so need you to be a brave girl.'

'I'll look after you, Mummy.'

'Oh darling, I know!' Erienne crushed her into an embrace and Lyanna clung on. Erienne could feel her agitation and worry. This was no place for a young child and the effect on her of the terrors to come was something Erienne would never have the chance to deal with. But right now, all Lyanna knew was that something was wrong and that everyone around her was feeling a deep tension. It would all make her very uncomfortable and insecure.

A knock on the door surprised her and she jumped, disturbing the moment. Lyanna pulled away and Erienne sat further up, pulling up the sheets to cover her breasts.

'Come in,' she said.

The door opened and Nerane came in carrying a tray on which sat two steaming mugs.

'Sorry to disturb you so early,' said Nerane. 'But The Unknown Warrior has asked that you raise yourselves.'

She smiled as she saw the family picture in front of her. Beside Erienne, Denser stirred and rolled over, grunting as he sat up.

'It seems such a shame to make you move,' said Nerane. 'You look perfect together.'

Erienne looked across at the half-asleep Denser. She saw his tousled hair, uncombed beard and his slack mouth open and laughed. 'Are you sure?'

'You know what I mean,' said Nerane. She left the tray on a table near the bed.

'What else did The Unknown say?' asked Erienne.

'The Dordovans are on the beach and spreading through the island. They'll encircle us soon. The Al-Drechar shield is up and steady, everyone is inside the house and you need to move from here soon because the doors to the wing need to be sealed and blocked.'

'Did he make you learn all that?' asked Denser, looking down and noticing his daughter. 'Oh, hello you.'

'Hello, Daddy.'

'At least I know why my back hurts so much,' said Denser.

'I don't think it's got much to do with Lyanna,' said Erienne.

Nerane had blushed and was backing towards the door. 'The Unknown Warrior says that next time he'll send Hirad to make you get up.'

'Incentive indeed,' said Denser. 'Thank you, Nerane. Tell him it won't be necessary.'

The old elf left, closing the door quietly behind her. Denser looked deep into Erienne's eyes and she felt a longing it would have been impossible to deny but for Lyanna between them. He reached out and put a hand to her cheek, which she covered with hers.

'So this is it, then,' he said.

'Yes, I suppose so,' said Erienne.

He nodded, his lower lip trembling. 'Just remember how much I love you,' he said, his voice barely above a whisper.

'And I'll love you, wherever I am,' she replied.

Lyanna squirmed. 'What's wrong, Mummy?'

'Nothing darling, nothing at all.'

*

Hirad placed the last of the Al-Drechar's beds in the kitchen, near to the stove to enjoy its heat.

'So did they get any of the assassins?' he asked.

'Three,' said The Unknown.

'Good going,' said Hirad. 'And no one got inside?'

'Not that we know. But Ren thought she saw a flyer. We can assume they've seen the orchard and know the size of the house. The Al-Drechar said no one touched the shield.'

Hirad sat at the table and drew his blade, honing its edge on a whetstone he'd borrowed from the Guild elves. He felt alive. There was a fight to come, the odds were stacked against them but The Raven were always to be reckoned with.

'So how long before they attack?'

'Any time,' said The Unknown. 'They aren't massed yet but it won't be long. We should get to our places.'

Hirad checked the edge of his sword and, satisfied, stood and sheathed it, automatically checking his daggers were also in their sheaths. The door to the dining room swung open and the Al-Drechar came in, supported by Guild elves.

'All right, ladies?' asked Hirad.

Myriell gave him a withering look. 'I had thought my days in the kitchen well and truly over,' she said.

'Well, we'll try and keep it as brief as possible,' said Hirad. 'Then we can talk about my dragons.'

He smiled and waited for them to pass before walking into the ballroom via the dining room, a worry nagging at him. He'd tried to speak with Sha-Kaan but had found his mind closed. Either that or dead. He hoped their rest would save them but he remembered Sha-Kaan's weary mind the last time they had shared contact and feared the worst. How they could do with their power today.

He shook his head and moved on, The Unknown limping beside him, having checked that the blocked entrances were as secure as they could be. Through the ballroom and down the corridor, the door to the Guild wing opened and Denser appeared, belting on his sword.

'In your own time,' said Hirad as he strode past.

'Ha ha,' said Denser.

'I'll ask the Dordovans to wait for you,' returned Hirad.

'If you wouldn't mind.'

'Hirad,' warned The Unknown. 'Come on.'

They carried on down the corridor. The Protectors were already on

station and in the near dark Hirad could pick out one of the elves in
the orchard, hidden under a fallen branch that had made an arch with
the wall. Further on down the corridor, they found Darrick prowling,
his sword as yet sheathed but his face taut with nervous concentration.

'Morning, General,' said Hirad, grinning, as they stopped by
him.

'Is he always like this?' asked Darrick.

'Always,' said The Unknown. 'You get used to it. Sort of.'

'All ready?' asked Hirad, feeling he ought to bring himself to order.
He felt strangely lightheaded, the thrill of imminent action charging
his mind and body. But he knew he couldn't afford to be unfocused.

'Just the door to the Guild wing to seal and we're there. We've got
a little breathing space, assuming we're right about the bombardment.'

'Should the elves be out in the orchard?' asked Hirad.

'The shield bleeds over the near edge of the orchard and it's a
calculated risk we have to take. I can't afford to be surprised there
and I don't want Dordovans seeing where our defenders are hidden.'

Hirad put out his hand and Darrick shook it warmly, doing
likewise with The Unknown.

'Just shout if you need more bodies,' said Hirad.

'And you,' said Darrick.

The Raven pair moved on, walking as fast as The Unknown could
go, across the entrance hall to where Ilkar was already waiting with
Aeb and the Protectors.

'We all ready?' asked Hirad.

'Spell shield already up,' said Ilkar, his voice reflecting his
concentration. 'It's covering the door.'

'Good,' said Hirad. 'Now where the hell are Denser and Erienne?'

Lyanna sat on a chair at the end of the kitchen table looking awfully
small and scared. Erienne was crouching by her, stroking her hair and
whispering to her, trying to calm her. Lyanna was clutching her doll
and, though she nodded occasionally, Denser could see her eyes
darting continually to the Protectors, who stood stock still around the
kitchen. He understood her fear.

He walked across to his family, past the sympathetic but slightly
unfocused gazes of the Al-Drechar.

'How's she doing?' he asked.

'Just about all right,' said Erienne.

Denser leant in and kissed Lyanna's cheek. 'You'll be safest here, you know,' he said.

'But I want to be with you,' complained Lyanna.

'It'll be dangerous out there, my sweet,' said Erienne. 'You'll be safer here with Ephy and Clerry and Myra, don't you think?'

Lyanna looked around the room her little brow furrowed. 'I don't like these men. Why have they got masks on? And why don't they ever say anything?'

Erienne looked to Denser who raised his eyebrows. This was hardly the time to try and explain the Protector calling to a five-year-old.

'They are special soldiers from where I come from,' said Denser. 'Don't worry about the masks, they wear them to make them better at fighting and they are in here just to look after you.'

Lyanna nodded. 'All right.'

'Now listen to me, darling,' said Erienne. 'It's going to be very noisy here and there will be lots of shouting and it will be scary. But you mustn't try to come and find us because it will be very dangerous for you. We'll be all right, don't you worry. Will you be brave for me?'

'I'll try,' said Lyanna.

'There's a good girl,' said Denser. 'Now if you get too scared, then go and cuddle one of the old ladies. They love you too.'

Lyanna nodded.

There was a crump which echoed through the house.

'It's started,' said Denser. He knelt and hugged his daughter. 'I'll see you a little bit later.'

'Bye Daddy,' said Lyanna.

Erienne hugged her too. 'Be a good girl and do what the masked men say, won't you?'

With a lingering look at their daughter, they left the kitchen and ran to join The Raven.

'On my order and not before!' roared Vuldaroq as the solitary FlameOrb soared away to splash against a shield. He turned to Gorstan, who had been the lead mage in Arlen. 'I want concentrated spells; I want as much of this house destroyed as you can manage but I expect you to stop before you exhaust yourselves if you are getting nowhere.

'He may have been an idiot to cast early but it was an education, was it not? That was not a shield from any College I've ever seen.'

'Yes, my Lord.'

'Right. Cast at will. And remember, advise me before the last spells are away. I have an attack to order.'

'Was that it?' asked Hirad. 'I—'

'Wow,' said Ilkar, rocking slightly and sensing significant movement in the mana. 'Here it comes.'

A moment's silence and then the spells thundered in. Like a herd of giant horses riding across the roof above them, FlameOrbs clattered into the Al-Drechar's shield. Light flashed all around them, orange, yellow and white sheeting through cracks in the barricades and washing across the orchard behind them. The shield fizzed as it struggled to repel the attack. Hirad hunched reflexively, the barrage of noise hurting his ears despite his hands over them. It was deafening, shuddering the floor beneath his feet and rattling the doors in front and the slate over his head.

He turned to see Erienne and Denser running up and he managed a smile but couldn't hear what the Xeteskian said to him, shrugging his shoulders and pointing at an ear.

Behind him, Orbs splashed down into the exposed orchard, sending flame scattering across the sodden trees, boiling away water and catching hold, crackling and spitting. Trotting to the barricaded doors, he looked out, saw no other trouble and jogged back, a thumb up in response to The Unknown's look.

More light and a crunching sound as a spell breached the barrier, thudding into the roof. All eyes looked up anxiously but elsewhere the shield was still holding and the noise right above them subsided as the barrage died away, to be replaced by echoing rumbles to their right.

'EarthHammer,' said Denser. 'They're attacking the wings.'

Hirad's ears were ringing from the attack. Behind him, the orchard was blazing in a swathe twenty yards wide and above they could just hear the sound of the one FlameOrb spell, eating at the wood and slate.

The noise increased over the wings. Vibrations rattled under their feet and the sound of a detonation echoed across the hallway, FlameOrbs exploding in enclosed spaces. In the first light of morning, the spell flashes were bright and stark, filling the shadows that still dominated the house.

'Aeb, alert your brothers and Darrick. They'll think they have an entry point,' said The Unknown.

'Yes,' said Aeb.

A further flurry of spells smacked across the shield above their heads and then for a few precious moments the world was quiet.

'Ready Raven,' said The Unknown. He drew his elven blade and tapped it one-handed on the stone flags at his feet.

Seamlessly, they formed up. The Raven's favoured chevron in the centre of a semi-circle that sealed the main entrance. Hirad stood to The Unknown's right, Aeb to his left. Three Protectors stood to either flank and behind knelt the mages.

'HardShield up,' said Denser.

'IceWind ready,' said Erienne.

The doors shuddered under heavy impact.

'Spell?' asked Hirad.

'No,' said Ilkar.

Another impact. The doors creaked ominously. Hirad shifted his stance, grip moving on his sword. He could hear shouts outside and the running of feet as the Dordovan soldiers massed. Bring them on, he thought, letting the metronomic sound of The Unknown's blade flow through him, bringing him the strength it always did.

'This time,' said The Unknown.

Third time, the battering-ram of a tree trunk crashed straight through the centre of the doors, sending splinters to bounce off Denser's HardShield. There was a roar from outside, the trunk was hauled out of the way and in the diminishing gloom Hirad could see a mass of armoured bodies charging his way.

Through the gap flashed arrows and crossbow bolts, again ricocheting off the shield and, hard on their heels, FlameOrbs savaged through the broken entrance, splashing against Ilkar's spell shield and setting fire to the wood surrounds.

'Holding,' said The Unknown, who hadn't so much as flinched as the spells and missiles came in. 'Here come the swords.'

And indeed, on the back of another pair of FlameOrbs, they did, pouring up to the doors and through, shouting as they came at the steady Raven line.

'Erienne, as you will,' invited The Unknown.

Behind them, Erienne stood. 'Duck,' she said.

The warriors did and the IceWind roared over their heads, smashing into the front rank of Dordovans, shouts cut off as they stumbled and fell, faces frozen in fear, fingers and weapons shattering as bodies struck the floor. The charge faltered and The Raven warriors stood.

'Come on!' roared Hirad. 'We're waiting.'

In they came. The Unknown's blade tapped, dagger in his left hand. The tapping ceased and The Unknown brought his blade up, left to right, and thrashed it through the guard of the first man, catching him in his upper chest. His blade carried on through the man's lower jaw, The Unknown's strength stopping him in his tracks and sending his body backwards, blood spattering all over.

Next to him, Hirad blocked a sword easily, jabbing with a fist as he thrust the attacker back. He stumbled but came on, feinting left and striking right. Hirad blocked again but this time reversed his blade back across the enemy's chest, seeing it slice through cloth and leather armour. The enemy gasped, staggered to his right and took a Protector axe clean through the top of his head.

The space in front filled with Dordovan soldiers. Left and right the Protectors, wide-spaced and double-weaponed, forged their awesome silent warfare. Aeb, his sword keeping Dordovans from the left side of The Unknown, was devastating with his axe, batting flat-bladed and delivering massive overheads and flank blows. But as the bodies fell, the press increased and The Raven were slowly edged back.

The Unknown caught a sword blow on his dagger and twisted the blade away left, opening up his opponent's chest. Needing no second chance, the big man plunged his sword through the chain mail, the man falling backwards. Wrenching the blade clear, his hip locked and he lost balance momentarily, stumbling forward, crying out in sudden unexpected pain.

Seeing an opportunity, a blow flashed in from the left. The Unknown, in no position to block it, waved his dagger in the way but saw the attack pushed aside by Aeb. The huge Protector thundered his axe through neck-high, catching the man just above the shoulder blade and carving all the way through to his spine. He was thrown into the enemy line. Not pausing, Aeb dragged The Unknown back, the line reformed.

Hirad, chopping down on a half-hearted blow, breathed a sigh of relief, dragged his opponent to him with his free hand, headbutted him on the top of his nose, thrust the stunned man away and ripped his blade through his groin. The Dordovan fell screaming.

Squaring up, Hirad sought his next target and then the doors from the orchard exploded behind him.

Darrick saw the mages flying above the orchard, moving fast and away out of sight. Turning back to his defence, he could hear

Dordovans advancing through the rubble behind the doors to the first wing.

To his right, a spell exploded against the second wing's doors, shattering them, the Protectors who had been standing aside, now turned into the action, blades chopping down and the sounds of dying men echoing into the corridor.

There was a thud in front of him and urgent voices sounding behind the doors.

'Clear,' he warned. The trio of Protectors flattened themselves against the walls. 'Let's get in there fast and we might get the mages.'

Slight nods indicated they both heard and agreed.

Without further warning, the doors rattled and burst in on their hinges, slapping back against the walls. Darrick turned his head away as dust and splinters sprayed out and the ForceCone spent itself against the orchard wall.

'Now!' he yelled, leading the charge into the corridor, the Protectors carrying swords only in the close quarters of the passage, flanking him.

Darrick laughed at the surprise on the faces of the mages and warriors he faced. He crashed his blade through the stomach of the mage immediately in front of him before he had a chance to move, Protectors on either side, the third just behind.

With awesome speed, they moved ahead, cutting and slashing into the Dordovans, chopping down mage and warrior alike, blood smearing the walls and the cries of the dying filling the corridor. Darrick came forward again but the enemy broke and ran, Protectors making to chase them.

'Stop!' ordered Darrick. 'Fall back.'

They ran back to the relative safety of the main corridor. Darrick glanced over his shoulder, figures were moving.

'Down!' he yelled.

They hit the ground on either side of the door, and rolled. A heartbeat later, FlameOrbs roared into the corridor splashing over the walls and thundering through the empty window frames, fires licking at exposed wood.

Darrick got to his feet and found the Protectors already standing, watching him.

'Patience,' he said.

That was something the Protectors had in abundance.

Ren scoured the sky, bow relaxed but arrow nocked and ready.

Shapes had rushed across, too fast for her or her people to follow. They were looking for trouble no doubt, angling to land inside the house while their forces occupied both Raven and Protector alike. She could hear the sounds of fighting from the front door and behind her, dull thuds signified attacks from the wings.

A whistle from her left and she looked. The Guild elf pointed up and right. Ren followed the finger. Eight mages, descending fast. The warning went round the orchard. Bows were bent, waiting.

Ren breathed deep and regular, watching her target as it moved, swirling in the air. The sky was lightening but clouds were gathering and the wind was getting up quickly, gusts whipping at the drifts of leaves in the orchard and fanning the flames to the right near the doors to the entrance hall.

Down they came. Wait, wait. Ren tensed the bow string that little bit more. Away. Her arrow sped into the sky, thudding into the neck of the mage who fell soundlessly from the sky. Right behind it, three more arrows sang through the orchard, two more mages fell. That left five still descending.

Ren nocked another arrow and glanced left. More shapes coming. More mages. A dozen.

'Fire at will, fire fast,' she called. 'Left and incoming.'

She let go another arrow which caught a mage on his arm. His wings flickered, steadied then disappeared and he screamed a long 'no' as he plunged to the earth, his body slapping on to the collapsed roof of the west wing.

More arrows flew into the air, two missing their targets that Ren could see but now half a dozen mages were down, wings dispersed and advancing quickly, spells being prepared as they came.

Ren could feel panic spread through the Guild elves. She fired again, taking another mage in the eye.

'Keep firing, keep firing,' she urged.

But the mages weren't looking to attack them. They were moving towards the doors to her right. FlameOrbs sailed out and the doors exploded inwards. More came, and then more, and the orchard was filled with fire.

Chapter 39

'Ward!' yelled Hirad as glass and timber showered their backs.

In front of them, the Dordovans came again. More and more light filled the orchard and screams echoed up into the air.

'Ilkar!' shouted The Unknown, battering his sword into the face of a Dordovan, the enemy swaying back, the blade catching the point of his jaw and splitting the bone. 'Drop the shield, check the rear.'

'No and yes,' said Ilkar.

Hirad evaded a weak attempt and buried his sword in the chest of his enemy. More spells detonated behind him.

'Unknown!' he said, blocking a thrust easily. 'Second perimeter.'

'Not yet. Keep going. We can still hold them here.'

And they could. The Protectors spread fear through the attacking Dordovans, their mages couldn't get any spells away through the press without sacrificing their own men and, with dead and wounded being hauled away, the floor was slick with their blood.

'Talk to me, Ilkar,' said The Unknown, punching out with his dagger hand. Beside him, Aeb took the sword arm clean off a Dordovan but suffered a cut to his right arm as he did.

'The Guild elves are broken, mages in occupation. I have the door.'

'Keep it tight Raven,' urged The Unknown. 'Let's go again!'

Hirad roared and struck out again, ignoring his protesting muscles.

Lyanna was very unhappy. She'd tried to sit at the table and draw shapes and play with her doll but the sounds from all around her were horrible. She'd seen the old ladies lying in their beds and making noises like they were hurt as bangs and crashes made the cups wobble on the table and the floor under her chair rattle.

She knew it was all down to magic. She could sense it but didn't understand how it was all made and when she tried to get inside the minds of the old ladies the rushing of the wind pushed her away and made her head ache. She cried quietly, hoping that one of the strange men would come and see how she was, but they just stood where they were and watched up at the windows or the open doors into the ballroom and the dining room.

The magic noises had stopped now but the old ladies had all become still. They were still breathing but their faces didn't look right. They were wet and very white. Lyanna got off her chair and walked across to them.

'Ephy?' she said, crouching by the frail elf. 'Are you all right, Ephy?'

Ephemere's eyes flickered open and she tried to smile. Her hand came up and Lyanna could see it trembling as it patted her cheek.

'We are so tired, Lyanna,' said Ephemere. 'Is it all right if I sleep for a while?'

'But Mummy said if I was scared I could be with you,' said Lyanna.

'In a little while,' said Ephemere and her hand fell away. She spoke again, her voice fading. 'In a little while.'

Lyanna stamped her foot. It wasn't fair. There was no one to make her feel better and she needed someone now. She needed Mummy. She knew what she'd been told but it didn't matter. She walked towards the door to the dining room where one of the masked men stood. She tried to squeeze past his legs but he put a hand on her shoulder and looked down at her.

'You are to remain in here,' he said. 'It is dangerous out there.'

'No,' said Lyanna, her anger growing quickly. 'I want my Mummy now, I'm scared.'

'It is safer in the kitchen,' said the man. 'I cannot let you leave here.'

Lyanna stepped backwards and the man released her shoulder and straightened. She tried to run past him but he stopped her easily, pushing her firmly backwards.

'No!' she shouted. 'Let me go.'

The man crouched to look at her and she could see into his eyes and they were horrible, like part of him had gone.

'Your mother will be very angry if you leave here. Stay.'

'You aren't allowed to stop me,' said Lyanna, not really understanding what she was saying but knowing it was right. 'There's things nearby you and they can make you feel very bad.'

The man in front of her flinched. 'Stay in here, please.'

'I don't want to.'

The man was quiet for a while. Behind her all the other men were walking towards her. Lyanna felt even more scared. She looked at them all, huge and strange. They wanted to stop her. They might even hurt her. That wasn't nice.

'I told you, and you wouldn't listen,' said Lyanna, feeling dispossessed from her mind and body. 'And I won't stay here, I won't.'

Inside her head, the wind grew and she heard a chattering. There were the things and there was a way to release them, it was easy.

In front of her, the man clutched at the sides of his head and screamed. He fell backwards, writhing on the ground, his legs pushing him across the kitchen floor, his body jumping and twisting. Lyanna backed away and looked up at the other men who stood stock still, hands clenching and unclenching. Her chin wobbled and she started to cry at the sounds the man made. He wouldn't stop screaming.

'I'm sorry,' she said, starting to run into the dining room. 'I'm sorry. Mummy!' Her cries echoed into the battle-filled house.

Aeb hesitated next to The Unknown and only just forced a thrust aside. Even so the blade nicked his hip and he grunted in pain.

'Aeb, Aeb,' said The Unknown, slashing wildly to keep the Dordovans back. They were pressing hard now and both he and Hirad were tiring. Behind them, Ilkar's shield held against the mages in the orchard. He was relying on the unflagging force of the Protectors but they had all slowed perceptibly, their attacks not delivered with the usual force. 'Aeb, speak.'

The Protector shook his head and smashed his axe through the shoulder of the man in front of him.

'Lyanna is free of the kitchen,' he said. 'She has invoked DemonChain punishment.'

'What?' The Unknown jabbed forwards, his blade blocked, not believing what he had heard.

'Our brother is suffering. We can sense his pain. It is . . . distracting.'

All the Protectors had backed up half a pace, forcing The Unknown and Hirad to do likewise. They could lose this very quickly. More Dordovans filled the gap, gaining in confidence. Beside him, Hirad jarred his hand as he clashed swords with his enemy. There was a fresh cut on his scarred cheek.

'Erienne!' shouted The Unknown. 'Loose the spell and get back to the ballroom. Ilkar, go with her. Lyanna is out.'

Erienne stood and cast FlameOrbs over the heads of The Raven, not pausing to see where they landed before turning and running towards the corridor.

'I can't leave this door,' said Ilkar.

'Go!' shouted The Unknown. 'Secure the second perimeter. Tell Darrick we're coming.'

The FlameOrbs landed, washing fire over the third rank of Dordovans and splashing fresh flame over already charred timbers. Panic spurred Dordovans on to the weapons of The Raven. The Unknown thrust his blade into the side of the man in front of him and slashed his dagger across his neck. Beside him, Hirad ducked and chopped into the legs of his opponent and the Protectors, forced into a flurry of action, made it count.

'Disengage on my word,' said The Unknown. Behind him, he heard Denser get to his feet. 'Now!'

A pace back and they turned and ran. The Unknown was slow but the Protectors surrounded him, one at each shoulder, picking him off his feet.

'Mages in the ballroom. Mages moving with us through the orchard,' said Aeb, his voice calm in the sudden chaos.

'Gods,' muttered The Unknown. 'Denser, keep that shield up.' He stared ahead as they turned the corner into the orchard corridor.

'Darrick!' roared The Unknown. 'Second perimeter. There's trouble in the ballroom. We've lost the orchard.'

Darrick was ahead, his sword moving quickly as he fought off attack from the first wing. The corridor was on fire, spreading along the wall of the orchard towards the ballroom, the heat intense. At both the other wing entrances Protectors were engaged in fierce fighting.

The Unknown saw Ilkar and Erienne run past the third wing. Moments later, a detonation split the air and fire gorged out. The quartet of Protectors never stood a chance, blown back against the wall, bodies seared, dead before they slumped to the ground. Fire washed across the ceiling, the after shock of the explosion shaking loose plaster dust into the air to mix with choking smoke. Dordovans poured into the gap running left and right.

Even before he asked it, the Protectors released their support, sprinting on with Hirad, and leaving The Unknown with Aeb, Darrick and Denser to marshal the rear defence. He prayed Hirad would break the way ahead quickly. If not, they would be trapped.

Lyanna came to a stop in the dark ballroom. There were more of the masked men there but they were not moving, just like the ones in the kitchen. She didn't know what she'd done but she knew it was wrong, only she didn't know how to stop it.

'Mummy, where are you?' she wailed, her eyes filling with tears. She clutched her doll tightly.

On the other side of the ballroom, she could hear people shouting and fighting and there were flames leaping and jumping. That would be where Mummy and Daddy were, helping to keep her safe. She chewed at her bottom lip, caught in indecision. She should go back to the kitchen to be with the ladies and see if the strange man was better. But she so wanted to be with Mummy. Probably she wouldn't be too angry but she didn't want to get into any more trouble.

Something was happening. She looked up to the ceiling of the ballroom which had a big hole to the sky. The sky was very cloudy and it was going to rain very hard again but that wasn't what caught her eye. There were men swooping in on wings, lowering themselves through the hole. One of them even carried another one in his arms.

There were six of them and she watched them, wishing she could fly like them. On either side of her, the two men with the masks moved again, running towards her. She screamed and ran away and they gave chase. One of them swept her up in his arms while the other turned towards the flying men. They all landed, the wings disappeared and the one who had been carried drew a long sword. She struggled to get away but the man held her too tight.

'Mummy, help me!' she shouted. 'Help!'

The room went cold and the first masked man fell. The one carrying her ran for the ballroom door. If she screamed loud enough, surely Mummy would hear.

Ilkar ran behind Erienne, hardly closing the distance between them at all.

'Erienne, slow down! The Protectors will handle it!' he yelled, but she didn't slow at all.

Twenty yards from the ballroom door, a Protector appeared in the opening, Lyanna shrieking in his arms. He was running but jolted violently, falling forwards. Ilkar felt the chill afterwash of an IceWind rush past him and knew the Protector's body had saved Lyanna's fragile life. The Protector crumpled, the girl trapped under him. She cried out and tried to shuffle clear but his weight was too much and her legs were trapped.

'Lyanna!' screamed Erienne and she upped her pace.

Ilkar tore after them, praying Hirad was close enough behind.

Gods knew how many of them were in the ballroom. He closed the distance at a flat sprint but time seemed to crawl. A Dordovan mage, ShadowWings live on his back, strode out of the door, looked up once then stooped to pull the Protector's body out of the way. Erienne slithered to a halt, a hand to her mouth, calling Lyanna's name over and over. The child herself held out her hands and begged for help. But Erienne wasn't going to get there in time.

Behind Ilkar an explosion sounded and his thoughts took on a terrible clarity. In front of him, a Dordovan mage leant down to snatch the Nightchild and take her back to Dordover where the threat of the One would be snuffed out forever. It would be so easy to let the mage take her, to not quite stop him. To make an effort so great that none could blame him for her loss. It would save the Colleges. It would save the fledgling new Julatsa.

For a Julatsan mage, it was the only decision that could be made. What had The Unknown said of him? That he wouldn't get in the way of someone killing her. Implying that for him the saving of his College was bigger than one life.

Was it, hell.

Ilkar didn't know what possessed him. It was something he'd never even dreamt of attempting before but his subconscious instructed his body without bothering to check with the rational part of his mind. He drew his sword, his only weapon, from its sheath and flung it down the corridor and time stopped standing still.

The sword flicked end over end. It wasn't a great throw but it was enough. Bouncing from the orchard wall it struck the mage flat on, sending him staggering backwards, concentration and wings gone. In that moment, Erienne dived towards Lyanna and pulled her free. The Dordovan mage came again but this time Ilkar grappled him around the middle and both man and elf tumbled back into in the ballroom.

Hirad lashed his sword through the first Dordovan throat, chopping through his windpipe and jugular and sending him crashing back into the corridor where he had come from. Beside him, a Protector overheaded with his axe, splitting the skull of the next through his helmet. Without pausing to extract the weapon, he snapped the sword from his back and drove it through, waist-high, into a third.

The barbarian roared, the blood rushing through his veins, feeling empowered and very, very angry. He batted away a strike to his midriff and laid a straight left hand punch on the enemy's nose.

Letting his momentum carry him on, he spun, taking the man in the face with his left elbow, then the right and finishing with the back of his right fist. The Dordovan went down with blood spraying from his shattered face and Hirad was in the middle of them. They never knew what hit them.

'Come on, you bastards!'

Facing them again and with his sword coming through, he thumped it into the forehead of the next victim, slicing through bone and seeing brain explode from the top of his skull as it compressed and shattered. He kicked out waist-high, his foot sweeping the body aside and leaving his path clear.

'Ilkar, I'm coming!'

There were more Dordovans ahead. Two Protectors ran past him, bludgeoning two of those who ran after Erienne and Ilkar before Hirad caught them up, his eyes seeing only red, and picked his next target.

'Move, move!' called Denser, desperately holding his concentration on the HardShield as arrows and crossbow bolts bounced off it. 'Stay behind me, attack only if they get inside a couple of paces.'

The Unknown was limping hard down the corridor, Aeb to his left and Darrick to his right. Ahead, Hirad had gone berserk and was causing confusion in the Dordovans spilling from the corridor entrances. They didn't know who to attack. Aeb made up their mind for them, charging in and beheading one with a clean sweep of his axe.

Ignoring his pain, The Unknown ran after him, each footfall sending his head swimming.

'Get to the kitchen. Third perimeter. Third perimeter!'

Aeb blocked with his sword and hammered low with his axe, taking the standing foot from a Dordovan mage who sank to the ground, clutching at the bloody stump. The Protector was battering a path, blocking the wing entrance and buying time, but he would soon be outnumbered. The Unknown surged on.

'Denser, stay with me,' he managed, every step with his damaged leg firing new agony up into his back.

'Right behind you, Unknown. I'll tell you when to run.'

The Unknown reached the mêlée and deflected the attention of two soldiers. The first came at him, sword raised to strike downwards. The big man might have been slow but he wasn't yet a complete cripple. He swayed right and swung his sword from the left, slashing the man across the stomach as he prepared to deliver his death blow. It was a mistake he'd never recover to learn from. The second was more cautious but was distracted by Aeb heaving his axe just past his nose to bury it in the face of another Dordovan. Seeing the chance, The Unknown threw his dagger which the soldier blocked well but then left himself hopelessly open. The Raven warrior carved open his stomach. The Unknown felt sick with the pain now. It carried through his back and into his head in waves, threatening to overwhelm him.

'Run!' yelled Denser.

The Unknown looked behind and swallowed hard. The Dordovans were charging now, abandoning range weapons for overwhelming numbers. Darrick came past him, shouting something he didn't catch.

'Aeb, we're going,' said The Unknown.

'Yes.' Aeb thumped the pommel of his sword into the face of a soldier and pushed him into the pack following.

He turned, grabbed The Unknown's arm and ran with him up the corridor.

'Get those doors ready!' called The Unknown, fighting the urge to vomit. He wasn't sure exactly how long he could stand up, let alone move.

Behind them, the Dordovans were gaining fast. It was going to be very close.

Ilkar rolled over, finishing on top of the Dordovan. He smashed both fists into the mage, hearing the back of his skull connect with the tiles and his grip go slack. Behind him, Erienne stumbled into the ballroom. He looked around. It was full of Dordovans.

'Oh Gods,' he said. He got up and ran low at the nearest mage, praying he wouldn't prepare in time.

Lyanna clung to her mother as she got up and ran back into the ballroom and towards the kitchen. The man with the sword came from nowhere and struck Erienne across the side of the face. She went down hard, Lyanna screaming as she tumbled from her mother's arms and slithered across the ballroom floor. She refused to cry and got up to run back to Erienne but the man stopped her, pushing her away.

'You're going back home to die, little one, but not before you see me kill your bitch of a mother.'

His voice wasn't right but she understood him.

'You don't hurt my Mummy,' she said, then raised her voice and shrieked. 'You don't hurt my Mummy!'

Ilkar staggered under an enormous pressure in the mana as he tried to attune to the spectrum, aiming to prepare as he ran. In front of him, six mages rocked as one, their hands clamping on their ears. Whatever they had been creating was gone. Ilkar would have killed the lot of them but the power assailing the mana pushed him to his knees. He groped around, looking for help. Hirad surged through the door, Protectors at his heels and, in the middle of it all, the mana light was pouring into Lyanna.

Hirad saw Selik standing over the prone form of Erienne as he burst into the ballroom. Lyanna was standing alone screaming but he couldn't worry about that now.

'Selik!' he said, advancing. 'I said there'd be another time.'

The Black Wing, sword in hand, swung to face him, his smeared features curling into a travesty of a smile.

'I knew I'd never get out of here alive but at least I'll have torn the heart from The Raven. First you, and then the bitch.' He kicked out, catching her in the stomach. She groaned where she lay. Lyanna screamed louder.

'Dream on, Black Wing,' snarled Hirad. He ran forward.

Every surviving pane of glass in the house exploded into a thousand fragments. Every piece of plaster cracked and fell. Beams ruptured, roof slates showered down and the floor rocked beneath them.

A great howling wind thrummed through the house. The orchard walls exploded outwards, the corridor pitched, its roof buckled and caved in. Hirad, like Selik, was flung from his feet. He rolled over, saw Lyanna stock still in the madness and then Ilkar, screaming in pain, blood running from his nose and ears.

The noise of the wind snatched the sound but he could see the agony.

'Ilkar!' The elf couldn't hear him. He had to get him to safety.

He dragged himself to his feet and fought the blistering gale for the few yards to where his friend lay hunched in foetal position, his face contorted. He tried to shout again but it was no use. He looked around, saw the Dordovan mages suffering the same fate, and fixed his gaze on Lyanna. If she wasn't stopped, every mage in the house would be killed.

Denser dropped to the ground as the floor heaved and split. The Unknown turned to help him, seeing the roof blast upwards above him and collapse all along its length, showering timber and slate everywhere. The Dordovan charge had faltered and broken, men covering their heads and running right and backwards, desperate to escape the destruction.

Wood struck The Unknown on the shoulder as he leant to pick the prone mage from the floor, the pain from his hip sending his head spinning. Wind, the like of which he'd never heard or felt before, pushed him flat, his face close to the Xeteskian's.

'Denser, what is this!' he shouted.

'Lyanna,' he managed through gritted teeth, a line of blood oozing from a nostril. 'Erienne has got to shield her. She's dragging it all in and she won't be able to . . . to hold it. Get them to the kitchen. The Al-Drechar.'

The Unknown thought he understood.

'Darrick, help me!'

'No,' said Darrick, yelling into his ear. 'I've got to find Ren. I can't leave her out there.' And he ran right towards the doors to the orchard.

The Unknown picked Denser up and turned to see Aeb fighting his way to the ballroom door. The big man staggered after him, turning his face against the hurricane and raising an arm to knock aside the hunks of plaster that flew at him.

Inside, the sound was even greater.

Aeb, if you can hear me. Bring the girl and Erienne. We have to get to the Al-Drechar.

Aeb looked over to The Unknown and nodded. Instantly, brother Protectors turned and started crawling across the floor. One encircled Lyanna with a huge arm, two others picked up Erienne. Behind The Unknown, the Dordovans were coming on again, leaning into the wind, picking their way across the rubble and their fallen comrades. Lyanna was buying them some time but, from the pain on her face, it was destroying her mind.

Chapter 40

The kitchen was an oasis of calm but keeping it that way was killing the Al-Drechar very quickly. All three sat up in their beds, hands clasped together, their shield pushing outwards, barely making it beyond the table in the centre of the room. Outside it, the mana was in havoc. Anything that hadn't been secured had been picked up and flattened against wall or shield. Mugs were shattered, chairs so much match wood and the table itself had been sliding across the floor to crush them when they had stopped it.

Ephemere fought to reach out with her mind, to bring Lyanna into the boundary, to calm her. But she was too far away and too far gone. For Erienne, the time was now or it would be never.

The door from the ballroom burst open. The defending Protector made to strike but instead bent to drag in Hirad and Ilkar. He slammed shut the door after them and stood ready again, impassive, unmoving, the gale picking at his clothing as he stood just within the boundaries of the shield.

'Where is she, Ephy?' moaned Myriell. 'We can't hold this.'

'Outside,' gasped Hirad. 'They're still outside.' He looked down on Ilkar who was mercifully still breathing and ran for the door into the dining room.

'Hurry, Hirad,' said Ephemere. 'Hurry.'

But he had no need to. Falling almost into his arms, a Protector stumbled in with Lyanna. He sprawled into the compass of the shield and the howling, splintering and tearing stopped as if someone had cut a rope and dropped a curtain. The Al-Drechar's shield had stopped the mana pouring into Lyanna, her mind not schooled enough to evade the lattice they had made.

Footsteps could be heard, gathering in volume and, as the shout to arms rang around the wreckage of the house and the Dordovans gathered themselves for one last surge, The Unknown hobbled in with Denser and supported by Aeb. They were followed closely by a pair of Protectors carrying Erienne.

On the ground in the kitchen, the tortured Protector was dead, killed by a brother. For him and his soul, it was blessed release.

'Get these doors blocked,' said The Unknown. 'We're out of time.'

'It has to be now, Erienne,' muttered Denser. 'Goodbye my love.'

The Unknown put him down and started to haul the table to block the ballroom entrance. Denser crawled over to Erienne who pushed herself groggily up on her hands. The pair of them looked at Lyanna, who lay stiff as a board in the arms of the Protector who'd saved her.

'Leave her, defend us,' said Denser.

'Yes, my Master,' said the Protector, laying her on the floor.

'Erienne?' said Ephemere gently. 'You know what it is you must do.'

Erienne nodded, pulled her child into her arms, lay back against Denser and prepared to enter the mind of the One, knowing she would never return.

Darrick ran right towards the north doors to the orchard, keeping below window level and in the deep shadows cast by the flames that still ripped through the trees. All around him, the quiet after the mana gale heightened every sound and he heard Dordovans shouting from behind but nothing from ahead. He reached the doors, which had splintered from their hinges, and crept into the blazing quadrangle, running to the right-hand wall which had been blown apart by Lyanna's brief but devastating mana gale.

Darrick's crouching run took him swiftly from shadow to shadow, his eyes fighting to focus in what was an alien landscape. Most of the trees were down, many turned to ashes by the Flame Orbs, and the fires still ate into the wet bark all over the orchard. The blue-tinged orange and yellow light leapt and danced in the natural wind that blew across the big open space. Already, he had seen the charred and twisted bodies of four mages and a male elf.

To his right, Dordovans ran up the ruined corridor towards the ballroom. Too many of them. Even given the Protectors in the kitchen and The Raven going to join them, there were too many enemies. It was only a matter of time before they were overwhelmed.

Darrick cursed himself for a fool. He had seriously underestimated the weight of mage attack that the Dordovans had thrown into the orchard and now it was up to him to change things. Until the orchard was taken, they'd been holding the first perimeter comfortably, wearing the Dordovans slowly down. He had really felt they could win and leave Erienne clear to do what she had to do. But now, it was desperate. And if the Dordovans broke through into the kitchen, everything would be in vain.

The Lysternan General carried on to the south doors. Five more Dordovan mages lay dead. Arrows had brought them down and their throats had been cut before the fires took their bodies. Darrick knelt by the last one, looking around. At least one elf had survived to wield the knife.

He waited, watching for movement, and felt the edge of an arrow against his neck.

'I should teach you some tracking skills,' said Ren, removing the arrow. 'What are you doing here?'

Darrick looked round. Ren was right behind him with another elf just behind her. She had an ugly burn across her right cheek and blood ran from a deep cut by her left ear. She was shivering.

'Looking for you,' said Darrick. 'The Dordovans are at the third perimeter. The Raven can't keep them away for long. We have to do something. Any ideas?'

Ren nodded. 'Just one.'

The surviving six Protectors went three to a door. The Unknown had dragged the table over to block one, its broad top covering it completely. Two of them leant against it, leaving the entrance from the dining room the only option for attack. The Dordovans took it.

Blow after blow splintered the timbers and the Protectors stood waiting, Hirad behind them. His lungs felt fit to explode, a piece of plaster had smashed over his head and his skull ached. But behind him, Erienne was sacrificing her life for her child and he was prepared to do the same to allow her to complete the job. Next to him, he heard the tap of a blade on the cracked stone flags. He looked across and met The Unknown's determined gaze.

'Ready for this?' asked Hirad.

'What do you think?' said The Unknown.

'What happened to Darrick?'

'He shouted something about going to find Ren. So he should. He put her out there, after all.'

'Oh,' said Hirad. 'He'll make a fine member of The Raven.'

'If he lives,' said The Unknown. 'Which I doubt.'

The Unknown's blade ceased tapping. Aeb was at his left, Hirad his right and Protectors made up the rest of death's welcome. The kitchen door splintered and in they came.

*

Darrick, Ren, and the other surviving Guild elf, Aronaar, ran across the eerily empty hallway and up to the main entrance. Bodies lay where they had fallen, puddles of blood left the way underfoot treacherous and the sounds of fighting echoed from the direction of the kitchen.

Ren put a hand out and stopped them just inside.

'There, under the trees opposite, like the coward I thought he was.'

Darrick strained his eyes and could see Vuldaroq, flanked by three mages and two soldiers. He was seated, apparently unconcerned by the death he had set in motion, just waiting for the outcome.

'You need to take the mages,' said Darrick. 'Make sure Vuldaroq is incapacitated as far as casting is concerned. They look like they escaped the gale out here. I'll take the swordsmen.'

'Both of them?' asked Ren.

'No problem,' said Darrick.

'Be ready,' said Ren.

She signalled Aronaar and the two elves slipped soundlessly out of the entrance, disappearing immediately into the shrubs to either side of the door. Darrick scoured the area for more Dordovans. He couldn't see any but the cover behind Vuldaroq about thirty yards away was deep. He'd have to trust the elven eyes.

He drew his blade, checked its edge and watched. Vuldaroq was talking to one of his mages, who turned and pointed down towards the beach. A birdcall sounded from the left, bow strings thrummed and two of the mages fell, arrows taking both in the eye.

Darrick ran out.

'Vuldaroq!' he shouted, deflecting attention for a vital moment.

He closed the gap quickly, watching the two soldiers move forward to block him while Vuldaroq and his surviving mage began casting. The bow strings sounded again. The fat Dordovan Tower Lord shouted in pain as an arrow burrowed into his right arm at the shoulder. His mage was not so fortunate.

Darrick ran on, aiming a blow at the first enemy who blocked clumsily and fell back a pace under the weight of the strike, sword jarring from his hand. A pace further on, the General clashed blades with the second soldier, a scared young man not ready for the fight. Darrick had no compassion. Able to keep an eye on the other soldier as he stooped to grab his blade, Darrick swung left to right, his opponent leaping back, hanging his sword out in a pathetic attempt at a block.

Darrick smashed it aside, stepped up and rammed his blade

through the soldier's stomach, pushing the body away with his foot, freeing his sword and reversing it across the chest of the second man whose guard wasn't ready. He fell on to his back, clutching at his ribs, gasping. Darrick stood over him and rammed his blade through the man's heart.

Looking up, he saw Vuldaroq already under the guard of Ren and Aronaar, Ren's dagger to his neck and Aronaar's bow sweeping the area, looking for threat.

'Bring him,' said Darrick.

The trio hurried Vuldaroq back to the house and into relative safety.

'You'll pay for this, Darrick. Desertion and now treachery against Lystern. You'll hang. I'll see to it personally.'

Darrick turned and grabbed Vuldaroq's injured arm, bringing a whimper from the mage.

'One more word and I'll bleed you right here, fat man,' he grated. 'Your unholy alliance with the Black Wings has brought us to this and now you are going to do my bidding. Understand?'

Vuldaroq was scared, Darrick could see it. His face was white with the pain of his injury and the sweat was dripping from his brow. To exemplify his point, Darrick twisted the arrow. Vuldaroq squealed.

'Understand?'

Vuldaroq nodded. They moved swiftly up the corridor, picking their way over bodies and rubble, the fighting getting nearer and louder with every pace. Darrick had his blade at Vuldaroq's back now, Ren and Aronaar just ahead as they approached the ballroom.

Inside, Protector bodies lay still and Dordovan mages moaned.

'Cover them, Aronaar,' said Darrick. 'Right, Ren, let's stop this thing.'

Erienne flowed gently over Lyanna's consciousness, feeling her tension and pain, and soothed them away. She burrowed deeper, finding the core of her magic, where the mana writhed and pulsated. She followed its tendrils to where they ate at her body, leaching her strength and destroying her. She reached out to ease the first ones from their hold but they lashed out and she felt a blow as if slapped that sent her mind reeling.

She gathered herself and came in again. Remembering the words of the prophecy. *The mother shall stifle the destruction within, laying her mind bare to its power and accepting the death herself that was promised to the Innocent. For the Innocent to fail, surely so must the mother.*

She moved in closer. At the centre of her child's mind, a monster was suffocating her. It sucked on the mana and gorged on her life energy, drawing both to it to make itself stronger, a living force with one aim, the death of its host. Dordover had triggered it and Lyanna had fed it unwittingly, the Al-Drechar too frail at the last to protect her from herself. And Lyanna was fading fast. Her last burst had fed it such power and it pulled the spirit from the tiny girl.

Focusing her mind and her mana energy, she surged in, the monster opening its claws to greet her.

No, Mummy.

Lyanna?

You mustn't go there. That's a bad thing.

But it's within you, my sweet, and it must be taken away or you will die.

But if you go there, it will kill you, too.

I know, darling. But I'll always be here, inside you to help you as you grow.

You won't. Erienne sensed crying. She crept further down. *You'll be dead. You can't die.*

There is another way.

Erienne halted. That had been another voice. Recognisable in an instant.

Ephemere, get out of my child's mind.

Erienne, Erienne, haven't you ever understood? This is not your child's mind. It is the mind of the One. The mana construct of us all.

What do you mean? Erienne's heart raced.

The One isn't like a College magic. It has form. It is an entity that, once awakened, joins with a mage mind to bring a single harmony. And now it is awake but it can't stay here.

Why not? Erienne felt a brief confusion before the import of Ephemere's words sank in and she felt herself go cold. *Don't you dare hurt her, you old witch, or by the gods I'll kill you myself.*

Lyanna can't feel pain any more. But her body is too young to contain what was awakened within her. We tried to teach her, to make her stronger. But she doesn't have the physical maturity to contain the One mind.

I can save her, Ephemere. Tinjata was very specific. Get away and let me do it.

He was wrong. He didn't read all the signs correctly. You are here because you are the mother of the child. Because you alone have the empathy the One mind requires to survive now the Innocent cannot. That is what you are laying open to the One. I thought you understood, Erienne,

Understood what?'

Oh, my dear Erienne, we aren't letting you into her mind to save her.

Hirad barely blocked the blow, the sword point nicking his right cheek to give him a cut to mirror the one he already sported. He lunged forward, his speed surprising the Dordovan in front of him who leapt back, his blade coming across his body to knock Hirad's aside.

Behind, they massed still and The Raven had nowhere to run any more. With Denser and Ilkar unable to cast, there was no backup and he felt himself tiring too quickly. Beside him, The Unknown grunted with every blow. One of the Protectors was down, another two plus Aeb were already carrying injuries, and the Dordovans were rotating their attackers where they could, keeping fresh while they wore their opponents down.

Hirad looked for a gap and hurried his sword in an upward arc, his enemy swaying back to dodge the blow. The man came in quickly and Hirad dropped to his haunches, the blade whipping over his head, coming up as he brought his own weapon down, clattering it through the back of the soldier. He dropped. Hirad backed up. He looked again over the heads of the enemy, trying to gauge their numbers. Too many. Too damn many.

'Unknown?' he said, using a two-handed grip to deflect a lunge to his head. He steered the enemy weapon aside and thrashed back quickly, his opponent stepping smartly back to evade.

'Keep going,' said The Unknown, though his breath was short and there was desperation in his voice. 'Believe.'

Beside The Unknown, Aeb clattered his axe into the chest plate of a Dordovan and he crashed backwards into his companions. Hirad's opponent was knocked off balance and the barbarian seized his chance, whipping his blade into the man's throat, seeing it torn out to spray blood high. The victim fell choking, hands dragged him aside and yet another moved up to take his place.

Something had to give. Hirad, his arms aching and lungs burning, roared to clear his head again and swore that it wouldn't be him.

∗

Darrick was in no mood to wait. They were behind the fight, looking at the Dordovan forces pushing inexorably on. He could see Hirad's sword rising and falling, blocking and sweeping. But he could also see the direction of the battle, and his friends would die.

'Call them off,' he said.

Vuldaroq said nothing.

'Ren, I think we should get their attention. Fire until they notice you.'

Ren sighed, stretched her bow and let go the arrow, seeing it slam into the back of a Dordovan neck. The man pitched forwards into those in front.

'Call them off,' repeated Darrick. His sword point dug a little deeper and his free hand rested on the arrow once more. 'If my friends die, so do you. I promise you.'

Ren fired again, another soldier fell and those at the back of the line were turning quickly. Some of them advanced. Ren nocked another arrow and bent the bow. Darrick moved his blade to Vuldaroq's neck and held up his free hand to keep the Dordovans back.

'Your move, fat man,' he whispered. 'Either we all live or we all die. Choose.'

Hirad could see movement at the back of the Dordovan press but couldn't see exactly what had caused it. Men were moving away and the shouts of encouragement had turned to those of warning. The pressure eased.

'Come on Raven!' he yelled, and though only The Unknown stood by him, the Protectors took up the invitation. They pushed.

Hirad thrashed his blade into the chest of his enemy, bending chain mail links in and winding him. The soldier couldn't raise a block and Hirad slammed his sword right to left and down into his stomach. Beside him, The Unknown overheaded, his blade clanging into a helm and stunning his opponent while Aeb's blade whispered through the air as it had all day, its point tearing the throat from an enemy.

There was shouting from ahead, urgent and quick. He thought he heard the order to disengage and the Dordovans paced back. He made to move in to keep up the attack but Darrick's voice stopped him.

'Hirad, hold!'

Confused, Hirad backed off.

'Cease,' said The Unknown. The Protectors stopped immediately. The Dordovans retreated into the dining room, there were still twenty of them, maybe more. Hirad, breathing hard, sweating and glad for the break, saw them part and then, through them, came Vuldaroq, Darrick's blade at his neck and Ren by him, bow flexed and ready.

Hirad smiled and was about to speak when Erienne came to, screaming.

She surged out of Lyanna's mind, murder on her lips. She had to warn Denser, had to let him know somehow. But the tendrils were snatching at her and with every passing heartbeat the monster invaded her, leaving Lyanna to die. For even as it fed on her, it sustained her while she gave it strength, like a parasitic host. Keeping her alive it leached all it could from her before discarding her for another. And the Al-Drechar weren't prepared to take the chance of losing what they had nurtured within her daughter and they were transferring it to another, more able host; and the match was perfect.

She clawed towards consciousness, fought the monster which locked on to her, suffusing her mind, showing her miracles, showing her power. She didn't want any of it. She wanted her child alive.

Her eyes flashed open, her heart trip-hammering in her chest. She looked down at Lyanna. The child was still, so still. A scream erupted from her lips and she was massaging Lyanna's arms, her chest, her back, urging her to breathe, for her pulse to beat and for her lips to move and her lungs to drag in air.

She could dimly sense Denser talking to her, calling, crying, shouting. There was a cacophony in her head. She put Lyanna on the ground, shaking off the hands that clawed at her, her mouth meeting her daughter's, breathing into her again and again.

But there was nothing but the roaring in her own head and the whispering that she was too late. She raised her head slowly, wiped the stray hair from Lyanna's beautiful face, saw her tears drip on those perfect cheeks and brushed her trembling fingers across her blueing lips.

'My poor little girl. I'm so sorry.'

Denser's arms were around her. Silence beat at her ears and the roaring died away.

'Let me go,' she said calmly.

He relaxed his hold. She shot to her feet, dragged the knife from her belt sheath and dived at Ephemere, plunging the blade over and over into the Al-Drechar's chest.

'Murderer!' she cried. 'Murderer!'

Strong arms pulled her away. She fought against them.

'You killed her, you bastards!' she raged. 'Fucking bitches, you killed her!'

She almost broke free but more hands held her arms down and the dagger was prised from her grasp. Denser's face came close to hers and he put a hand to the back of her neck and pulled her towards his heaving shoulders.

'They killed my baby,' she whispered. 'They killed my baby.'

And then there was darkness.

Hirad was shaking. He didn't understand. Lyanna was lying dead on the floor of the kitchen and Erienne had torn the chest from Ephemere while the other Al-Drechar looked on, too dazed or weak to do anything about it. The Unknown had dragged her away and Aeb had taken the dagger from her.

He turned, bloodied sword in hand. Ilkar was sitting slouched, semi-conscious. Darrick had marched Vuldaroq into the midst of them, the Dordovan soldiers falling back, looking to their wounded and casting wary eyes at the Protectors, the only men still ready and willing to fight.

Hirad heaved in a breath. Denser was crying, Erienne in his arms. He had retreated with her to a chair and sat there, oblivious to everyone around him. The barbarian turned to Darrick who was holding his sword still at Vuldaroq's neck.

'Thank you,' he managed, though it felt like utter failure.

Darrick shrugged. Out in the dining room, the Dordovans stood in a confused silent group, covered from the kitchen door by Ren and Aronaar, who had moved back from the ballroom.

'Hardly matters does it?' said the General.

Hirad shook his head. He looked down on Lyanna's still form and over at the hideous bloodied mass that had been Ephemere. Flanking her, Myriell and Cleress sat, eyes closed, each with a hand covering one of their dead sister's.

Vuldaroq cleared his throat. 'Would you mind moving this?' He waved at Darrick's sword point. 'For rather obvious reasons, I no longer represent a danger.'

'Hirad?' asked Darrick.

'Whatever,' said the barbarian. 'We can't kill him, so we might as well let him go.' Darrick sheathed his sword and Vuldaroq relaxed.

Hirad looked at The Unknown. The big man's gaze was locked on the body of the child.

'Unknown?'

'All for nothing,' he said. 'Poor little mite. She never stood a chance.'

'But we had to try,' said Hirad.

'Always doomed, wasn't she?' The Unknown pointed at the Al-Drechar. 'And they knew it.'

'What now?' asked Hirad.

The Unknown looked up, his eyes moist. 'First, I suggest the Dordovans pick up their wounded, bury their dead, and leave. The battle is over. Then, I really haven't got a clue.'

Movement at the periphery of Hirad's vision had him spinning. A man, if you could call him that, shoved his way to the front of the Dordovans massed around the kitchen door. He had one hand to his head from which blood dripped steadily. He was swaying on his feet, blood ran from a badly bandaged wound on his leg and his eye was unfocused.

'Selik,' grated Hirad. He hefted his sword. 'One man who doesn't get away alive.' He crossed the space quickly and raised his sword to ready. 'Defend yourself. I'd hate to cut down an unarmed man.'

Selik dragged his sword from its sheath and waved the Dordovans away, nodding.

'You I can take.'

But The Unknown stepped in between them, facing his friend.

'No, Hirad,' he said. 'The fight is over. It would be murder.'

Hirad looked at him, his blood boiling for him to strike the Black Wing down, but The Unknown held his gaze and spoke softly.

'Hirad, we have a Code.'

'Yes,' said the barbarian. He put up his sword and pointed a finger at Selik. 'One day, The Unknown won't be there and I'll be waiting. Remember that every day when you wake up.'

Selik spat on the dining room floor. 'Honour. It'll be the death of you, Coldheart. Now, Vuldaroq, when are we going to leave this bastard island?'

'Come walk with me, Hirad,' said The Unknown.

It was late in the afternoon and so much had changed. The Dordovans had gone back to their ships, taking their wounded and Selik with them. Whether the Black Wing made it to Balaia was a matter of some conjecture but Hirad rather hoped he did. He wanted the satisfaction for himself.

Ilkar was once again watching over Thraun and he remained a

mystery. Soon, they would have to wake him and see if he was either man or wolf inside the hybrid body. Denser had taken Erienne out into the gentle sunshine and had laid her on a grass bank near some of the ancient graves to sleep under a WarmHeal spell. It would do nothing to ease the agony of her mind, but it gave her body respite from the trauma. And Darrick walked alone, no doubt picking over the holes in his tactics and wondering whether anything could have been made different. Elsewhere, the six surviving Protectors, including Aeb, conducted ceremonies for their dead.

The Unknown limped beside Hirad as the two old friends wandered out through the rubble of the house and down the path towards the beach.

'How will she cope do you think?' asked the big man. 'Either of them for that matter.'

'Erienne?'

'Who else.' The Unknown fell quiet for a few paces. 'Losing a child, however it happens, must be a devastating blow. But it's happened to Erienne twice. First the twins, now Lyanna.'

'We'll be here,' said Hirad.

The Unknown smiled. 'I know but she'll need so much more. Imagine. All her children are dead. Her spirit will be shattered. Her belief in herself as a mother gone. I doubt it's something she'll ever really come to terms with. Lyanna was her world.'

'Denser's the key, isn't he?' said Hirad. 'He's the only one that can really share her grief or understand what she's going through and make her believe in herself again.'

'And he'll need our help too. This is going to be a difficult time. Mostly for Erienne and Denser but we're all going to need patience and tolerance in abundance. You included.'

'Point taken,' said Hirad.

The friends walked on, Hirad seeing a faraway look in The Unknown's eye. He didn't think the walk had been just to remind him to keep his temper.

'What is it?' he asked.

'Can you feel those who need you most?' asked The Unknown.

'How do you mean?

'Well, do you know inside that they are alive and waiting for you?' explained The Unknown.

Hirad shrugged. 'I guess so. Put it this way, if Sha-Kaan was dead I would feel it.'

'So he isn't?'

'No,' said Hirad shaking his head. 'In fact, he might even enjoy this climate for a time. Heat and humidity. Much more like home.'

'I hope so.'

'You're thinking about Diera and Jonas, aren't you?'

The Unknown stopped and rested against a fallen tree.

'I just want to know they're all right.'

'Well, you'll be home soon enough.'

'No, not soon enough,' said The Unknown. 'Soon enough is now, today.'

Hirad walked on, hearing the big man limp after him, his left leg dragging a little.

'And you expected to feel them inside you?' he asked after a pause.

'I suppose so,' said the Unknown. 'Silly, isn't it?'

'Not at all.' Hirad put an arm around his shoulders. 'They'll be fine. Tomas will have looked after them.'

They rounded the right-hand corner and crunched across the sand. Myriell was standing there, Ren by her side, looking out to sea. She turned as they approached.

'So, Raven men,' she said, her voice tired and weak. 'Why so glum?'

'We aren't used to failing,' said Hirad.

'Failing?' replied Myriell. 'Who says you've failed.'

'Lyanna is dead,' snapped The Unknown. 'We came here to save her. We failed.'

'I understand how it looks to you,' said Myriell. 'And I understand Erienne's reaction. It saddens us too that we have lost two sisters. But Lyanna was a very special child and she will never truly be gone. Only her body is at rest.'

'What are you talking about?' asked Hirad. 'You killed her, didn't you?'

'She was dead already,' said Myriell. 'You have to believe that.'

'It's Erienne you have to convince, not us,' said Hirad.

'I know.' Myriell's eyes glinted with sudden energy. 'But you have to understand that you haven't failed. Far from it. You mark me well, Raven man. You have just secured this world a saviour. And this world will need a saviour, believe me.'

'I don't get it,' said Hirad.

'Erienne,' said Myriell. 'What she now carries has to be kept safe. It is fortunate the Dordovans thought their job done with the death of poor Lyanna. The One is a power that cannot be allowed to fade from this dimension, not yet. It isn't easy to describe in words you would understand but the fabric of magic and of the dimensions is strained, out of alignment with the natural order, and the One is the binding. Until that fabric is settled once again, the One is critical to everyone, even those that believe it an evil force.'

Hirad frowned. 'So if Erienne dies, the world dies with her?'

'Oh, there would doubtless be a new order but the chaos that would reign across Balaia and interdimensional space would seem like the end of the world to those who witnessed it. Keeping the One in existence for now is infinitely preferable, believe me.'

'Oh, I see,' said Hirad.

'You don't, but you will,' said Myriell, smiling. 'Now I wonder if you two youngsters will carry me back to the house. I'm feeling very tired.'

'Youngsters?' said Hirad. 'She can't mean you, Unknown.'

'Remember what I told you about my fist?' said The Unknown.

They picked the old elf up and chaired her from the beach.

James Barclay was born in 1965 and was raised and educated in Felixstowe, Suffolk (not Folkestone, Framlingham or Farnborough but Felixstowe) where his parents live to this day. The third of four children, James gained a BA (Hons) in Communication Studies from Sheffield City Polytechnic. Fancying the life of an actor, he travelled to London to train. He still lives there now. Currently, um, 'resting' from acting, he works in the City as an advertising and copywriting manager for a leading investment house.